PRAISE FOR THE NOVELS OF ALLISON BRENNAN

TELL NO LIES

"Allison Brennan is always good but her latest and most ambitious work ever…is downright spectacular…. A riveting page turner as prescient as it is purposeful."
—*Providence Journal*

"Bestseller Brennan's intriguing sequel to…*The Third to Die*…[has] fast-paced action…[and a] well-constructed mystery plot."
—*Publishers Weekly*

"Engaging from the beginning… Those who enjoy thrillers and detective novels with lots of action will appreciate the multiple possibilities that Brennan presents before sharing who the bad guys really are."
—*Bookreporter*

THE THIRD TO DIE

"A lean thriller starring a strong and damaged protagonist who's as compelling as Lisbeth Salander."
—*Kirkus Reviews*

"Fans of Jeff Abbott and Karin Slaughter will find this crime novel hard to put down."
—*Publishers Weekly*

"Brennan's broadest and most expansive novel yet, as much Catherine Coulter as David Baldacci, with just enough of Thomas Harris thrown in for good measure. A stellar and stunning success."
—*Providence Journal*

"Leave all the lights on…you'll be turning the pages as fast as you can. *The Third to Die* is the first in Brennan's amazing new thriller series. Dive in and enjoy this nail-biter."
—Catherine Coulter, *New York Times* bestselling author of *Labyrinth*

Also by Allison Brennan

The Third to Die
Tell No Lies
The Sorority Murder

For additional novels by Allison Brennan,
visit her website at www.allisonbrennan.com.

THE WRONG VICTIM

ALLISON BRENNAN

mira

mira™

ISBN-13: 978-0-7783-1230-7

The Wrong Victim

Recycling programs
for this product may
not exist in your area.

Copyright © 2022 by Allison Brennan

All rights reserved. No part of this book may be used or reproduced in any manner whatsoever without written permission except in the case of brief quotations embodied in critical articles and reviews.

This is a work of fiction. Names, characters, places and incidents are either the product of the author's imagination or are used fictitiously. Any resemblance to actual persons, living or dead, businesses, companies, events or locales is entirely coincidental.

For questions and comments about the quality of this book, please contact us at CustomerService@Harlequin.com.

Mira
22 Adelaide St. West, 41st Floor
Toronto, Ontario M5H 4E3, Canada
BookClubbish.com

Printed in U.S.A.

To my sister-in-law Peggy Brennan: sister, friend, great aunt to our kids and an all-around wonderful person. I'm so glad we live closer now. Maybe someday we'll be in the same city!

THE WRONG VICTIM

1

A killer walked among the peaceful community of Friday Harbor and retired FBI agent Neil Devereaux couldn't do one damn thing about it because he had no evidence.

Most cops had at least one case that haunted them long after the day they turned in their badge and retired. For Neil, that obsession was a cold case that his former law enforcement colleagues believed was closed. Not only closed, but not a double homicide at all—simply a tragic accident.

Neil knew they'd got it wrong; he just couldn't prove it. He hadn't been able to prove it thirteen years ago, and he couldn't prove it now.

But he was close.

He knew that the two college boys didn't drown "by accident"; they were murdered. He had a suspect and he'd even figured out *why* the boys had been targeted.

Knowing who and why meant nothing. He needed hard evidence. Hell, he'd settle for *any* evidence. All his theory got him was the FBI file on the deaths sent by an old friend, and the ear of a detective on the mainland who would be willing to investigate if Neil found more.

"I can't open a closed death investigation without evidence, buddy."

He would have said the same thing if he was in the same position.

Confronting the suspected killer would be dangerous, even for an experienced investigator like him. This wasn't an Agatha Christie novel like his mother used to read, where he could bring the suspect and others into a room and run through the facts—only to have the killer jump up and confess.

Neil couldn't stand to think that anyone might get away with such a brazen murder spree, sparked by revenge and deep bitterness. It's why he couldn't let it go, and why he felt for the first time that he was close…close to hard evidence that would compel a new investigation.

He was tired of being placated by the people he used to work with.

He'd spent so long following dead ends that he'd lost valuable time—and with time, the detailed memories of those who might still remember something about that fateful weekend. It was only the last year that Neil had turned his attention to other students at the university and realized the most likely suspect was living here, on San Juan Island, right under his nose.

All this was on his mind when he boarded the *Water Lily*, his favorite yacht in the West End Charter fleet. He went through his safety checklist, wondering why Cal McKinnon, the deckhand assigned to this sunset cruise, wasn't already there.

If he wasn't preoccupied with murder and irritated at Cal,

Neil may have noticed the small hole in the bow of the ship, right above the waterline, with fishing line coming out of it, taut in the water.

"I'm sorry. It's last minute, I know," Cal said to Kyle Richards in the clubhouse of West End Charter. "But I really need to talk to Jamie right away."

"It's that serious?" asked his longtime friend Kyle.

"I cannot lose her over this. I just can't. I love her. We're getting married."

At least, he hoped they were still getting married. Two months ago Jamie finally set a wedding date for the last Saturday in September—the fifth anniversary of their first date. And now this whole thing was a mess, and if Cal didn't fix it now, he'd never be able to fix it.

You already blew it. You blew it five years ago. You should have told her the truth then!

"All right, then. Go," Kyle said. "I'll take the cruise. I need the extra money anyway. But you owe me—it's Friday night. I *had* a date."

Cal clapped Kyle on the back. "I definitely owe you. I'll take your next crappy shift."

"Better, give me your next corporate party boat." Corporate parties on the largest yacht in their fleet had automatic eighteen percent tips added to the bill, which was split between a typical four-man crew in addition to salary. Plus, high-end parties often paid extra. Drunk rich people could become very generous with their pocket cash.

"You got it—it's next Saturday night, the Fourth of July—so we good?"

Kyle gave him a high five, then left for the dock.

Cal clocked out and started for home. He passed a group of sign-carrying protesters and rolled his eyes.

West End Charter: Profit Over Protection.

Protect Fish Not Profits!
Hey Hey Ho Ho Ted Colfax has to go!

Jeez, when would these people just stop? West End Charter had done nearly everything they wanted over the last two years—and then some—but it was never good enough.

Fortunately, the large crowds of protesters that started after the West End accident had dwindled over the last two years from hundreds to a half dozen. Maybe because they got bored, or maybe because West End fixed the problem with their older fleet, Cal didn't know. But these few remaining were truly radical, and Cal hoped they didn't cause any problems for the company over the lucrative Fourth of July holiday weekend.

He drove around them and headed home. He had more important things to deal with than this group of misfits.

Cal lived just outside of Friday Harbor with Jamie and their daughter. It was a small house, but all his, his savings covering the down payment after he left the Coast Guard six years ago. But it was Jamie who made the two-bedroom cottage a real home. She'd made curtains for the windows; put up cheery pictures that brightened even the grayest Washington day; and most recently, she'd framed some of Hazel's colorful artwork for the kitchen nook he'd added on with Kyle's help last summer.

He'd wanted to put Jamie on the deed when she moved in with him, but she wanted to go slower than that. He wanted to marry her, but she'd had a bad breakup with her longtime boyfriend before they met and was still struggling with the mind games her ex used to play on her. If that bastard ever set foot back on the island, Cal would beat him senseless.

But the ex was far out of the picture, living down in California, and Cal loved Jamie, so he respected her wishes not to pressure her into marriage. When she found out she was pregnant, he asked her to marry him again—she said yes but wanted to wait.

"There's no rush. I love you, Cal, but I don't want to get married just because I'm pregnant."

He would move heaven and earth for Jamie and Hazel—why didn't she *know* that?

That's why when she finally settled on a date, confirmed it with invitations and an announcement in the San Juan Island newspaper, that he thought it would be smooth sailing.

And then she left.

As soon as he got home, he packed an overnight bag while trying to reach Jamie. She didn't answer her cell phone. More than likely, there was no reception. Service was sketchy on the west side of the island.

He left another message.

"Jamie, we need to talk. I'm sorry. Believe me, I'm sorry. I love you. I love Hazel. I just want to talk and work this out. I'm coming to see you tonight, okay? Please call me."

He was so frustrated. Not at Jamie—well, maybe a little because she'd taken off this morning for her dad's place without even telling him. Just left him a note on the bathroom mirror.

Cal,
I need time to think. Give me a couple days, okay? I love you, but right now I just need a little perspective.
Jamie.

Cal didn't like the "but" part. What was there to think about? He loved her. They had a life together. Jamie and their little girl, Hazel, meant everything to him. They were getting *married* in three months!

He'd given her all day to think and now they needed to talk. Jamie had a bad habit of remaining silent when she was upset, thanks to that prick she'd dated before Cal. Cal much preferred her to get angry, to yell at him, to say exactly how she felt. Then they could move on.

He jumped in his old pickup truck and headed west, praying he could salvage his family, the only thing he truly cared about. Failure was not an option.

★ ★ ★

That night Kyle clocked in and told the staff supervisor, Gloria, that Cal was sick, and he was taking the sunset cruise for him.

"Are you lying to me?" Gloria asked, looking over the top of her glasses at him.

"No. Well, I mean, he's not *sick* sick." Dammit, Kyle had always been a piss-poor liar. "But he and Jamie had a fight, I guess, and he wants to fix it."

"All right, I'll talk to Cal tomorrow. Don't you go lying for him."

"Don't get him in trouble, Gloria."

She sighed, took off her large glasses and cleaned them on her cotton shirt. "I like Cal as much as everyone, I'm not going to jam him up, but he should have come to me. I'll bet he gave you his slot on the Fourth, didn't he?"

Kyle grinned. Gloria had worked for West End longer than Kyle had been alive. They couldn't operate without her.

"Eight people total. A party of four and two parties of two." Gloria handed him the clipboard with the information of those who had registered for tonight's sunset cruise. "Four bottles of champagne, a case of water, and cheese and fruit trays are on board. You have one minute."

"Thanks, Gloria!" He ran down the dock to the *Water Lily*. He texted his boyfriend as he ran.

Hey, taking Cal's shift, docking at 10—want to meet up then?

He sent the message and almost ran into a group who were already standing at the docks. Two men, two women, drinks in hand from the West End Club bar, in to-go cups.

"Can we board?" the tallest of the four asked.

"Give me one minute. What group are you with?"

"Nava Software."

Kyle looked at his watch. Technically boarding started in five minutes; they'd be pushing off in twenty.

"I need to get approval from the captain." He smiled and jumped over the gate. He found Neil Devereaux on the bridge, reading weather reports.

"You're late," Neil said without looking up.

"Sorry, Skipper. Cal called in sick."

Neil looked at him. "Oh, Kyle, I didn't know it was you. I was expecting Cal."

"He called out. Everything okay?" Neil didn't look like his usual chipper self.

"I had a rough day."

Rough day? Neil was a retired federal agent and got to pick any shift he wanted. Everyone liked him. If he didn't want to work, he didn't. He had a pension and didn't even *have* to work but said once that he'd be bored if he didn't have something to do. He spent most of his free time fishing or hanging out at the Fish & Brew. Kyle thought he was pretty cool for a Boomer.

"Your kids okay?" he asked.

Neil looked surprised at the question. "Yes, of course. Why?"

"You said you had a rough day—I just remember you talking about how one of your kids was deployed or something."

He nodded with a half smile. "Good memory. Jill is doing great. She's on base in Japan, a mechanic. She loves it. And Eric is good, just works too much at the hospital. Thanks for asking."

"Four guests are waiting to board—is it okay?"

"There's always someone early, isn't there?"

"Better early than late," Kyle said, parroting something that Neil often said to the crew.

Neil laughed, and Kyle was glad he was able to take the skipper's mind off whatever was bothering him.

"Go ahead, let them on—rear deck only. Check the lines, supplies, and emergency gear, okay? No food or drink until we pass the marker."

"Got it."

Kyle slid down the ladder as his phone vibrated. It was Adam.

F&B only place open that late—meet at the club and we'll walk over, k?

He responded with a thumbs-up emoji and a heart, then smiled at the group of four. "Come aboard!"

Madelyn Jeffries sat on the toilet—not because she had to pee, but because she didn't want to go on this cruise, not even for only three hours. She didn't want to smile and play nice with Tina Marshall just because Pierce wanted to discuss business with Tina's husband, Vince.

She hated Tina. That woman would do anything to make her miserable. All because Pierce had fallen in love with *her*, Madelyn Cordell, a smart girl from the wrong side of the tracks in Tacoma.

Pierce didn't understand. He tried, God bless him, but he didn't. He was from another generation. He understood sex and chivalry and generosity and respect. He was the sweetest man she'd ever met. But he didn't understand female interactions.

"I know you and Tina had somewhat of a rivalry when we met. But, sweetheart, I fell in love with you. There's no reason for you to be insecure."

She wasn't insecure. She and Pierce had something special, something that no one else could understand. Even *she* didn't completely understand how she fell so head over heels for a man older than her deadbeat father. Oh, there was probably some psychologist out there who had any number of theories, but all Madelyn knew was that she and Pierce were *right*.

But Tina made her see red.

Tina, on top of this pregnancy—a pregnancy Madelyn had wanted to keep quiet, between her and Pierce, until she was

16

showing. But somehow Pierce's kids had found out last week, and they went ballistic.

They were the reason she and Pierce decided to get away for a long weekend. Last night had been wonderful and romantic and *exactly* what she needed. Then at brunch this morning they ran into Tina and Vince, who were on a "vacation" after their honeymoon.

Madelyn didn't doubt that Tina had found out she was here and planned this. There was no doubt in her mind that Tina had come to put a wedge between her and Pierce. After five years, why couldn't she just leave her alone?

Just seeing Tina brought back the fearful, insecure girl Madelyn used to be, and she didn't want that. She loved her life, she loved her husband, and above all, she loved the baby inside her.

She flushed the toilet and stepped out of the stall.

Tina stood there by the sink, lips freshly coated with bloodred.

Madelyn stepped around her and washed her hands.

"Vince took me to *Paris* for our honeymoon for two glorious weeks," said Tina.

Madelyn didn't respond.

"*I* heard that you went to *Montana*." Tina giggled a fake, frivolous laugh.

It was true. They'd spent a month in the Centennial Valley for their honeymoon, in a beautiful lodge owned by Pierce. They went horseback riding, hiking, had picnics, and she even learned how to fish—Pierce wanted to teach her, and she found that she enjoyed it. Fishing was relaxing and wholesome, something she'd never considered before. It had been the best month of her life.

But she wasn't sharing that with Madelyn. Her time with Pierce was private. It was *sacred*.

She dried her hands and said, "Excuse me."

"You think you've changed, but you haven't. You're still the little bug-eyed girl who followed me around for years. I taught you how to walk, I taught you how to attract men, I taught you how to dress and talk and act like you were *somebody*. If it wasn't for me, you would never have met Pierce Jeffries. And you took him from me."

"The boat leaves in five minutes." Madelyn desperately wanted to get away from Tina.

"Vince and Pierce are going into business together. We'll be spending *a lot* of time together, you and me. You would do well to drop the holier-than-thou act and accept the fact that I am back in your life and I'm not going anywhere."

Madelyn stared at Tina. Once she'd been in awe of the girl, a year older than she was, who always seemed to get what she wanted. Tina was bold, she was beautiful, she was driven.

But she would never be satisfied. Did she even love Vince Marshall? Or had she married him because of the money and status he could give her?

Madelyn hated that when she first met Pierce she had thought he was her ticket out of poverty and menial jobs. She hated that she had followed Tina's advice on how to seduce an older man.

Madelyn had fallen in love with Pierce, not because he was rich or powerful or for what he could give her. She loved him because he was kind and compassionate. She loved him because he saw her as she was and loved her anyway. But when he proposed to her, she'd fallen apart. She'd told him that she loved him, but she could never marry him because everything she was had been built on a lie—how she got her job at the country club, how they first met, how she had targeted him because he was wealthy and single. She would never forgive herself; how could he? His marriage proposal had been romantic and beautiful—he'd taken her to the bench where they first had a conversation, along the water of Puget Sound. But she ran away, ashamed.

He'd found her, she'd told him everything, the entire truth about who she was—a poor girl from a poor neighborhood who pretended to be worldly and sophisticated to attract men.

He said he loved her even more.

"I knew, Madelyn, from the beginning. But more, I see you, inside and out, and that's the woman I love."

Madelyn stared at her one-time friend. "Tina, *you* would do well to mind your p's and q's, because if I tell Pierce to back off, he'll back off."

She sounded a lot more confident than she felt. When it came to business, Pierce would listen to her, but he deferred to his oldest son, who worked closely with him. And Madelyn had never given him an ultimatum. She'd never told him what to do about business. She'd never have considered it, except for Tina.

Tina scowled.

Madelyn passed by her, then snipped, "By the way, nice boob job."

She left, the confrontation draining her. She didn't want to do this cruise. She didn't want to go head-to-head with Tina for the next three hours.

She didn't want to use the baby as an excuse…but desperate times and all that.

Pierce was waiting for her on the dock, talking to Vince Marshall.

"Would you excuse us for one moment, Vince?" she said politely.

"Of course. I'll catch up with Tina and meet you on the boat."

She smiled and nodded as he walked back to the harbormaster's building.

"What is it, love?" Concerned, worried, about her.

"I thought morning sickness was only in the morning. I'm sorry—I fear if I get on that boat, I'll be ill again. I don't want to embarrass you."

"Nonsense," he said. He took her hand, kissed it. "You will never embarrass me." He put their joined hands on her stomach. The warmth and affection in his eyes made her fall in love with him again. She felt like she loved Pierce a little more every day. "I can meet with Vince tomorrow. I'll go back to the house with you."

"This business meeting is important to you, isn't it?"

"It might be."

"Then go. Enjoy it. I can get home myself. Isn't that what Ubers are for?"

"A sunset is not as pretty without the woman I love holding my hand."

She wanted him home with her, but this was best. They had separate lives, at least in business; she didn't want to pressure him in any way, just because she detested Tina. "I will wait up for you."

He leaned over and kissed her. Gently. As if she would break. "Take good care of the woman I love, Bump," he said to her stomach.

She melted, kissed him again, then turned and walked back down the dock, fighting an overwhelming urge to go back and ask Pierce to come home with her.

But she wouldn't do it. It was silly and childish. Instead, she would go home, read a good book, and prepare a light meal for when Pierce came home. Then she would make love to her husband and put her past—and that hideous leech Tina Marshall—firmly out of her mind.

Jamie already regretted leaving Friday Harbor.

She listened to Cal's message twice, then deleted it and cleaned up after dinner. Hazel was watching her half hour of *PAW Patrol* before bath, books, and bed.

Her dad's remote house near Rogue Harbor was on the opposite side of the island from where they lived. Peaceful, quiet, what she thought she needed, especially since her dad wasn't here. He was an airline pilot and had a condo in Seattle that he lived in more often than not, coming up here only when he had more than two days off in a row.

She left because she was hurt. She had every right to be hurt, dammit! But now that she was here, she wondered if she'd made a mistake.

Cal hadn't *technically* cheated on her. But he also hadn't told her that his ex-girlfriend was living on the island, not until the woman befriended her. She wouldn't have thought twice about it except for the fact that Cal had hidden it from her.

She had a bad habit of running away from any hint of approaching drama. She hated conflict and would avoid it at all costs. Her mother was drama personified. How many times had young Jamie run to her dad's house to get away from her mother's bullshit? Finally, when she was fifteen, she permanently moved in with her dad, changed schools, and her mother didn't say squat.

"You should have stayed and talked it out," she mumbled to herself as she dried the dishes. The only bad thing about her dad's place was that there was no dishwasher.

But Cal was coming to see her tonight. He didn't run away from conflict. She wanted to fix this but didn't know how because she was hurt. But he had to work, so she figured she had a few hours to think everything through. To *know* the right thing to do.

"Just tell him. Tell him how you feel."

Her phone buzzed, and at first she thought it was an Amber Alert, because it was an odd sound.

Instead, it was an emergency alert from the San Juan Island Sheriff's Office.

19:07 SJSO ALERT! VESSEL EXPLOSION ONE MILE OUT FROM FRIDAY HARBOR, INJURIES UNKNOWN. ALL VESSELS AVOID FRIDAY HARBOR UNTIL FURTHER NOTICE.

Her stomach flipped and she grabbed the counter when a wave of dizziness washed over her.

She turned on the small television in the kitchen and switched to the local news. She watched in horror as the news anchor reported that a West End Charter yacht had exploded after leaving for a sunset cruise. He confirmed that it was the *Water Lily* and did not know at this time if there were survivors. Search and rescue crews were already out on the water, and authorities advised all vessels to dock immediately.

Cal had been scheduled to work the *Water Lily* tonight.

Hazel laughed at something silly on *PAW Patrol*. Jamie caught her breath. Then suddenly tears fell. How could—? No. Not Cal. She loved him, and even if they had problems, he loved Hazel more than anything in the world. He was the best father she could have hoped for. Hazel wasn't planned, but she was loved so much, and Cal had made it clear that he was sticking, from the very beginning. How could she forget that? How could she have forgotten that Cal had never made her feel inadequate, he'd never hurt her, he always told her she could do anything she wanted? He was always there for her...when she was bedridden with Hazel for two months. When she broke her wrist and Hazel was still nursing, he held the baby to her breast every four hours. Changed every diaper. He sang to Hazel, read her books, giggled with her in makeshift blanket forts when thunder scared her.

And now he was gone.

There could be survivors. You have to go.

She couldn't bring Hazel to the dock. The search, the sirens, the fear that filled the town. It would terrify the three-year-old.

But she couldn't stay here. Cal needed her—injured or not, he needed her and she loved him. It was as simple as that. Rena would watch Hazel so Jamie could find Cal, make sure he was okay.

"Hazel, we're going home."

"I wanna sleep at Grandpa's!"

"I forgot to feed Tabby." Tabby was a stray cat who had adopted their carport on cold or rainy nights. He wouldn't come into the house, and only on rare occasions would let Jamie pet him, but she'd started feeding him. Hazel had of course named him after a cat on her favorite show.

"Oh, Mommy! We gotta go rescue Tabby!"

And just like that, Hazel was ready.

Please, God, please please please please make Cal okay.

Ashley Dunlap didn't like lying to her sister, but Whitney couldn't keep a secret to save her life, and if Whitney said one word to their dad about Ashley's involvement with Island Protectors, she'd be grounded until she graduated—and maybe even longer.

"We're going to be late," Whitney said.

"Dad will understand," Ashley said, looking through the long lens of her camera at the West End Charter boat leaving port. She snapped a couple of pictures, though they were too far away to see anything.

She was just one of several monitors who were keeping close tabs on West End boats in the hopes that they would catch them breaking the law. West End may have been able to convince most people in town that they had cleaned up their act, and some even believed their claims that the leakage two years ago was an *accident*, but as the founder of IP, Donna Bell, said time and time again, companies always put profit over people. And just because they hadn't caught them breaking the law didn't mean that they *weren't* breaking the law. It was IP who documented the faulty fuel tanks two years ago that leaked their nasty fuel all over the coast. Who knew how many fish had died because of their crimes? How long it would take the ecosystem to recover?

"Ash, Dad said not a *minute* past eight, and it's already seven thirty. It's going to take us thirty minutes just to dock and secure the boat."

"It's a beautiful evening," Ashley said, turning her camera

away from the *Water Lily* and toward the shore. Another boat was preparing to leave, but the largest yacht in the fleet—*The Tempest*—was already out with a group of fifty whale watching west of the island in the Haro Strait. Bobby and his brother were out that way, monitoring *The Tempest*.

Ashley was frustrated. They just didn't have people who cared enough to take the time to monitor West End. There were only about eight or nine of them who were willing to spend all their free time standing up to West End, tracking their boats, making sure they were obeying the rules.

Everyone else just took West End's word for it.

Whitney sighed. "I could tell Dad the sail snagged."

"You can't lie to save your life, sis," Ashley said. "We'll just tell him the truth. It's a beautiful night and we got distracted by the beauty of the islands."

Whitney laughed, then smiled. "It is pretty, isn't it? Think those pictures are going to turn out? It's getting a little choppy."

"Some of them might," she said.

Ashley turned her camera back to the *Water Lily*. The charter was still going only five knots as they left the harbor. She snapped a few pictures, saw that Neil Devereaux was piloting today. She liked Neil—he spent a lot of time at the Fish & Brew talking to her dad and anyone else who came in. He'd only lived here for a couple of years, but he seemed like a native of the small community. She'd talked to him about the pollution problem from West End, and he kept saying that West End had fixed the problem with the old tanks and he'd seen nothing to suggest that they had other problems or cut corners on the repairs. He told her he would look around, and if anything was wrong, he'd bring it to the Colfax family's attention.

But could she believe him? Did he really care or was he just trying to get her to go away and leave West End alone?

Neil looked over at their sailboat, and both she and Whitney waved. He blew the horn and waved back.

A breeze rattled the sail, and Whitney grabbed the beam. "Shit!" she said.

Ashley put her camera back in its case and caught the rope dangling from the mast. "You good, Whit?"

"Yeah, it just slipped. Beautiful scenery is distracting. I got it."

Whitney bent down to secure the line, and Ashley turned back toward the *Water Lily* as it passed the one-mile marker and picked up speed.

The bow shook so hard she thought they might have hit something. Then a fireball erupted, shot into the air along with wood and—oh, God, people!—bright orange, and then black smoke billowed from the *Water Lily*. The stern kept moving forward, the boat in two pieces—the front destroyed, the back collapsing.

Whitney screamed and Ashley stared. She saw a body in the water among the debris. The flames went out almost immediately, but the smoke filled the area.

"We have to help them," Ashley said. "Whitney—"

Then a second explosion sent a shock wave toward their sailboat, and it was all they could do to keep from going under themselves. Sirens on the shore sounded the alarm, and Ashley and Whitney headed back to the harbor as the sheriff's rescue boats went toward the disaster.

Taking a final look back, Ashley pulled out her camera and took more pictures. If West End was to blame for this, Ashley would make sure they paid. Neil was a friend, a good man, like a grandfather to her. He...he couldn't have survived. Could he?

She stared at the smoking boat, split in two.

No. She didn't see how anyone survived that.

Tears streamed down her face, and as soon as she and Whitney were docked, she hugged her sister tight.

I'll get them, Neil. I promise you, I'll prove that West End cut corners and killed you and everyone else.

MONDAY

2

Nine people dead.

FBI Special Agent in Charge Mathias Costa, head of the Mobile Response Team, stood at the end of the Friday Harbor pier and looked east where the *Water Lily*, a private charter, had exploded three days earlier. All remnants had been cleared since, but he could picture it... He'd read the reports, he'd seen the photos, he knew what explosions did to flesh and bone.

This wasn't the first bombing he'd investigated. He couldn't allow the past to cloud the present.

Matt needed this minute alone, to focus his attention on the case at hand, to be the leader his team deserved. When he and his boss, Tony Greer, came up with the concept of the Mobile

Response Team, he knew that he'd be assigned difficult and challenging cases all over the country. It was harder when he knew one of the victims. Though he hadn't seen former FBI agent Neil Devereaux in years, he had been to his retirement party; he'd attended his wife's funeral. Neil had been a solid agent, the type of cop most agents aspired to be. Dedicated, trustworthy, smart.

And Neil was Tony Greer's closest friend. It was all Matt could do to convince Tony to stay in DC and let Matt work the case without the assistant director breathing down his neck. Fortunately, Tony hadn't worked in the field for more than a decade, and didn't push hard to join Matt.

The San Juan Islands were uniquely beautiful and Matt could see why Neil had chosen to retire here. Not only was he originally from Washington State, but the islands were a piece of paradise for those who loved boating, fishing, and fresh salt air. A hundred and seventy-two islands dotted the archipelago, though most of the population lived on the main island, San Juan Island, where Friday Harbor was located. Matt had never been here before, an oversight, he realized, because he liked the environment.

The San Juan Islands Sheriff's Department patrolled the inhabited islands—all twenty of them—and fortunately, the sheriff was more than happy to have the FBI take over this investigation. The crime rate was low, violent crime almost nonexistent. The bombing had thrown the entire community into shock, and Matt needed to give them peace.

The only way they would find peace was if he and his team found the bomber and brought him to justice.

And that was something Matt was very, very good at.

He heard someone walking down the pier toward him. He glanced over his shoulder, saw his longtime friend and colleague Catherine Jones, one of the FBI's top forensic psychiatrists. This was her first case since returning from an extended sabbatical after her sister had been murdered nearly a year ago. He was glad she was here, though Catherine had changed. He wasn't certain the changes were for the better. She still maintained her regal appearance, attractive and calm, yet cool and unapproachable to anyone who didn't know her. She was still one of the smartest people he knew. But she seemed even more aloof, more distant, sharper-edged. Matt had hoped getting back in the field would give her the final push she needed to reclaim her life after her sister was murdered, but for the first time, he wondered if he'd pushed too hard, too soon.

It's been a year since Beth died.

"I thought I might find you here," Catherine said when she approached and stood next to him.

"I wanted a minute," he said.

Together they stared out over calm waters. Already, three days after the explosion, a variety of boats dotted the horizon. In the distance he could see a ferry coming from Anacortes, the closest port to the islands, an hour east. Life went on. He was grateful for the fact, but he still mourned the eight people he had never known—and especially, the one person he did.

"The sheriff has been more than accommodating," Catherine said. "We have a conference room dedicated to the investigation, and he's assigned two deputies full-time to assist—Redfield and Anderson. More if we need them."

"It's nice to have local law enforcement support."

"Agreed." Catherine paused, then said, "Are you thinking about the Tucson Bomber?"

He was, but he didn't want to talk about it.

"You caught him," Catherine reminded Matt.

"Not before he killed thirteen people."

It had been one of the worst cases of his career. Hell, maybe *the* worst. The Tucson Bomber had targeted children. There was nothing worse than holding the body of a dying child in your arms.

Until he faced the fifteen-year-old boy who had committed those horrific acts and saw nothing in his eyes. The kid had no soul, no remorse, no joy, no sorrow. He was empty inside. His only emotion was excitement when he watched things explode.

And no one, not even Catherine, could understand why a fifteen-year-old boy from a good, middle-class family would put a bomb in an elementary school. The fatalities could have been so much higher, but thirteen dead was thirteen too many.

Kara would understand.

He pushed the thought from his head. Yes, Kara would understand. She understood even what he didn't say, and at times the silence between them was as calming as their deeper conversations. He should talk to her...just to reconnect. As soon as they were assigned this case, she'd physically and mentally stepped away from him, and he already missed her. He understood why—they were working a case, she was on his team, and they needed to keep their relationship on the down-low.

He just didn't want to. And that would get them both in trouble.

"I'm here, Matt, if you want to talk," Catherine said.

"I know. Thank you." But he didn't want to talk about it. To Catherine—or even to Kara. Sometimes, the past needed to stay in the past.

"Let's focus on this case," Matt said. "Michael is still in Seattle with ATF, analyzing the bomb fragments. They already identified the explosive as C-4—hard to get, tightly regulated, easy to work with. Tracing the explosives is a top priority, and Michael is pushing ATF on that."

Agent Michael Harris had been Matt's first hire onto the Mobile Response Team. He was a former Navy SEAL who had an exemplary military record, and Matt had helped recruit him into the FBI when he retired from active duty. He was Matt's key field agent here because of Michael's expertise with munitions. He understood ATF in-speak and would cut through all the bullshit so Matt didn't have to. One thing Matt excelled in was delegating, which was why he picked the best of the best for his team, each agent with a different specialty.

"Will Michael be here tonight?" Catherine asked.

"Fifty-fifty. He serves us better riding ATF. Jim is talking to the ME about the victims," Matt added. Jim Esteban was a forensics expert who Matt had recruited away from the Dallas Crime Lab. He'd met Jim several years ago at a joint training session at Quantico and they'd been friends since. No one could analyze a crime scene like Jim. He was the equivalent to a full team of forensic scientists. "We should have a solid forensics report before the end of the day to help re-create the explosion. I have Kara interviewing witnesses and the family of the survivors. I'll put one of the officers with her, which should help speed up the interviews. Ryder will retrieve Neil Devereaux's personal files and computer, since Neil was obsessed—Tony's word, not mine—about a Washington cold case."

"The Mowich Lake drownings?"

Mowich Lake was in the Mount Rainier National Forest, several hours southeast of the San Juan Islands. The case was one of Neil's last before he'd transferred to DC, more than a decade ago.

"Yes. Neil was convinced the boys were murdered, but there's no evidence of that. Tony sent him the FBI files on the case, which was open-and-shut." Matt would assign the second SJSO deputy to Ryder Kim. Ryder was an analyst, not an agent, and Matt wanted him protected.

Matt turned to walk back to the sheriff's department.

"Are you okay, Mathias?"

He glanced at his old friend. "Yes. I'm okay, Catherine."

The old demons would stay in the past. He'd solved the Tucson Bomber case and he would solve this one.

When Matt and Catherine arrived back at the sheriff's station, the sheriff, John Rasmussen, greeted them. The sheriff's department doubled as the courthouse and housed a small jail, but inmates were generally taken across the strait to Yakima County for any detention that lasted longer than a few days.

San Juan Island had fewer than seven thousand permanent residents—half the population of the entire county, which was confusingly called San Juan Islands County—though there were nearly twice as many people here now, at the height of the tourist season. That made Matt's job doubly hard. Was the explosion the work of a visitor or a resident? It would be far too easy to plan an attack and escape via water up to Canada, which was closer than the mainland of Washington State. Virtually everyone had a boat, and between the inhabited and uninhabited islands, there were plenty of places to hide out, especially in the warm summer months.

"Your man Kim has set up the conference room. It's all yours," John said. "Anything you need, you let me know."

"You mentioned on the phone last night that the charter company had received threats. Do you have those here?"

The first priority was to determine the target of the attack, whether West End Charter was the target, or one of the individuals on the boat.

John walked over to the tallest stack of folders on the table. It was more than a foot high.

"I took the liberty of prioritizing the threats. My office has looked at all these cases as they came in, and most of the threats were verbal assaults. But the red cases—I flagged those—the biggest threat is from a group called Island Protectors, IP for short. They have a variety of causes, some pretty good, some way out there. They've been critical of West End Charter for years, but it all came to a head two years ago when a damaged boat leaked oil into a protected inlet. The EPA and the state environmental review commission investigated, determined that it was an accident. A valve on the fuel tank had been recalled and West End had twelve months to retrofit their fleet. They were in the process, hadn't gotten to that particular boat. West End paid for the cleanup, paid a fine, decommissioned the boat, took all others off-line until they were retrofitted, and were cleared by both federal and state regulators. Cost the company a pretty penny, but they complied. Yet IP hasn't let up. Their ultimate goal is to get rid of all gas- and diesel-powered boats."

"Isn't that most boats?" asked Catherine.

The sheriff nodded. "Kayaks and rowboats aren't going to get you across the channel quickly, that's for sure, and not when the weather is inclement. If Island Protectors gets what they want, it would kill the tourism industry. Sightseeing, whale watching, and fishing tours are the bread and butter for our summertime businesses, and West End is the largest charter boat company here."

"Any specific person issuing the threats?" Matt asked.

"The signed letters have lower priority, in my opinion," said John. "The leader of Island Protectors is Donna Bell, and she had a long op-ed in the paper a few months back, but never sent anything to West End directly, at least under her name. I've known her most of my life—we were in school together. Good people, though we don't always see eye to eye on things. She'd never condone something like this." He waved his hand toward the photos on the whiteboard of the *Water Lily* wreckage.

Matt raised an eyebrow. "I hear a *but*."

"Donna is old-school, like me. IP draws a lot of younger activists who don't have our common sensibilities. They protest and chant and get in people's faces. They're not going to send a threatening letter, but they might get in Ted Colfax's face—he and his brother and sister own the company, since their dad died a few years back. Anyway, I talked to Donna Saturday, right after the explosion Friday night. I might have been a bit rough with her—she clammed up, thought I was accusing her. I wasn't, but her people are not her, if you get my drift."

"I do."

"Even though I pissed her off, I should be there if you decide to talk to her. She's not going to be forthcoming with the FBI." He put his hands up in a shrug. "No offense."

"Any assistance is welcomed," Matt said. "I want to talk to her today. Is there anyone involved with IP who might be capable of this? What about the two who were arrested last year for vandalism?" He tapped another file and opened it, glancing through it as John spoke.

"Craig Martin and Valerie Sokola. Craig has lived here with his mother and brother for years; Valerie is his girlfriend. They are both on probation, and to be honest, this is out of their realm, in my opinion."

"I'll still want to talk to them."

"I'll track them down."

"First, West End Charter, then Donna Bell, then the vandals."

"Donna is like Mother Goose," said John. "She draws all these young idealists into her life, but she's a true believer. A lot of these kids have different backgrounds—spoiled entitled brats, if you ask my opinion."

Matt walked over to the whiteboard. Catherine was already in the middle of reorganizing the information.

He tapped two names. "McKinnon and Jeffries. Both were supposed to be on the boat but weren't."

"Correct. My deputy, Marcy Anderson, said she and one of your agents would be following up with them. I know McKinnon. He's lived here for the last six years, was in the Coast Guard before that. Has a fiancée and a baby. Madelyn Jeffries is the wife of one of the victims."

Catherine cleared her throat. "Pierce Jeffries? Money could be a motivating factor. The Jeffries estate is extensive."

Matt turned to Ryder Kim, who was quietly working in the corner. He'd already hooked them up to the FBI system, and set up individual workstations for each team member. He had filled the refrigerator with fruit, and several boxes of organic granola bars—and the less-healthy energy bars that Kara seemed to live on—were stacked next to water bottles. Ryder was worth his weight in gold and Matt didn't know what he'd do without his organization skills. But sometimes he was so quiet and studious that Matt forgot he was in the room.

"Ryder, contact Zack in DC and have him go over finances, insurance policies, business dealings starting with Jeffries then going to…" he looked at the other victims on the board "…Marshall, Nava Software, and the others, in that order. Kara will follow up with the next of kin."

Zack Heller was the newest member of Matt's team, but he was still working on the complex white-collar crime aspect of their last case and Matt needed him in DC to finish the paperwork. He could assist them easily enough from the East Coast.

Catherine asked, "Is Mrs. Jeffries still on the island?"

John nodded. "I asked her to stay for a few days. I would say she's in shock."

"What are you thinking, Catherine?" Matt asked her.

"She is the much younger wife of a very wealthy man, married five years. I find it suspicious that she left the boat immediately before it set off."

"You look into her background; Kara will talk to her, then exchange notes. There would certainly be far easier ways to kill your spouse and avoid suspicion."

Still, prisons were full because of stupid criminals, and greed was one of the most common motives.

Ryder walked over and handed Matt a printout. "This was in the news this morning. A blog."

Matt skimmed the document. A blogger reported that the four owners of Nava Software had recently turned down an offer from a major competitor to buy their company. "Why is this important?"

"According to the rumors, the competitor thought he had a sale and then they pulled out last minute, creating a ripple effect for the competition. Stocks were affected. It might be something Zack understands—the financial fallout and if it's big enough to suggest a motive."

"Send it to him as well, and Catherine will look into each victim as she puts together the profile."

"Profile?" John asked.

"Catherine is a forensic psychiatrist, one of the best from the FBI's Behavioral Science Unit. She's going to put together profiles of the victims as well as the bomber, so we can narrow our focus. Right now we don't know the target, have no known motive, and multiple victims who could have been involved or at risk."

Catherine said, "Though the *Water Lily* bombing was clearly a domestic attack, the question remains as to whether it was a solo bombing—which might suggest that *one* of the victims was the target—or was it the first, and there's more to come?"

"I don't like the sound of that, one bit," John said.

"We need to keep it in mind and act accordingly," Catherine said. "If it's the first, then the victims were collateral and the target is most likely West End Charter or the boating industry as a whole."

John said, "ATF was all over the place this weekend with bomb dogs. They inspected all of West End, headquarters plus boats, as well as the larger ferry system. They've added security to the ferries—we have hundreds of people who go back and forth every day, thousands on the weekends. If someone wants to create full panic, that's the way they would do it."

"The FBI has no chatter that there was or is any planned attack in this area, but they're on alert," Matt said. "If something changes, we'll be the first to know."

"What I should have said," Catherine clarified, "was that if there's another attack on West End Charter, it's likely someone in that stack of papers is responsible." She gestured to the threat pile John had compiled.

"Ryder," Matt said, "take one of the deputies with you to Neil's house to gather his files and computer."

"Deputy Redfield is available," the sheriff said.

"Thank you, Sheriff," Ryder said. "I need a little more time to finish setting up the network, then we'll go."

The sheriff turned to Matt, held up his phone. "The Colfax family of West End are expecting us, if you're ready. They're pulling together all the information you asked for."

It seemed everyone was cooperating, which gave Matt hope that they could solve this case before anyone else died.

3

Kara Quinn stared at the business cards she'd received from the FBI printing office before they'd left DC last night. The official FBI logo in one corner, stamped in gold. In tiny print on the bottom right was the DC headquarters address and the mobile number that went directly to Ryder Kim. Centered in the middle was her name and title.

Kara Quinn
Special Consultant
Mobile Response Team

She pocketed the card.

Twelve years of working her ass off to earn the rank of detective in the Los Angeles Police Department, gone. She couldn't even use her title because the FBI didn't have detectives, and even though she was still technically employed by LAPD, she couldn't do her job. The card was proof that it was over. Her identity as a cop, gone.

She'd never be able to go back, not in the capacity that she'd once served. And *fuck* if she was going to sit at a desk all day long because she'd been burned.

Kara was depressed and angry. She'd been so proud of her job. She'd worked hard and *earned* every collar, every promotion, every case she'd been assigned. She'd *earned* everything she had. Her small beachfront apartment she had to give up. Her friends—few and far between—but they were *hers*. No longer. Either dead or unable to associate with her because her LAPD boss thought it would put her in danger, or them.

The only thing she had was her badge. Because *technically* she was on loan to the FBI.

On loan indefinitely.

Meaning, forever.

Someday, she would destroy the federal agent who had turned her life inside out. Kara would never forget. Forgiveness? Hell no. Not after he got her partner killed.

The one thing she had was time. She didn't need revenge—*justice*—today. She could wait for payback.

Deputy Marcy Anderson met her out in front of the sheriff's department. Kara had appreciated that Matt had kept the briefing short and sweet—she liked having a job to do in the field, and she detested meetings. She and Marcy would be reinterviewing two teenagers who'd witnessed the explosion, then Madelyn Jeffries, the young widow who was supposed to be on the boat but bailed last minute. She'd planned to also interview Cal McKinnon, but he asked if he could come in tomorrow morning

41

to talk because he had family matters. Matt cleared it, so Kara would interview him tomorrow morning at eight.

"Agent Quinn, right?" said Marcy, the local deputy.

"Detective Quinn," she said. "Long story. Call me Kara."

"Marcy. My truck's right over there." She gestured. "It's only a couple minutes' drive to the Fish & Brew. We could walk, but later we'll need to drive to the Jeffries place, which is up the coastline a few miles."

Kara walked with her to a Ford Bronco in the lot. Kara was short—barely five foot four *if* she stretched and walked tall and wore shoes. Marcy towered over her. Kara didn't mind being on the shorter side. She could more easily blend in and take on different roles. Plus, being short helped her look younger, a huge plus when she went undercover in high schools and on college campuses.

When you still worked undercover.

"So am I ever going to hear the story of what a detective is doing working with the feds?"

"Sure, over a beer one night."

Kara wasn't here to make lifelong friends, but a beer with her temporary partner might be a needed diversion later on.

But Marcy just looked at her quizzically, as if she wasn't ready to settle for that answer. Maybe she had a point. They were thrown together on this case, they knew nothing about each other, and if Kara was in that position, she'd want to know more as well.

"It's a long fucking story that pisses me off every time I tell it," Kara said. "Short version? I put a bad guy in prison, he lied about how it went down, someone important believed him, he's out pending trial but had plenty of time to put out a hit on me. Going back to LA right now isn't really an option. I helped Costa's team with an investigation, they thought I did a good job, so here I am."

Kara slid into the passenger seat of the department-issued

Bronco without waiting for a comment. Yes, she was still angry. Yes, she wanted to go back to her life and LA and the way things were. But that was foolhardy, along the lines of unicorns and Santa Claus type of fantasy.

Marcy checked her gear, then jumped in and looked at her. "Long version over beers?"

"Sure," Kara said, though she really didn't have more to say. "And then I expect your story of how a big-city cop adjusts to tiny-town America."

"Fair enough." Marcy headed east toward the waterfront. "Pete Dunlap owns the Fish & Brew, a couple blocks up from the harbor. Tourists come in, too, but it's a favorite among locals. If you like fish and chips, best in the state—not just on the island. Small menu but everything is good. If you don't like fish, the hamburgers are the bomb."

"Now I'm hungry."

"I already ate lunch, but I'm happy to get you something."

Kara laughed, pulled an energy bar out of her pocket. She'd grabbed three from Ryder's stash because she didn't know how long she'd be out.

Marcy grimaced. "If I don't have three meals a day, I'm crabby."

As soon as Kara walked into the Fish & Brew, she knew she'd be back. This was just the type of pub she gravitated toward. Rustic, dark—but not too dark. Sports on the televisions, a full-stocked bar, large selection of microbrew beer, and virtually every seat with a view of the entrance or rear exit. She might come here tonight alone. She didn't think it was all that far from the house the FBI was renting.

Kara did *not* like the idea that everyone on their team was sleeping under the same roof. She needed her privacy. Kara had lived on her own since she was eighteen. Even before she was eighteen, she'd had little supervision and a lot of freedom. She didn't even have her own apartment in DC yet—Matt's boss,

Tony, had set her up in a short-term rental while she looked for a place. She felt like she was in limbo, and being thrown in with her team—living in the same damn house—she felt invisible walls closing in on her.

The longer she lived with this new situation, the more she regretted agreeing to work for the FBI.

Don't lie to yourself. Working for the FBI was your only option if you wanted to continue being a cop. And if you're not a cop, you're nobody.

"Great, isn't it?" Marcy said.

"My kind of place," Kara agreed.

Marcy walked over to the bar and motioned to the bartender—thirtysomething, light brown skin, short black hair, hazel eyes, and well-defined muscles. "Damon, this is Kara Quinn with the FBI. We're here to talk to Pete and the girls. He's expecting us."

"He's in his office, you know where that is, Marcy. Go on back."

As they walked through the pub, Marcy said, "Damon is Pete's brother-in-law. He had a football scholarship for college, shattered his leg senior year. Too bad, because he was good, everyone said. But he's also smart, graduated and now teaches math at the high school in Bellingham, works for Pete in the summers when the pub is busy."

"Young for a teacher." If all Kara's teachers were that young and handsome, she might have liked high school a lot more.

Marcy laughed. "I think he's thirty-two, thirty-four, somewhere around there. We go to the same gym. There's not a lot of options on the island. There's a CrossFit gym, and a regular gym. Damon and I do CrossFit. You should join us while you're here."

"I'm not a gym rat unless it's raining," Kara said. "I'm more of a runner." And not so much running as jogging. Alone.

"I know the best places to run."

Great, Kara thought. *I don't want a running buddy.*

But she didn't say that.

The office door was open. Pete was in his forties, had a darker complexion than his brother-in-law, kept his curly black hair very short, and wore thick, black-framed glasses as he perused a stack of invoices on his desk.

"Pete, hello," Marcy said. "Thanks for agreeing to talk to us."

Pete looked up, taking off his glasses. He had a Black Clark Kent thing going on. Cute with the glasses, very sexy without them.

Kara had to stop thinking about men as sex symbols and bedmates. Especially in light of the fact that she was sort-of, somewhat, kinda involved with someone.

Marcy introduced Kara, then said, "Are the girls here?"

"They're finishing up their summer classes—overachievers, both of them," said Pete. "When I was a kid and summer came? My brothers and I were out on the boat from sunrise to sunset. Or hiking over on Orcas. The thought of going to summer school made my skin crawl."

He looked at a clock on the wall. "They'll be here in a few minutes. I texted them, told them you wanted to talk again. Whitney's excited—she loves crime shows and is talking about being a cop, though at your suggestion, Marcy, I'm gently pushing her toward the Coast Guard. She loves being on the water, so it would be a good fit. Ashley, though—don't get me wrong, both my girls were devastated by what happened Friday night. But Ashley is very empathic. She's heartbroken."

"I promise we'll respect Whitney and Ashley's sensitivities," Marcy said.

"I appreciate that."

Kara asked, "How well did you know Neil Devereaux?"

"Very well," he said. "In fact, I'd call him a friend. He's been coming in regularly, several times a week, since he retired here nearly three years ago. Bonded over football. You know, Damon was almost drafted by the Raiders before his accident. Me, my blood bleeds blue and green for my 'Hawks. Neil and I had that in common. We even caught a game together last season."

The sound of two teenagers talking over each other came in through the back, and the group turned as the girls halted in the doorway.

The taller girl said, "Hey, Deputy Anderson. How are you?"

"Good. Whitney, this is Kara Quinn with the FBI," Marcy said. "Whitney Dunlap, and her sister, Ashley."

Pete said, "Let's go to the back room. It's bigger and we can sit down and talk."

He led the way down the hall that was covered with photographs of what appeared to be locals posing with fish of all different sizes. He turned and motioned to a room filled with six empty rectangular tables, each that could fit six comfortably, or eight close friends.

The back room could be closed off for private parties, and Pete closed the accordion doors now to give them privacy from the late-lunch diners. The room also had access to an outside eating area.

They sat and Kara said, "Thank you both for agreeing to talk about this again. I know this isn't easy, but it helps our investigation."

Whitney, taller but younger than her sister, said, "You want to see if our story changes, or if we remember something else?"

"Yes, though it's not about your story changing," Kara said, mildly amused. "You're not a suspect. But witnesses often remember something they didn't think about during an initial interview. It's why most cops will tell you, if you think of anything else, call. So while I know this is difficult, I need you to go back to Friday evening and tell us what you saw. But we're going to start at the beginning because I've found that helps keep a recollection clearer. Your dad said you're taking summer classes. When did you leave school on Friday?"

"Noon," Whitney said. "I'm taking chemistry and Spanish 3,

so I can take Spanish 4 next year with Ashley because we want to go on a mission trip after she graduates. Each class is an hour and fifty minutes."

"They don't care about that," Ashley said quietly.

"I do," Kara said. "I care about whatever you want to share. Sometimes, talking about things that are normal helps you remember other details. Where do you want to go on your mission trip?"

"La Paz," Whitney said. "They have an orphanage there, and last year a group from our church went and they did a presentation about their experience. It was so amazing. Ashley wants to be a teacher, so working with kids is perfect."

"And you want to…?" She left it open-ended because she wasn't sure Pete was right that he was being "gentle" about being a cop versus Coast Guard.

"I don't know yet. I really want to work for the sheriff's department. I did an internship last semester, and it was just *so* totally fascinating. And Sheriff John is so nice. He talked to all of us in the program—like he really wanted to, you know? But then Officer Marcy, she talked about the Coast Guard, which sounds totally cool, too, so I really don't know. But if I'm in the sheriff's office I can go into search and rescue, which I would love and I'm the best swimmer, but Dad says go to college first—"

Pete reached out and rubbed the back of his daughter's hand. "Baby, you're rambling."

"Sorry. I talk too much when I'm nervous."

"You talk too much when you're not nervous, too," Ashley said, not quite under her breath.

"Whichever career path you decide, I'm sure you'll be good at it," Kara said.

Ashley was observant. Sometimes it was the quiet ones who saw more than anyone.

But Whitney was the people pleaser and, though younger than her sister, clearly more comfortable talking to strangers.

"After school," Kara prompted, "you went out on your boat. Around one? Later?"

"Twelve thirty," Whitney said. "We went over to the north side of Shaw Island. Our best friend lives there. She broke her leg last week and we wanted to cheer her up and surprise her with a picnic. Then we got to playing games at her house and talking and left."

"What time was that?" Kara asked. She appreciated that Marcy was letting her run the interview. She hadn't wanted a partner but agreed with Matt that having a local cop with her would be an asset.

"Six, a little before. We're supposed to be back by eight. It usually takes about forty-five minutes to sail from Shaw back to the harbor, but it was such a gorgeous night, we took our time. And Ashley wanted to take pictures," Whitney added. "She's an *amazing* photographer."

Pictures... Kara needed to come back to that.

"In your original statement, you said you passed the *Water Lily* as it was coming out of the port after seven p.m."

"Yeah."

"How fast was the boat going?"

"Not very. It was still in the control area."

"Between four and five knots," Ashley said.

"Five miles an hour," Pete explained.

Ashley nodded. "We were coming in and had just turned the sails to slow down as we approached the harbor. Neil waved to us—we waved back. He blew his horn to say *hi*."

She looked down at her hands.

"You were close enough to recognize Neil?"

"He was in the bridge—we were just shy of maybe a hundred yards? They didn't have a big wake, so I wasn't worried about getting caught up in it. I think Neil was waiting until we passed by before picking up speed. He was real considerate like that." Ashley bit her lip.

"So you passed each other and then he increased speed. About how long after you waved did you see the explosion?"

"I didn't," Whitney said. "We'd passed the *Water Lily* and I dropped a line and went to pick it up. I heard the explosion."

"I saw it," Ashley said quietly. "I had turned around to tie the line and the bow just…burst. They were going at least fifteen knots by then, maybe more, he'd picked up speed, and it was like the boat just collapsed into itself. People…" Her voice cracked.

"It's okay," Kara said quietly.

"They just fell off the boat. Thrown off, I guess. The boat kept moving forward after the explosion—momentum."

Whitney took her sister's hand. "I turned around and there was smoke where the boat was supposed to be," Whitney said. "And then I saw the back of the boat, but the front was just… gone. The stern was bobbing, tilted, and…we wanted to go back to help, but then there was a second explosion."

"The fuel tank," Marcy said. "It was the fuel tank, according to the reports."

The sisters nodded in unison but Kara didn't think they really registered what Marcy was saying. "The alarms were going off in the harbor and the search and rescue boats were coming and we couldn't… I mean, we couldn't do anything," Ashley said. "I wanted to. We wanted to."

"There was nothing you could have done," Kara said. "There were no survivors, and you would have put yourselves at risk if you got closer. But your instincts are good."

Pete cleared his throat. "You did the right thing, girls."

"When you got to the port, what did you do?"

"Called our dad," Whitney said. "He was already there."

"I heard the explosion," Pete said.

"Did you stay at the dock?"

"Yeah, everyone was watching. Dad helped us with our boat."

"Could you see the *Water Lily* from where you were standing on the dock?"

"Not really. And the fire went out real quick, but there was still some smoke, so we knew where it was, but we couldn't see anything."

"It was a mile out of the harbor," Ashley said.

"Before you returned to the harbor, did you notice anything else—like another boat in the area, whether you knew them or not?"

"There were a lot of boats," Ashley said, "but we were the closest to the *Water Lily*."

Pete asked Kara, "Are you thinking that this was intentional?"

Kara looked him in the eye. "It was intentional," she said. "We know that a bomb was planted in the bow of the boat and we're working with ATF to determine exactly how it was triggered. It could have been by timer or cell phone or radio or someone on the boat. So if the girls saw another boat near the *Water Lily*, that might help us. Not necessarily a suspect, but another witness we're unaware of."

"Why?" Pete asked. "Why would someone do this?"

Any number of reasons, but Kara didn't comment.

Marcy said, "That's why the FBI is here, Pete. To help us solve this quickly. We don't want people to be scared or worried."

"Ashley, you were taking pictures," Kara said, remembering what Whitney had said earlier. "Can you share those?"

"Why?"

She sounded defensive.

"Because the FBI is real good at getting all the data out of an image. You might have captured something you didn't see with your bare eye—something that could help us with the investigation."

She frowned, didn't comment. Why was she reticent?

"Is it those IP nuts?" Pete asked.

"They're not nuts, Dad," Ashley said.

"Most of them are," he responded.

"No one in IP would do this," Ashley pushed back.

"We'll talk about it later," he said.

Something to pursue, Kara thought. Was Ashley part of Island Protectors? Did she know people who were? That might be helpful—but Kara realized she would have to talk to Ashley without her dad. First, Ashley wouldn't be as forthcoming around her father. And second, her dad clearly didn't like the group and might interrupt, causing friction with his daughter and Kara the inability to get potentially useful information.

"Thank you for your time," Marcy said as she got up. "Pete, if we need anything else, we'll call."

"Thank you."

"Ashley." Kara remained sitting. "Your camera. Is it digital? Did you use your phone?"

"I have a digital SLR I got for my sixteenth birthday."

"I need those pictures."

"Of course," Pete said. "Ashley, where's your camera?"

"It's at home."

"We can email them," Pete offered.

"If you wouldn't mind," Kara said, "I'd like to take the camera or the memory card and our technology expert can download the data directly to the FBI server. If there *is* anything important, we need to establish a direct chain of evidence. But we'll replace the card."

"I'll bring it to the station this afternoon," Pete said.

"Thank you."

She thanked the family for their time, then left with Marcy.

"What are you thinking?" Marcy asked when they climbed back into her Bronco.

Kara wasn't used to a partner—not working a case like this. She primarily worked alone, and she didn't have a complete thought formed in her head.

"Ashley is seventeen, correct?"

"Yes. Why?" asked Marcy.

Generally, law enforcement could talk to minors without parental consent—and because Ashley wasn't a suspect, Kara didn't see an issue with it. The issue was that the sheriff had promised their dad that he could be present during any questioning.

The sheriff—not the FBI. Kara didn't want to make things difficult for Marcy after the FBI left, and she didn't necessarily want the sheriff interfering if he thought Pete should be present. So she deflected Marcy's question and asked, "What do you know about this group, IP?"

"Typical environmental activist group," Marcy said. "Some of their members get out of line—vandalism, trespassing, things like that—but I can't see any of them being violent."

"Matt said in the briefing that IP had been investigated for threats made to West End."

"True, and two of their members were arrested and fined, got probation—community service—for vandalizing one of the West End docks last summer. Since then, they've been pretty much well-behaved, other than general protesting and whatnot. Really, I think they're harmless."

Kara knew Matt planned to interview the two vandals. Being on probation helped because, as a term of their probation, they were required to cooperate with any police investigation.

"What are you thinking?" Marcy continued.

"I'm trying to see a bigger picture," Kara said, leaving it at that. Kara didn't have a uniform, and while she was in law enforcement, she was also an outsider in this community. Someone who would be gone in days or weeks, at the most. She was pretty certain she could get Ashley to talk about IP and anyone she might be concerned about—but not with anyone in authority present.

"Let's hit Madelyn Jeffries and see what she has to add."

4

The Jeffries vacation home was larger in every way than most primary homes—soaring A-frame roof, broad picture windows, a front door you could drive a truck through. But at the same time, it blended in beautifully among the trees, almost invisible even in its vastness. As soon as Kara started up the front steps, she realized the expansive deck had one of the best unobstructed views of the ocean that she'd yet seen. She'd bet a month's pay there was a hot tub around back with that same view, something big and relaxing. Oh, yep, Kara could be happy here. She didn't need the big house—one room would suffice—but she would kill to have a place on the water.

"Madelyn Jeffries is twenty-nine," Marcy said as they approached the door. "Married to Pierce Jeffries, the deceased."

"The notes I have say you talked to her Friday night?"

"No, the sheriff notified her on Friday night. Tom Redfield and I went to follow up with her Saturday morning, to ask why she'd decided not to go on the sunset cruise."

"And?"

Marcy shrugged. "I didn't buy her answer. That she wasn't feeling well. Might not mean she's involved in anything illegal, but she's probably inheriting his money, and word is he's worth tens of millions. I'm sure there's a will. He has three kids, none of whom were happy he married a younger woman. Two of his kids are older than she is."

"Is that motive for murder? Kill their daddy because they don't like their new mommy?"

"No, but maybe Mrs. Jeffries killed her husband for his money."

"And eight other people?"

Sure, it was possible, and Kara had seen enough shit in her thirty years to know it could happen, but did Madelyn have the knowledge to make a bomb? To obtain the C-4, know where to place the device to cause maximum damage, be calm enough to walk her husband to the boat, then leave in an Uber?

It would take someone extremely cold to do that.

Or she could have hired someone, but there would be a trail. Unless she had a young lover, maybe a former Navy SEAL like Kara's colleague Michael Harris, who could make and plant a bomb and would ostensibly know where to steal C-4.

A place to look, but there were a lot easier ways to kill someone than bombing a boat.

Kara went into every interview with an open mind and said as much to Marcy. "It seems," Kara added, "that you don't like this woman. Do you know her personally?"

"No—never met her until Saturday. I know of her, though, because she and her husband are often on the island and the locals keep tabs and gossip. This island has only seven thousand people and everyone knows everyone's business."

Kara could relate to that. "I spent my high school years in a small town in eastern Washington."

It was because of these small-town biases that it was a good idea that the FBI's Mobile Response Team had been sent out. On the one hand, having local authorities who knew the people involved, who understood the local dynamics of the population, who had experience and knowledge in the area, was crucial. But having an outsider with no preconceived ideas about a person or suspect was an added benefit.

They rang the bell. Kara stepped back out of habit; Marcy looked around the area. It was quiet and remote; tall redwood trees growing close together prevented Kara from seeing any neighboring houses, north or south.

A petite older woman with no makeup, wearing jeans and a fierce expression, answered the door. "This isn't a good time," she said, looking specifically at Marcy.

Marcy said, "We're following up on Mrs. Jeffries's statement. We're in the middle of our investigation and it's crucial that we verify every detail. Or Mrs. Jeffries can come down to the sheriff's office and talk to us there."

The woman glared at her.

Kara said, "Ma'am, I'm Kara Quinn with the FBI. We are working closely with the sheriff's office to find out who committed this horrific act. Mrs. Jeffries was understandably upset after the event, and no one wants to pressure her into reliving what happened, but it's important for us to talk to her now, while that evening is still fresh in her mind. She may have seen or heard something that can help us find who did this."

"Her husband is *dead*. She's grieving."

"I promise," Kara said, "we'll respect Mrs. Jeffries's privacy and grief."

"Mama."

Madelyn Jeffries walked up behind the older woman. She was substantially taller, elegant, and beautiful, even though her pale, tearstained face made it clear that she'd been crying. She wore no makeup and her hair was pulled back into a sloppy bun. She was dressed in pressed jeans and a black blouse, wore diamond stud earrings, and played with the wedding ring on her finger.

"You don't need this right now, Maddie."

Madelyn motioned for Kara and Marcy to enter. She introduced her mother, Anne Cordell, and said, "My mother is looking out for me, which I appreciate." She gave her mother a small smile, but her eyes said more—like, *enough, I've got this.* "May I get you anything?" she asked Kara and Marcy. "Coffee? Water?"

"No, thank you. Let's sit wherever you're comfortable."

Kara watched Madelyn closely, without making it obvious. Kara knew con artists—she'd been raised by two of the best— and she didn't think Madelyn's grief was fake. Her mannerisms— the way her eyes watered when she looked at her wedding ring, her slow, deliberate movements—seemed genuine, like that of a woman processing the loss of a man she loved.

On the wall above the fireplace was a portrait—an actual painting, Kara noted—of Madelyn and Pierce Jeffries. Not a wedding portrait, but a painting of a casual depiction of them having a picnic, with huge mountains behind them. Pierce, in his fifties, was attractive for an older guy. He sort of had that debonair Sam Elliott thing going on, without the mustache. But the painting was…surprising, thought Kara. Very romantic and sweet. While she didn't have a romantic bone in her body, she recognized the feeling.

She commented, "That's a lovely painting. Did you sit for it?"

Madelyn stared at the painting and said nothing for a long minute. Tears leaked from her eyes. She ignored them at first, then turned to Kara and gave her an awkward smile as she wiped her cheeks. "It was Pierce's idea. That was based on a photograph from our honeymoon in Montana. We were on a picnic and he set up his camera. I thought he was just taking scenery pictures—he was a wonderful amateur photographer. I didn't know what he did with it until he gave me that painting on our first anniversary."

She turned away and led them to the outside deck. "Do you mind?" she said. "I really love being outside. Pierce and I would sit out here every evening and watch the boats. Well, he'd work, and I'd watch. It's peaceful."

"It's a beautiful day," Kara said.

Marcy looked uncomfortable and Kara didn't know why. Was she rethinking her assessment of Madelyn from the other day?

Anne brought out a box of tissues, handing her daughter two. She took them and dabbed her eyes. It was a dainty maneuver but seemed appropriate for her.

Kara wanted Madelyn relaxed, so she talked a bit about the view, the house, then asked about her honeymoon. Madelyn and Pierce had been married for just over five years. They'd returned to Montana for their five-year anniversary last month.

Kara noticed that Madelyn's hand rested on her stomach. She kept an eye on it, curious.

"You came here to San Juan Island often?"

"Yes—several times a year. We have a house in Bellingham, which is about a three-hour trip, so we come here at least one weekend a month—except in the winter. Sometimes I come here alone; usually, when Pierce is traveling for work."

"You didn't travel with him?"

"Sometimes, but if it was a short trip, where he was filling his days and nights with work, I didn't want him to be distracted, thinking he had to entertain me."

"What exactly did Mr. Jeffries do?"

Kara knew, of course—he owned in full or part several different companies across multiple industries. His business reputation was solid, according to Matt, and Zack in DC was digging deeper into his finances to make sure they hadn't missed anything.

"He had a knack for seeing the diamond in the rough," Madelyn said wistfully. "He would look at a fledgling company and know whether he could save it, make it blossom, he used to say. He's well respected in that world."

"And you? Do you work with him?"

"No. I have no marketable skills."

"Nonsense," Anne said. To Kara and Marcy she said, "Maddie has two degrees from the University of Puget Sound—in English and history."

"I didn't say I was unintelligent, Mama. Just that unless I go back to school for a teaching degree, what would I do? Pierce valued education, and we talked about books and history all the time. I've read more since I graduated than I did in school and enjoy it a lot more now." She looked out at the water.

Kara said, "You told Deputy Anderson on Saturday that you didn't join your husband on the sunset cruise because you weren't feeling well."

"Yes."

"Why did he go without you? A sunset cruise seems romantic."

Tears again. "He offered to come home with me, but I knew he wanted to talk to Vince Marshall about a business venture. I don't know the details, so don't ask me—I never cared about the details. Justin—Pierce's oldest son—would know. But it was important to Pierce, so I told him to go, I'd see him at home, and then…" She took a deep breath but couldn't stop the tears. "I thought I would be okay, but I miss him. I want to rewind time and insist he come home with me. I should have been on the boat and died with him."

Anne squeezed her hand. "No, Maddie, do not talk like that."

"Madelyn," Kara said, her voice calm but firm, "walking to or from the boat, did you see anyone who acted odd? Out of place?"

She was shaking her head. "I was angry. I wasn't paying attention."

"At your husband?"

"Of course not. At myself for letting Tina get under my skin."

"Tina Marshall?"

"I knew her in college. She was a year older than me, and we were in the same sorority. But…she was… No. I'm not going there. She's dead, and I didn't want her dead. We had disagreements in the past, but that's irrelevant."

Kara heard a car in the driveway. Two doors slammed and Madelyn jumped.

"Are you expecting company?"

"No."

Anne got·up and walked to the edge of the deck, where she could see the driveway below. "I don't believe it!" She turned back, hands on her hips. "You don't have to talk to them, Maddie. Go to your room."

"Who are they?" Marcy asked.

"Pierce's children," Anne said. "Brats, all of them."

"No, Mother, they're not. They're grieving, too. And Justin has been kind—"

"I don't trust any of them after how they treated you when you married Pierce."

Family drama, Kara thought. She shot a glance at Madelyn. She was pale and distressed.

The bell rang multiple times. Pause. More buzzing.

Anne, hands clenched, started for the door, but Kara said, "Ma'am, let Deputy Anderson get the door."

Marcy gave her an odd look, but Kara tilted her head toward the front of the house. "Authority," she said under her breath as Marcy passed by her. Marcy exuded authority in her uniform, and Kara wanted to make sure these people remained calm.

As soon as Marcy went in the house, Kara turned to Madelyn. "Are you pregnant?"

Madelyn looked stricken. "How did you know?"

Kara gestured to Madelyn's hand that was on her stomach. "Did your husband know?"

"Yes," she squeaked. "We found out last month. I'm thirteen weeks now. It's why we went back to Montana for our anniversary, to quietly celebrate. I wanted to keep it a secret as long as possible, but—"

"But what?"

"A week ago Pierce's children found out. I don't know how. Maybe I left something on my desk they might have seen. They were not happy— I should say, Kimberly and Josh weren't happy. Justin was nice about it, to be honest. After a rocky beginning, he and I, I guess, developed a mutual respect. His fiancée had a lot to do with it, I believe. She and I became friends and she's… well, Robin is a wonderful person. Or maybe he decided that whatever made his father happy wasn't something he wanted to mess with."

When Madelyn said *whatever made his father happy*, Kara saw a hint of steel in Madelyn. Kara wasn't going to judge the marriage or the age difference or whether Madelyn was a gold digger. Unlikely or not, it seemed that Madelyn and Pierce had a relationship that had worked for them.

Kara knew a thing or two about unlikely relationships.

"Madelyn," Kara asked, "did you know of any threats against your husband or his business? A disgruntled employee or an investor who wasn't happy?"

She shook her head. "Justin would know. He and his father were very close. They worked together, talked almost every day."

Justin Jeffries moved up on Kara's to-talk-to list.

Before she could ask another question, Marcy returned, followed by a man and woman in their late twenties.

"You are a piece of work," said the woman—Kimberly, Kara surmised.

Marcy stepped toward her. "Ms. Jeffries, remember what I said?"

"You don't know—"

"I mean it," warned Marcy. "This house belongs to Madelyn Jeffries and you are here at her pleasure. This is a difficult situation, and we're going to act like adults."

The young man said, "I hope you're asking her about what she had to gain from our father's death!"

"I've gained nothing, Josh," Madelyn said, "and lost everything."

"You liar!" Kimberly said. "Daddy changed his will, and you have *half of everything*! And to top it off, you get a quarter of what should be split between my brothers and me because you got yourself knocked up! Is that why you killed him now? So you get more money? I'll prove you set this up, you bitch!"

Marcy whistled between her fingers with such shrieking power that Kara was genuinely impressed. She had always wanted to be able to do that.

Kara said to Marcy, "Can you take Madelyn and her mother inside, get all contact information for family and friends and personal lawyer? I'd like to talk to Ms. and Mr. Jeffries."

"And who the fuck are you?" Kimberly said.

Kara took out her badge. She loved this part of her job. "Quinn, FBI. Sit."

"You can't be a fed."

Her badge said LAPD, so she handed Kimberly her new business card.

"Sit. Now."

Kimberly sat, staring at the card. Her brother joined her on the cushioned wooden couch.

After Marcy led the others inside and slid the door shut, Kara said, "I'm sorry for your loss."

"That's rich," Kimberly snorted.

"Nine people died Friday night and my team came from DC

to find out who did it and why." Kara was determined to be patient with this unpleasant woman. "We are pursuing all leads. We do not know at this time whether your father was a specific target or an innocent bystander, but it would help greatly if you could leave your animosity toward your stepmother outside of this investigation."

She said *stepmother* on purpose because she knew it would piss them off, and she didn't like either of these people. Their father was dead, and they verbally attacked a pregnant widow.

"Well, maybe," Josh said with quiet venom, "you should look at who profits from his death."

"Do either of you work with your father in his business?"

They shook their heads. Kimberly crossed her arms and glared at Kara.

"So your brother Justin is the only one who knows about your father's business dealings?"

"He's probably screwing her," Josh said. "That's why he changed his tune about her. When our father first got remarried, he felt the same as us about that gold-digging bitch."

"I'll be sure to ask Justin," Kara said. "In the meantime, when was the last time *you* spoke to your father?"

They didn't say anything.

"You don't remember? Can I show you a calendar?"

The siblings exchanged a glance. Then Josh said, "A week ago Sunday. We have dinner every Sunday unless Dad is traveling."

"And why is that hard to remember?" Kara asked.

"It was a clusterfuck," Kimberly sniped. "Because of that woman. She's come between us and our dad, and now she's having a baby. I'm going to demand a paternity test."

"You might as well tell me exactly what happened at the dinner last week because I will find out. If you hold back, it might make me think that you were angry enough at your father to kill him."

"How dare you!" Kimberly said. "I *loved* my father! He was being used, and I just wanted him to see that."

Josh put his hand on his sister's arm. Finally, he was showing some common sense and trying to calm his sister.

"Dad asked us to leave," he said.

"Why?"

"Because Kimberly found out that Dad changed his will to include an unborn child."

"I would think the terms of your father's will were confidential. Did he discuss this with you?"

Neither said anything. Okay, a friend or relative or someone in the law firm had squawked.

"And I assume you didn't want any alterations to his will?"

Kimberly tilted her chin up. "I wanted Dad to understand that she was using him for his money, and now that she was pregnant, she was never going away."

"You didn't think he loved her?"

"I'm sure he did. Dad is amazing in every way, but he was conned. Madelyn doesn't love him."

"Why do you think that?"

"She was twenty-four when they got married, he was already fifty-one! What do you think? Nearly thirty years age difference? And she came from *nothing*. Dead broke. Worked at a country club as a *waitress* and basically flirted and seduced rich single guys, looking for a free ride. She loves his *money*."

"How. Dare. You."

Madelyn stood in the doorway. Kara was angry at herself that she hadn't noticed the woman's return, and irritated that Marcy hadn't kept her inside.

"It's true," said Kimberly.

"Out."

"This was Daddy's house!"

"It's my house. I want you to leave, and I never want to see you here again. I will call the police if you return. Deputy Anderson said I don't have to let you in, and that if you refuse to leave I can call her. I will, so help me God."

"This isn't over," Kimberly said.

Josh took her hand. "Let's go, Kim."

"I hate you," Kimberly said, tears starting to fall. "You turned my daddy against me."

"I will say this one time," Madelyn said, steady as a rock. "Your father loved you tremendously. Your anger and selfishness hurt him, but he never stopped loving you. I hope you realize that one day."

They left, and Madelyn sat heavily in a chair. She looked worn out. "I don't know if I can handle those two on my own."

"I need to talk to Justin," Kara said. She handed Madelyn her business card, and said, "If you think of anything, Madelyn— what you saw, heard, something that comes back to you about that night, or something Pierce said that might have worried him—call me. Day or night. I wrote my cell phone on the back, so you can reach me directly."

"Thank you for being kind. Justin will be here tomorrow. He wanted to come sooner, but he was in Japan when…when the boat…" She cleared her throat. "Anyway, it's been a long trip, and he's grieving, but he assured me he would be here tomorrow before noon. I'm sure he'll want to speak with you as well. And please, when you find out what happened, will you tell me? If Pierce was the target, or someone else? Or…no one? I read in the newspaper that it might have been an act of domestic terrorism." Tears pooled in the young widow's eyes as she looked at Kara. "Why, in a civilized society, would someone kill so many people to make a statement?"

Maybe because some people weren't civilized, Kara thought.

5

With both Matt and Ryder gone, and Jim Esteban, their forensics expert, in a private office reviewing the autopsy reports and other forensic evidence, Catherine Jones sat in the large conference room the sheriff had provided them, blissfully alone.

She needed more information about the bomb itself to create an accurate profile of the bomber, because each bomb had a distinctive signature. Was it a one-time detonation, or had the killer used a similar device before? If it was unique enough, it could point to a pattern—or a person.

It could be that the bomb malfunctioned. Perhaps the loss of life was unintended—especially if it was set as a political statement. If that was the case, guilt may set in and expose the perpetrator.

The ATF was first on scene and had already collected physical evidence from the boat. They'd determined the type of explosive and the location of the bomb; they were unsure yet of *how* the bomb went off. Michael Harris was with the ATF today because he had extensive experience in this field. That information would help her hone her profile of the bomber.

Zack Heller, their white-collar crimes expert in DC, was reviewing West End Charter financial records, as well as those of each of the victims—in case insurance or money was a motive.

C-4 was an explosive material that was not easy to come by but easy to work with, which suggested to Catherine that this was a deliberate, intentional act by a man of above-average intelligence.

Virtually every bomber was male.

There were two types of domestic terrorists. The first wanted to instill fear for a political purpose, and while they used violence as a means to create fear, they didn't intentionally set out to kill anyone. They would vandalize, intimidate, harass, throw rocks and bottles, and might set fire to empty buildings. These types might also turn a peaceful protest into a violent attack against property, not caring about the cost, only the reaction. They might set a bomb, but only if the chance of killing someone was minimal. They recognized that murder would distract from their cause.

The other type killed because it was a bigger stage—they wanted attention, they wanted to destroy, they wanted to maim and murder because it was a Statement with a capital S. They had a bigger agenda. Either the terrorist was a lone wolf—someone who was disgruntled in every aspect of his life and latched on to a political cause—or the attack was part of a bigger plan among a group of like-minded people who wanted to create fear and friction within society. Any deaths were necessary for a greater agenda, and murder birthed fear.

The chances this was a foreign attack or a sleeper cell target were slim to none. The FBI had a strong counterterrorism component, and there had been no chatter about any terrorist activity in the Pacific Northwest, and no organization had taken credit for it. After three days, their intelligence community would have picked up some talk of it. In addition, most foreign terrorists would go after a bigger target or mass casualties: a government building or an icon of America, like the 9/11 attack on the World Trade Center and the Pentagon. If they were to target a boat, they would have picked a ferry with hundreds of people as potential casualties.

A cruise ship could be a target, Catherine mused, but a small charter boat? This was either domestic terrorism, an insurance scam, or the planned assassination of one person, masked under the deaths of nine.

Of course, she couldn't discount that they were dealing with a sexual bomber. They were similar to serial arsonists, where they obtained sexual or personal satisfaction at the act of fire or explosion itself. But she'd already reviewed all known arson fires in the Pacific Northwest and there was nothing even close to what they had with the *Water Lily*. The team in DC was expanding the search in case the bomber was a visitor to the San Juan Islands and had started his violent explosions elsewhere. But so far, nothing.

Such serial arsonists—or bombers—started small. The fire or explosion created sexual excitement, and like many sexual predators, when small crimes no longer satisfied, they sought *bigger, more*—larger fires after small; physical attacks after verbal attacks; murders after assault.

Serial criminals, whether they were arsonists or rapists or killers, followed an identifiable pattern. They *grew* over time, with the speed of that growth directly related to their psychology and environment, as well as external stressors and the control they had—or didn't have—in their personal lives.

A serial bomber operated in a similar way as an arsonist, but generally didn't act on their dark impulses until later in their life, at least well into their twenties. They were often antisocial and might have a long list of misdemeanors in their criminal record. They were almost always from broken or violent homes where they'd had no support and no healthy outlet for their anger.

Catherine considered the Tucson Bomber, whom Matt had arrested. Trevor Thompson had fit none of the usual criteria for a serial bomber—which was why Catherine now sought to assess the West End bombing with a totally open mind.

While Thompson *had* started with smaller bombs set in empty buildings or in the middle of the desert, he had quickly escalated. Matt had worked with the ATF on the investigation after a recognizable pattern emerged from abandoned building to *closed* businesses. It was when Thompson targeted an empty school that Catherine had been brought in to do an assessment as to whether this bomber would escalate and take lives. She had determined that yes, he would.

The confirmation of her assessment came when a bomb went off in the teachers' lounge in the middle of the day—but no one was injured. ATF determined that the bomber was becoming more proficient in his bomb making. Each bomb was bigger, better designed than the last.

And then Thompson killed when he set off a bomb in a classroom during school hours.

He was caught because he was young. He might have been brilliant in how he designed his bombs, but he didn't account for security cameras, witnesses, fingerprints, and DNA. The ATF traced some of his supplies, he was found on camera at several different sites, and his prints were found on part of a device that had survived the blast. Matt led the raid that arrested him, but it had been a tough case for him—as it would be for any agent where eleven of the thirteen victims were children.

So far in this case, they didn't have any hard evidence. The lack of prints or DNA on recovered components suggested this bomber was more experienced and mature. They were still combing over security footage, but the key angles revealed nothing suspicious. If he was a pro, they might be able to trace him through the device itself. That was the ATF's job, but so far, this bomb had not matched any known bombers. While awaiting a better analysis of the bomb debris itself, Catherine turned her focus to the victims.

Neil Devereaux was a twenty-seven-year veteran of the FBI until he retired three years ago at the age of fifty-five. Catherine had met Neil several times through Tony Greer, the assistant director who oversaw the Mobile Response Team.

Born in Vancouver, Washington, he'd been assigned to the Seattle field office after graduating from Quantico. Shortly after, he met his wife and they had two children. His son, Eric, now twenty-six, was a medical resident in Washington, DC, and daughter Jillian, twenty-five, was currently serving in the Navy and based in Japan. Neil's wife, Christina, died eight years ago of cancer, he hadn't remarried, and according to Tony, he wasn't involved with anyone else.

Christina was his true love. I was at her funeral and believed Neil when he told me there would never be another.

Nearly thirteen years ago, Neil had transferred to the DC office. His son was starting high school at the time and he'd been given a promotion, plus Catherine knew from Tony that Neil had endured some conflicts with his colleagues over the investigation into the suspicious deaths of two college students, Brian Stevens and Jason Mott. Neil had initially been called in to assist when the boys had been found dead on a federal campground, drowned in the lake. It had been ruled accidental, yet two years ago, Neil had requested the old files from that case. Tony had the Seattle office send them to him, even though that wasn't standard protocol.

Now the Seattle office was going through all of Neil's past cases and determining the status of bad actors he'd crossed paths with over the years in a professional capacity. Revenge or retribution was a powerful motive, which placed Neil near the top of their list as a target, after West End Charter itself.

Next, Catherine looked at Cal McKinnon. He had called in sick—domestic issues—and thus escaped death. He was a veteran of the Coast Guard, honorably discharged, went to community college in Seattle for two years, earned an AA in Business Tourism, then relocated to the San Juan Islands when he took a job with West End Charter nearly six years ago. Two years later Jamie Finch, a local waitress, moved in with him, and a few months after that they had a daughter, Hazel, who had turned three last month.

What would be his possible motive for the bombing? If he was having financial trouble, he could have set it up for the insurance money for his family, but then he would have to be the one dead—not Kyle Richards. It seemed on the surface that McKinnon was simply lucky.

Still, the agents on her team needed to dig deeper to make sure he didn't have unsavory associates, unknown financial trouble, or enemies. McKinnon being the target was lower on the list—and nothing in his file or his personality suggested he had set it up. Target? Low. Suspect? Low.

Kyle Richards wasn't scheduled to be on the boat, so the chance that he was a target or a suspect was next to zero. She put him at the bottom of the list. They would need to verify he wasn't suicidal, but it seemed pretty far-fetched based on the timeline.

The Nava Software group that had been on board would be looked at closer. She had all their names and addresses—all from Seattle, here for a company retreat—but everyone seemed to have a low profile. No one was married, they were all under thirty-five, no known threats or mental health issues. One of the Seattle agents was talking to the staff in their office and family members to determine if there had been any threats against the company or any of the individuals. And FBI in DC was running deep background checks on all four. A computer blog had reported that an investor had wanted to buy out Nava, and the company declined, but Catherine didn't see that as being a strong motive. Pending further investigation, she didn't think the group was the bomber's target.

Vince and Tina Marshall, married last month, lived in California, though Tina was originally from Washington. They arrived on San Juan Island Thursday morning, and their reservations had been made only two days before. That seemed odd to Catherine, but she wasn't spontaneous—she planned out everything. Taking a vacation last minute would stress her out. Other people didn't seem to mind.

Still, last-minute trips were often a red flag.

Vince Marshall, forty-eight, was a wealthy entrepreneur who owned a vineyard in California—where he lived—and a software company in Seattle, and he was an investor in several other companies—some of which he'd bought, then sold to be disbanded. Unlike Pierce Jeffries, Marshall was not a self-made man; he had inherited the vineyard and used family money to buy the software company—a trust-fund businessman. Catherine had known many such trust funders growing up, and they were not fondly recalled.

She sent a note to Zack to analyze Marshall's various businesses. If someone lost their company because of Marshall's business decisions, they might go after him. And in the articles that Catherine read were hints of shady business practices. Perhaps they were even shadier than suggested.

Though a bomb would suggest organized crime, and she didn't see indications of that in the paperwork in front of her. Again: looking into that was a job for Zack. Those unknowns put Marshall higher on the list than the others.

Marshall was on his third wife, Tina née Foster. There was extensive divorce material on Marshall, even with no children from any of his marriages. Split assets, anger, accusations of infidelity on both sides. So common, she thought with a slight sneer. With a lot of money involved, that could be a motive worth exploring. Perhaps talking to his two ex-wives. But women, again, didn't generally use a bomb to kill.

Marshall's current wife was from Tacoma, Washington. *Hmm*... so was the Jeffries widow, Madelyn Cordell Jeffries. They were a year apart in age.

Catherine switched databases and pulled up personal information. Madelyn and Tina had both graduated from the University of Puget Sound. They were members of the same sorority—and both had worked at a golf course in Olympia, south of Tacoma, every summer while in college.

That connection seemed unusual, unless this trip was planned for the old friends to get together. Possible. She made a note to ask Mrs. Jeffries about her relationship with Tina.

There was little data on Tina Marshall. She had gone to work for Marshall's winery as an event planner three years ago... This was interesting. Marshall's second marriage dissolved a year ago.

Would a bitter spouse kill after their divorce?

Or maybe they were both the target.

Yet revenge killings rarely took out innocent bystanders on purpose.

Catherine made a note to look into Marshall's second ex-wife, and she put the Marshalls higher up on her list of potential targets.

That brought her to Pierce Jeffries.

He was a self-made man, born in Seattle to immigrant parents from Poland. He was the fifth of seven children.

On paper, he seemed to be a philanthropist, and there was little negative press on him in the gossip rags or the business magazines. His oldest son worked with him day-to-day. He married when he was twenty, had three children. His wife died ten years ago of an aneurysm. It had been sudden and unexpected.

He married Madelyn Cordell five years ago, when she was

twenty-four and he was fifty-one. According to the engagement announcement, they'd met at the country club where Madelyn worked and Pierce was a guest of a business associate. Pierce called it "kismet," even though it took Pierce two months to convince Madelyn to join him for dinner. After that dinner—which lasted more than six hours and they talked about everything from their favorite books to World War II to Impressionist art—they saw each other whenever possible, and Pierce proposed four months later.

In the article, Pierce was quoted: "I fell in love with Madelyn during that dinner, but I feared I'd chase her away with a quick proposal."

The accompanying photos were staged. The couple looked happy, and the piece didn't reflect the fact that Pierce's children were unhappy with the engagement.

Twenty-seven-year age difference. Catherine didn't understand what a beautiful young woman had seen in a man old enough to be her father, other than money. Of course, psychologically there were a host of other issues to consider—was Madelyn's father in her life? Did she equate love and sex with older men? Had she been abused or groomed from a young age to be attractive to older men—or to want an older relationship herself? Catherine wouldn't be able to determine any of that until she sat down with Madelyn Jeffries. But the fact that she had left the boat before the explosion that killed her husband, *and* there was substantial money involved, suggested a strong motive.

Reviewing her notes, Catherine had three focus points: West End Charter as the target, either for business/insurance reasons or as a domestic terrorist attack; Neil Devereaux as a target by an as yet unidentified criminal Neil put behind bars, or related to the cold case he was investigating; and Pierce Jeffries as a target of his young wife.

She updated the whiteboard and added her notes. This helped her to visualize the information and discern connections that might not otherwise be obvious. She wished she had a private room to do so. Catherine didn't like having to explain her shorthand to strangers, but Matt had assured her that this conference room was theirs to use for the duration of the investigation.

Her phone beeped. It was a text from Kara Quinn, the LAPD detective who Matt had brought onto the team—that seemed an odd arrangement to Catherine.

Kara's text read: Jeffries not the target unless a business motive pops.

Catherine frowned. How could Kara possibly know that after just one interview with the widow? Jeffries was by far the wealthiest person on that boat; he was worth more than a quarter of a billion dollars.

Kara was unqualified to make that determination, and if she had evidence to prove her assertion, she should be more specific.

Catherine almost picked up the phone to call her, then thought better of it. This would be better to discuss during their debriefing later that day.

A wealthy businessman with heirs and a young wife was clearly a potential target. If Madelyn Jeffries wasn't the perpetrator, her stepchildren could be. Perhaps they didn't want to share their inheritance with her. This was a potentially volatile situation, and worth looking at closely. Family dynamics were complicated.

Her phone rang and she made a huge mistake—she answered it before looking at caller ID.

"Catherine Jones."

"I have been trying to reach you for a week, Catherine."

She automatically straightened her spine, even though her posture was already perfect. "I'm sorry, Mother," she said automatically. She glanced up, relieved the door was closed.

"On Friday, what time will you arrive?"

"I won't be coming."

Silence. Charlotte Harrison had mastered silence as a weapon long before Catherine was born.

"I'm working. I'll call you later."

"Unacceptable," Charlotte said. "There is a memorial service at the church Friday evening, seven p.m. You will be there."

"I will likely not be there, Mother."

"Your only sister was murdered a year ago."

"Stop." Catherine did not want to do this now.

"I spoke to Chris," said her mother. "He's bringing Elizabeth. I thought you had reconciled with him."

The last thing Catherine wanted to do was talk to her mother about her marriage. She and Chris went through a rocky spot, and that was on her. But they were good—not that she would share that with her mother, who would make a snide comment designed to make her feel small and worthless.

No, actually, the last thing Catherine wanted to do was talk to her mother about Beth. She missed her sister more than anything and would have died to save her. Deep down, she knew that her mother would have preferred that outcome.

"Mother, I'm working on an important case and I don't know that we'll be finished by Friday."

"This is more important."

"I can't have this conversation now."

"This is the problem, Catherine Anne. You have always put work before family. It's why Chris left you."

Her blood boiled. "Chris did not leave me."

"That is not important," her mother said dismissively. "My daughter was murdered by a man obsessed with *you* and you have the audacity to tell me you can't be bothered to come to a prayer service honoring her *life* on the one-year anniversary of her *death*?" Her mother's voice rose at the end of each phrase.

"I cannot speak now. I will call you later."

"Do not hang—"

Catherine disconnected the call. She was shaking. She was

forty years old and she still avoided her mother whenever possible.

She put her palm on her forehead; she was clammy. How could her mother still elicit such a strong physical reaction in her?

As a forensic psychiatrist, Catherine understood human psychology better than most people, but when it came to her own life she was a mess. She knew—intellectually—that her physical reaction to her mother was based on her perceptions from childhood, how her mother had treated her compared to how she had treated Beth; how her mother blamed Catherine for events out of Catherine's control. Consequently, Catherine's choices in life—from college to career to marriage—had been designed to separate her from her mother. Separate and punish her mother, she supposed, for loving Beth more than her.

Yet Catherine loved her sister with everything she had. Beth had been the best the world had to offer. Beautiful, talented, kind, compassionate, without a mean or vindictive bone in her body. How had she and Catherine come from the same parents? Genetics was a mystery, how the same two parents could create a happy optimist and a brooding pessimist.

Catherine never resented her sister for her joy; instead, she was drawn to her, as if some of Beth's joy might rub off on her.

Catherine picked up her phone and pulled up a picture of Beth. She was everything Catherine was not. She was bright, happiness etched in every line of her face. Her hair was a few shades lighter than Catherine's dark brown; her eyes a few shades brighter than Catherine's dull hazel green. She should be walking on earth instead of lying dead six feet underground.

Catherine scrolled through more photos, remembering her sister, remembering when everything in her life was right. Her daughter, Lizzy, who was named after Beth, adored her aunt. They were so much alike… Lizzy could have been Beth's daughter.

Her finger scrolled too fast, and she hit a photo of Beth and

Matt from years ago, when they had still been in love, when Catherine thought that her best friend would be her brother-in-law and everything in her life would finally be perfect.

Matt ruined it, like he did with every relationship he'd ever had.

She had to find a way to get over this. Knowing the anniversary of Beth's death was Friday could interfere with Catherine's ability to do her job.

No, admit it. You agreed to come out here, nearly three thousand miles from your mother in Pennsylvania, because you didn't want to go to the memorial service. You didn't want to be working in DC or home in Virginia or anywhere within a hundred miles of Shenandoah National Park, where Beth was murdered. You couldn't get much further without leaving the continental United States.

Catherine tried not to lie to herself; she recognized that she'd run. Fled from Chris's affection and attention and his understanding. She didn't want to be told it would be okay. Her life had been anything *but* okay since Beth was murdered.

Killed because of Catherine.

Killed because Catherine didn't realize the killer she had profiled was so obsessed with her, that he wanted her attention so badly that he would kidnap her sister to get it.

And then Beth was dead.

The door opened and Catherine put down her phone.

Jim Esteban walked in. She was glad it was Jim, who was comfortable like a favorite uncle or kind mentor. A little overweight, a little too chatty, extremely smart yet a tad clueless about interpersonal situations. The job he worked brilliantly, but Catherine would never have to worry that he might ask how she was feeling, or notice that she was out of sorts.

He grabbed a water bottle and drained half of it, then poured coffee while he spoke. "Except for the captain, who was on the bridge, directly above the bomb, and the Marshalls, who were standing on the bow, everyone else on the boat died of drowning, with a secondary cause of blunt force trauma."

Catherine shifted gears, relieved to think about the deaths of strangers over the death of her sister.

"They were unconscious from the blast when they hit the water," stated Catherine, picturing those grisly events.

"*Bingo.* The Marshalls and Neil took the brunt of the explosion— they would have been dead no matter what. And there were other injuries that would have been life-threatening—broken bones, internal injuries, what you might expect from a violent explosion. But drowning takes five to ten minutes."

"Were all the bodies recovered?"

"Yes. The drowning victims were all intact; the other three were positively identified. No one on the boat that wasn't supposed to be there, either."

That had been one possible scenario: that an unknown suicide bomber had hidden in the hull of the boat until detonation.

"Any word from Agent Harris on the bomb mechanism?"

"Nope. He's still down in Seattle. Don't know if he'll make it up here tonight, at least not before dark. Did you make any progress?"

"Some," she said.

"If you don't need me, I'm going to head over to the house for an hour. Since Matt wanted to hit the ground running, I haven't had a breather. Just need a catnap."

"I'm good. Still reading through files and I have some calls to make."

She was relieved when Jim left. She liked him, but she felt like she had to be *on*, for lack of a better word, when anyone was around. She needed to process her mother's call, then refocus on the task at hand.

She glanced down at her phone and again saw the message from Kara Quinn. Now, that she could do! If Quinn wasn't going to seriously dig into the lives of the Jeffries family, dismiss suspects based on a brief interview without explanation, someone had to do it.

6

When he and John arrived at the West End Charter main office, Matt thought everyone who worked there still looked shell-shocked, even after three days. More than two dozen people sat together outside their cubicles, or stood in small groups. This was a third of their operation—the rest worked in security, maintenance, or in the club.

John knew every person he saw—one of the nice things about working in a small jurisdiction as a cop. Also, when the crime rate was low, residents trusted law enforcement more, and that developed a good working relationship between business and the police. But it also meant there could be a blind spot if someone you knew and trusted was involved in a crime.

John had called ahead, and the three owners of West End Charter—the Colfax siblings—had set up the conference room with coffee and pastries. Matt gladly took the coffee. He'd been up at three in the morning to catch the flight out west and was feeling sluggish now that it was after lunch—and close to the dinner hour on the East Coast, where they'd flown from.

The Colfax family had founded West End Charter with two boats more than fifty years ago. Since, it had grown to a fleet of forty that included charters, boat rentals, and guided tours. Their kayak rental business was thriving. Directly south of the main Friday Harbor port, they also had a harbor leased from the state for ninety-nine years, and they rented out a small number of extra slips there to long-term visitors.

Ted Colfax was the oldest, forty, and he appeared to have a quiet, even temperament.

Lynn, his sister, midthirties, was divorced and had taken back her maiden name. Not that it meant anything, but Matt always kept an eye out for family motives, past and present, whenever there was a crime that could have a financial component. Lynn was the accountant for the company and seemed to have a solid head on her shoulders.

Adam Colfax was the youngest brother, at least ten years younger than his sister, and clearly a hothead. Matt could tell not only because he had once been a hothead—and sometimes his Cuban temper still got the better of him—but because of Adam's inability to sit still or talk without an accusatory tone.

"You still don't have answers, John?" Adam said after introductions. "It's been three days. We have the damn protesters back because they think the explosion was a malfunction of our boat!"

Matt had spotted the IP protesters lining the street leading to West End property. They chanted and carried signs with rather generic messaging about saving marine life, but hadn't obstructed traffic.

John said, "I've already given a statement to the press that the preliminary investigation indicates that it was an intentional bomb, not a mechanical problem or accidental error."

"And they don't listen!"

Ted cleared his throat and said, "John, ATF was here all weekend inspecting our boats and property and they found no other bombs. We are remaining closed today out of respect for the families, but we're cleared to continue operations unless you tell me there's a reason we shouldn't."

"That's a business decision," John said. "At the moment, I can't tell you whether your business was the target or not."

"So you don't know anything more than you did Friday night," Adam interjected.

Matt said, "We know the bomb was planted in the bow of the ship, and the explosive used was C-4. That's something we can trace because it's hard to get and is heavily regulated, but tracing takes time. C-4 is easy to handle—it won't go off spontaneously. We ran preliminary background checks with the ATF on all your staff, and so far, everyone is clean."

"I could have told you that," Adam said. "We run backgrounds on everyone when they're hired."

"Be that as it may," Matt said, "we have to do the same. We appreciate your cooperation with security footage and access to your records. It helped us get a jump on the investigation over the weekend."

"But you didn't find anything?" Lynn asked, trying to sound hopeful.

"Not yet. Unfortunately, the security footage is only from building entrances and immediate exterior," Matt said. "It wouldn't show anyone approaching a boat from the water."

Ted shook his head. "It's our fault. We didn't foresee something like this."

"There's no blame there," Matt said. "And we don't know exactly *when* the bomb was planted. We're working backwards from the time the *Water Lily* set off. It could have been planted weeks ago."

Ted shook his head. "We inspect our boats regularly. Our maintenance people would have found it."

"How regularly?"

Lynn slid over a file. "These are the maintenance records for the *Water Lily* for the last six months. Ten days ago, the yacht was fully inspected. That means every inch was covered, both interior and exterior and a full exam of the engine. The *Water Lily* was last out Wednesday night. Ted took it out."

"I didn't go down into the hull, so I couldn't tell you whether the bomb was there or not," Ted said. "But I took a group of sightseers all around Orcas Island, and we had no problems."

"Who was your crew?"

"Cal McKinnon. He works full-time, year-round. He didn't do this."

"We have to talk with everyone. Cal passed our initial background check, but he canceled his shift last minute on Friday."

"Cal and his fiancée had an argument. He didn't get into what it was about, but Jamie had left, taking off to her dad's place on the other side of the island with their daughter, and Cal wasn't handling it well. I was surprised, to be honest, because Cal and Jamie have been together for five years, almost since Cal moved to the island. They're not, I don't know how to say it, a problem couple."

Lynn said, "What Ted means is they don't have drama. The idea of them arguing about anything substantive is almost laughable."

John asked, "Did Cal tell you what the argument was about?"

Ted shook his head. "I didn't ask, just told him if he needed anything to let me know. Cal is family. Not by blood, but family just the same."

Matt didn't see a motive yet, but Cal might know more than

he was saying. The charge of "accessory after the fact" could be a powerful motivator to encourage someone to talk.

Which brought up another problem with small communities—they tended to protect each other. They didn't want to believe the worst of their neighbors, and the idea that someone they knew could have killed nine people was foreign to them.

"And have you talked to IP?" Adam said. "Because they've vandalized our property before. Printed libelous accusations in the newspaper. They've—"

"Adam," Ted said. "John knows what he's doing."

"They are behind this! I know it. That Valerie bitch—"

"Adam, that's enough," Lynn said.

"Donna is stubborn and idealistic," Ted said, "but she's not violent."

"Donna? She has no control over these people." Adam waved his hand generally toward the front of the building. "Two of her people vandalized our dock last year."

John said, "And they paid for it, Adam. They're still on probation."

Adam wasn't backing down. "It cost over seventy thousand dollars to repair and the insurance doesn't cover all of it. Not to mention our rates went up because of all the little bullshit those people have done to our property—things we couldn't get them on."

"They're paying restitution," John said. "Graffiti and chanting is a long way from murder."

"Maybe they didn't plan for anyone to be on the boat," Adam said. "It malfunctioned or something and went off."

Matt didn't need people to start speculating and talking about this outside of the investigation. He said, "We are investigating every threat made to West End. What I need from you is information. You gave the sheriff all the threats you've received, correct?"

"Yes," Lynn said. "I've been tracking them, and anything that seems over-the-top I send to John right away. On Saturday, I gave him copies of everything we have."

"Have there been threats aimed at any of you personally, not specifically the business?"

They all shook their heads.

"If you receive anything—mail, on the phone, a computer message—no matter how innocuous, I need to see it. No one has taken credit for the bombing, which suggests it's probably not politically motivated. We're also looking into the lives of each of the victims. Other than Neil and Kyle, did you personally know anyone else on the boat?"

"I knew Pierce Jeffries pretty well since he bought vacation property here on the island five years ago, after he married Madelyn," Ted said. "He wanted to retire here, at least part-time, but that was years from now. He's a good man. Both him and his wife are avid sailors. We had a lot in common, so sometimes had a drink at the West End club. He shared business advice freely—he could have charged a fortune for his counsel. In fact, two years ago, when we had the recall issue that ended up leaking oil and caused IP to target us in the first place, he gave me a game plan to fix the problem, both on the business end and the PR end. I followed it to a T, and we've been doing very well, even after the economy tanked."

That was Matt's unasked question. Though he wouldn't rely solely on Ted Colfax's assessment—he wanted outside verification of West End's financial strength.

"And did you know Madelyn Jeffries?"

"Pierce never came to the island without her. Quiet, beautiful young woman, very nice. I didn't know her as well as I knew Pierce, but he seemed devoted."

"And what about his family? Was there friction that he married someone that much younger than him?"

"If there was, Pierce didn't mention it. But he didn't gossip. Honestly, he was a throwback to another era."

"I know Madelyn," Lynn said. "We became friendly. She didn't have friends here, and when Pierce was on business calls, she'd lunch here—said our club was more comfortable than the Harbor House."

"Which is?" Matt asked.

"The premier country club on the island," John said. "Anyone who's anyone in Washington belongs, though most of their members don't even live on the islands, just vacation here."

"The Jeffries belonged—it's where Pierce did most of his business," Ted said. "But to relax, he came here."

Lynn agreed. "I didn't like seeing her eat alone, so often I joined her. Madelyn was standoffish to most people because she felt they were judging her as a gold digger. Once you got to know her, you realized why she and Pierce had such a successful marriage. She's far more mature than her age suggests, and very knowledgeable about art and books, but not in a snooty way. I like her. I went out to see her yesterday, to find out how she's holding up. Her mother was there, so I didn't stay long, just gave her some food I had the kitchen prepare."

"And how was she?" Matt asked.

"In shock, I would say," Lynn said. "She seemed lost."

"Why all these questions about the Jeffries?" Adam asked. "They are good people. You need to be looking at IP!"

"Adam," Ted said quietly.

"It's okay," Matt said. "I'm used to people telling me how to do my job." He addressed Adam directly: "I have to look at all possible motives, suspects, and victims. Pierce Jeffries was by far the wealthiest person on that boat, and money can bring out the worst in people. So I need to look at anyone who might hold a grudge, or who might benefit from his death."

"I would look at his rotten kids before Madelyn," Lynn said. "I might be biased because I like Madelyn, and she's rarely spoken about her family situation. But they were here in the spring for a long weekend, and Madelyn stayed a few days longer. I asked her about it because it was unusual. She said Pierce had to go to New York and she wanted a few days without family drama. She regretted saying it, tried to backtrack—as if she feared I'd talk to a gossip rag. But it was more how she said it—it clearly bothered her. Later I learned there was a write-up in a business magazine where Pierce's daughter cruelly insulted Madelyn. It hurt her."

Matt made a mental note to have Catherine read and assess that article and the relationship between Madelyn Jeffries and the family. But back to West End. "I need a list of every employee who was let go over the last year, or any employee who was let go over the last five years who you think might possibly have a grudge."

"There's no one."

"No one?"

"We haven't fired anyone this year. Like I said, this is a family business," Ted said. "Small and lean. We hire locals. My kids work here. Lynn's daughter works here in the summers—she's in high school. I know everyone on the staff personally. There are people working here who've been here for twenty years, who our dad hired. People have left—usually because they moved off the island. We have a lot of temporary summer hires—a lot of college students. I recruit for the summer from University of Washington and hire ten to fifteen extra staff. It's the nature of the business—we don't do a lot of charters in the middle of winter."

"Neil Devereaux worked year-round?"

"Yes, part-time. As needed—and we always needed him in the summer. Plus, because he was a former FBI agent, there were a few jobs I wanted him to take."

"For what reason?"

"A few years ago I found out that one of my charter boats had been used to smuggle drugs from Victoria into the islands.

I didn't know how or who, so I asked Neil to do the run for a few weeks. He figured out who it was and how they did it."

"An employee?"

"No. It was someone who bought a ticket, once a month, working with a dockhand in Victoria. They're both in prison now, thanks to Neil."

"I'll need any files you have on that case," Matt said, "just to cover bases."

"I'll get them for you," Lynn said and wrote on her pad.

"I remember the case," John said. "I can pull the arrest record."

"You think some guy who is doing five years for smuggling blew up our boat and killed people?" Adam said with a distinct frown.

"I don't think anything at this point," Matt said. "But like I said earlier, I need to cover every possible angle."

A knock on the door interrupted Matt's next thought. A young man opened the door. "Ted? The protesters outside blocked access to the club, and it's getting a bit volatile. Raul and his team are there, but they still won't leave."

John stood. "I'll take care of it."

"May I go with you?" Ted said. "This is my business. I know some of those kids. I can talk to them."

"Go ahead," Matt said. "I only have a few more questions."

When they left, Matt asked the others, "Who is Raul?"

"Head of security," Lynn said. "He's worked here forever, was one of our dad's closest friends. He has a crew of six—we've never needed more. After Friday, he hired on additional security for the rest of the summer. We don't want anything like this to happen again. They're inspecting the boats every morning now."

Doubling security must have cost them, but it was a smart move, Matt thought.

He finished up by asking Lynn for a few files and information about security that she didn't have with her. She left the room and Adam was about to follow, but Matt asked him to stay.

"I can see that you're both upset and angry about these events," Matt said.

"Wouldn't you be?" Adam demanded.

"We don't know if IP is involved—or anyone in the group. Know that my team will be investigating every possible theory. We follow the evidence. But your animosity could be a hindrance, and I don't want to have to talk to you about it later."

"It's been three days!"

Adam ran both hands through his hair and paced. He was the outward persona of how Matt sometimes felt. But experience, training, and age had taught him to contain his natural frustrations.

"Multiple agencies are working the evidence. We know a lot, Adam. Far more than we did Friday night. We have some of the best people in the country working this case, here, in Seattle, and in DC. I don't give up. The bomber will face justice."

"You believe that?"

"I do."

"It would really help," Adam said, swallowing some of his anger, "if you could get it out that this wasn't West End."

"Meaning?"

"What, you haven't ruled us out? Do you actually think that Ted or Lynn or I blew up our boat and killed our crew and all those people? That we could be that...*cruel*? Heartless? Risk all that legal fallout and destroy our business?"

"Like I said, we must investigate every possible scenario. Insurance payouts are a powerful motivator for struggling companies."

Matt had intentionally baited Adam to see what he would say or do. It was clear from his shocked expression that Adam was stunned by Matt's words. Insurance scams were a dime a dozen, but hard to get away with—and Matt sensed that the savvy Colfax family would know that.

"Insurance? We have replacement insurance on all our boats. We don't get like, what? A cash settlement? We get a new boat. For what? Nine lives? We want a new boat, so we kill nine people? I can think of half a dozen ways to get a new boat without killing anyone! If that's one of your theories, it's idiotic. I hope you know what you're doing, because right now, I'm having doubts."

"We'll be looking at your insurance documentation—which is one of the things I asked Lynn to get for me—and can verify everything you've said. One thing to mark off the list—but I have to mark everything off the list."

Adam wanted to argue but kept his mouth shut.

Matt didn't honestly think it was an insurance scam, mostly because of exactly what Adam said—West End wouldn't benefit.

Though insurance could be a factor; life insurance on one of the victims. At this point, among the Nava Software folks, only one had life insurance, a small policy that benefited a sister. The Marshalls had dual policies, benefiting each other—so that wasn't a clear motive. Neil had a small policy that was part of his pension plan—that was split evenly between his two kids. But Jeffries? He had a substantial life insurance policy, and the beneficiary was his wife. If she predeceased him, it was split evenly between his mother-in-law and his three children.

"If you have any questions," Matt said, "call me. I'll tell you as much as I can about the investigation. But the last thing I want to hear is you—or anyone, frankly—making accusations or confronting potential suspects."

Adam nodded stiffly. Matt turned to leave. Then Adam said quietly, "Kyle was my boyfriend. We'd been involved for—well, a while now. About a year."

"Was it secret?"

"We didn't announce it in the paper, but we're both out, so it was pretty obvious to people who knew us."

"Are you telling me this because you think Kyle being gay could be a motive for murder?"

"No. I'm telling you because I loved him, and it hurts that he's gone."

Matt commiserated. "Like I said, my team is the best. We'll find out who did this. Talk to me if you need to talk about the case, but don't let your emotions dictate your actions. It never ends well."

7

The sheriff had called out two deputies to manage the protesters. They were a small group, but he was irritated when he climbed into his Bronco. "There's no reason for this," John said. "West End hadn't done anything, not that we know of, at any rate, and the only thing that works with these kids is threats of arrest for trespassing. They back off, but as soon as I leave, they start causing problems again. Then I have to put a couple deputies out there, pulling them from patrol. It really ticks me off."

"What are they protesting?" Matt asked. He looked in the side mirror as they drove off. There were about two dozen people, mostly young, with signs he couldn't quite make out except for the one that said *Save the Whales*.

"Like I told you before, two years ago there was a recall of a valve on the fuel tanks for about half of the West End fleet. They were given one year to retrofit their fleet, which they'd started to do. They could have pulled all the affected boats, but because they're a relatively small operation, they didn't—and weren't mandated to by law. But one of the boats leaked oil into a protected inlet and Donna went ballistic, used small print in the valve recall to sue West End for negligence. They ended up settling with the EPA, paid a fine, pulled all the remaining boats, and paid for the cleanup. Donna lost her suit. Before that, IP was mostly about protecting marine wildlife and trying to limit shipping in the Haro Strait—which is both a federal and international issue. With West End, she was able to localize her concerns, and that helped with her fundraising, in my opinion."

"Now I'm beginning to see the bigger picture."

"I'm going to make it clear to Donna Bell that West End is innocent in the explosion. Maybe she can get them to back off."

"What if they aren't?"

John glanced at Matt. "Are you seriously thinking that the Colfax family is behind this?"

"I'm not saying anyone specifically is involved—not yet," Matt said. "But even if they are low on the list, we haven't ruled any of them out." He tapped the files next to him. "My analyst will go through the financials and insurance records and see if there's a motive. And my investigators will look at personal motives."

"I know this family."

"John, you know everyone on the island."

"That makes me good at my job."

"I agree. I trust your judgment over anyone else."

"Why do I hear a *but* in there?"

"Being close to a situation can give us blinders. You run a tight department. You know the Colfaxes and I trust that your assessment is good. At the same time, having an outsider verify the information is necessary—not just to work the case, but to make sure that nothing slips through the cracks. When we turn this case over to the AUSA for prosecution, we need it to be airtight. If I get a thread that seems more plausible than another, I will pursue it until the lead is proven or unviable."

That appeased John, and they headed to Donna Bell's house, a five-minute drive south from West End, just outside the town limits. She had a pretty spread on the water: a cozy bungalow with a wide porch, surrounded by a lot of land and trees. A large hand-painted political sign advocating a yes vote on a local measure faced the road, which didn't see much traffic.

"What's that?" Matt asked. "There's not an election coming up, is there?"

"Local election in the fall. IP got a business tax increase on the ballot that would be earmarked for environmental issues. It's not going to pass. The 15,000 people who live in San Juan Islands County, most of them either own a business or work for a business that might cut their hours if the tax goes through. She tries every four years. Last time, she got closer—the initiative had a thirty-nine percent yes vote."

They weren't out of the truck before Donna stepped out of her house and stood on the porch, glaring their way.

Matt and John walked up the stone path. "Hello, Donna," John said, taking off his hat. "May we come in for a minute?"

"I've already said my piece, John," Donna said. "You have something to add, you can do it from there."

Matt stepped forward. "I'm Matt Costa, FBI Special Agent in Charge of the Mobile Response Team."

"I don't care if you're the second coming of Jesus Christ, you're not coming in."

Matt didn't waver. "I'm happy to ask my questions out here. We can do it standing, or maybe we can sit in those chairs under the tree?" He gestured to the right of the house, toward a grouping of plastic chairs under a huge oak tree.

Donna looked him up and down, not holding back her

disdain—whether toward him or law enforcement in general, Matt couldn't tell.

"Five minutes, that's it. You insult me or mine, you can take a hike."

"Thank you," Matt said.

They walked over to the chairs and Matt waited until Donna claimed her seat before he sat. She was a petite woman, not even five feet tall, but her attitude more than made up for her slight stature.

Matt gave Donna a brief rundown on the Mobile Response Team and why he was tasked with this case. He wanted her to feel like she was in the know, and he would be doubly happy if she would spread the information far and wide. If anyone in IP was involved in the bombing, they needed to know that federal law enforcement was closing in on them.

Once he was finished, Donna said, "Is that supposed to impress me, Agent Costa?"

"I'm just giving you information, Ms. Bell."

"But you're here right now because you think someone in my group put a bomb on a boat."

"No."

She raised her eyebrows and pursed her lips. "Don't lie to me, Agent Costa."

"I'm here to discover the truth. If that leads me to your organization, I will find out. I have no preconceived notions about Island Protectors or anybody involved. John here says you're honest and straightforward, so I'm being honest and straightforward with you. We don't know who bombed the *Water Lily*. This could be a one-time attack designed to kill one specific person—or it's the first of a series of bombs, and I will do everything in my power to prevent anything else like this from happening again.

"What I need from you, Ms. Bell," Matt said, "is any information that might help us. For example, we know that the overwhelming majority of bombers are male. A profile would suggest he is highly detail-orientated, above average IQ, and takes pride in his ability to plan. Often socially distant, he is less likely to work with a partner. The spectacle of the explosion is more important than the destruction itself—usually, a bomber is motivated to be destructive before latching on to any cause. If this is a specific target bombing, then the profile would change. Murder would be the focus, and the bomb is simply the mechanism."

Donna's expression changed from self-righteous anger to interest as Matt spoke, which emboldened him.

"We're pursuing both possibilities," Matt continued. "IP is the largest environmental group on the island and has had long-standing issues with West End Charter. We both know that good groups with nonviolent missions can have misguided—or downright evil—people within them. Not the group's fault. Whoever planted that bomb is solely responsible for the deaths of nine people. What I'm asking from you is to think about the people who are involved with IP. The bomber most likely wouldn't talk about bombing specifically but might be prone to advocating more militant actions to promote your cause. And because this is a tourist town, also consider any new members—maybe a seasonal hire, who comes to meetings or joins your protests but no one knows him, though he says all the right things."

Donna leaned forward. "If you think I'm going to sic the FBI on any of my members, John clearly didn't tell you who I am."

"I want you to look at your people and assess them critically."

"And what if I'm wrong? What if I look at a new kid—call him John Doe—and think, well, he's not from here. He's quiet. Just showed up one day and picked up a sign and helped with a project. Oh, no, he's suspicious. Better turn him in to the law."

"You're a smart person, Donna. You know what I mean."

"Yes, I do. And I'm not going to let you or John here give a rectal exam on any of my people and then when you catch them in a misdemeanor send them up the river to do a year and change."

"That's not how I operate."

"That's how *all* of you operate."

Matt had thought because of her interest in what he said that Donna would prove more helpful.

"What do you know about the vandalism last year?" Matt asked.

Donna glared at John. "You dragging those poor kids through the wringer again?"

"They did it, Donna," said the sheriff. "They were caught on security tape. Craig admitted it. They're lucky they didn't do jail time."

"Because jail is such a good idea for a couple of idealistic kids who made a mistake. You're a piece of work, John."

"You'll remember I recommended probation, not jail," John said, not backing down.

"Oh, how we rewrite history. They had no record, no one would have convicted them. You just convinced yourself that you were being the do-gooder here, when they are going to be in debt for a decade to pay off the restitution!"

"They caused a lot of damage, Donna."

This wasn't getting them anywhere. Matt intervened. "I'll be talking to the two in question, hope to remove them as suspects. It's a long way from vandalism to murder."

"Damn straight," she said.

"I'm not asking you to betray anyone," Matt continued. "I'm asking you to watch. To assess. And let me know if anyone is behaving out of character."

"You're wasting your time," Donna said. "I know my people, and no one would do anything like this. I'm done. I've given you more than five minutes. Now you can leave."

Matt handed her his business card. "If you change your mind."

"I won't."

But she took the card.

Maybe her animosity was real, maybe it was for show. But Matt hoped John was right and Donna was someone who wouldn't stand for her group being taken over by radicals.

Driving back to the station, Matt wished he'd listened to Kara and let her come to the island quietly and infiltrate the group. She would have then been in a better position to watch people. But he'd needed all hands for interviews and evidence analysis, so an undercover operation wasn't a realistic option.

"Back to the station?" John said.

"Do you know where Martin and Sokola are now?"

"Yep. They should both be at work. Want to pay them a visit?"

"No. I want them to come down to the station. I'm not saying they're involved, we have no evidence either way, but they are persons of interest because they have already targeted West End Charter."

"Matt, I don't think arresting them is going to help here."

"I don't want to arrest them. I want you to ask them to come down to the station at their convenience after work today, or first thing in the morning. Keep it friendly, but I want them on our turf."

"That I can do."

"In the meantime, let's head back to the station. I want to go over their files with a fine-tooth comb. Do you know if either of them would have access to explosives? Do they work in construction or have family members in construction? Or the military—it's harder to get C-4 off a military base, but not impossible if you know someone."

"Craig Martin has lived here since his parents divorced, about the time Craig was starting high school, ten or so years ago. Bobby is four or five years younger. He graduated high school a year ago, but I heard he's going to UW in the fall, working now to save up money. Their mother is a nice gal, owns a hair salon here—a lot of the women like her. My wife goes to her every six weeks like clockwork."

"You didn't answer my question."

"I don't know much about their dad. Craig went to college for two years in Bellingham but dropped out. A bit lazy, in my opinion. Bobby has worked a variety of jobs—a smart kid, will do anything to save up money. This summer I heard he was working as a janitor in the high school. Not something you see most nineteen-year-old boys aspiring to do, but he needs the money for college. Plus, he works weekends processing fish on the north end of the island. Not a fun job, I did it a couple summers in my youth, but it pays real well. I respect that."

"So do I, but I need to know if they can access explosives."

"You'll have to ask."

"And what about this Valerie?"

"She came to the island a couple years ago. Followed Craig, I believe, got her college degree in environmental science. Works at the coffee place. Not too friendly, but Craig's smitten. After we arrested her last year, she didn't have any family calling about her. A bit of a loner, but the Martins have taken her in as one of their own."

It was a long way from vandalism to murder...unless the murder was unplanned. They could have wanted to blow up the boat, and not realized that it was being used. But why? If IP's beef with West End was for a fuel leak that was fixed two years ago, why were they still targeting the group? Was it really what John said, that they wanted all motorboats banned from the area? That seemed not only unrealistic but foolhardy in a community that relied on ferry service and a tiny airport to get on and off the island.

If they were guilty, Matt would ferret it out during interrogation. And based on the sheriff's comments, Craig Martin would cave first.

Matt called Ryder to find out where he was in processing Neil's house. He didn't answer.

Ryder always answered his calls.

"How far to Neil Devereaux's house?" he asked John.

8

Neil Devereaux's house was walking distance from West End Charter. It wasn't much—bedroom, living room with a counter that served as the kitchen, and a small den—but the deck, which was twice the size of the house, boasted a choice view of the water.

Ryder Kim and Deputy Tom Redfield entered the dead man's home that afternoon. It smelled musty from being closed up for three days, and warm, either because of the summer heat, or the heater had been on.

"What are we looking for?" Tom asked.

"Any files related to criminal investigations, his past cases, and specifically information about the two students who died near

Mount Rainier. You take the bedroom and living room, closets. I'll take the den. Oh, and check for any information about Brandon Fielding."

"Fielding was a pyramid scam, right?"

"Yes, and he was released from prison six months ago. He threatened Agent Devereaux in court."

"Fifteen years is a long time to hold a grudge."

Not really, Ryder thought, but didn't say anything.

His paternal grandparents had never forgiven his dad for marrying a non-Korean wife. They subtly criticized his mom every time they came over—how the house was never clean enough, dinner mediocre, or her clothing inappropriate. It didn't seem to matter that his mother, like his father, was a doctor (a microbiologist, while his father was a surgeon), or that she was as brilliant in her field as his father in his. His parents had been married for thirty-five years, and yet his grandparents had never changed.

Ryder didn't understand why his dad never stood up for his mom, nor did he understand why his mom didn't fight back—especially since in every other situation she stood up for herself and spoke her mind. *Tradition* wasn't a good excuse, but it was the only one his parents offered him.

His one act of rebellion had been joining the Army. He had been premed in college and planned to follow in his parents' footsteps. The decision to join ROTC while in college had changed his entire life.

He'd expected that his father would never forgive him. Ryder was surprised but happy that his judgment had been wrong. His father embraced him, told him to follow his own path.

Still, the grudge that his grandparents held suggested to Ryder that some individuals could be unforgiving—perhaps even to the point of murder. Brandon Fielding maintained he had been wrongly imprisoned because of Neil Devereaux's perseverance, and clearly bore a grudge.

Ryder sat down at Agent Devereaux's desk and rubbed his

forehead. He wasn't generally prone to headaches, and this one had come on suddenly, but he dismissed it as a consequence of his upside-down routine today. He hadn't exercised, his breakfast was far earlier than normal, and he hadn't had time to find a healthy lunch, resulting in eating snack food. By tomorrow he would be back to his routine.

Devereaux had an old PC on his tidy desk, off. Ryder unplugged the cords and put the computer aside to take to the station.

The retired cop didn't have a lot of personal mementos in his den, save for one photo on the wall. It was several years old, Ryder knew, because his wife had died eight years ago, and Mrs. Devereaux was in the photo. The kids looked to be teenagers. It had been taken on a boat, and Ryder recognized the marina in the background, near Chesapeake Bay. Now the two kids had no living parents, and while grown, they were grieving. Ryder wanted to find out what happened, to give them peace, but would they ever have peace?

Ryder loved his parents; if they were gone, he would be alone. He was an only child; he wasn't close to his father's family; his maternal grandparents had died years ago. Did Neil's kids, Eric and Jillian Devereaux, have other family? As they lived half a world apart, they must feel isolated and alone.

Ryder hoped to help find Eric and Jillian justice. He believed he would. His boss, Matt Costa, wasn't a man who gave up, which was one attribute that Ryder admired—as well as his ability to delegate and the deep trust he placed in his team. Ryder didn't want to let him down.

After setting the computer aside, he went through the desk drawers. Most were empty, which seemed odd for a man obsessed with a cold case. Where were the files? His notes? Was everything on the computer?

While most of the drawers were empty or filled with unrelated documents like Devereaux's personal financial records, in the bottom drawer Ryder found two thick files about the Mowich Lake drownings, which he pulled out.

Two college seniors—Brian Stevens and Jason Mott—had drowned in Mowich Lake near Mount Rainier on Memorial Day weekend, shortly after finishing their third year of college. Though the deaths were suspicious, one body recovered first had a toxic level of alcohol in his system. The second body, recovered months later, was inconclusive. The ME concluded that the young men drowned, with a secondary cause of alcohol poisoning and hypothermia. Specifically, it appeared they were so wasted they fell off their boat and drowned in the icy water. They went missing that weekend, but the timing was uncertain—they were reported missing by their parents Tuesday morning when they didn't return from the camping trip.

He would analyze the files in detail back at the station, but gave a cursory look at the information. Devereaux had meticulous notes attached to every article and record on the case, all laid out cleanly, and Ryder could easily follow his train of thought. But Devereaux had what Ryder always thought of as the proverbial "gut" that many cops talked about, and something Ryder lacked. He came across a sticky note with a question that made sense—but Ryder would have never thought to ask it. For example:

Witness A reported unidentified third male at campsite—before or after deaths?

Another note was also cryptic—

TOD inconclusive, water temperature near freezing. Witness B reports seeing Brian and Jason on Sunday at sunset by their tent—did they go to the lake Sunday night or Monday morning?

Devereaux had photos from the campsite, but there'd only been one official photo after the boys had disappeared, with their equipment still at the campsite, taken on his cell phone by the ranger who was first contacted after the boys didn't return.

Based on the time stamps and notes, the other photos were taken by Devereaux at a later date.

Brian's body was found on a rocky shore the Wednesday after their disappearance, but Jason's body wasn't discovered for nearly three months until it floated to the surface near the middle of the lake. Devereaux had a map of the lake with two marks indicating where the bodies had been found—substantially far apart.

Scientifically, it didn't cause Ryder any suspicion. If the boys had been drunk and out on a boat, it might stand to reason that one died faster than the other. Brian could have attempted to swim to the boat or shore, then succumbed to the icy water. While the distance from shore to shore was less than a mile at the widest point, he could have been disorientated.

But several notes related to the boat itself: *Why it hadn't been checked for fingerprints. How it ended up on the opposite shore from Brian's body.*

Ryder's head pounded. He didn't like taking pain relievers, but he might have to pop a couple of Tylenol if the throbbing didn't subside on its own. He'd ask Deputy Redfield if there was a juice bar in town—he thought he'd seen one. Ryder preferred vitamins and diet when fixing what ailed him.

Ryder was not confident he would be able to do what Matt expected of him: to determine if Neil Devereaux had uncovered important evidence that may have led to his death. The accidental deaths were well-documented, and Devereaux's subsequent investigation hadn't yielded any additional information that Ryder could see that might be cause to reopen the case.

Ryder flipped through Devereaux's address book, but his eyes blurred. He squeezed them shut, rubbed them, opened them again. He didn't feel any better. Something was wrong...

"Tom?" he called out. "I need to step outside."

Redfield didn't answer. "Tom?" Ryder called again.

He rose from the chair, immediately felt dizzy as a wave of nausea overcame him. He staggered and fell to his knees. He heard his phone ringing. It was in his pocket, but it sounded like it was ringing underwater.

You've been poisoned.

How? If both he and Redfield were ill, that wasn't food. What was it?

Gas?

No, this was carbon monoxide. The realization hit Ryder immediately. Odorless gas. Dizziness. Fatigue. Nausea.

He crawled, focused on the door. Fresh air. He needed air.

Call Matt. Call 911. Where's Tom?

He reached into his pocket for his phone, but was unable to dial.

He collapsed before he reached the door.

Matt called Ryder a second time as John pulled up behind the deputy's cruiser parked on the gravel driveway leading to Neil's small house. Again, no answer. He couldn't dismiss it as poor cell coverage because he hadn't had any trouble sending and receiving calls in Friday Harbor.

"Tom's not answering, either," John said.

Matt jumped out of the Bronco and John followed him. They approached the house cautiously, but quickly, looking in every direction to assess if there was a threat. It was quiet. He could scarcely hear traffic from the nearby downtown area.

All the blinds were drawn in the house. The front door was solid wood, no glass panes, nothing to see inside. He tried the knob; it was unlocked.

He pulled his gun. He didn't know what to expect. He knocked. "Ryder! Tom! It's Matt Costa. I'm coming in!"

He pushed open the door and stepped back. Silence. No movement.

"Agent Kim!" he called, as he stepped inside. John stood at the threshold.

The house was musty and there was an underlying scent Matt

couldn't identify. To the left was a kitchen area separated from the living room by a bar counter. To the right was a narrow hall leading to a small office, and Ryder—lying facedown on the wood floor.

"Clear the house," Matt told John as he squatted to check Ryder's pulse. He was responsible for this young analyst; how could this happen?

Ryder's pulse was strong, but he was unconscious.

"Matt!" John called. "Tom is passed out in the bedroom!"

"Call for paramedics," he said. He didn't know what was going on, but if both Tom and Ryder were unconscious with no visible signs of injury, that suggested something they'd eaten or inhaled. There were no signs of vomit, there could be a gas leak, but Matt didn't smell any gas.

"John, call the gas company."

Matt turned Ryder over and grabbed him under his arms and pulled him out of the house. He moaned and Matt was relieved. Matt put him on the lawn, made him stay down. "Ryder?"

"I'm. Okay."

"Stay put. I'm going to help John with Deputy Redfield."

Matt went back in and John was struggling with Tom, who was taller than the sheriff. Matt picked Tom up the same way he'd picked up Ryder, and motioned for John to get his feet. They carried him out.

"Are you sure we should be moving him?" John asked.

"I think there's a gas leak, something—I don't know. I don't smell anything, but something caused both of them to pass out. Maybe the heater was on, or the pilot light got blown out. But it needs to be checked out."

Tom hadn't regained consciousness yet, but Ryder was trying to sit up.

"Stay," Matt said.

"I need to get the files."

"You need to stay put. The gas company is on its way."

Ryder shook his head. "Carbon. Monoxide. I recognize my symptoms. I just need fresh air."

"And oxygen, if I remember EMT training."

John said, "I'll turn off the main gas line."

He went around back.

The ambulance arrived shortly after John returned. The paramedics gave both Tom and Ryder oxygen. Ryder insisted he felt better. Tom had come around, but was disorientated and complained of a headache. He was put on a gurney to be transported to the small island hospital.

Ryder insisted that he was fine. "Matt, don't make me go."

"You need to have your vitals checked."

Ryder looked at the paramedic. "You can do that, right? I'm fine. I was an Army medic. I know I'm okay."

"It's up to you," the paramedic said.

"It's up to me," Matt said.

Ryder scowled, and Matt didn't think he'd seen his analyst so irritated.

"Check him out, give us both the stats, and we'll make the call."

Kara and Deputy Anderson pulled up then. Anderson went to talk to John, and Kara came over to Matt. "What the fuck happened?" she said. "We were almost to headquarters when Marcy heard on the radio that a deputy and agent were down here. I recognized Neil's address."

Matt always appreciated Kara being straight to the point.

"Gas company is on its way, but Ryder and Deputy Redfield were both passed out when I arrived. I came when Ryder didn't answer his damn phone. Ryder thinks carbon monoxide, but that seems suspicious. Though, the house is old—it's possible."

"He's okay?"

"He's a medic, doesn't want to go to the hospital. Says he's fine."

Kara glanced over at Ryder, clearly concerned. Matt wanted

to touch her for support, but that would be inappropriate here, in front of others. It had become harder for him to keep his feelings for Kara locked down, especially since they'd been able to spend so much time together over the last month. He wondered if she had the same problem.

Probably not. She never talked about how she felt, what she wanted, if she was happy with their relationship. Except when they were alone, in bed, and he was her sole focus. He wanted that every night, but that just wasn't possible, for a variety of reasons. She'd made it clear that everything about them was one day at a time. It was becoming increasingly more difficult to live that way.

The gas company pulled up. As soon as they cleared the area, Matt needed to secure the house and retrieve the computer and files Ryder had been boxing up before he collapsed.

Kara turned to Matt. That's when he saw what he wanted to see, just a hint of intimacy. "Hey," she said, "he looks fine. I'll talk to him. He can't lie to me."

"Okay."

"This was an accident, right? Do you think our team was targeted? Or the house?"

"I can't make that assessment until I talk to the gas company, and I don't know when they'll be done with their investigation." He reached out, brushed the back of his hand against the back of hers. "Meet at headquarters, one hour?"

"I'm heading there now. I'll take care of Ryder." She winked at him, her back to the crowd, and it was exactly what he needed.

He walked over to John and the head of the gas company to talk about Neil's house. If this wasn't an accident, they were going to have to shift the focus of their investigation. Because if Neil Devereaux was the target, they needed to know why.

9

Kara convinced Ryder to go to the short-term rental for an hour or two. "Shower, drink water, take aspirin, relax," she said. "You still look a bit queasy."

He agreed, and Marcy dropped him off. Kara walked him in to make sure he didn't pass out. She didn't think he would— but she felt a bit overprotective of Ryder. Sure, he'd been in the Army and he had gone through the FBI academy and he was a medic, but he was still an analyst and they needed to keep an eye on him. And she liked him.

"You feel up to it, I'm going to convince Matt to take us to the Fish & Brew for dinner."

"I will," he said. "I'll be at the station soon."

"No rush. Seriously."

Kara jumped back into the Bronco. "He okay?" Marcy asked.

"He's fine. Headache. It's been a long day for us."

"Want to grab a bite?" Marcy asked as she pulled into the parking lot behind the sheriff's station. "I have paperwork, but I'll be done in thirty."

Kara was starving, but it was nearly five and Matt wanted everyone to debrief. She also hoped he had answers to what had knocked Ryder out.

"Work calls," Kara said.

Marcy seemed to be a competent cop. Kara liked that she was quiet and observant, but she also didn't want to be her BFF. At the same time, they'd be working together for the foreseeable future, so Kara needed to keep it friendly. She was good at playing the part but wasn't in the mood right now.

"I run most mornings at five thirty," Marcy said. "If you're up for it."

Kara didn't want a running partner, but hadn't she just been thinking she needed to play nice?

"That I can do."

"There's a great path along the water, north of the harbor, that's just over five miles round trip. Meet me at the main harbor entrance."

"I'll be there."

Kara headed to the conference room and Marcy went down the opposite hall.

Catherine was the only one there.

Kara grabbed a water bottle from a mini fridge and eyed the energy bars—she'd already eaten three, and the thought of another made her feel sick. Ryder would never stock up on junk food. She'd have to remember to grab chips and trail mix sometime tomorrow.

She drank half the water in one long gulp. "You heard about what happened at Agent Devereaux's house."

Catherine looked up at her.

"Yes."

"Where's Jim?"

"He'll be here momentarily."

Kara wasn't sure what to make of Catherine. She'd met her Sunday morning during their initial debriefing on the bombing and she'd been standoffish, which normally didn't bother Kara. She wondered if their conversations back in March, when Kara was involved in the Triple Killer investigation and Catherine was working the case from DC, had something to do with it. Kara was blunt—if she had something to contribute to a conversation, she did. She was a cop, after all—she knew what she was doing when it came to murder and mayhem. Not everyone appreciated bluntness.

Kara took a seat and looked at the whiteboard. Catherine had been busy—she had the victims listed and ranked them high or low as potential bombing targets. Then she noted potential motives on the other side. Right there in a starred box was Madelyn Jeffries.

Kara drained her water bottle and tossed it in the recycling can. "Madelyn didn't kill her husband," she said. "I'd move her to low. Cross the *t*'s and dot the *i*'s, but it's not her."

Catherine said nothing, continuing to read the file in front of her.

Kara was tired, hungry, and her first instinct was to argue. Instead, she bit her tongue and stared at the board, trying to see the evidence as Catherine saw it.

Sure, on paper, a young, beautiful wife, middle-aged rich guy—the perfect recipe for murder. But people weren't paper. Stereotypes could be true, but reliance on them got cops in trouble.

Kara didn't think that Pierce Jeffries's kids had the guts to murder anyone, and she didn't get the vibe that they wanted their dad dead—though if Madelyn had been on the boat and

Pierce had stepped off, she'd believe it. They hated their stepmother and were clearly unhappy with the idea that she was pregnant with their half sibling.

She needed to follow up with Justin Jeffries, who had worked with his dad. Madelyn said he was fair, and he spent the most time with his father. Business? Maybe. But not personal unless there was a deep scandal they hadn't yet uncovered.

Let Catherine think what she wanted, no skin off Kara's nose.

"She's pregnant," Kara said.

Catherine again looked at her before speaking. "Excuse me?"

"Madelyn Jeffries. A little over three months. Her stepkids heard about it last week and pitched a fit, then showed up at the house while I was there and accused her of killing their dad."

"And you still don't consider her to be a suspect."

"She loved him. She didn't kill him." Damn. Why couldn't Kara keep her mouth shut to keep the peace? "You would come to the same conclusion if you sat down and talked to her."

"Love and hate are often two sides of the same coin."

"Yep. Not this time."

"Psychological profiling is a lot more than a single interview, Detective Quinn."

This conversation was getting them nowhere, and the longer it went on, the angrier Kara would get. Profiling was a tool in a cop's tool chest. She often talked to the department shrink in LA, especially when she was working with CIs, to get a better sense of how far she could trust them. But it was a *tool*. Nothing beat one-on-one interviews, assessing tone and body language and information from the witness or suspect, comparing that with evidence. Which was, Kara knew, a part of profiling. When she had traffic detail, reading a driver was essential in determining whether they were a threat or just ticked off about being pulled over. Wrong judgment could get you injured or worse.

So profiling—yeah, Kara appreciated it, but Kara wasn't an idiot, and she would bet her badge that Madelyn had no part in killing her husband. Why Catherine couldn't at least see that or acknowledge Kara's experience and professional assessment, Kara didn't know. She couldn't quite read Catherine.

Yet.

But she would.

Catherine began typing on her laptop, and Kara walked over to the whiteboard and took pictures of the information.

The typing stopped.

"What are you doing?"

Kara took another picture.

"To study later."

Catherine had no answer to that and went back to the laptop. Kara resisted the childish urge to stick her tongue out at the shrink.

The sheriff walked in, pushing a cart with two boxes and a computer. "The gas company said the house is clear. Your boss wanted me to bring these here, from Agent Devereaux's house."

Kara helped him unload the files. "Did they determine what happened?"

"Your guy, Kim, was right. Carbon monoxide poisoning. It's an old house, don't know why Neil didn't have carbon monoxide detectors. But they're still investigating the how, whether accident or not. Matt said he'd be here shortly."

"How's Deputy Redfield?" Kara asked.

"He'll be fine. They're keeping him overnight because his oxygen level was low. He was in the back of the house, searching closets and under beds, and carbon monoxide settles. I'll let you all know when I know exactly what happened."

"Appreciate it," Kara said as the sheriff left.

She looked through the files just out of curiosity. Everything appeared to be about the Mowich Lake drownings, and there were a lot of sticky notes.

Marcy Anderson walked in. "Kara, here's the information you wanted about Justin Jeffries."

"Great, thanks," she said.

"Now I'm really leaving. Time to hit the gym or I'll never do it. Unless you need me?"

"We're good, thank you."

"Tomorrow morning, don't forget."

"I won't."

Kara resisted the urge to roll her eyes. It probably wasn't fair to the cop—it was a small town, and she was friendly. Maybe she didn't have anyone to run with, and Kara fit the bill.

"Why did you need information on Justin Jeffries?" Catherine asked.

"To follow up on my conversation with the widow and get Justin's take on the marriage and pregnancy. Already heard from the other two kids. He's supposed to be in town tomorrow."

"I think we should reassess how we approach the Jeffries family," said Catherine.

Kara leaned back in the chair, balanced on the back two legs, which helped her control her building tension. "Oh?" she asked casually.

"We can't dismiss Madelyn Jeffries simply because she charmed you."

It took all of Kara's self-control to *not* jump down Catherine's throat. "I wouldn't use that word."

With an eyebrow raised, Catherine spoke slowly, as if Kara was an idiot. "My job is to analyze behavior and psychology and determine whether someone is a viable suspect. I haven't ruled out Madelyn Jeffries, and on paper she has a solid motive."

Kara leaned forward, her chair dropping to the floor louder than she intended. "My job," she said, equally slowly, "is to find out who blew up nine people, and Madelyn Jeffries was not involved."

"You cannot know that."

"You analyze behavior and personality? So do I. I spent more than an hour with her and she's not guilty." Now Kara was going out on a limb, because she rarely made a definitive statement like that.

She also knew in her gut that she was right. And she wasn't going to let some shrink make her feel incompetent or stupid because she disagreed.

"With all due respect, Detective," Catherine said dismissively, "it's not your job to determine who is and is not a suspect. I understand that you're used to working alone, but you're now part of a team of highly trained and experienced investigators. I'll take your opinion under advisement."

Kara stood up and walked out. She needed five minutes to get her head on straight or she was going to explode.

She wanted to take Dr. Catherine Jones down a peg or three. *Damn*, was she angry.

She strode out of the building. The warm salt air wrapped around her and she breathed in deeply. Anger wasn't going to do her any good. It wasn't going to solve this case or get her off this team.

Kara didn't know if she fit in here. She didn't know if this was what she was meant to do.

And what are you going to do, Kara? You can't go back to Los Angeles and work undercover. Your cover was blown. You can't even go to LA and be safe. You have people gunning for you. Literally and figuratively.

She'd never fit in anywhere.

Well, that wasn't true now, was it?

She turned away from the sheriff's station, not looking back, and in that moment she didn't know if she wanted to go back.

The truth was, while she always felt like an *outsider*, she always *fit in*. Because she changed who she was—who she had to be—*to* fit in. Being an undercover cop meant she could be anyone. It had been a game for a long time, a challenge, and she was good at it. It had also been her job. But now, fitting in on this task force job meant ignoring her instincts and being treated like a rookie cop?

Nope, not going to do that. She *couldn't* do that.

She stopped walking when she hit the shoreline. She'd walked six blocks and should probably double-time it back to the station for Matt's debriefing. Instead, she stared at the water and sailboats, soaking in the sun, and thinking this might be the last case she worked with the Mobile Response Team.

10

Ashley Dunlap called out to her sister that she was taking their dog, Dakota, for a walk. She hustled the husky out the door before her sister came downstairs to join her.

Walking briskly down the street and around the corner, she steered Dakota into the small park where Bobby Martin was waiting for her.

Dakota greeted Bobby with a vigorous hand-licking; Ashley greeted him with a kiss.

"You're shaking," he said.

"Did you talk to your brother?"

"Of course. But you shouldn't be worried. Craig had nothing to do with that explosion."

"The FBI said it was intentional. That someone planted a bomb."

"Craig wouldn't do anything like that, but I talked to him. He says no one with IP would do such a thing. I mean, he hates West End, but he wouldn't hurt anyone."

She frowned. She didn't think that Bobby's older brother had anything to do with it, but Craig *had* been arrested last year for vandalism.

"Ash, what are you so upset about?" He put his arm around her, and they sat on the bench. Dakota lay down at her feet, his head up, watching kids playing on the swings across the park. She looked at their entwined hands, hers darker than Bobby's. His palms rough because of his part-time work at the fish processing plant; hers rough from sailing. She liked that—they both were active, they both loved the outdoors, they both loved the island.

It was nearly six o'clock but still light enough to play, and Ashley was nostalgic. Her mother had taken her and Whitney to this park almost every day when they were little. She'd been ten when her mom died, and only three months before that she had told her mom she was too old for the park.

She wished she had one more day with her.

"Ash? You okay?"

She pushed away the thoughts of her mom and her childhood.

"I know it was awful," Bobby continued, "and I'm so sorry you had to see it, but no one we know did this. No one we know *could* do anything like this."

"Neil is dead. And Kyle. We know those people, and they're just...gone. My dad is positive it's IP, and he's so mad... He doesn't understand."

"We're not violent. You know that. And Craig isn't violent. He just did something stupid and he's paying for it now."

"Has the FBI talked to him?"

"The FBI asked him to go down to the station tomorrow, but I don't know if he will."

"He's on probation. He has to."

"I don't think that's true."

Ashley was pretty sure she was right but didn't correct her boyfriend. And truly, she didn't think Craig would do this—she'd known him for years, and he didn't seem to have a mean bone in his body, just like Bobby.

She bit her lip. She didn't want to say it, but she'd been thinking about it all day.

"What?" Bobby asked, as if reading her mind.

"Valerie is a lot… Well, she's kind of radical."

"We're all considered radical in the eyes of people like your dad."

"He just doesn't understand what's at stake. But you know what I mean—Valerie's different. She's just— I don't know."

"Look, I don't like her all that much, either, but she cares and is dedicated, and that's what's important, right?"

"I don't think your brother would have vandalized the pier last summer if she hadn't egged him on."

Ashley hadn't liked Valerie ever since she'd moved to the island two years ago. She couldn't really put her finger on *why*, just that Valerie was so angry all the time and was—well, kind of a bitch. She hated that word, but it fit her. Bobby didn't like her, either, but he never said anything to his brother because for some reason Craig thought she was amazing, and he was in love.

"Ash, what did the FBI say that has you all worked up?"

"Whitney told them that I was taking pictures. They wanted to see my camera—my dad took the memory card and just *gave* it to them."

"What are you worried about? Do you think Craig…anyone… is on that disk? I mean, no one we know did this. You *know* that. So what are you worried about?"

"I don't know… I mean, it's just pictures, but it wasn't just the *Water Lily*. The pictures I took last week are on there, too, and what if they ask me about that? What do I say? What if they talk to my dad?"

"You know what my mom says? Don't borrow trouble."

"I'm not! This is real, it's happening. My dad is going to find out...that I..." She couldn't say it.

Bobby hugged her tight. "Baby, don't do that. It's going to work out. I promise."

"You don't know that. And it's not just the pictures or the FBI... What if something happens *again*?" She didn't want to think about it. Watching the boat explode, seeing the bodies flying in the air, had been the worst thing that ever happened to her, other than when her mom died.

"Ash, don't do that to yourself. Did the FBI tell you if there was a lead or something?"

"Not really. They mostly asked about what Whitney and I saw, what we remembered, if we saw anything suspicious, things like that. I wish we had—I wish we could help find who did this. Maybe the pictures will help..." She put her head in her hands. Her dad was going to ground her forever if he found out she had been volunteering for Island Protectors. He just didn't understand how important this was to her!

"The FBI talked to Donna today, too," Bobby said.

She jerked her head up. "They don't think she did this!"

"I don't think so. Craig just said that the FBI and sheriff went out there today and Donna was pissed off. Are you coming to the meeting tonight?"

"I want to, but—"

"We'll skip the social hour. Your dad goes back to the restaurant after you guys have dinner, right? Meet me after that."

She bit her lip. She shouldn't, especially on top of her dad giving that memory drive to the FBI. But she'd made a copy and she needed to get that to Donna. Maybe Donna would figure out what was going on and prove that no one in IP had anything to do with this.

"Whitney won't rat you out, will she?"

"No—I'll tell her I'm just going on a walk with you. She thinks we're romantic. Okay, I'll meet you. But we can't stay late."

He kissed her and she hugged him. She loved Bobby so much, but her dad wouldn't understand. He was good friends with Ted Colfax, so the Martins were off-limits because of what Craig had done. It had been stupid, Craig knew that, and Bobby had nothing to do with what his brother had done—why couldn't her dad separate them in his head?

Bobby had taken the last year to save money for college, but he was leaving for the University of Washington this fall. She planned to join him there next year, but she was going to miss him when he left. Still, when she went to college her dad would have nothing to say about who she dated.

That thought didn't make her feel good. She loved her dad so much and she hated keeping this secret from him, but he could be so damn stubborn about things. Especially boys. "We just have to be careful," she said. "I don't want my dad to even suspect, especially now."

"I wish you'd come clean with him," Bobby said. "I don't like sneaking around."

"I don't, either, but you're nineteen and graduated last year and he's weird about things like that. Plus, he knows about Craig and the dock and has seen you protesting... I don't want to make him mad." *You don't want to disappoint him, either.* Ashley didn't like when her dad was angry or upset, but sometimes, his quiet disapproval was worse than anything.

"I don't want to hide how I feel all summer."

"Let me think about the best way to tell him, okay? Maybe... when this whole thing is over and the FBI tells him that no one at IP had anything to do with that awful bomb."

He kissed her. "Text me when you're leaving tonight, and I'll meet you outside the library."

"I love you, Bobby."

He hugged her tightly. "I love you, too, Ash. It's going to be okay. I promise."

11

Matt walked into the conference room and said, "Quick debrief. It's after six, and we have a lot on our plate tomorrow."

He glanced around. Catherine was writing on the whiteboard, Ryder was at the table on his laptop.

"Ryder, what are you doing here? Kara said she took you back to the house."

"I showered, drank water, and found a juice bar walking back here." He held up a disgusting-looking green smoothie, half-gone. "I feel good, sir. I promise."

Matt didn't expect anything less from Ryder, but he didn't take what had happened lightly. "The gas company is still investigating, but they confirmed carbon monoxide and that it came from the heater. With no one going in and out since Friday, all windows closed, it built up. It was stronger in the bedroom, which is why Deputy Redfield was affected more."

"Accident or intentional?" Catherine asked.

"They're leaning accident, but they're doing a full investigation, and the fire department has an arson investigator who has experience with all manner of gas leaks. We'll have more answers tomorrow."

Matt continued, "Where's Kara and Jim?"

Ryder said, "I texted them—they're coming. Jim is on a call in the sheriff's private office."

Matt nodded toward a box on the table. "Is that from Neil's house?"

"Yes, sir. The FBI file is there, and all Agent Devereaux's notes on the Mowich Lake drownings. But his desk was nearly empty—this was everything there, and so far, nothing that points to what he thinks happened, why he thinks the college students were murdered. I'll go through his computer tonight and tomorrow."

"Good. Two agents are talking to Brandon Fielding as we speak. I should be getting their report shortly. Zack reported that Fielding is broke, he doesn't have any expenditures that point to hiring the bomber, but we'll cross him out once we can verify his alibi and background."

Jim and Kara walked in together. Jim was laughing at something Kara had said, and she had a grin on her face. She sat down next to Ryder. "I'm starving," she said. "Can we make this fast?"

Jim pulled out a chair across from Kara. "I heard about this pub not far from here."

"The Fish & Brew," Kara said. "I was there earlier, interviewing our teenage witnesses—I've been starving ever since."

Matt said, "Business first, then we'll head over there. I haven't had good pub fish in a long time. First—I talked to Michael and he'll be here tomorrow morning. He's at the ATF lab and they have confirmed that one-half a brick of C-4 was used in the explosion. No other accelerant was detected, and it was the fuel from the boat which caused the second explosion. They believe the bomb was motion activated, based on the speed of the boat, and are running a series of tests to determine exactly how it detonated. This is Michael's area of expertise, and I'm pleased that the ATF has pulled him in. We'll get answers faster with Michael running point."

Ryder said, "I booked him on a direct flight from Seattle that arrives at eight tomorrow morning."

The airport was tiny and supported only small planes, but they had regular routes from both Bellingham and Seattle, a half dozen flights a day. The sheriff's department had three helicopters and John said Matt could use one if they needed to get to the mainland quickly.

Matt told the group what he'd learned from the Colfax family and Donna Bell. To start off, he wanted to rule out IP. "I won't say that they're the number one suspect—as a group or any of the individuals—but unless we find a personal motive against one of the victims, they are our most logical suspects." He nodded toward the whiteboard, where Catherine had laid out her theories. "I see you agree, Catherine?"

"Yes, based on the actions of other radical environmental groups, it's not implausible, though I don't think it's the group specifically. They are an organization known to the FBI but are not on any watch list. There have been no reported warning signs. It's more plausible that an individual within IP could have used their cause as a justification to act on his darker impulses. All that said, I haven't ruled out other motives."

"Tomorrow morning I'll be speaking with the two individuals on probation for vandalism against West End," Matt said.

"A formal interview?" asked Catherine.

"I pitched it as routine." He looked at her whiteboard notes, had more questions, but turned to his forensics expert. "Jim? You've been chatting with the ME."

"Yes, as well as the head crime scene investigator that Snohomish County sent over on Friday since San Juan Islands County doesn't have a dedicated crime scene unit. ATF is handling the boat and all evidence from the explosion; Snohomish County has collected a wide spectrum of potential evidence from the docks. So far, nothing pointing to a suspect. I went over the autopsy reports with the ME and, as expected, there are no red flags with any of the victims. Three victims were killed by being, essentially, blown up; the other six victims all died by drowning with a secondary cause of blunt force trauma from the blast."

Kara immediately thought about what Ashley and Whitney told her, that they'd wanted to help when they saw a body floating in the water. She asked Jim, "Does that mean if the rescue crew got to the boat faster, they could have saved those victims?"

"No. At least, not in my professional judgment. Blunt force trauma was severe, rendered the victims unconscious, and most would have died from their injuries within minutes to hours, but they drowned first. One victim, for example, had a broken neck. This was a violent explosion and the explosion is the ultimate cause of all the deaths, but for medical record purposes, we have to list the exact cause.

"All remains have been identified, everyone is accounted for," Jim continued. "We confirmed that Agent Devereaux was not intoxicated, no common drugs in his system, nothing that would even hint that he was at fault. Same for the deckhand, Kyle Richards. They've sent a panel to the state lab for a more thorough screening, just to cover their bases."

Of course, they hadn't believed Neil was drunk, but every investigation like this required a full tox screening of the pilot.

"I don't feel the need to go to the mainland and double-check the ME," Jim said. "He's done as much as I would have in the same situation and he's been transparent from the beginning. Yet I feel I don't have much else to do here."

Matt disagreed. "You're more than a forensics expert, Jim— you're also a cop. I need you to review all the security footage. The sheriff's department collected disks from every business within a two-block radius of the dock and they looked at it, but it's a lot of data and I need fresh eyes. If there's an anomaly, anything out of place, I need to know. And I want you to work with the gas company to confirm their initial assessment, and assist in any investigation if the carbon monoxide leak was intentional. If someone tampered with Neil's heating system, we need to know that as well. It will help us narrow the focus of our investigation. If you need help with the security disks, Ryder will be here analyzing Neil's data."

Jim nodded. "I can do that."

"Sir," Ryder said, "I asked Kara to help because Neil wrote a few vague cryptic questions I can't find answers to. I hope I didn't overstep."

Matt thought it was odd but didn't comment. Ryder was sharp as a tack—he shouldn't need anyone's help. "We're a team, we use all our resources, so if you need a second set of eyes, you got it. Kara—your witness interviews."

"Nothing was said that wasn't in the initial police report, other than learning Ashley Dunlap had been taking pictures that day. Maybe Jim can go through that as well—she was taking pictures just before the explosion."

"Excellent. Where's the camera?"

Kara gestured to the table, which had a collection of evidence bags. "Her dad dropped off the memory chip this afternoon. I told him we'd return or replace it. I'd still like to talk to Ashley without her dad, Pete, around."

"Why?"

"I won't go so far as to say that she's hiding incriminating information, but I sense she has information that might help."

"Accessory after the fact?"

"No. More like…" She paused, then said, "Pete doesn't like Island Protectors. Thinks they're a bunch of nutjobs. He said so when I talked to the family today. Ashley pushed back on that, then clammed up, which tells me she sympathizes with the group, may know people in the group, may even be part of the group. If we are running a theory that someone associated with IP may be responsible for this bombing, we need an *in* there—and you just said that the head honcho, Ms. Bell, wants nothing to do with us. I need to get Ashley talking to me—but not around her father, and probably not around her sister. Whitney isn't someone who can keep a secret."

"How old is Ashley again?" Matt asked.

"Seventeen." While state laws varied, cops could generally talk to children over the age of fourteen without a parent or advocate being present or even notified. They were clear with Ashley.

"Okay, good call. Do it." Matt looked up at the board. "And the widow, Mrs. Jeffries. She's listed here as a high possibility. You interviewed her, correct?"

"Yes, I did," Kara said. "She's not involved."

Catherine cleared her throat.

Matt looked from Kara to Catherine. *Oh, shit.* Now he felt the tension in the room. It had been there from the beginning, but now it was almost tangible.

"You disagree, Catherine?"

"Based on what we currently know, it's more likely that someone affiliated with IP is involved, or if the gas leak was intentional, that Neil is the target; however, Madelyn Jeffries is our second most viable suspect. She has the most to gain financially."

"You think she's capable of killing nine people?" Matt asked.

"I need to interview her and do a psychological profile to make that determination. I've done extensive research on her background and marriage and cannot rule her out. I also think it's suspicious that Mrs. Jeffries knew one of the other victims, Tina Marshall. They were in the same sorority and had worked together at the country club where Mrs. Jeffries met her husband. That avenue needs to be explored."

Matt turned to Kara. Her face was completely blank, and he would have thought she was disinterested except for one small tell: she was sitting perfectly still. Kara never sat still. She rocked in her chair, she rolled her feet, she played with her watch. She was a fidgety person. Except when she was angry. When she was frustrated, she paced. When she was *really* angry, she froze.

"Kara, what did Mrs. Jeffries say or do that had you believing in her innocence?" Matt asked carefully.

She didn't answer. She was looking straight at Catherine until Catherine averted her eyes. What on earth had gone on between them before he got here?

"Kara," Matt urged, "you must have a reason."

"I interviewed her, she's pregnant, she loved her husband, she wasn't involved."

"Did you ask her about knowing any of the other victims? Ms. Marshall?"

"She indicated," Kara said, "that she'd let Tina Marshall get under her skin prior to the boat leaving dock. That was the reason she had left."

"So she lied to the police," Catherine said. "The first opportunity she had to speak to law enforcement, and she lied about why she wasn't on the boat."

"At that moment, she was in shock, having just learned that her husband was dead. She felt guilty that she hadn't asked him to come home with her," Kara said. "She told her husband she wasn't feeling well—morning sickness—because she had a confrontation with Tina and didn't want to be around her."

"Did you ask her what the confrontation was about?" Matt asked.

"I was about to when two of Jeffries's kids showed up and

caused a scene. But she was up-front about knowing Tina Marshall."

"Don't you think you should have continued that line of questioning?" Catherine asked. "She lied to the police, she knew two of the victims, she had clear motive—"

"Motive? Because her husband was rich?"

"Yes. It's a common motive for murder."

"Her grief was real."

"Guilt can be misinterpreted for grief."

"I may not be a fucking psychiatrist, but I can tell the difference."

Matt had to defuse this. "We need more information," he said. "Then we'll reassess and determine the best course of action with regards to Mrs. Jeffries. Catherine, find out everything you can about Mrs. Jeffries's friendship with Mrs. Marshall, and we'll proceed accordingly."

Matt had led many teams over the years, and he had dealt with team members who disagreed and some who flat-out didn't like each other. But he hadn't expected this between Catherine and Kara.

Why not? Two strong-willed, extremely independent cops who are used to leading their own investigations.

He went to the next name on the list. "Vince Marshall. Catherine, you ranked him as the third most likely target, along with Neil."

Catherine said, "Records show that he has had ups and downs in business, multiple lawsuits both settled and pending, so I asked Zack Heller to review the financial and legal information to determine if he might be the bombing target. As far as Neil, we haven't ruled out all his previous arrests—including Brandon Fielding, who threatened him in court and was released six months ago from prison, but as you indicated earlier, he didn't have the means to accomplish this. And there's Neil's personal investigation into the drownings on Mowich Lake. Until we have those answers, he will remain on the list. Nava Software is lower, but Zack is looking into a potential buyout by an investor that didn't go through, to make sure there isn't something we're not seeing there. And finally, *Water Lily*'s two deckhands are all but cleared. Kyle Richards wasn't supposed to be on the boat—he has no history of depression, hasn't been suicidal. Cal McKinnon seems to have a viable reason for calling out sick, though that's pending our interview with him. He's low on our suspect list, and so far, nothing in his background would suggest he might be a target, but we'll continue down that path until we completely clear him."

"McKinnon is coming in here first thing tomorrow morning," Ryder said. "Kara is meeting with him."

"Kara, after you talk to him, let me know if the assessment changes, as target or suspect. Ryder, continue the background checks on all the victims as well as McKinnon and the Jeffries family, use DC as needed. Good work, everyone. For less than ten hours on the ground, we've accomplished a hell of a lot."

12

As they were leaving the conference room, Catherine pulled Matt aside. "I need to call Lizzy before she goes to bed. Would you mind walking with me to the house?"

It was an excuse, but one she knew Matt would accept.

He said to Ryder, "Go on ahead. I'll meet you at Fish & Brew, if you're still up for it?"

"Yes," Ryder said. "I'll tell the others."

Catherine and Matt walked out of the sheriff's station and headed up the hill to their rental house. "Spill," he said.

"I read Kara's file," she said. "Why is she on this team?"

"Because she's not FBI?"

"No. Because she's a borderline sociopath."

Matt tensed as they stopped at the corner to wait for a light to change. "That's uncalled-for."

"You don't see it?"

"Just because you disagreed about Madelyn Jeffries?"

"No, that is not the primary reason, though she should have deferred to my judgment," Catherine said. "I'm not saying I'm right, but I have far more experience and training. That is not, however, relevant to my concerns."

"I've read her file as well. What's your specific concern?"

How did Catherine explain? She could see it—why couldn't Matt? Was it because she was a psychiatrist with nearly two decades of experience? Because she understood sociopaths better than others?

"She has no college degree," Catherine said. "She entered the police academy after getting her GED. They gave her an exemption on age requirements because she was recruited into a specialized program to send officers undercover in high schools to root out drug dealers."

"Like that old television show, *21 Jump Street*," Matt said with a grin, trying to lighten up the conversation. But Catherine couldn't allow him to do that. This was serious; Matt needed to take it seriously.

"She is reckless and volatile, and I've seen those traits in cops before. They get killed or get someone killed. She has fatally shot six suspects in the line of duty. That is high for her department, for *any* department, even considering her high-risk assignments. However, my primary concern lies with her inability to separate herself from her job. She worked undercover for nearly twelve years. She comes to conclusions based solely on her opinion, not on facts or evidence."

"I don't think that's true."

"The situation with Madelyn Jeffries, for example. She hasn't considered the plethora of evidence that shows that Mrs. Jeffries married Pierce Jeffries solely because of his money. The public comments by his family, the fact that she was much younger, poor, and dated several older men before Jeffries, according to an article in a reputable magazine. I tried to explain that to her, but she cut me off and refuses to consider that as a motive."

"I think," Matt said slowly, "that she comes to quick conclusions based on her experience as an interrogator and investigator. We all do it. You do as well."

"In this case, it's a mistake. And I am a psychiatrist. I'm trained to make these assessments. Matt, looking at Kara's background, I'm skeptical. So I ask again, why is she on this team? She has no qualifications to be an FBI agent."

"She was an asset on the Triple Killer investigation."

"Which took place while she was on administrative leave after she killed a suspect."

"Who threw a knife in her back," Matt said. "I am familiar with the case. If you read her files, you know that she went undercover for nearly a year to end a human trafficking ring that was bringing in Chinese nationals for the purpose of slave labor."

"I did. She spent eleven months in that role, and only two hours with the police psychiatrist after her informant was killed. Then she shot to death one of the suspects, and the other allegedly fell from a roof and suffered major injuries. She was the subject of a federal investigation for civil rights abuse—"

"Stop right there, Catherine. Tony looked into that investigation and it was bullshit, opened by an agent who was reprimanded because of Kara's testimony in a case years before this one."

"I don't think either of us—or Tony—knows the whole story. Why did you even want her on this team?"

"It wasn't solely my decision, but I'm glad she's here. After the Triple Killer case, Kara went back to LA and her cover was blown. Her partner had been killed, and she couldn't work in the field anymore. Her boss talked to Tony and they worked out an arrangement for her to be on my team until she testifies against the trafficker she took down. It's going to be a year to eighteen months before the trial."

"I know Tony gave you veto power over every hire. You should have vetoed her."

Catherine didn't understand why Matt hadn't. He didn't always play by the rules, but he wanted a team that did. He had always expected 100 percent loyalty and competence.

"She's a maverick," Catherine continued. "Worse than you ever were. And in these volatile times, when law enforcement is always under a microscope, Kara Quinn is a relic of the past. You need to cut her loose."

Matt didn't say anything, and Catherine took that as a sign that he knew she was right.

"The sooner, the better," Catherine said, "before she puts our team at risk."

"Give Kara a chance. She has great instincts and a different kind of experience that is valuable to our team."

They'd reached the house. Catherine walked up the stairs to the wide front porch; Matt stayed at the bottom.

Catherine turned to face him. "Would you at least keep an open mind?"

"I could say the same thing to you."

She bristled. "Fair enough."

"I'll save you a seat at the pub."

"Ryder had food delivered earlier. I'll make a sandwich. I'm not in the mood to socialize." She hesitated, then said, "My mother called today."

Matt didn't say anything, but by his expression, he knew exactly what the call had been about.

"I'm not going to the memorial service," Catherine said.

"Is that why you're here? To avoid the anniversary of Beth's death? Or your mother?"

"Subconsciously, those are two of the reasons. But I'm not

lying to myself, Mathias," she said. "Beth was murdered three hundred sixty-one days ago. I'm glad you remember."

His face darkened. Why had she said that? Why did she have this need to keep hurting Matt because he didn't love her sister?

"I'm going to eat. Say hi to Lizzy for me."

As he walked away, she felt a twinge of guilt. She walked into the house and shut the door. Waves of negative emotions washed through her. Her anger with Matt. The overwhelming sadness of losing Beth—her sister and best friend. The feeling she deserved to be alone; the guilt of what she put her husband and daughter through when she had walked out.

It didn't matter that she and Chris were back together, that they were living under the same roof, that she loved him—she loved him so much it hurt. She had put him through pain because she couldn't handle her own pain. What kind of psychiatrist did that make her? What kind of human being?

She went to the kitchen and opened a bottle of wine she'd bought earlier in the day. A decent chardonnay from an Oregon vineyard. She poured; sipped. Pulled out her cell phone and hit Home.

Home. She had to remember she still had one.

Chris answered.

"I'm sorry," she said. "It's late."

"It's only ten here. It's great to hear your voice."

She sat down, sipped more wine, closed her eyes. She loved this man so much; she wished she were home. "It's been a long day."

"Tell me."

"You don't—"

"Yes, I do."

So she told him everything: about the case, her concerns about Kara—and Matt's blindness about her—the call from her mother.

"You say the word, I'll be there."

"I'm okay." She paused. "I hurt Matt on purpose."

"About Beth."

"Yes. I need to get over this. I thought I had, but…" She couldn't complete that thought. It made her seem shallow. Vindictive.

"Matt's a good man, but he's always put his career over all else. He's a friend, and I know deep down you care about him. But a friend would also recognize that Matt and Beth were incompatible."

"You believe that?" Her voice cracked.

"Yes. And you had to have seen it as well. Beth loved him, but she was okay when he walked out. You weren't. You can't continue to blame him for not loving your sister."

"I don't."

She was lying.

She admitted as much.

After a long silence, she said, "How do I get past this?"

"Meet me at the memorial."

"No. I can't face my mother *and* her husband."

"You need closure."

"Not… Just no."

"Is it this bombing case?"

"I'm not walking away from it."

"I wouldn't expect you to. But twenty-four hours to grieve would give you some peace. Lizzy and I will be there. She wants to go, and I'm not going to deny her that."

"Protect her from my mother's drama?"

"Sweetheart, Lizzy is the smartest eleven-year-old on the planet. She isn't going to be swayed by rhetoric and emotion."

"She's still a child."

"I would like you to come."

"I'll think on it."

"Do. I'll get Lizzy."

"Is she still awake?"

"She's not supposed to be, it's after ten, but I suspect she's reading."

Catherine wished she were there, told Chris exactly that. "I love you, Chris."

She didn't say it often enough.

"I love you more."

She believed he did.

Kara was glad Catherine wasn't with them at the pub. At this point, she wouldn't even care if Matt showed up. That meeting at the sheriff's office had been total bullshit.

She stood outside with Jim, who was on the phone while Ryder got them a table. She breathed in the fresh ocean air and tried to push aside her frustration.

Kara knew she didn't play well with others, as her old boss Lex Popovich had told her on more than one occasion. So what? She did a fan-fucking-tastic job and she was right 99 percent of the time. Something like this? No-brainer. She'd met Madelyn Jeffries, and the woman wasn't a killer. She couldn't even conceive of it, Kara figured, and thus she wouldn't have hired someone to kill her husband. Catherine hadn't met the woman, instead basing her profile on what she'd read and her own biases.

Kara was beginning to understand Dr. Catherine Jones's narrow focus. The doc was rarely challenged by her peers because she was so smart—*book* smart, that is. Probably always the smartest person in the room. She was at all times calm, cool, collected. Spoke well. Had she ever lost her temper? Probably. But it was rare, and people respected the ability to keep emotions in check. People respected education and doctorates and all that.

Kara had none of it. She'd never gone to college. She had street smarts in spades, and she'd survive anything put in front of her—she had no doubt if the world fell apart that Catherine would cower in her ivory tower and Kara would survive on the street. Zombie apocalypse? Bring it on.

Maybe that wasn't fair. Maybe Kara was projecting her own biases on Catherine: her animosity toward schooling and psychiatrists and other people judging her.

At the same time, Kara had confidence in her assessment. She might be a total fuckup in her life, but she was never wrong on the job. She *was* her job.

And Catherine Jones was a shrink who thought she knew who Kara was.

Like hell she did.

"Who you planning on killing?" Jim asked her as he ended his phone call.

She turned to him. "That obvious?"

"You're a million miles away with an expression like you're plotting dastardly deeds."

"Not murder. Wanna beer?"

"Sure."

"Trust me?"

"Absolutely."

She grinned and they walked inside the pub. She nodded in the opposite direction of the bar and said, "Looks like Ryder found a table. I'll get a pitcher."

Kara walked over to the bar while Jim joined Ryder across the pub. Owner Pete Dunlap was working behind the bar wearing a white polo shirt, bright against his dark skin. "How are the girls?" she asked, sliding onto a vacant stool.

"Good. Thank you for how you handled the situation. I was worried, but they seem to be adjusting okay. Knowing what they saw... It pains me. They shouldn't ever have to see anything like that."

"If they need to talk to anyone, I'm here. Just let me know."

"Thank you." He smiled at her. He was an attractive guy, a bit on the edgy side, but exactly the kind of guy Kara would jump in the sack with in a heartbeat.

Except she was conflicted about her love life right now.

Not so much conflicted as...well, hell. What was she? She wanted Matt Costa. She shouldn't—he was now her boss.

He wasn't your boss when you first slept with him.

But things had changed and she didn't know what to do. All she knew was that when she saw Matt, if they weren't actually *working*, she wanted to take him to bed. Was that even healthy?

"I'm going to get my team a pitcher of..." She looked at the offerings written on the chalkboard behind the bar. "That dark blond microbrew. It good?"

"My favorite," he said with a smile.

"I'm serious. I like good beer. I prefer a good porter, but it's an acquired taste and I don't think my guys over there are up for it."

"You'll like this. It has a bite, but it's light."

He started pouring.

"Hey, that Herradura Reposado, can you pour me a shot?"

He glanced over at her with a surprised grin.

"Sure. Wish I could join you."

Kara had a weakness for good tequila. Downing shots in front of her team probably wasn't wise, but after today she needed it, and it wasn't like she was on duty.

He finished the pitcher, put it down. "How many?"

"Ryder doesn't drink, my boss is on his way, so three. And a club soda with lime for the straight guy." Meaning, non-drinking. She didn't think Ryder was straight, but she hadn't said anything because he hadn't said anything. She didn't want to accidentally out him.

Pete took three chilled pints from the bar fridge.

"Whitney thinks you're the greatest thing since sliced bread," he said.

"Hardly."

"No, really. You're young, smart, an FBI agent."

"I'm not."

He glanced at her, eyebrows questioning, as he reached over for the bottle of Herradura. She didn't feel the need to explain.

He poured a shot—and a bit extra—and put a saltshaker and slice of lemon on a plate.

"Save it." Kara picked up the shot glass and said, "To Neil. May he see justice."

She drained the tequila—*God, that is good*—and put the glass down.

"I'm not an FBI agent," she explained. "I'm actually an LAPD detective currently assigned to the FBI. Long story."

"Sounds like a good one."

She winked. "It is."

"Tell me?"

He was flirting. She could see it in how he looked at her, his tone, his body language. The way he leaned forward, attentive. Focused.

Damn.

This was why she avoided relationships. Men like Pete Dunlap pushed all the right buttons.

But then there was Matt.

He was quite the button-pusher, too.

"Maybe I'll give you the whole story another time. If you're right about this beer, I'll be back."

"Hold up." Pete pulled out a shot glass and poured a dark beer into it from the tap; put it in front of her. "Not porter—a good stout from a microbrewery in Bellingham."

She smelled it. Drank it. Heaven.

Kara smiled. "I'll definitely be back."

She carried the pitcher in one hand, had the three cold pints stacked in the other along with the club soda, and walked to the table.

She put everything down, and poured beer for her and Jim.

"Three mugs?" Jim questioned.

"Matt will be here, Catherine won't, Ryder doesn't drink."

Ryder gave her a half smile.

"Catherine told you that?" Jim said.

Sometimes, though a brilliant forensic dude, Jim was clueless.

"No," Kara said, then drained half her beer. Yes, it was good. Not as good as the stout Pete let her sample, but good.

"I'm starving," she said. "You know what you want?"

"You haven't even looked at the menu."

"Fish and chips. House specialty. I saw someone eating at lunch and I've wanted it ever since." She motioned for the waitress.

"Shouldn't we wait for Matt?" Ryder asked.

Catherine was probably busy giving him an earful about her. "Go ahead and wait. I'm not. I had three energy bars for lunch. I need real food."

"Hi!" the waitress said with a genuine smile. "I'm Rena. What can I get for y'all?"

Kara ordered, and so did Ryder and Jim. They chatted for a while—Jim, mostly, talking about his three grandchildren and the apartment his daughter and son-in-law were building for him in his own basement.

She liked Jim a lot. He had the Columbo cop vibe but was very much into his family. She wondered what it would have been like to have a dad like Jim Esteban. Better than her dad, that was for sure.

Matt came in just as their food came out.

"You couldn't wait?" he asked.

Kara ate a fry. It was hot, but so good. She sprinkled malt vinegar over everything. "Ryder, I told you we should have waited." She wrinkled her nose at the analyst, who just shook his head at her.

"I wasn't serious." Matt poured the rest of the pitcher into his mug.

"Neither was I," she said and ate another fry, watching Matt without letting on that she was watching him.

He didn't look at her. Preoccupied. Stared at his beer as if trying to think of what to say. She could almost hear his internal debate.

Should I tell Kara what Catherine said? Ignore it? Address it one-on-one or in a staff meeting? What if Catherine is right?

She knew him, even after only three months. Catherine had definitely said something to him about her, and he was thinking it over.

Dammit. Catherine and Matt had a history. Kara didn't think that they had been involved romantically—she didn't get that sex vibe from them—but they had clearly been friends for a long time. Back when they were working the Triple Killer investigation, Ryder had told her that Matt and Catherine had gone through Quantico together. And Matt was friends with her husband and godfather to their daughter. That made them tight.

Matt ordered the same thing she had. She offered him some of her fries while he waited; he shook his head. He told the table Michael's theory about the detonation had been confirmed. According to their skilled munitions expert, the bomb on *Water Lily* had been set to detonate when the boat reached a speed of between eighteen and twenty knots.

Jim nodded. "A line or weight was probably attached to the device, dropped in the water, and when the boat reached that speed, the tension ignited the charge and *boom*."

Matt looked impressed. "In a nutshell, that's exactly it."

"Simple and smart," Jim said.

"So simple that anyone can do it?" Kara asked.

"Simple enough that you don't need to be an expert like Michael to create this device," Matt said, "though some basic skills would be necessary."

"The internet has a wealth of subversive information," Ryder said. "My cybercrime class at Quantico went deep into studying the dark web for a week."

"I'm familiar with the dark web," Matt said, "but someone still needs access to C-4 and they most likely need basic engineering knowledge."

"Or someone who practiced," Kara said. "Couldn't they have ignited a much smaller bomb somewhere else? In the middle of the ocean? Something that wouldn't arouse suspicion, might not even be noticed?"

"Definitely," Jim said. "If I were going to plan something like this, I would want to know that it was going to work."

"It depends on the motive—if it was to cause death or destruction."

"Or both," Kara said, eating the last of her fries.

"Do you have a theory?" Matt asked. The first direct question he'd asked her tonight.

"Nope."

She was beginning to formulate a theory, but it was still rough around the edges. She didn't think it was the environmental group because it was overkill. If they'd blown up the boat while docked in the middle of the night, yep, she'd buy it. Aim at West End, make a statement, whatever. But killing nine people? The fact that Michael proved that the bomb was designed to go off when the boat was moving fast—out-of-the-harbor-area fast—told her someone on board was the target.

"I think you do," Jim said. He drained his beer.

"I'm going to finish my interviews first," she said. "And review Neil's notes with Ryder. Speaking of that, Ryder, we need to reach out to that woman listed on his calendar. Mott?"

"Jessica Mott, a sister of one of the dead college students," Ryder said. "I have her contact information."

"Why is she important?" Matt asked. "Do you think she has information about Neil's investigation into the cold case?"

"It's likely," Ryder said. "Her name is in his address book with multiple contact numbers and emails. He met with her in

January in Seattle, and last year she came up here twice to meet him. I left a message for her earlier and asked if she would be willing to talk to us, possibly come up and look at Neil's files."

"Why do you need her to come here?" Matt asked.

"I think something's missing," Ryder said, "but I don't know what. The information about the Mowich Lake drownings seems complete, but I don't know for certain. And Neil's desk seemed... I don't know, empty. Except for the cold case."

"If you think it's important, make it happen."

Rena the waitress returned to take their plates. "How was everything?"

Kara said, "Amazing."

"I know, right? Best fish on the island, and that's saying something. Can I get you another pitcher?"

"I wish, but I have an early morning." She glanced at Jim and Matt, and they concurred.

The place was bustling. "Busy," Kara said. "Are you covering all these tables?"

"Yeah, but people are mostly patient, and Pete helps a lot. Jamie will be back tomorrow."

Kara's instincts twitched. That was Cal McKinnon's fiancée. "Jamie Finch?"

"Yeah," Rena said with a smile. "I'll finally get a night off, can't wait. I'm going to put my feet up and binge-watch Hallmark Christmas movies. Yes, Christmas in July. I'm a sucker for happy endings." She laughed good-naturedly and walked away with all the empties.

"What was that about?" Matt asked.

"McKinnon's girlfriend. Finch," said Kara. "I'm still trying to figure out what's going on there. I'm interviewing him in the morning, then I think I'll talk to Jamie as well. Just to check it off." She looked at Matt. "I still plan on talking to Justin Jeffries."

"Take Catherine with you."

She didn't say anything.

Matt didn't explain. Kara wasn't happy at the thought of partnering with Catherine, but she couldn't do a damn thing about it.

Except be right.

13

Kara told the others that she'd meet them back at the house.

She needed time alone to process all that she'd learned today, and to try to understand Matt's reliance on Catherine.

And, honestly, she wanted to be alone.

As Kara rounded the street corner, she realized being alone wasn't going to be an option tonight. She spotted Ashley Dunlap walking briskly down the sidewalk, away from the Fish & Brew. Kara turned her body toward the closest storefront as if she were a tourist, but kept her eyes on Ashley. A boy—probably eighteen or nineteen—stood across the way, waiting for her. When she reached him, he kissed her. Then they held hands and walked down the alley that ran parallel to the main road.

Right toward the library where IP held their Monday night meetings. Kara had seen the signs all over downtown. They started at seven thirty for a meet and greet, eight thirty for the meeting.

It was already nearly eight thirty. She didn't have much time.

Kara walked into the souvenir shop. "Honey, we close in five minutes!"

"That's all I need," she said with a smile. She was wearing jeans, which was good—they blended. She quickly assessed her options. Hippie hippie hippie...but not too overboard.

Sale on sweaters. Perfect. A long sweater, open, no buttons. It was soft and the muted fall colors helped it not look brand-new. A hundred bucks on sale? *Jeez.*

The clerk said, "The sweaters are all handmade by a local knitter. These are the last two we have—she delivers more next week, if you're still in town."

"It's beautiful," Kara said, hiding her sticker shock. Maybe she could get Matt to expense it. No, she'd give it to her grandmother. Her birthday was at the end of summer, and it was exactly something Em would love.

She also grabbed a retro Greenpeace T-shirt, a pack of gum, a water bottle, a travel-size hair gel bottle, and anti-bluelight glasses. They weren't prescription or magnified but looked real. Glasses were one of the best ways to quickly change your appearance. At the last minute, Kara added a tube of bright lipstick. She never wore lipstick on duty, so this was a good way to alter her looks, even if it made her stand out.

She thanked the clerk and went out to the alley. No one was around. She took off the blazer and black T-shirt she wore. Her hair didn't quite reach her shoulders. The humidity made it curly, so she poured the water on her head to dampen her hair, pulled out her comb and brushed it through, then grabbed the firm-hold gel and squeezed a liberal amount into her hands. She ran her hands through her hair and slicked it back completely.

She dried her hands on the Greenpeace shirt—which made it look both used and retro—and then pulled it on. She pulled her pocketknife from her pocket and cut a hole in it, then tore it so the edges would be frayed and appear worn.

She put on the sweater, then assessed her appearance with the camera in her phone. She still looked too much like Kara Quinn. She added the lipstick—God, she hated lipstick—then the glasses. Smiled. Much better. She didn't even think Matt would immediately recognize her.

She packed her personal clothing into the plastic bag and started toward the library. She found a bush halfway there where she stowed her bag. The nice thing about the sweater was that it was long and flowing, so her gun was completely concealed. No way in hell was she going into a situation without her weapon. Did it once—never again.

Never say never.

She'd do anything she had to but preferred having her weapon on her. And it wasn't like she could hide her gun behind a bush like she did her clothes.

The meeting had already started by the time she slipped in and stood in the back. There was punch and cookies and brownies on a table along the wall, but she never ate or drank anything she didn't know the origin of. Probably safe here, but it was a hard habit to break.

Ashley and her boyfriend were sitting in the rear of the room, next to Craig Martin and Valerie Sokola. A young girl was talking about their plans for protesting West End this week. They were making signs tomorrow with the theme of demanding answers about the explosion.

"We can't just believe what the police tell us," the girl said. "We need answers, real answers, and independent verification. But we can't forget the real reason we can't trust West End—we have no independent verification that they retrofitted all their boats properly. Until they provide that documentation and allow our experts to inspect their ships, we will continue this fight!"

Applause, then the girl added that Island Protectors would be joining with a Seattle-based environmental group in September for a large protest along the waterfront to bring attention to motorboats killing marine life in Puget Sound.

Kara realized she should have told Matt where she was going. Dammit, she wasn't used to working on a team like this. She pulled out her phone, sent a quick text message:

UC with IP at library, going dark for an hour.

She made sure it went through, then deleted the message, put the phone on silent, and pocketed it.

A woman sitting nearby was staring at her. Yep, Kara was a stranger. She would stand out. Kara nodded to her and kept listening while also taking in the crowd.

She didn't know if—relatively speaking—this was a big or small environmental group; she'd never infiltrated one before. There were forty people here, tops. There were enough chairs for sixty. Kara took a water bottle from the table—something sealed that she could open herself—and sat down near the woman who hadn't taken her eyes off her since she walked in.

Didn't want her to think that Kara was intentionally avoiding her.

She also happened to be right behind Ashley Dunlap, who didn't give her a second glance.

Kara popped a piece of gum in her mouth and chewed. Sipped her water. Observed and listened.

When the speaker was done, Donna Bell rose, and all side conversations ended.

"I've talked to most of you already. I see one or two new faces." She looked directly at Kara. "I won't be long tonight. Late this morning I had a visit from the FBI."

Someone swore loudly, others under their breath. Several anti-police comments rolled through the room.

Donna put her hands up. "I'm not a fan, but the sheriff has always treated this group with respect, so I was willing to listen. But it's clear to me that they are focusing on Island Protectors and they specifically asked me to report on anyone who is acting suspiciously."

Kara was pretty certain that wasn't how Matt would have put it, but it was an interpretation, she supposed, especially if you didn't like law enforcement as a rule.

"That's bullshit, Donna," someone said.

"I agree. I know that no one here had anything to do with what happened to West End's charter boat. The sheriff said it was a bomb and I'm sure you've seen ATF all over the place, but they haven't released many details, so I'll take their comments with a grain of salt. As Brenda said earlier—" she gestured toward the girl who had been speaking when Kara first walked in "—West End has never been transparent with us, and until I see an official report that is clear as to the cause of the explosion, I'm not going to buy the talking points.

"What I want you all to know," Donna continued, "is that you don't have to talk to the police *at all*. They have no evidence, nothing, that points to anyone specifically, and they're clearly sniffing around. I detest these fishing expeditions, because they will take small bullshit crap—like personal-use drugs—and parlay that into years in prison. So I'm telling you this now: if anyone gets called in, you don't have to go. If anyone gets arrested for any reason, call me and I'll get you a lawyer. I'm not going to let anyone here get railroaded."

"Donna," Craig said, "the sheriff called both Valerie and me to come in and talk to them. We have to go; we're still on probation. We had nothing to do with this, but they have this way of twisting everything around and you don't know what end is up."

"If they had any evidence, they wouldn't have *asked* you to come in," Donna said. "They would have arrested you. Which tells me again: fishing. Because of your past mistake, they want the easy path."

Craig looked worried and scared.

Valerie scowled. "I'm not going," she said. "They can't make me. They can't just use this probation as a free pass to haul in all the usual suspects."

"I agree," Donna said, "but if your probation gets revoked you might have to go before a judge and face possible jail time. We would fight it, but sometimes cooperating is more helpful. I'll call Larry and have him meet you at the station in the morning, all right? He'll represent you and Craig and make sure your rights are protected. Listen to him, do not answer any questions he doesn't tell you to answer."

"I don't think we should have to talk to them at all. They have no evidence it was us. Or anyone."

Craig said quietly, "Val, shh."

"Don't. It's not fair. They're not asking everyone else in IP to come in, just us."

Donna said, "Valerie, I understand how you feel. And they still may come after the rest of us. I'll deal with that if it happens. But for now, basic cooperation. Don't give them anything they don't ask for. Listen to Larry, and everything is going to be fine."

There were grumbles throughout the room.

Kara wasn't sure about those two, Craig and Valerie. They didn't look like killers, but Valerie was definitely angry. Hostile. She might act rashly—maybe, as Matt had suggested earlier, setting a bomb and not realizing it might actually kill people. Maybe she got Craig to go along with it.

The *why* bugged her. Domestic terrorism was a thing; anger at the government, at a group of people, at a business. But anger aimed at a specific business like West End tended to be personal.

Maybe it was personal for Valerie. That was definitely worth looking into.

Donna said, "Now, all this being said, if any of you know anything about the alleged bombing—if you saw something that might help the police, or if you overheard someone talking about it—come to me. I'll get the information to the police, and no one has to go in and make official statements. Clearly, if an individual is responsible for killing nine people, we want them to be brought to justice. But that doesn't mean any of us have to give up our rights to help the police do their job."

There was silence, a few nods.

Ashley raised her hand.

"Yes, Ashley, you have something to add?"

Ashley rose, had an awkward, nervous smile on her face. "Um, the FBI came with a San Juan deputy, to the Fish & Brew. My dad wanted Whitney and me to talk to them because we, um, saw the explosion. They were both very nice, very professional. I, um, just wanted to share that."

Donna nodded. "Not all FBI agents are jerks like the one I had to deal with."

Kara couldn't wait to share that tidbit with Matt.

"You were a witness," Donna added. "Of course they'll want to follow up. You and your sister doing okay?"

Ashley nodded. "It was awful. And I know most of you here, and I know you wouldn't do anything like that. But I wanted to share what I knew. The FBI agent said it was a bomb and the ATF is working on figuring out how it was triggered. And it got me thinking that there could even be more bombs around here and I wouldn't even know what they look like."

"Honey, we don't know what's going on," Donna said, "but I'm pretty sure that West End's boat was targeted for a specific reason and that you have nothing to worry about."

Did she know that for a fact, Kara wondered, or was she trying to make a scared teenager feel better?

"But in the future," Donna said, "you should always have a

lawyer present when you talk to the police, and especially the FBI. Even innocent people need to protect their rights."

"You're right. I'll remember that. I won't do it again. Thank you, Donna."

Ashley's boyfriend took her hand, and she sat down again.

Well, shit, Kara thought. Would Ashley really not talk to her now? Kara had been certain she'd talk alone, but if she felt emboldened by Donna's speech, she might clam up.

Donna answered a few questions. No, they weren't going to stop protesting West End. Yes, Donna would use the IP legal fund if necessary. Yes, they would continue to meet here on Monday evenings, and she would be at the big Fourth of July protest.

"We need to amp up the pressure. West End is going to have to admit that they cut corners, that their boats continue to pollute our waterways even after the so-called 'retrofitting' of their fuel tanks. Until they open up their books, their maintenance records, their routes, their growth plans, we aren't going to sit back and wait for them to toss us a bone. If anyone sees any evidence, take lots of pictures. It's how we caught them two years ago, and it's how we'll catch them now."

They ended the meeting and Donna was instantly surrounded by her fans—that's the vibe Kara was getting from the group. They were groupies. They loved and trusted this woman. She watched as Ashley and Bobby waited their turn to talk to Donna.

Kara planned to quietly slip out, but the woman who had her eye on her from the minute she walked in came over. "I haven't seen you here before."

"I don't live here. I'm a grad student at Gonzaga. Emily." She always used her grandmother's name when she couldn't use her own because it was easy to remember.

"Jane. You're a long way from Spokane."

Suspicious. It didn't really matter if they knew Kara was a cop or not. She had what she needed. "I'm here with my girlfriend for a week. I tried to get her to come with me, but…" She shrugged. "I saw the sign earlier today, and I have to come up with a thesis by next month and I'm stumped. I thought maybe I'd get an idea listening."

"What's your major?"

"I have a degree in psychology, but I'm getting my master's in nonprofit administration."

"I didn't know they had a master's in that."

Kara knew for a fact they did. Her grandmother had wanted her to go to Gonzaga when she graduated from high school, so Kara had read a few brochures to make Em happy and even toured the college, though college was never going to be in the cards for her.

"It's a terrific program." She had no idea whether it was a good program, just that it existed. "I've gone to several community organizing meetings and I've been working through a couple of ideas for a thesis. I have to get it to my advisor in six weeks or I'm totally screwed."

"I can introduce you to Donna, if you'd like. She's been a community organizer for most of her life, and she knows everything about running a small nonprofit."

"That would be great, but you don't have to do that."

"I don't mind."

Jane moved directly to Donna's side, as Ashley and Bobby were talking to her. Kara stood half behind her, not positive that her "disguise" would prevent Ashley from recognizing her this close up. But the girl barely looked at her.

"I made a copy," Ashley was saying.

Kara didn't need to hear the beginning of the conversation as she watched Ashley hand a memory chip over to Donna.

Donna pocketed it immediately. "Thank you for this. I'll look at them. If the FBI steps out of line, I'll put up a wall."

"I'll go out next weekend, too," she said. "I'll find something. I just need to put in more time."

"Because of you, we have a solid photo journal of West End activities over the last three months. It's only a matter of time before they violate the regulations, and we'll have the proof—because of you. Just be careful, sweetheart."

"I'll go with you, Ash," Bobby said, his arm around his girlfriend. "Thanks, Donna."

Donna smiled, turned to Jane. "You brought a new member?"

"No, Emily is here on vacation. She's working on a thesis."

"Oh?" Donna turned to Kara. She didn't look suspicious, but she was shrewd and Kara was going to have to be at her best. "On what?"

"I'm still trying to come up with the idea. I'm getting my master's in nonprofit administration and have been going to community groups all over Washington trying to get ideas for my thesis. I'm leaning toward the challenges of community fundraising in times of recession, but it seems too... I don't know, boring."

"I'd be happy to talk through your ideas with you. We need more people who understand the business end of nonprofits. We have the ideas and the heart. We need to make sure we can pay for it. How long are you going to be here?"

"Through next weekend."

"Where are you staying?"

"An Airbnb on Park." Park was a long street that she had to walk down to get to where the FBI was actually staying, so she hoped Donna didn't get more specific where Kara's evasive answers might be called into question.

"I'm free tomorrow for coffee," Donna said.

That was fast.

"My girlfriend made plans for us—we're going to hike Bell Point Trail, have a picnic lunch. Do you have a card or something? I can call you Thursday or Friday and see if you're free."

Donna gave Kara her number, which Kara put into her phone. "Thanks."

"Jane can join us," Donna said. "She used to run a nonprofit in Oregon, didn't you?"

"If you can call it that," Jane said. "We were constantly fund-raising, and though our overhead was barely existent—we had a donated space, most of the people who worked there were volunteers—we didn't have enough time to do what we wanted."

"Which was?" Kara asked, wanting to turn the conversation away from her to anything else.

"Housing rights. It was always a battle, every year, to pull together the budget and make it stick."

Kara's phone vibrated. She looked at it; a question mark from Matt.

"My girlfriend is looking for me," she said. "I should go. I didn't tell her I was going to be this late."

"I look forward to talking to you more," Donna said. "What college did you say?"

"Gonzaga."

"I know the head of the environmental sciences department there, Wayne Epicott. Do you know him?"

"No, I was a psychology major. I had one intro class my freshman year, Professor Parks or Parker or Parkinson... I don't remember. The only interesting thing we did was hike up Antoine Peak." She smiled, said goodbye, and got out of there before Donna had any more questions. Kara figured she was just being sociable, but she could have also been testing her. Kara hadn't formed a stand-up backstory, and didn't want to be trapped.

Kara wouldn't actually meet with Donna unless Matt thought she should, but Kara sensed that Donna would figure out she was a cop pretty quick—the only reason she didn't have her pegged yet was because she hadn't see her working today. But it was clear after that meeting that Donna had a lot of eyes and ears around town, and by the end of day tomorrow Kara's cover would be blown.

In the parking lot, she saw Ashley and her boyfriend talking to Craig Martin and Valerie Sokola. Valerie was agitated, waving her arms around, and Ashley looked intimidated. Craig finally got Valerie into their car, and Ashley hugged her boyfriend. She was crying? Why?

Jane came up to her. Kara had sensed someone was watching her—now she knew who. "Need a ride?"

"No, I'm good. I like to walk." She jerked her finger toward the group. "There was some drama. I think that woman who was sitting in front of me made that kid cry."

Jane dismissed her comment. "Ashley is a sweet kid. I'm sure she's fine. And Bobby wouldn't let anyone mess with her."

Kara just stared at her blankly.

"Don't worry about it. Sure you don't want a ride?"

"I'm sure, thanks."

"Call Donna, I know she'd love to talk. She likes to help people, especially young people."

Kara laughed. "I'm not that young."

"What, twenty-five?"

"I wish. Thirty. I went to grad school late."

"I wish I had your skin. You look way younger."

"I get it from my grandma. She doesn't look her age, either." Kara smiled and said goodbye, then left.

Bobby—why did that name sound familiar?

Right. Craig Martin had a brother named Bobby.

It might not mean anything. Except...tears could signify guilt.

Ashley wasn't the type of personality to plant a bomb, whether or not it killed anyone. But she *was* the type to feel guilt if she had information she knew she should share, but it might get someone she cared about in trouble.

Someone like her boyfriend's brother.

Yet...she had freely given Donna a copy of the photos she took. And based on what Ashley had said, she'd been following West End boats for some time, taking pictures and trying to catch them violating environmental regulations.

Kara definitely wanted to talk to her one-on-one, but she needed to figure out exactly how to approach the teenager.

She walked toward Park Street, collected her bag of clothes from behind the bushes near the corner—making sure no one saw her—and headed to the FBI house.

14

It was after ten by the time Kara walked into the house. She was beat and thought for once she might possibly get a good night's sleep. All the travel yesterday and then hitting the ground first thing in the morning today—yeah, she was ready to pass out for five, maybe six hours. Bliss.

When she walked in, everyone except Jim was in the dining room, which Ryder had turned into a workroom. The table was large enough for a printer and multiple laptops and was a comfortable place to talk about the case or work.

Still wearing her disguise, Kara greeted the others. "Great, almost everyone is here. I can give you a rundown all at once."

Matt did a double take when he saw her. She almost grinned.

If she was still wearing the glasses, she wondered if he would have recognized her?

Catherine cleared her throat.

Ryder didn't look at her.

Matt said, "I got your text."

"Why do I feel like I'm coming in after curfew and am about to be grounded?"

"Kara, I—well, I feel you should have called to discuss your idea. You're known to the community as a member of our task force, and it could have been awkward."

"No one recognized me, no one will. I sat right behind Ashley Dunlap, who I interviewed this morning—she didn't give me a second glance. I got myself introduced to Donna Bell and she wants to have coffee with me to discuss her nonprofit." She pulled the glasses out of her pocket and put them on. "The point is, I know how to blend in, I know how to infiltrate a group, and even if they pegged me for a cop—which they didn't—it doesn't matter because I don't need to go back."

Catherine said, "Matt's point is that your presence *could* have created problems for our investigation, in addition to the necessity of having backup in case the situation turned bad."

"I wasn't infiltrating Antifa or the Aryan Brotherhood," she snapped. Maybe she shouldn't have, but what was Catherine's problem? "I have information to share, then I'm going to bed."

"We need to address this breach of protocol," Catherine said, focusing on Matt, not Kara. "We could be dealing with an entrapment issue when we talk to Martin and Sokola."

"That's bullshit," Kara said. "I didn't even talk to them. We were in a public place, anything they said was in a public place."

"In the future," Matt said, cutting off something Catherine clearly wanted to say, "let's talk about these ideas first, okay? Kara, you're part of a team now, and I know you are used to doing things your own way. But we need to weigh multiple angles and—"

"I would have lost the small window of opportunity I had," Kara said. She was not backing down on this. "Look, here's the information you need. When Craig Martin and Valerie Sokola show up tomorrow, they'll be with a lawyer named Larry that Donna is retaining for them. Donna also told everyone else— including young Ashley—they don't have to talk to any cop, and if they get arrested or harassed, to call her and she'll get them a lawyer. Ashley gave Donna a copy of all the pictures she turned over to us—and apparently, the teen has been tracking West End boats for quite some time, taking lots of pictures, so maybe we can find out if she has anything else we can use. Oh, and Donna told everyone there, all forty of them, that if they have information about the bombing to call *her*, not the police, and she'll talk to the sheriff. There's a big protest on the Fourth of July that they're preparing for. And Donna thinks you're a jerk, Matt. Good night."

She walked down the hall to the small room she'd claimed because she didn't want to be upstairs with everyone else.

She was not going to put up with this bullshit from Dr. Catherine Jones. The woman didn't like her, fine. But she wasn't going to be treated as a rookie cop who didn't know what she was doing. *Hell* no.

She stripped and walked into the small bathroom off her room. She took a long, hot shower, mostly because she was so frustrated. She washed out the gel, scrubbed her face, stood under the water until she felt calmer.

When she was done, she pulled on a tank top and panties, keeping her sweats draped over a chair, her shoes on the floor next to her bed, in case she had to run out quickly. She sat down at her laptop and banged out an "official" report and sent it to Matt. Just the facts. What she saw, why she followed Ashley Dunlap, everyone she met, spoke to, what they said, how they sounded, and why she thought *if* Craig Martin or Valerie Sokola was responsible they could nail Craig on the guilt card.

He was no killer, and if he bombed the boat his guilt would be eating him up.

Then she added her opinion.

Craig Martin wants to belong as well as do good. He's head over heels for Valerie, but he's also a family kid—close to his kid brother. He's not a criminal at heart, though I'm not surprised he followed his girlfriend down that path. Valerie Sokola is a crime waiting to happen, but you can't arrest her on that. She's angry and volatile and an agitator. If there's any more vandalism in town, my money is on her. She's the kind of activist who would throw rocks at cars and hit cops in the eye with a laser. But murder? I don't see it. Make sure you separate the two if you run at them. Valerie won't talk, but Craig will—just play on the tragedy and he'll break down if he was involved, or if he has useful information.

Earlier, she had longed for a good night's sleep, but now she was tense. She stared out the lone window into the night and wished she wasn't in the same house as the others.

She heard people walking around upstairs, then the house fell silent.

It was midnight.

She left her room and, without turning on the kitchen light, opened the fridge and pulled out a beer. Twisted off the cap. Drank. Sat down on the counter and considered her options.

She'd expected Matt to back her up. Not because they were sleeping together, but because she was right—and he should have seen it. He should have been there for her, professionally.

And he wasn't.

Matt walked into the kitchen wearing nothing but boxers.

"Kara," he said, surprised.

"Good night," she said, putting her beer down and sliding off the counter.

He took her arm. "You're angry."

"No, of course not." She stared at him. "Angry? Me? Being lectured like I'm a fucking rookie cop who doesn't know my ass from a hole in the ground?" It took all her willpower to keep her voice low.

"I'm sorry I came off like that—"

"You didn't. She did. And you didn't back me up."

"It's a matter of protocol."

"Bullshit."

"Please—I miss you."

"Miss me?"

"You're going to make me say it?"

"Sure, why not? What do you miss, Matt?" She was angry, but she also could see Matt's point—to a degree. She probably should have given him more detail before she walked in, but she did the right thing and she would stand by it.

And truth be told, she did miss having Matt in her bed. It had been nearly a week since they had a whole night together, and maybe that sexual frustration was adding to her feeling of being disconnected from everyone here.

He put his lips on hers, lightly. He touched the small scar on her face that she got last month, that may be there forever or could completely heal. She didn't care which. But he caressed it intimately. Too intimate, especially for her current emotions.

Kara wasn't going to go light now.

She pushed her body against his and he backed into the counter. Every muscle in his body was rock-hard, and if they were alone in this house, they would be having sex in less than a minute—the only things separating them were her panties and his thin boxers.

Matt groaned as she touched him between the legs; she kissed his neck, behind his ear exactly where he liked it. His hands went immediately to her ass and squeezed, pulling her even closer. She bit his earlobe, kissed the back of his neck, and when his warm mouth came down on the sensitive part of her chin, right below her jawline, she gasped.

Damn, she wanted him.

But the last thing she needed was anyone walking in on them. She stepped back, breathing heavily.

"Let me—"

"No. Not here. Not with an audience." She started back down the hall, already regretting her decision.

"Kara," Matt said. "You did good tonight."

She stopped, couldn't face him, and said, "You should have said that in front of Catherine."

TUESDAY

15

After the economy went in the toilet two years ago, Garrett Washington hadn't been able to find a decent job until now. It wasn't like the security gig paid great, but because it was a short-term assignment and they wanted someone with experience, he did okay. It was better than doing nothing. He'd lost his business and wanted to build another when things started looking up, but recently he always seemed to be behind the eight ball. His wife was a nurse, so she could find work, but she'd started traveling to make better money. She didn't like it—she wanted something permanent, preferably in Washington. They talked every night at five. Their son, who'd just turned fourteen, was staying with Meg's parents this summer. Garrett missed his kid something fierce, as much as his wife, but this job was only until Labor Day, and he was making nearly three times as much as he'd been making as a handyman.

He walked back into the West End Charter security office and turned in his equipment. "Gorgeous night," he said to Bruce, who was running the desk. Garrett didn't mind the hours. 5:00 p.m. until 3:00 a.m. Two paid thirty-minute breaks to grab a bite or take a snooze. And this was paradise. He was bringing Meg back here sometime, maybe for a second honeymoon. Their twentieth was coming up next year.

"It is, it is. Uneventful, thank goodness. Heard you and Hank chased some teenagers off the pier, drinking beer and tossing the bottles in the water."

"Told them if we saw them again after hours, they'd be taken into the sheriff's station. Should have seen the look on their faces."

Bruce chuckled. "Hank said one of them was the Billings kid—his dad is on the town council, bet Hank will be calling him up tomorrow." He typed on the keyboard, leaned back. "You're clocked out, see you tomorrow."

"Tomorrow."

Garrett pulled on his warm jacket. Even though it was a pleasant evening, it was cold, and he had an eight-block trek to his apartment. He didn't mind. The apartment was rent-free for the whole summer. So what if he had to share with another guy? He barely saw the dude because he worked days and Garrett worked nights. Every dime that Garrett didn't need to eat was going into his business fund. He *would* start a new business as soon as he had the seed money.

And he liked this gig. The people were nice, the weather was great, and he found it a lot less stressful than looking for work in the city.

Tonight he was particularly happy. Meg had told him she had a line on a permanent position in Olympia. It would mean their son had to start high school in a new city, but these days Olympia was much safer than Seattle, and they'd even be closer to Meg's family. Garrett liked her parents, and got along great with both her brothers.

It was a win-win. Garrett was optimistic.

The night had turned chilly from the wind coming in from the north, but it felt good after walking the grounds for the last ten hours. Still, he pulled his neck gaiter up around his neck and walked along the pier, where a short staircase led to the street. But then he heard the sound of knocking in the boathouse.

He hesitated, listened.

Silence.

If the Billings kid and his friends had come back, Garrett would definitely take them in. But he'd thought Hank had scared them silly. Garrett knew that if *his* son was sneaking around at two in the morning, the kid would be grounded for a month. That time of night was when teenagers got into trouble—or trouble found them.

He pulled his small flashlight from his jacket pocket and wished he had the heavy-duty light West End provided him, but he'd turned that in with his other equipment. He shined the faint light around, seeing nothing out of the ordinary.

Still, one couldn't be too careful.

He walked over to the boathouse. Though it was accessible from the water, the door from the dock should be locked.

He walked over to check just to make sure.

It was open.

Garrett reached into his pocket for his radio, but it wasn't there. Right, he turned in his equipment when he clocked out.

"Security!" he called into the boathouse. "Who's there?"

Silence. Well, shit, someone must have forgotten to lock up. The knocking was likely the door blowing in the breeze.

He didn't have his keys, but he didn't want to walk back to the security office. He pulled out his phone to call Bruce and

alert him. He'd send someone over. They had at least two people patrolling the grounds at all times.

As he scrolled through his contacts, he saw movement to
his right. He turned, saw someone—he thought it was a man,
shorter than him, about five-ten and in a heavy coat—moving
in the near-dark. Before he could react, a brick came down on
his head and he fell to the ground.

He groaned, tried to reach up to protect his head, but the
brick came down again even harder.

Garrett didn't feel anything after that.

16

Though the end of June, the early morning was unusually brisk. Kara expected it—she'd lived outside Spokane for most of her teenage years. The Pacific Northwest could get hot in the summer, but the cool mornings—especially on the water—were her favorite time of the day.

She pulled on her running pants, a tank top, and a thin windbreaker. No one else was awake in the house. She drank a full water bottle, filled her Hydro Flask, then ate a piece of toast with half a banana. She wasn't one for breakfast but knew from experience that she'd get a better workout if she had something in her stomach. She started a pot of coffee for when she returned and headed out to the harbor on foot. It was still dark, though the sky was lighting up to the east. As she walked the six blocks to the harbor, she enjoyed how the thin red line turned orange, the deep blue sky turning purple. The vast horizon, the reflection off the water, the peaks of Orcas Island across the bay, dark against the sky, all reminded Kara that she was just one small part of a bigger world. It was both inspiring and heady.

Three hours of sleep had left her sluggish, but the morning breeze and brisk walk helped invigorate her. She needed clarity about her life but didn't expect it now or later. Where she stood with the FBI team. If there was any hope of her getting back to her job in LA. What was going on with her and Matt and if she should trust her feelings—something she did in the job, but rarely in a relationship. For her entire life, sex had been about sex. Pleasure was pleasure, and as long as the guy knew what he was doing and wasn't an asshole, that was all that mattered to her.

Until Matt.

She didn't want to think about that.

She wouldn't get clarity about her professional or personal life, so the next best thing was clarity about this case: something she could control, something she could turn around in her head and solve.

And she *would* solve it, whether Catherine Jones thought she was competent or not.

The Friday Harbor port was tiny. There were two primary piers—one for the ferries that went out to the islands as well as the mainland, and one that was part of the yacht club, reserved for private boats. West End Charter was to the south, only partly visible from the main harbor, partly hidden as a wide cove cut inland. They, too, had a club, but the boats on their pier were all charters of the company.

Marcy was waiting for her in front of the main harbor across from the ferry dock, stretching against a metal railing. The streetlights were still on, even as the sun crept over the harbor. A smattering of high clouds made the morning picture-perfect.

The island was growing on Kara—the water, the fresh air, the trees—but it had a population similar to tiny Liberty Lake, where she'd lived with her grandmother during high school. One thing Kara didn't like was when everyone knew everyone else's business—especially hers. There were few secrets in small towns, which gave her the confidence that they'd solve this case quickly. Someone knew something.

"Morning," Kara said when she approached. She did a couple of squats, then stretched her hamstrings. "We went to the Fish & Brew last night. You were right, amazing. I could eat there every night."

Marcy laughed. "When it comes to food, I'm never wrong. Ready?"

"Lead the way."

They started off at a slow jog, heading north, past the yacht club. "The run is just over five miles. I do it at least three times a week. Down the main street, then we turn off on a road that leads to a broken dock at the edge of the water. A few houses out there, not many. I usually take a water break, stretch, head back. Good?"

"Good."

Kara wasn't a die-hard runner. She worked out mostly to release energy. She preferred more physical and competitive exercise routines—she and her old partner Colton used to spar together. That was a great workout, and fun to boot. Some of the cops at her precinct would put together racquetball tournaments that tended to be cutthroat near the end. She rarely won, but almost always made it to the final round.

When Kara ran, she preferred to be alone, but making friends among local law enforcement was one of her unspoken job descriptions. After the case down in Arizona, Matt and Tony had sat her down and said that she had a knack for getting people to trust her—not just because she worked undercover, but because she'd been a local cop, too. Local cops tended to gravitate to her.

In Liberty Lake you had an in because you were from the area, but it was more than that—you instill trust and loyalty among the men and women in blue, and that's something we need when we go into small communities.

She instilled loyalty because she could play any part that was necessary. It was a knack she'd always had. Being raised by two con artists meant Kara read people better than most cops.

Which was another reason it burned her that Catherine didn't trust her assessment of Madelyn Jeffries. You could only learn so much from a book or files. The one-on-one conversation said a whole lot more, and if every one of Kara's interrogations was going to be second-guessed and duplicated, they would never make any forward progress on the case. Matt had to take a stand on this, or Kara would.

When they moved off the main road, Marcy picked up the pace and Kara easily kept up with her, even though Marcy had much longer legs.

Halfway down the two-lane road, the water came into view on the right. A few houses sat right on the water, but it still felt like they were in the middle of nowhere. Kara understood why Marcy liked this stretch.

Maybe, Kara thought, if she survived being a cop, in thirty years she could park herself on the water, not caring about the gossip of a small town. She could investigate insurance fraud, or maybe turn into that old broad the British lady wrote about all those years ago…a busybody. What was her name? Marble? Kara could sit on her front porch and solve crimes the cops couldn't.

Boring, but if she made it to sixty and was forced to retire, she'd do it in a place like this because of *water*. It's what she'd loved about growing up in Liberty Lake, what she loved about her apartment in Santa Monica, and what she loved about this job here in the San Juan Islands. Especially considering their last big assignment had sent them to the middle of the desert at the beginning of summer, this was like sitting down with a hot fudge sundae with extra fudge and cherries.

By the time they reached the end of the road, Kara felt more herself. Marcy slowed the pace and jogged down a worn dirt path toward the shore. There was an old shed and a dock that had collapsed into the water. Kara was surprised that a storm hadn't swept it completely away. Maybe it was because they were in a small inlet that protected the rotting wood from complete destruction.

And right now, as the sun was rising quickly, it was pretty damn spectacular.

"I found this spot shortly after I moved here," Marcy said as she stretched. "I love it. Sometimes on my day off I'll walk out here with a blanket and sit down and read for an hour or two. You can't even see the houses, and this is public land. No one seems to know about this place—I've never seen anyone, except other joggers or someone walking their dog."

"Why'd you leave the big city for here?"

"A lot of little things. I think it was the hostility toward police in Seattle that finally sent me packing. I mean, people call us because they have a problem but treat us as if their problems were our fault."

"Welcome to twenty-first-century policing."

"We got hit hard in Seattle a few years back, and I felt like I just couldn't do the job anymore. At least, I didn't feel like I was making a difference. So when this opportunity came up, I jumped. Who wouldn't want to live and work up here? Winter kind of sucks, it can be boring as hell, but then I go running along the coastline and feel...well, like I'm where I'm supposed to be. Home."

Kara wondered if she would ever find a place she felt was home. In thirty years, only her grandma's place even came close.

"I thought maybe I could settle down, you know?" Marcy continued. "A quieter life, find someone who appreciates me, have a baby. I'm thirty-four and single—I don't have a lot of time."

"A lot of women don't even get married and they still have a kid."

"Is that what you plan to do?"

She asked it as if it was a serious question.

"I'm not having kids."

"Why? Don't you like them?"

"Sure, they're little people, I like them, but the world sucks. I'm not going to bring a kid into this mess." She paused. "Maybe, down the road, I'd adopt an older kid, you know, someone who was dealt a bad hand." She'd met a couple of kids in her undercover work that she'd wanted to help in the worst way. Sometimes she could.

Most of the time she couldn't.

"But hey, you want a kid of your own. Who am I to say squat?"

"Do you think you'll ever go back to LAPD?" Marcy asked. "Or do you like working with the FBI?"

It took Kara a second to remember she'd given Marcy the quick version of her situation in LA.

"If I have the opportunity? I'd go back. But things are up in the air right now."

Marcy looked at her, expecting more, but Kara didn't feel like sharing. Even though it was nearly four months ago, the whole fiasco was still raw. In fact, this way-too-personal conversation was giving her palpitations.

"We should head back," she said. "I need to shower, then I'm interviewing McKinnon and following up with Justin Jeffries."

"I'll go with you."

"I'd like that, but I'm stuck with our department shrink."

It seemed Marcy wanted more chitchat, but Kara was done. She headed up the steep path toward the road, Marcy following behind her. Maybe the deputy was lonely here—leaving her friends and family behind in Seattle. But Kara just never did well in the buddy role.

One thing Marcy was right about: this was a terrific run. Just long enough to get a good workout, but not too difficult. Kara felt invigorated, and she might just have to venture out here alone tomorrow.

Kara picked up the pace when they reached the dirt road and Marcy ran alongside her. By the time they reached the town, they ran in the bike lane because there was no one else out. Still early, and the morning commute hadn't really started. Someone in a small Jeep honked and waved; Marcy waved back. Kara ignored them.

As they approached their meeting spot next to the harbor, Kara heard a horrific sound at the same time as the ground shook. She almost thought *earthquake*, then she looked south, beyond the harbor, and saw a ball of fire shoot into the air, followed by a plume of black smoke.

Another bomb, and it had exploded at West End Charter.

Before Kara could formulate a sentence, a second explosion roared louder than the first. She stumbled; Marcy caught her so she didn't fall on her ass.

As they watched, the fire quickly burned out, and the smoke seemed to fade. What the hell happened?

Simultaneously, Marcy and Kara sprinted toward the explosion.

17

Matt let the sheriff's department secure the scene. They had the necessary manpower and knew what they were doing both on land and water. ATF was on their way and would take over the forensics end of the investigation, and Matt's agent Michael Harris was with them.

But Matt was in charge of the overall operation, and the sheriff went out of his way to tell his deputies that if Matt gave an order, consider it coming from him.

Fifteen minutes after the explosion, the sheriff had secured the perimeter and a fireboat had extinguished the boathouse fire.

Kara was working crowd control. She had her badge out and around her neck but was still in her jogging clothes. Matt knew she was okay—she had called him right after the explosion to tell him the location and that she was already on scene. But seeing her in person was a relief. She'd been close to the blast. Three minutes later and she would have been running past the boathouse when it detonated.

At first glance, the damage didn't look extensive. From his vantage point, the side of the boathouse had been taken out by the bomb but the fire had been short-lived. Based on Kara's description, Matt surmised that the first explosion had been C-4, and the second explosion a fuel tank. Other boats moored nearby had only minor damage.

He needed Michael here ASAP to tell him what the hell had happened. That the second target was the West End Charter boathouse pretty much confirmed that West End had been the target of both attacks.

That put someone in Island Protectors at the top of their suspect list.

Matt wasn't going to play nice again with Donna Bell when they spoke, and he planned on talking to her as soon as possible. After he talked to the two vandals on probation.

The fire chief approached Matt along with one of his men. "Agent Costa? There's one victim. We found him when we were clearing the dock."

"ID?"

"Adult Black male approximately six foot based on our visual. The sheriff says you're in charge here. I can walk you through the safe zone. We're keeping people off the pier until we can ensure that the supports haven't been damaged, but the walkway along the dock is safe."

Matt motioned for Jim, who jogged over to him carrying a large backpack.

"We have a body."

Jim's face fell. "I need the ME from Snohomish here ASAP, but I'll take the sheriff's team and start processing."

"What you know, I know," Matt said. "Michael is on his way with the lead investigator with ATF. ETA, forty minutes. I want to know if the dead guy is the bomber as soon as possible." It wouldn't be the first time a bomber was killed by his own device.

Kara called him on his cell.

"What?"

"Turn around."

He did and saw Kara at the opposite end of the dock, stopping Ted Colfax from breaking the police line.

"I'm coming. Don't let him cross." Matt couldn't risk having a civilian screwing up the evidence. He ended the call, turned to Jim. "Go."

Jim motioned to the two sheriff's deputies who doubled as crime scene investigators. Then Matt strode down the walkway to where Kara was talking to West End's owner.

"Is there a body? Dammit, your agent won't tell me anything!"

Matt was mindful of the eyes and cell phones all over the place. He didn't need anyone listening to this conversation.

"Detective Quinn," he said, "thanks. Keep the perimeter until the sheriff's people relieve you, which won't be long." He motioned for her to watch the crowd, but he probably didn't have to remind her. Bombers, like arsonists, often lurked at the scene among bystanders.

"I need to know, Costa," Ted said. "What happened? Was anyone hurt?"

Matt walked Ted toward the administrative building, but they didn't go inside. He found a private place where no one could listen in.

"Yes, there's a body. Black male, adult, that's all I have right now."

"Garrett." Ted closed his eyes, rubbed them with his fingers. "Dammit."

"Garrett who? Employee?" He didn't remember the name from the list he got from Lynn Colfax.

"Washington. Garrett Washington. Security. New hire, he started Saturday. His roommate called me when he heard the explosion. Garrett gets off at three in the morning; his roommate starts at six. I doubled security, rented a couple apartments for these guys through Labor Day. Just to patrol because... But Garrett wasn't on duty. Why was he there?"

"We're investigating. I assume you ran a background check?"

"Of course! Why? You don't think— No. No way, that makes no sense. He lives outside Seattle. He wasn't even here before Saturday afternoon."

"Okay, that's a start, but I'll need to verify that. I also need to talk to the last person who saw Garrett."

"Bruce Dingham. He runs the night crew. He's been with me for years. Shit! What's going on? Why is this asshole killing people?"

Matt had theories, but without more evidence, that's all they were. "ATF is on their way, along with a munitions expert who has investigated dozens of bombings."

"I just can't believe those kids would do anything like this!"

"Kids?"

"Island Protectors. They're mostly high school and college kids. But I suppose after all the crap that happened a couple years ago, some of these kids think that it's okay. But this isn't vandalism. This is murder."

"First, we don't know who is doing this, so keep your theory to yourself. I'm investigating every angle. Can you call Bruce in?"

"He's still here." Ted looked around. He saw his employees standing outside the main building, others near the club entrance, some crying, all shocked. "I'm going to have to close until we know... Dammit! I didn't want to do this. These people count on me. I employ more than a hundred people during the summer. And..." He took a deep breath.

"Do what you need to do, be available. Where's Bruce?"

Ted led him to a small building next to the administrative building. A simple sign read SECURITY OFFICE.

Bruce was upset—he'd liked Garrett, a good guy down on his luck after losing his business—but he had nothing of import to add except two things: the exact time that Garrett Washington clocked out (3:03 a.m.) and the fact that he and his partner had run off teenage boys who'd been drinking on one of the docks—including a fourteen-year-old named Mickey Billings, the son of a town council member.

Matt turned to Ted. "When your brother and sister arrive, I need to talk to them. But make it clear *not* to make any statements to the press or others about what happened until we have more information. If you're comfortable, you can refer everyone to me."

"What about Garrett's wife?" Ted asked. "He only worked for me a few days, but damn, he was a good guy. He's married, has a kid. What am I supposed to say to them?"

"I can call her," Matt said.

"No. He was my employee, my responsibility. I'll do it."

Ted walked toward the administrative building.

Matt saw Kara standing on the edge of the dock. She wore sunglasses and was watching the crowd. Deputy Anderson was there, in uniform, moving people along and keeping order along with a half dozen other deputies. The Coast Guard had arrived and were keeping boats out of the containment area. The sheriff had two teams of dogs out, inspecting every boat at West End. When they were done with West End, they'd move over to the harbor. The ferry service was delayed. If Matt had his way, he would cut off all boat service for twenty-four hours or more until they had a grasp on what they were dealing with here.

But that might not be realistic. He'd already got a report from the sheriff that they were not sending any ferries until noon; they would reassess then and decide whether it was safe.

They'd locked every port across all islands while security inspected every boat.

Matt walked up to Kara and said, "I have a potential witness I need to interview. May be nothing, but worth following up. Keep me in the loop."

He had more to say, but not with a nearby crowd eager to hear. He knew Kara was angry with him about last night—the Jeffries interview, plus how he reacted after her impromptu undercover work in IP. And he wasn't quite sure how to react to their make-out session in the kitchen.

Kara glanced at her watch, then without looking put her arm out to stop a kid who was trying to go through the line. "Back off," she said.

"You're a cop?" he said with a grin.

"That's what they tell me. Stay on that side of the tape."

His phone rang. It was Jim. Matt stepped away and said, "News?"

"Some. The victim's skull was crushed, likely before the bomb detonated. His body is in surprisingly good condition—it was close to the explosion, there's shrapnel embedded in his flesh, but the blast went up and out, not wide, so we should be able to determine cause of death from the autopsy."

"Is he our bomber?"

"Like I said, head beaten in before the explosion, I'm guessing not. Again, autopsy will confirm, but my very educated guess is that he's been dead four to six hours. Definitely dead before the bomb went off. The good news is the fire was contained and burned out quickly. Bad news, the water from fire and rescue didn't help us preserve evidence. Fortunately, the body was partly protected from the roof that came down. We're going to bag him up and take him and the boat he was lying in to the mainland. The ME is already on his way and I'm going to assist, if you don't mind."

"That's why you're on this team. Anything you find, let me know."

"He was hit over the head with a brick or block of cement, I'm fairly certain. I can see some debris embedded in his scalp, and it's not deep enough to be from the blast. The guy was six feet, but if someone within a couple inches either side of that used both hands and came down hard to whack him, he'd be on his knees. The rest was child's play."

"Good work." Matt didn't need the details until Jim confirmed.

His cell vibrated. It was Michael, so he ended the call with Jim and answered.

"Tell me you're here," Matt said.

"Just landed at the sheriff's helipad. We'll be there in five minutes. Victim?"

"One, security guard, blunt force trauma most likely cause of death, dead four to six hours."

"Caught the bomber in action, not the bomber?"

"That's my guess. We have a good time window. He got off just after three a.m. and the boathouse was maybe a five-minute walk from the security office. That's when it happened. I need everything you and ATF can give me on this bomb."

"We're on it."

Kara didn't mind crowd control, and she had taken extensive video of the spectators, on the chance that the bomber showed up to view the results of his destruction. Unfortunately, based on the location, he could be in any number of stores or restaurants across the street, and the dock that led to the Friday Harbor ferry building was open to pedestrian traffic, which consisted mostly of people watching police and fire. He could be anywhere.

Kara knew what she was doing, and if he was watching nearby, one of her shots caught him. They might not be able to find him among the throng of people, but she didn't miss anything.

It was after eight, and Ryder told her Cal McKinnon was waiting for her at the sheriff's department. She walked over to Marcy. "Duty calls. You have enough people here?"

"We're good. If you need me, please tell John. I hate crowd control. If not, maybe drinks tonight?"

"Fifty-fifty. We'll touch base this afternoon."

Kara left and walked to the sheriff's department, and the desk sergeant told her McKinnon was in the smallest conference room. "Is that okay?"

"Perfect," she said and followed his directions down the hall and to the left, on the opposite side of the building from where the FBI was set up.

McKinnon stood as soon as she entered. "Are you Kara Quinn?"

"Yes, Detective Quinn, working with the FBI. Sorry for my attire—I was jogging when the explosion hit and didn't have time to change."

"Was anyone hurt? I heard someone might have been killed, but the news didn't confirm."

"One person died. I can't tell you any more than that yet."

"God, this is so awful."

She motioned for him to sit down; he did.

Cal was a pleasant-looking guy. Twenty-nine, according to his driver's license. Dark hair, a bit on the long side, curled up at the ends. Eyelashes that belonged on a girl. Dimples. Blue eyes. A bit skinny. No record, two parking tickets—both paid—and honorably discharged from the Coast Guard.

"I want to follow up on your statement from Friday night. At this point, the FBI is running the investigation with the full cooperation of the sheriff's office. I have your statement taken by Officer Redfield."

"Yeah. Whatever you need. Anything."

"Start with why you didn't go to work that night."

"Kyle." His face fell and he closed his eyes.

"Kyle Richards," she prompted. She wanted him to tell the story in his own way.

"I liked him. He was a good kid. Doing the five-year college plan but would have graduated next year. Anyway, I asked him to cover because Jamie and I had an argument, and I wanted to make things right. Jamie's my fiancée."

Everything he said tracked with what he'd told Redfield. "What was your argument about?"

"A misunderstanding." He paused. "Why? Is that important?"

"I need to confirm your alibi."

She wanted a reaction. His reaction was confusion. "Alibi? Why?"

"You were supposed to be working on the *Water Lily*, and you called out last minute."

"Oh." He didn't sound suspicious. "It's kind of complicated."

"You should know that I'll also be talking to Jamie. Just to make sure everyone's statements line up."

"Jamie? Why? She's so upset about this. She loved Neil. I mean, like a dad, not like a guy. Her dad travels a lot. She rarely sees him."

That, Kara hadn't known. "Jamie knew Neil? How well?"

"She works at the Fish & Brew. He came in a lot, they became friendly, and then when her car was in the shop, he loaned her his truck for a week. Just... I mean, no strings. He even watched Hazel a couple times when our babysitter canceled last minute."

"Hazel is your daughter?"

He smiled, a genuine smile. He pulled out his phone and showed her a photo of a toddler with curly dark hair and big blue eyes.

He took another lingering look at the photo, then put his phone facedown. "Anyway, Neil has a daughter Jamie's age. He misses her a lot because she's in the Navy, stationed in Japan. He hadn't seen her since Christmas. I think he enjoyed spending time with Jamie and Hazel."

"Did Neil ever talk to you about an old case he was investigating?"

"About those college kids who drowned? Yeah, a bit. Why?"

She didn't answer. "Did he share with you any details about what he'd uncovered? Why he thought it wasn't an accident?"

"Not really. I mean, sometimes he would just talk things out when he was working on the boat, you know? So not really telling me anything, just chatting."

"Can you give me an example?"

"Uh—why?"

"Cal, it's not a trick question."

He shrugged. "Well, okay, um…a couple weeks ago we were working, a charter gig—big extended family wanted a sightseeing tour. They got off at Orcas for a picnic, and Neil and I were talking while we waited. He asked me about holding grudges."

"Grudges?"

"Yeah, like, how long did I hold a grudge. I said I didn't. Life's too short, you know? I think when I was younger I kind of did— like my best friend in high school stole my girlfriend and I didn't talk to him for the rest of the year, and intentionally drilled him in batting practice—I was a pitcher in high school, but didn't go to college. I could have, I guess, but I didn't know what I wanted to do, and I've always liked the Coast Guard. My grandpa was in the Navy."

"And Neil? Grudges?" She pushed him back to the subject. "Did he tell you why?"

"No. We talked about high school and sports and football—I don't really like football, but I know enough to get by."

"And you didn't find the question a little odd?"

"It was kind of Neil's way. He always had these hypothetical questions that really didn't have answers, you know? Like he was trying to figure things out but didn't quite say what he was trying to figure out."

"Where can I reach Jamie?"

"Today? Well—she's working tomorrow at the Fish & Brew. Eleven thirty to eight. Today she's at her dad's place on the other side of the island but will be back before dark. You want me to have her call you?"

Kara considered. Cal seemed forthcoming, and the second bombing pointed more fingers at IP, but she still couldn't get Neil's investigation out of her head, or the gas leak at his house.

Still, she needed to verify what Cal said. She slid over her card. "Yeah, have her call me to set up a time. I'll go to her. Just to clarify, when did you hear about the *Water Lily*?"

"Jamie told me. After Kyle took over, I drove to her dad's place to talk, so we could work things out. She looked like she'd seen a ghost, told me that the TV news reported a boat explosion. We watched more of the news together, then I left and came back here—to West End, I mean. Told her to stay at her dad's until we knew what was going on. I drove back out there on Saturday—and we worked everything out. Mostly."

"Worked what out?"

"We've been engaged for years and she finally set a date—September—but then she felt insecure because she ran into one of my ex-girlfriends. Jamie had…well, let's just say she had a shitty boyfriend before me. I love her, I love Hazel, and she now knows it. I mean she *knew* it, but now I think she believes it, you know? But she keeps thinking that we're too perfect. Which is stupid. I mean, she's not stupid, but the idea that we can't be happy because then something bad will happen, that's just wrong thinking. So we're good. She's nervous, was getting cold feet about the wedding—we've been living together for nearly four years, but I want Hazel to have married parents. I guess that sounds old-fashioned, but whatever. And I know she wants it, but her parents had a crappy marriage, and she says she doesn't want to mess things up. Like she even *could*, you know?"

Cal was genuine. Nice guy, a bit on the beta side, loved his girl. Kara would confirm everything—because she'd met a couple of so-called "nice guys" who were total two-faced jerks or turned into assholes when they drank. She didn't see that with Cal, and everyone who knew him had the same story: he was loyal, friendly, loved his family, enjoyed the quiet island life.

"One last thing. Did you know anyone on board other than Neil and Kyle?"

"No—I mean, I knew *of* Mr. Jeffries. He was friends with Ted. But I think I only met him once or twice, when I was working. I bartend at the club when I'm not working a charter."

"And his wife?"

"No, Mrs. Jeffries didn't come into the bar, but I think I saw Lynn—that's Ted's sister—having lunch with her a couple of times in the dining room."

"Tell me about Island Protectors. They have a beef with West End because of a fuel spill?"

He rolled his eyes. "I want to support their cause—I mean, I'm all for protecting the environment, I recycle everything, we even used cloth diapers for Hazel. But they're wrong about West End. The fuel leak was really an accident. They were in the middle of retrofitting their boats. Yeah, they probably should have decommissioned all the affected boats until they could fix them, but then they would have had to lay off staff, and they are one of the top three private employers on the island. And the Colfax family has been here forever, they love the islands, they would never intentionally cause damage, you know? I think they—IP—just got a bee in their bonnet, as my grandpa used to say. One mistake—an accident—and they laser focused on them. I mean, I get it, the fuel leak could have been devastating, but they cleaned it up fast and there were no long-term consequences. Sometimes, I think people just like to stir up shit because they like to stir the shit."

"Anyone in particular stand out to you? Someone who held a more…specific grudge against them?" She intentionally used the word he used when talking about Neil.

He shook his head. "I really don't know those people but—well, I shouldn't say this."

"Yes, you should."

"Pete's been so good to Jamie, gave her time off during the pregnancy, always adjusts her schedule when she needs it. I don't want to hurt him."

"You won't."

"I think Ashley—well, she's a great kid. Both of his girls are. But I've seen her hanging out with the IP group. Pete would be livid if he knew. He's close to Ted—they went to school together, have been friends a long time—in their graduating class, they're two of maybe a half dozen that stayed on the islands. That kind of bonds people. I don't want to get her in trouble, but if anyone knows those people, it's her."

Confirmed everything Kara had learned about Ashley, but hearing a different perspective was helpful.

"Okay. I might need to ask more questions, and if you think of anything else, call me. Anytime." She got up but he stayed seated.

"Are you really going to talk to Jamie?" asked Cal.

"Yes," Kara said.

"Can you just be… I don't know, nice?"

"Was I not nice to you?" She was mildly humored, mildly suspicious.

"I mean…okay…flat out, Jamie and I had a fight about one of my ex-girlfriends. I kinda didn't want to say anything because she's a cop, and I know you guys are all friends."

Kara's instincts twitched. She sat back down.

Marcy's voice popped into her head. *"Cal's a good guy. We were in the Coast Guard together."*

She waited.

"So last year, my ex-girlfriend—well, not even really an ex-girlfriend, we only went out for a short time, like a half dozen times—she moved to the island. I was surprised, but whatever.

I didn't say anything to Jamie because she had finally set a wedding date and I kind of didn't think it was important."

Kara could see what happened a mile away. Insecure girl, ex-girlfriend.

"And?" she prompted when Cal hesitated.

"And then Marcy just started following me."

"Officer Marcy Anderson," she said to confirm.

"Yeah. I know, it sounds totally weird, and maybe I was wrong. Because I confronted her—"

"When did you confront her?"

"In the spring. Late April, I think. It was a Friday. Jamie was working—Friday has the best tips from the Fish & Brew, and Pete loves Jamie, she's been working there for years, so he always lets her have Friday nights. I had worked the day charter, so I was off at five. I went to pick Hazel up at her babysitter, and Marcy pulled me over. I'd seen her all over town—she came up to me when she first moved here, wanted to go out for drinks. I told her I was involved with someone. That we had a kid. And she told me that she hadn't been following me, it's just a small island, and she came here because Seattle had gone half-crazy and she wanted a quieter life. I guess…she seemed disappointed, but…"

"And?" she prompted.

"She kept showing up! Like, Jamie and I would take Hazel to the park—Marcy was there, running through the park. Hazel and I went to surprise Jamie at the Fish & Brew for her birthday last month and there was Marcy. I'd see her running by the house a couple times a week. And she'd look my way and she knew that I saw her…and she just ran by. I was a bit freaked out, but it *is* a small island. Still, I should have told Jamie."

"You didn't." Relationships didn't work when there were secrets.

"I should have, I know it, and I hit myself every day…and then on Thursday, Jamie had the day off and took Hazel to the park. Marcy talked to her. Said something like she had hoped to meet, that she was in the Coast Guard with me, and told her not only about our relationship, but about how I saw her in Seattle five years ago. That was after I'd met Jamie, but we had only gone on a few dates. I went to Seattle for the weekend for a friend's wedding. Marcy was there, mutual friend. I drank a lot, we ended up in my hotel room, and it was a total mistake. That's when I realized I really liked Jamie. I mean, yes, I cheated on her, but I didn't, you know? We'd only gone out a couple of times."

"I see what you mean." Kara could picture it as clear as day. "And you withheld this information from Jamie."

"We'd gone on *two dates*. I liked her, but I didn't think Jamie was into me. When I got back, we saw each other again, and it changed, you know?"

"So then Marcy told all this to Jamie." Kara didn't see how this was relevant to her investigation, but there was something off. Why hadn't Marcy told Kara that she'd been in a relationship with McKinnon?

"Jamie was so upset, so angry... I tried to explain, but she took off, went to her dad's place with Hazel on Friday morning. And that's why I called in sick that night. I had to make things right. I was wrong, so wrong, and Jamie's been hurt before."

"Where's her dad's place? The mainland?"

He shook his head. "Across the island. You can drive across the island in an hour. He has a cabin on the water, in a cove. It's nice. He's rarely there. Jamie has a bad habit of running from confrontation. But I needed to explain everything...well, we need to talk more, but she didn't call off the wedding, and that's a big plus."

Kara wondered what was going on with Marcy. It could be innocuous. It might be more serious. But she couldn't just let this go.

How she was going to address it—that was something she needed to think long and hard about.

18

Matt and John went to interview Mickey Billings, the fourteen-year-old who'd been drinking beer on the edge of West End property the night before. He was short with big hands and feet, which told Matt he would be going through a growth spurt in a year or two.

Though at first he denied being there, under the glare of his father, Mickey came clean.

"Yeah, I spent the night at Andy's house," he said, brushing his long brown bangs out of his eyes. "We snuck out at midnight. We weren't doing anything wrong."

Matt didn't comment.

"We each took one beer from Andy's dad's fridge, that was

it. Because we didn't want him to notice. And we weren't getting drunk. We just wanted to get out and, I don't know, just, you know."

Matt knew. He had done the exact same thing when he was a kid. He never intended to get into trouble, but there were a few times where the situation had gone south, quickly. Nothing good happened on the streets after midnight. Of course, Friday Harbor was a whole world different than Little Havana.

"Who else was with you?" Mr. Billings asked. *"Everyone."*

"Andy and Jake. That's it. I swear, Dad."

Matt said, "Two security guards told you to leave. Do you remember what time that was?"

"Um, about one, a little after. We got down there at twelve thirty, were just talking—I swear, we weren't doing anything bad."

"Sneaking out of the house after midnight. Drinking."

"One beer, Dad!"

"You're fourteen, Mickey. That's one beer too many. But to be honest, I'm angrier about you leaving the house without permission. No one knew where you were. Something could have happened... We'll talk later."

The kid frowned, looked at Matt. "I'm sorry."

"You'll have to talk to your dad about that. What I want to know is if you saw or heard anything last night. Before or after the guards told you to go home."

He shrugged.

"Mickey!" his dad snapped.

"No, sir," Mickey said to Matt.

"Let's do it this way. You left Andy's house at what time? Be as precise as you can."

"About twelve twenty, twelve twenty-five."

"And did you go directly to the pier?"

"We went by Jake's house, he came out, and he's like just a few minutes from the pier. Um, about twelve thirty, a little after."

"How long were you at the pier?"

"Forty-five minutes? Maybe an hour before the guards told us to leave. They, um, promised they wouldn't say anything."

"One of those guards died in the explosion," Matt said. "He told the office of his encounter with you."

Mickey's face fell. "Really? Ohmygod I'm so sorry."

Mr. Billings put his hand on his son's shoulder and squeezed.

Matt asked, "When you left, did you see anyone? I looked at the pier where you were—you would have to pass the boathouse on your way off West End property."

He shook his head, then hesitated. "There was a boat. I mean, there's boats everywhere, I know, but someone was on this one, about a hundred feet out, a little more, from the end of the pier. I wouldn't have noticed except that a reflection caught my eye. The moon wasn't out, so I thought it was the guards following us, with their flashlight or something. But they'd gone the other direction, and we went back the way we came."

Matt pulled out a detailed map of the area. "Where was the boat?" He pointed. "This is the pier where you and your friends were. This is the boathouse. You walked…here?" He moved his finger along a path.

"Yeah, though we cut through this part," Mickey said, dragging his finger along a parallel path. "Because there's a gate at the stairs that leads up to the road, but if you go along the beach, you can cut through the Johannessens' property here."

Mickey studied the map. "The boat was about here." He pointed to a spot between the pier and the boathouse, but about a hundred fifty feet out in the inlet.

"And you saw someone on the boat?"

"I mean, not really? I guess—there was someone, but it was just a dark blob."

"Did you hear anything? A motor?"

Mickey frowned. "Not then, but when we were sitting on the pier earlier I heard a motorboat going south but didn't see it. There's a lot of people who go out at night, so I didn't really think about it. And it wasn't going fast, there wasn't a big wake or anything."

"You have a good memory. And that was about one thirty?"

"Yeah. We got back to Andy's just before two, I think. We were a little wired, you know, getting caught and all. Played some video games... We'd just fallen asleep when we heard the explosion." He looked at Matt with big eyes. "I'm really, really sorry someone died."

"I know. Thank you for your help."

"I helped?"

"Yes. Now I know how the bomber got to the boathouse without being caught on the security cameras."

19

Kara thought it was a waste of time for her and Catherine to follow up with Madelyn Jeffries while Matt and Michael focused on the recent bombing. Madelyn had no motive to go after West End, and the idea that she would set off a second bomb—and bludgeon a guard to death—was ludicrous.

Kara needed to follow up with Jamie Finch, to find out what Marcy Anderson had been doing following Cal—if she had been following him—and help Ryder go through Neil's files on the Mowich Lake drownings. She shouldn't have to repeat her interview from yesterday when she knew damn well that Madelyn Jeffries was innocent.

The only reason she didn't push back on Catherine about

the interview was because they needed to follow up with Justin Jeffries, the oldest son, to determine if there had been threats against his father or anything unusual that happened that might have led to him being a target. That's what Kara wanted to determine. It was Catherine who wanted to reinterview Madelyn, and just the thought of it made Kara's blood boil.

But she remained as calm as possible.

Justin had originally agreed to talk to them at the sheriff's station, but because of the second bombing and the emergency vehicles downtown, Kara arranged to meet him at the house. She didn't think it was odd that he was staying there, but Catherine made a snide comment about it. She had read everything about the Jeffries family and believed what the kids believed— that Madelyn was a gold digger. Kara didn't even try to change her mind. What was the point? Catherine had no respect for her or her opinion.

For a shrink who was supposed to be open-minded and non-judgmental, Catherine Jones seemed to fall into stereotype traps. Kara didn't say it, but she wanted to.

She really, *really* wanted to. Take the doctor down a peg or two. But she bit her tongue, for now.

Kara drove. She didn't ask Catherine if she wanted to drive to the Jeffries house. Since Matt had the rental, she'd borrowed a car from the sheriff's pool.

She and Catherine were silent during the ten-minute drive. That was fine with Kara. She was still angry about last night and didn't want to risk a conversation with Catherine turning into a confrontation.

A tall, attractive man in his midthirties opened the door after Kara knocked. Justin Jeffries looked like a younger version of his father.

"Detective Quinn?" he asked.

"Yes," Kara said. "And this is Dr. Catherine Jones with the

FBI. Thank you for agreeing to meet with us today. I'm sorry for your loss."

"Madelyn said you were kind to her yesterday when my brother and sister came by. I want to apologize for their behavior. It's been a roller coaster."

"Tragedy does that."

"This wasn't about my father's death." He rubbed his eyes, motioned for them to enter. "Can I get you anything?"

"No, thank you. We won't take much of your time."

"Of course. Madelyn's outside on the deck, if you don't mind talking out there?"

"Actually," Catherine said, "if we could speak to you alone first, that would be helpful."

He looked skeptical but motioned for them to take seats in a spacious office off the foyer. He moved papers from the center of the desk, stacking them to the side, and closed his laptop. "I decided to work from here for the next few days, even before they shut down the ferries this morning. Do you know anything more about the explosion? I assume it's the work of the same culprit."

Justin spoke old-fashioned. He acted older than his years.

"We can't comment on the investigation," Catherine said formally, "but we're following all leads. You worked directly with your father."

"Yes. I— There's a lot to take care of, but my dad was very organized. He already had a plan in place, should something happen to him. I just didn't think we'd implement it. I thought we'd have time—my dad was healthy and happy. I never thought…" He paused, cleared his throat. "What do you need?"

"We're pursuing all avenues of investigation," Catherine said, "and looking at each of the victims to determine if one of them might be a target."

"The news this morning said the target was West End Charter."

"They may be, but we haven't ruled out other possibilities."

He nodded for her to continue.

"Did your father receive any threats?" asked Catherine. "Any pending lawsuits, hostile perhaps?"

"No. My dad was respected in both business and his personal life."

"Yet some people were skeptical of his marriage to Madelyn."

"So?"

"She's substantially younger."

"So?" he repeated.

Justin was a man who had firm control over his emotions and reactions, but he was becoming angry. Subtle, but present.

Kara enjoyed it. She hoped Justin tossed them from the house.

Catherine said, "It's a motive."

"Because Madelyn is nearly half my dad's age, you think she killed him and eight other people. What a sad world you live in, Dr. Jones."

"I didn't say that."

"Yes, you did. You said it was a motive. Do not say a word of this to Madelyn. She is barely holding it together, and she's pregnant with my brother or sister. She's family. You want the truth? The truth is I had a few doubts about Madelyn at the beginning because I know there are unscrupulous people out there. I'm a lawyer and a businessman, and I deal with a lot of them. But I have always trusted my father. If you knew him, you would trust his judgment as well. Madelyn loves him. I knew it the minute I saw them together, though it took me a few months to accept her. My father is not a fool and is not easily manipulated."

Catherine didn't back down. "Did you know that he changed his will?"

"Of course I did. He doesn't do anything that impacts the family without discussing it with me. He told me about the baby weeks before my sister found out. I was the one who suggested he change his will to protect their child. Because I know Kimberly, and she's vindictive. Angry. I get it—she was very close to Mom. Our mom died when she was fourteen—that's a hard time. I miss my mom, of course, but I've always been closer to my dad. Kimberly—she just refused to see Madelyn for who she is, but more than that, she refused to accept that our father was capable of making his own decisions.

"No one in the family is left out of the will. My father loved Kimberly just like he did my brother and me. He forgave her for how she treated Madelyn, for how she behaved in private and in public. I'm not as forgiving, but for my dad I will be, provided she grows up. So no one in the family has a financial motive. My brother has a master's degree in economics and works for the stock exchange. He's brilliant, makes plenty of money on his own without the need for his inheritance. My father didn't believe in trust funds, but he gave each of us seed money when we graduated from college to do with as we saw fit. Because Joshua is a mathematical genius, he parlayed his graduation present into a sizable nest egg. Kimberly wasn't as frugal, but she owns her own business and it's in the black. Dad bought her a condo in Seattle. As far as me, I work for the family business, I make a salary—a very good salary, but I earn every dime."

Catherine was not dissuaded. "Madelyn doesn't work."

"I don't understand why you are fixated on her." He looked at Kara. "You met her. Do you think she could kill nine people in cold blood?"

"I think anyone is capable of murder," Kara said honestly. "We have to cross off every possibility."

Catherine tensed next to her, but Justin relaxed, nodded. "I get it. I know how this looks to the outside world, but you didn't know my dad. I did. He was my hero. Kind, smart, brilliant really. He loved all of us. But he loved Madelyn more than anything. And if you had seen them together, you'd have seen the same thing. My dad had no enemies, no threats, no business deals gone bad. He wasn't the target, personally or professionally."

There was a knock on the den door and a woman—as attractive as Justin Jeffries—stepped in. "I'm sorry to disturb you, JJ, but you wanted to talk to Blaine as soon as he called. He's on Madelyn's cell phone."

"Tell him one minute." He smiled at the woman and they exchanged a look that told Kara they were involved.

She closed the door and Justin said, "That's my fiancée, Robin. I have to take this call—Blaine O'Malley is my father's personal lawyer and I know that Madelyn isn't up to talking about the estate right now, but there are some things that need to be done sooner rather than later."

"We still need to talk to Madelyn," Catherine said.

Kara admired Catherine's ability to remain completely calm and unfazed. Did she recognize that this was a complete waste of time or was she still convinced that Madelyn Jeffries had something to do with her husband's death?

"All right, but please be kind."

"You'll be on the island for how long?" Kara asked.

"At least until Friday. I'm trying to convince Madelyn to come back and stay with Robin and me in Seattle until she feels ready to go back to the house in Bellingham. She's having a difficult time making decisions right now. Please just—be gentle with her."

"Of course," Catherine said.

What was the shrink really thinking? She was hard to read. But Kara would figure her out. There wasn't a person she hadn't figured out yet. Some took longer than others.

Justin whispered to Robin, and the woman—she had to be a model, Kara thought, with her long legs and amazing hair—escorted her and Catherine to the deck.

"Maddie, sweetie," Robin said in a soft tone. "The FBI is here to talk to you."

Madelyn was sitting in a chair, staring at the water. She had a blanket on her legs, no makeup, and her hands were clasped over her stomach.

It took her a full ten seconds to turn her head and face them.

"Detective... I forget your name. I'm so sorry."

"Kara."

"Kara. That's pretty. Pierce and I haven't talked about names yet for the baby. Pierce loves his rose garden. Rose is a pretty name. Robin, do you think Pierce would like Rose for the baby?"

Robin sat down next to Madelyn. She was clearly concerned. "Pierce would love any name you liked."

"I don't know." She stared off at the water again.

Robin looked at Kara and Catherine with an expression that said *do you have to do this now?*

Catherine said, "Mrs. Jeffries, I'm Dr. Catherine Jones, with the Behavioral Science Unit of the FBI. I'm helping to investigate the explosion on the *Water Lily* and I have only a few questions for you. Are you up for it?"

She slowly turned to face her. "Questions. Yes. What do you want to know?"

"I want to confirm some of the information you told my colleague, Detective Quinn."

"Quinn?" She looked at Kara. "Oh. Yes. Kara Quinn. Okay."

Robin looked at them. "Is there any way we can do this later? Justin and I are going to be here at least until Friday, if not longer."

"I'll be brief," Catherine said.

"Please," Robin said, protectively.

Kara was interested to see where Catherine was going with this.

"Mrs. Jeffries—"

"Please, call me Madelyn. I don't like formalities."

"Madelyn, why did you change your mind about going on the sunset cruise?"

Madelyn looked like she hadn't heard the question, just stared at Catherine.

"Madelyn?" Catherine pushed.

"Cruise. I—I should have gone. I should have been stronger."

"Stronger? What do you mean by that?"

"Tina... I didn't want to spend three hours with her. I was being selfish. We—once I thought Tina was the most beautiful, smartest girl in the world. She got me a job at the country club. She taught me how to present myself. But we..." She stopped talking as if she had lost her train of thought.

"You and Tina...?" Catherine prompted.

Madelyn said, "I should have been with him."

Robin cleared her throat. "Maddie, don't."

"He wanted to come home with me, but I said no. He wanted to talk to Vince about business. I don't even know about what, but it was important to Pierce, and I didn't want to take it from him. I..." Her voice trailed off again.

"We're done here," Robin said emphatically.

Kara stood. She agreed. Catherine also rose. "Thank you, Mrs. Jeffries."

Madelyn didn't look at her.

On the way out, Catherine turned to Kara and asked quietly, "Was Madelyn that disconnected when you spoke to her yesterday?"

"No. She was more engaged, a bit slow to answer, but she understood that Pierce was dead. She was teary, but functional, and she stood up to her stepkids."

Catherine had her phone out and was scrolling through her contacts as Robin walked them to the door. "Robin, you need to get Madelyn into therapy as soon as possible. I know an outstanding therapist in Seattle, if you want to take down his contact information. He doesn't accept many new clients, but if you mention my name, he'll take her."

"She's grieving," Robin said. "We'll be here for her."

"She's disconnected from what has happened. She doesn't speak about Pierce in the past tense, and while that is not unusual, it's her tone and mannerisms that have me concerned. The fact that she regressed from yesterday is disconcerting. Under no circumstances should you leave her alone for a length of time."

Robin looked out onto the deck where Madelyn still sat. "Are you saying she's suicidal?"

"Not consciously. I don't think she has a conscious thought to kill herself, but she is not connected to the present, and needs to find a way to process what has happened. Until then, she may not know what she's doing. In fact, if you contact the doctor I recommend, he may come up here for a private consult."

"I'll take good care of her. I love Maddie like a sister, and I will do anything to help her get through this. I'll talk to Justin. I'm sure he'll agree."

"And while I understand this is a sensitive family situation, for at least the next few days, keep Pierce's other children away from her. The emotional stress isn't good for the pregnancy."

"Thank you for your concern. I promise, we'll take care of Maddie."

They left, and in the car Kara said, "That was really nice."

"I'm not a cold bitch, Detective."

"You can call me Kara."

Catherine didn't say anything.

"Do you believe me now?"

"I didn't disbelieve you."

"You thought I was unqualified to make the call on this."

"Yes, that is true."

Kara was almost surprised she admitted it. While it angered her, she appreciated Catherine's honesty. Yet she didn't elaborate. And by her tone, Catherine still didn't trust Kara's skills and experience.

Kara drove them silently back to the sheriff's station.

20

Kara left Catherine in the FBI conference room and drove to the high school in the center of town. It was time for summer classes to end, and she wanted to talk to Ashley Dunlap alone.

Ten minutes after she arrived, she saw Ashley and Whitney exit the building together. She got out, approached the girls.

"Agent Quinn!" Whitney said with a grin.

"Detective Quinn, but you can call me Kara."

"You have more questions? Dad said if you had any questions, it's okay to talk to you, you know, follow-up questions."

"Actually, I was hoping to talk to Ashley alone for a minute, if that's okay?" Kara wished she could have grabbed Ashley alone, but the girls seemed to be together all day long, so that would have been more difficult.

Ashley looked apprehensive but said, "Whit, it's fine. I'll meet you at home."

"Are you sure? Do you want me to call Dad?"

"*No,*" Ashley said emphatically. "Seriously. It's *fine.* I'll be back before you get the leash on Dakota."

Reluctantly, Whitney left, and Kara turned to Ashley. "Craig and Bobby Martin. Talk."

"I don't have to talk to you," she said.

"Do you want to follow Donna Bell's advice, or do you want to help catch the person who killed ten people?"

Her face fell. "Someone died this morning?"

"A security guard. Caught the bomber in the act, bludgeoned to death. He had a wife, a kid." With Ashley, being blunt was the best way to get her to talk.

"Craig and Bobby would *never* hurt anyone. If that's what you think, I'm definitely not talking to you."

"I want the truth. I know you gave Donna Bell a copy of the photos you gave to me. I know you're dating Bobby Martin, and I suspect your dad doesn't know about it."

Her dark eyes widened. "How? Who told you?"

"I'm a detective. I detect." She had to give her something to latch on to, so she said, "I don't think Bobby had anything to do with the bombings, and I doubt his brother did, either. It's a long way from vandalism to murder."

At the word *murder*, the girl involuntarily shuddered.

"But two bombings targeting West End property tells me someone really doesn't like them." That was a theory, but Kara's gut told her somebody in particular was a target, not West End as an entity. Maybe the killer had thought Ted Colfax was going to be piloting the charter that night. Maybe the killer had been targeting Neil Devereaux because of an old case.

But why the second bombing?

"Island Protectors is not a violent group," Ashley said defiantly.

"I didn't say it was."

"You implied it."

"No, I didn't. Tell me about Valerie."

"Why?"

"Because she made you cry."

"How do you know?"

Kara didn't say anything. Ashley was stunned she knew, but she hadn't put Kara and the stranger together last night.

Finally, Ashley said, "I don't like her, and neither does Bobby. But Craig loves her, and Bobby loves his brother."

"Do you think that she's capable of violence?"

"If I say no, you might charge me as an accessory."

"That's bullshit. The only way you'd be charged as accessory after the fact is if you learned who did it but didn't come forward. I don't think you had anything to do with the bombing, Ashley."

"I would never hurt anyone. I can't—I still have nightmares. I see—the bodies. Floating."

Kara felt for the girl. "I would, too," she said softly. "Ashley, you need to tell me what you know."

"I don't know anything about what happened!"

"Yesterday when I talked to you, you clammed up as soon as your father criticized IP."

"Because he doesn't know I go to the meetings. He doesn't know I've been following the charters for months, taking pictures, trying to catch them violating environmental regulations so we can shut them down. He's friends with Mr. Colfax, and he would never allow me to follow what I know is right. And—he doesn't know that I'm seeing Bobby. Bobby is nineteen, which isn't a big deal, but when his brother was arrested last year, my dad just went off on IP. My dad is kinda rigid about things, you know? I just can't talk to him about any of this stuff, and next year Bobby and I will be in college together, University of Washington, and then he can't do anything about it."

Kara was sympathetic to Ashley. Being a teenager was tough, especially when you and your parents didn't see eye to eye. At the same time, Pete Dunlap was doing the best he could, raising two girls after his wife died, even if he was overprotective. Kara had no intention of having kids, but she'd probably be overprotective, knowing what she did about the world.

"Please don't tell him," said Ashley.

"I have no reason to talk to your dad about your love life," Kara said. "Are you close to your family?"

"Of course I am. I love my dad so much—he just doesn't understand about Bobby, and I don't want to argue with him."

"In my experience, the truth always comes out, eventually. The question you need to ask yourself is: do you want to be the one to tell your dad or do you want him to hear about it from someone else? I grew up in a small town. There are no secrets for long."

Ashley didn't comment.

"Valerie?" Kara turned the conversation back to the reason she wanted to talk to Ashley in the first place.

"She's a bitch, but she's not all that smart, if you know what I mean. I don't think she could make a bomb or anything like that. She's all talk, no action—except for convincing Craig to vandalize the West End pier last year. But they got caught because she's stupid."

"Okay," Kara finally said. If Valerie was involved, Ashley didn't know. And that was going to have to be good enough—for now. "Ashley, I want you to be careful around the people at IP, at least for the next few weeks. We don't know who set those bombs, and we don't know why, but if someone in the group is involved, I don't want you caught up in that. If you see or hear anything that causes you concern, you have my direct number. I know that Donna told you to call her first, and if you want, go ahead. But it'll delay the investigation and create layers of legal bullshit that could prevent us from getting a warrant or catching the guy before he strikes again."

"You think he's going to set another bomb?"

"Why stop now? He has the attention of the town, of three law enforcement agencies, and West End Charter. Honestly, I think he's just getting started."

Matt pulled Catherine aside when she came into the station. "Where's Kara?"

"I don't know. She dropped me off and left."

"I have Valerie Sokola and Craig Martin in two separate rooms. They have the same lawyer, Larry Barker, so we can't interview them simultaneously. Barker's a jerk, but a smart jerk. I have one of the deputies tracking down Martin's brother."

"What happened?"

"An anonymous call came into the hotline. Claimed Bobby Martin was walking near West End, heading south, early this morning—didn't know the exact time, but between four thirty and five."

"Anonymous?"

Matt was skeptical like Catherine, but the information should be easy to prove.

"Doesn't mean they had anything to do with the bombing, but we need to talk to Bobby as well as Craig. Michael is going over security footage with one of the deputies and maybe we'll catch him on it. But in the meantime, I'm going to ask him. Who do you want to talk to first?"

"Craig," Catherine said without hesitation. "If the sheriff is correct, he's the one most likely to cave under pressure."

Kara had said the same thing, but Matt didn't remind Catherine of that. He needed his team to get along.

They notified the attorney, and a few moments later went into the interview room to talk to Craig.

Larry Barker went through the standard bullshit about how

his client was there of his own accord and they could walk out anytime they wanted. Matt didn't push back, not yet. He didn't have cause to arrest Craig—he had no evidence that he'd been involved—but he did have cause to question him because of past criminal actions against West End.

"Where were you last night between three and four a.m.?" Matt asked.

"Home," Craig said. "I didn't do anything. I swear to God, I didn't do anything."

Barker said, "Just answer the question asked, Craig."

"But I didn't. I didn't set any bombs. You said three and four, and I was home. My girlfriend and I have an apartment on Carter."

Matt knew that from his file.

"What time did you get home?"

"After the IP meeting last night. It broke up around nine forty-five. Val and I went to get food, and got home at eleven. And that was it. Watched TV, went to bed. I swear."

"Craig," Barker said, putting his hand on the young man's arm. "Agent Costa, I know that the security guard was killed shortly after his shift was over, at three a.m. My clients were home together at their apartment at that time. You have nothing, and we're going."

"No, you're not," Matt said. "Your clients need a better alibi than each other, considering they were arrested last year for vandalizing the dock adjacent to the boathouse that exploded this morning. I have a morgue filled with ten dead. Ten people, including friends of yours, Mr. Martin. I know you graduated high school with Kyle Richards. You both played baseball together, isn't that right?"

"Yeah. Kyle and I were friendly, well, until last year."

"What happened last year?"

"You don't have to answer that," Barker said.

Catherine said, "Is it because of the vandalism? Was Kyle angry because of what you and Valerie did?"

"Yeah, exactly. I mean, it was so stupid and I'm really sorry. I'm still paying for it. I apologized to all of them, and Kyle—but you know." Craig shrugged.

Catherine asked, "Was Valerie home last night?"

"Yeah—" he began at the same time that Barker said, "You don't have to answer that."

"But she was! I don't want them to think Val could have done this. We were both home. We were together all night. I swear to God, we didn't set that bomb."

"Do you know who did?" Catherine asked.

"No. If I did, I'd tell you. I'd tell you so you'd know it wasn't me or Val. But I don't know who would do this. I swear to God, I don't know."

Valerie wasn't as forthcoming. She only gave yes and no answers, but ultimately confirmed everything that Craig had said. Matt had no option but to cut them loose.

"Well?" he asked Catherine.

"I don't think either one of these kids are capable of planning something like this, though we should keep the pressure on them for a while, in case I'm wrong."

Deputy Redfield approached them. "Bobby Martin is here. I have him at my desk."

Matt followed the deputy and saw a taller, skinnier version of Craig Martin sitting there, a ball cap twisted in his hands. "Bobby Martin?" Matt said.

He stood. "Yes, sir."

Polite.

"Thank you for coming in. This won't take long." Matt introduced himself and Catherine. "Can we get you a Coke? Water?"

"No, sir. I have to get back to work. I mean, I can go back to work, right?"

"Of course. This won't take long." Matt led him to a small conference room. Bobby hadn't asked for his lawyer, and Matt didn't want to make him uncomfortable or suspicious. He closed the door and motioned for him to take a seat. "I called you in because a witness saw you walking along the edge of the West End property between four thirty and five this morning. Were you there?"

"I— Yes, sir, I was."

"What were you doing so early?"

"I, well, I went to see my girlfriend."

"Oh."

"Not like that!" He actually blushed. "Um, her dad doesn't know about us. He, um, well, she's not ready to tell him. She met me at the park at four in the morning, just to talk. She's been having nightmares and called me in the middle of the night."

"Nightmares?" Catherine asked.

"Yeah. Ashley—Ashley Dunlap. She witnessed the *Water Lily* explosion and she saw Neil—well, it was awful, and she doesn't want her dad to know she's having nightmares about it. So she called me, and I walked over. I only live a mile away, and I don't have my own car."

Dunlap. Exactly what Kara had told them last night.

"How long were you with Ms. Dunlap?"

"Forty-five minutes, maybe. It was cold, and I had to get ready for work—I'm a janitor at the school in the mornings, then I work at a restaurant near the pier most days, and then when they need me I go out to the fish warehouse on the other side of the island, usually weekends."

John Rasmussen was right—Bobby seemed to be a responsible, hardworking kid.

"Did you see anything when you were walking by West End? A person, hear a boat, an argument, anything out of the ordinary?"

He shook his head. "No. It was quiet. I saw a guy walking

216

his dog. I think only one car passed me the entire walk home. I didn't go to West End—I was on the street. After my brother—well, you know that my brother and his girlfriend got in trouble there last year."

"Yes, we know."

"You talked to him, right? He said he was going to talk to you today."

"We did."

"And he's not in any trouble, right? Craig wouldn't do this. You have to believe me."

"At this point," Matt said, "we're in the middle of our investigation and I haven't ruled anyone out."

"Fuck." Then he cleared his throat and mumbled, "Sorry."

"Has anyone with Island Protectors said or done anything that made you suspicious?"

"Donna said we didn't have to talk to you."

"You don't. You don't have to say anything. That's not going to stop us from investigating."

"I like Donna, she's great, but if I knew anything about anything, I'd tell you. I swear. And I don't. Everyone is nice, everyone just cares about the environment. All we want is to protect our island."

"Do you believe that West End is violating environmental laws?"

"I don't think they care about protecting the environment, you know? I mean, they don't have to actually violate the law to not do more to stop polluting our water. The fuel leak two years ago was serious, but they just act like business as usual. But that doesn't matter—no one I know would do anything like this."

"What about a new person? Someone who showed up this summer maybe—not a local or someone you know."

He shook his head, then hesitated. "Well, there was this woman last night. I'd never seen her before."

"What did she look like?"

"Um, short—I mean petite, I guess you say. Short blond hair. Glasses. She talked to Donna for a while after, but I didn't talk to her. Jane did. Jane Hicks. She's a stylist at my mom's salon. I know her pretty well."

"Did this stranger have a name?"

"I don't know. But I saw her walking away from the library. She didn't have a car or anything. Does that help?"

Kara. That was the only explanation, but Matt confirmed by asking Bobby how the woman was dressed. He didn't remember. "Just casual? I think she was wearing jeans. A long sweater."

Matt let Bobby go after giving him his business card and asking him to contact him about anything suspicious.

"What do you think?" he asked Catherine.

"While sociopaths can lie smoothly, I didn't sense he was being deceptive in any way."

"I need to confirm his statement, but since Kara already has a relationship with Ashley Dunlap, I'll have her do it."

He sent her a message.

Michael Harris walked in. He was usually impeccably dressed in a suit and tie, but with his work at the docks, he was dressed in khaki pants and a black T-shirt that matched his skin. He smiled widely. "Good, two birds."

Matt motioned for Michael to follow. "Let's head to the conference room so Ryder can hear what you have to say."

"I know Jim's on the mainland assisting in the autopsy; where's Kara?"

Matt didn't know. "In the field." She was, he was certain. He just wished she had shared her plans with him.

Once they were settled in the large conference room with Ryder, Michael shared the details about the bombs.

"Preliminary tests show both bombs used the same material— in fact, chemically, the same C-4. This means the C-4 not only came from the same manufacturer, but the same batch. The mechanism, however, was different." Michael used a blank area of the whiteboard to illustrate. "The *Water Lily* device used a motion trigger. A weight was extended through a small hole in the bow, attached to a fishing line. When the boat reached twenty knots, the weight pulled down enough to cause a spark here—" he drew "—to ignite the C-4 and create the explosion. It was simple and effective. The device was encased in a simple metal box—ATF and I are leaning toward a small toolbox and we may be able to narrow the brand with additional tests."

"A toolbox could have easily been overlooked during an inspection," Catherine said.

Michael concurred.

"So you don't know when it was placed on the boat," Matt said.

"No, but based on the maintenance records and trip records, it had to have been set *after* the boat docked Wednesday night. The *Water Lily* didn't go out Thursday night, so that gives us less than a forty-eight-hour window."

"And how does the first bomb differ from the boathouse bomb?" Catherine asked.

"The second bomb was *not* motion-triggered, but set on a timer for six thirty a.m. We recovered a significant portion of the device, and ATF is taking it to their lab as we speak. We're guessing half a block or less of explosive, but they're going to run through a simulation to confirm. Our guess is that the two bombs used in total one brick of C-4 that was from the same batch and most likely was split in half to make these two bombs."

"Bombers rarely deviate from their established MO," Catherine said. "Unless," she added, "they are improving their bombs. Is a timer more effective than a motion trigger?"

"Not necessarily. Each bomb was set, in my opinion, for the best outcome for the situation. Motion for the boat, timer for the boathouse. Both practical devices."

"Why not a timer for the *Water Lily*?" Matt asked.

"It depends on his goal. If he wanted to make a statement but not kill anyone, he would set it for the middle of the night—use a timer. But the motion trigger guaranteed that not only would the boat have one or more people on it, but that it wouldn't detonate *until* it was going a specific speed—a speed which guaranteed it would be away from the shore and other boats."

Matt looked at Catherine. "The boat—a *person* was a target. If West End was the target, he would have set a timer. And the second bomb was a clear de-escalation."

Catherine was thinking. She said, "You may be correct. If the bombs were in the other order, I would assume the first was a test run, the second bigger and more violent. But this second bomb was almost an afterthought."

"Why?"

"Perhaps to steer us away from a specific target," Catherine said.

"Shift the entire investigation to West End?" Michael asked.

"Two West End targets, that would be logical," Catherine said. "And it's still a possibility, especially if the killer thought Ted Colfax or someone in the family would be in the boathouse at six thirty."

Matt shook his head. "Ted gets into his office between seven and seven thirty most mornings, which I confirmed with his secretary. His brother and sister don't come in until eight thirty. The guard who was killed was off duty, but he passes the boathouse on his way home."

"So he saw or heard something and went to investigate," Michael surmised.

What the hell was going on? Matt turned to Ryder. "Where are we on Neil's cases?"

"I'm meeting with Jessica Mott tomorrow. She may have some information about Neil's investigation into her brother's death," Ryder said. "She told me over the phone that Neil believed they were murdered and was also interested in another allegedly accidental death that she brought to his attention. But six months ago, he told her over lunch that he didn't want her coming to the island anymore, that he was concerned about her safety. He didn't say why."

"She can't give us the information over the phone?"

"She told me everything she knew, but I asked if she could come here to go through Neil's files. I believe some things are missing, and when she told me about the other accidental death he was looking at, I couldn't find anything about it in his notes—he only has information about the drownings. I believe her input will be valuable."

"Okay. And Neil's computer?"

"He used his computer primarily to Skype with his children and send email. I've been going through his email, but it's not archived and it's taking some time to re-create the messages. The emails auto-delete after two weeks, but I cloned the hard drive and sent it to the Seattle office. They think they can un-delete the files."

"So nothing so far."

"No, but I have his contact list and have been putting names to the emails."

"Good. What about Brandon Fielding? Did Zack report back? Seattle?"

"He may have had a grudge against Neil, but the Seattle office confirmed his alibi. Fielding hasn't left Seattle since being released from prison. He is bitter, according to the interviewing agent, but doesn't have the means or ability to hire someone to do the job for him. Zack says there's nothing in his finances that said he could afford it, and he's dug down. Assistant Director Greer's staff has ruled out many of Neil's previous cases—either the felons are still in prison or were cleared. He has only a few more to review."

They were back at the beginning. Island Protectors had dropped down the suspect list—not off it, because Matt didn't know what was going on—but the second explosion made no sense in the grand scheme of things, especially if someone from IP was involved. It could be an individual, unaffiliated with the group, who might have a personal grudge against West End, but so far, no one fit that bill.

Matt said, "Michael, follow up with ATF every step of the way. We need to know where the C-4 came from. Right now, that's our only real lead. Catherine, motive. We're back at square one. Victim profiles, any like crimes, what are we looking at? And, Ryder—keep digging into Neil's files and let me know if Ms. Mott says anything that gives us a new direction. Until then, this is what we have." He motioned to the files in the room, the whiteboard with Catherine's meticulous script. "The answers are here. We just have to find them."

21

After talking to the FBI detective, Ashley walked slowly to her dad's pub feeling out of sorts, almost guilty—except she had nothing to feel guilty about. She hadn't hurt anyone. The idea made her sick. She had hardly been able to sleep since last Friday. Every time she fell into a deep sleep, she relived in slow motion Neil's body flying up, out of the boat. She couldn't stop the image and she desperately wanted to.

She opened the door of the Fish & Brew. Uncle Damon was chatting with Timmy and Sam, two old veterans who were here almost every afternoon. Sam was missing a leg from the Vietnam War, a war that seemed so far removed from Ashley that she barely remembered learning about it in American History last year. But now, looking at Sam's right pant leg knotted just below his knee, she could picture exactly how it had happened.

Her stomach churned.

"Good afternoon to you, Ash," Uncle Damon said with a smile.

"Hey," she mumbled.

"You okay?"

"Long day at school," she said as she passed by and walked down the hall to the kitchen to get some water. She needed something to settle her stomach. But the smell of fish and hamburgers had her stopping outside the swinging doors. She put her back against the wall and closed her eyes, willing herself to stop thinking about the bombing.

It didn't work.

Something Valerie said last night came back to her.

"It's karma, Ashley. What goes around comes around."

"How can you say that?" she had said, tears burning in her eyes. "People died."

"I'm not saying it's good, but West End has been fucking the environment for years and Mother Nature doesn't like that shit."

"No. That's not how it works," Ashley said, defiant. "God doesn't work that way."

"God." She snorted. "Right."

"Knock it off, Val," Bobby said. Ashley was used to being ridiculed for going to church and wanting to do missionary work, and she appreciated Bobby standing up for her.

"You knew Kyle," Ashley said. "He was a great guy."

Val shrugged. "But he worked for those people. And you know, it could have been an accident, something that West End screwed up and they're the ones who got those people killed."

"That's not what the FBI said."

"The FBI lies all the fucking time. You can't believe anything a cop says."

Ashley didn't believe in karma or any of that stuff. How could she think that Sam had one leg or Neil had been blown up or her mother had died of cancer was because of something they did? No. They were good people who had bad things happen to them because bad things happened.

Ashley didn't like Valerie, but she couldn't picture Valerie setting a bomb or killing anyone. She could picture her doing other things, though. Should she have said something like that to Detective Quinn?

No. Being a bitch wasn't a crime. She wasn't going to rat on Valerie just because she didn't like her or her style. But she seemed so...*callous*...about what happened.

"Ashley!"

She jumped. She hadn't seen her father step out of his office, behind the kitchen.

"Dad, what's wrong?"

He looked angry. Really, really angry.

"Did something else happen? After this morning? What's wrong?"

He said, "Tell me the truth. Did you sneak out of the house this morning and go to the park with Bobby Martin?"

"I—" She had never lied to her dad. Well, lies of omission, but she'd never lied to his face.

He stared at her.

"Yes," she said, her voice a squeak.

"Why would you do that?"

"I—I—"

"Are you trying to lie to me?"

"No!" Had the detective told him? "How did you find out?"

"That's what you care about? To find out who *told* me that you've been sneaking out of the house in the middle of the night? To meet with a boy? Apparently everyone knows. You had your sister *lying* to protect you."

"Whitney? I never asked her to lie."

"Good thing, because she can't lie to save her life, and I sure as hell don't understand how you can."

"I didn't lie to you, Dad."

"You've been seeing that boy for the last year and didn't tell me. Behind my back. Sneaking out of the house."

"I'm sorry."

"No, you're not. You're sorry you were caught."

"I love Bobby."

"So why keep your relationship a secret? Because you know he's bad news."

"Bobby's working three jobs to save up for college. He's nice and kind and he loves me."

"His brother vandalized a dock that could very well have hurt people, and he and his girlfriend could be behind these bombings."

"You don't know anything."

Her dad looked angry...and sad?

"Because I trusted you, you were able to run around behind my back and do whatever you wanted. You clearly have no respect for me or my rules."

"Because they're unfair! It's not fair to blame Bobby for Craig's past mistakes."

"Go home. You're grounded."

"You can't do that!" But her dad was right. She may not have directly lied, but she knew how he would react to the truth and she had hidden everything from him.

"You're still seventeen, you still live under my roof, and I will never tolerate lying and manipulation and sneaking out of the house. What if something happened? We may live on an island, but bad things happen here just like the big city. Go home. We'll talk tonight."

"How long?"

"I'm so disappointed in you, Ashley. I never suspected you would do this. Never." He stared at her and she saw he was near tears. That made her own tears come. She'd never wanted to hurt her dad.

She turned, walked out the back door, and ran all the way home.

Pete watched his daughter leave, then sank into his office chair, pinched the bridge of his nose. The tears burned his eyes. He pushed them back, but they were there, making his head hurt.

He'd never had to punish his girls. They were good kids. Great kids. Smart kids. And he was having a hard time believing that his baby had been lying to him for so long. It was like he didn't even know her. It hurt.

Damon stood in the doorway. "Hey, weren't you a little hard on Ash?"

Pete looked up at his brother-in-law. "Stay out of it, Damon."

"She's a good kid. She's not out doing drugs and robbing liquor stores."

"I don't have a lot of rules. She broke every single one of them."

"I just think—"

"I will deal with my kids as I see fit. You can go."

Damon turned and left. Pete kicked his door closed.

If his wife were alive, this wouldn't have happened. Did Ashley think she couldn't talk to him? They'd been so close when she was little. When Whitney was off at the playground befriending every kid she met, Ashley was content to sit with him on the bench, or play ball with the dog, or swing and watch everyone else. Ashley had always come to him for advice, but after Wendy died when Ashley was ten—an awful time to lose your mother, especially for girls—things changed.

He wanted his little girl back, but he was so proud of her and the young woman she had become. At least, until he found out she'd been lying to him.

Wendy, I don't know what to do. I miss you so much. Are you there?

I need your help, baby. I need your help with our daughter because I'm lost, and I don't want to lose her.

Pete put his head in his hands and prayed. He wasn't much for praying, but Wendy used to, and he didn't know what else to do.

When Kara walked into the conference room, Ryder was in the corner on Neil's computer, and Catherine was at the conference table reading files.

"Matt is looking for you," Catherine said.

She glanced at her phone. "Must not have been looking too hard," she said. "No messages."

Catherine clearly wanted Kara to fill her in on what she was doing, but Kara wasn't going to be micromanaged by someone who wasn't her boss. Hell, she didn't even let her boss micromanage her. She agreed to write reports—that was part of being a cop—but bureaucratic bullshit would be the death of her.

She walked over to the whiteboard to refresh herself on the case. An analysis of the bombs had been added, but that was the only new thing, other than a question mark after Island Protectors under the possible-suspects list.

Maybe Catherine was thinking the same thing as Kara. Most bombers escalated as they continued their destructive spree, but the second bomb seemed anticlimactic and caused far less damage and loss of life than the first bomb.

One other change. Neil Devereaux's name had a star next to it. If he had been the target, that meant the second bomb was intended to distract them.

At least Madelyn Jeffries had been moved to the bottom of the list. She didn't need any more police involvement in her life—until they could give her answers about her husband's murder.

When the door opened, Kara turned around. Marcy walked in. "The sheriff wanted to know if you needed me for anything." She spoke to the room but looked at Kara.

Kara was about to say no, but Catherine said, "Officer, I

haven't received any of the files from Seattle about Nava Software. You were originally with Seattle PD, correct?"

"Yes, ma'am."

"Would you mind following up with them? I ran the criminal records, there's none, but I still need any civil records and if any of the victims had a restraining order at any time and if so, who and why. Our FBI office there has contacted the families and talked to the office staff, but I still have holes. Here, you can take my file—you'll see what I still need."

"Happy to." She took the folder from Catherine.

"Thank you," Catherine said with a faint smile, then looked back at her stack of information.

Kara left the room with Marcy, mostly because she wanted to get away from Catherine.

"Run again tomorrow?" asked Marcy.

"Sure," Kara said. "Same time, same place?"

"Great." She motioned to her jogging clothes. "You didn't get a chance to change?"

"Nope."

"John—the sheriff—would have a heart attack if I didn't put on the uniform."

"I used to be an undercover cop—you should see some of my outfits."

"Maybe we can get a drink later. Or tomorrow. I'd love to hear more about your story."

"Sure. Text me."

Marcy walked away, and Kara considered going back to the house and taking an hour to recharge and change. Instead, she went back to the conference room. Ryder had asked her earlier to help with Neil Devereaux's cryptic sticky notes.

She sat down with the files, next to where Ryder was working on Neil's computer. "How you feeling?" she asked as she pulled out Neil's calendar.

"As I told everyone else when they asked, I feel good. Clean eating and regular exercise—I bounce back fast."

"Is that a jab?" she teased.

"I would be the last person to tell you how to live your life."

"Which makes you my bestie."

A small sigh came from across the conference table where Catherine was working. Kara chose to ignore her, and focused on the calendar.

Neil had a calendar dedicated to detailing the last year for Mott and Stevens, and he'd circled January 1. No further information on that date—just the circle.

"Ryder," she said without looking up, "did you run this date in Neil's computer? January first? Emails, subject or body, as to why it might be important?"

"I haven't received the report back from Seattle on what they were able to re-create in his emails. I only have two weeks here. They promised they'd have it by the end of today."

"It was important," she said. "He circled *and* starred it."

Kara's phone beeped. She looked down: a message from the Coast Guard personnel office.

After she'd talked to Cal this morning, she'd sent an official request to the Coast Guard to confirm service for both Caleb McKinnon and Marcy Anderson. Military offices were stingy with personnel records, but they were usually good about giving the basics—enrollment, position, service years, terms of discharge. Basic employment stuff.

She opened the email and viewed the summary reports for both McKinnon and Anderson, side by side. They overlapped sixteen months, which confirmed McKinnon's statement. Marcy had already been serving for a year when Cal was assigned to the Seattle division. Marcy worked in the logistics office, not on a ship. Cal had been a mechanic, worked primarily on dry dock. Neither served directly on a ship, but that didn't surprise Kara.

The Coast Guard had a far broader commission than people usually thought, and required a large support team.

Kara did a little more digging and found a roommate for Marcy during that same time. A twitch in the back of her mind told Kara that Marcy's stalking situation was something to consider. It might be nothing. It could be a guy blowing something out of proportion. And Kara still had to follow up with Jamie to find out what she really felt when Marcy confronted her about her past with Cal. Maybe it was nothing, casual, an *oh, I'm so sorry, I thought you knew...* kind of conversation.

Or not.

She couldn't put any of this up on the whiteboard because she didn't want Marcy or any other deputy to see her train of thought. It was probably nothing. Because no matter how Kara sliced it, Marcy's motivation to bomb the *Water Lily* was slim.

But it was possible...

Which was why Kara added Cal McKinnon's comments about Marcy's alleged stalking to her unofficial report for Matt. Just to cover all the bases.

She left a message for Marcy's old roommate and went back to analyzing Neil's notes. An hour later, she was too tired to process any other information and put the file next to Ryder.

"We need to find out who Neil was talking to in Seattle. He had a source for some of these notes. It's a cop—just my guess based on how he worded things. But he didn't put a name anywhere. We need to talk to that person."

"Every time I think I'm making progress in retracing Agent Devereaux's steps in how he was investigating this closed case, I end up with more questions," Ryder said.

"Like?"

"His contact list. I've identified nearly everyone in his list. He has detectives in several Washington cities on the list, half the law enforcement here in the islands, dozens of FBI agents. I don't know if these were personal friends, or if any of them—or which ones—were involved in helping with his inquiry. He has several people attached to the University of Washington campus police. Mott and Stevens went there, so I think that's the most logical place to start. I've called the campus law enforcement liaison office and they're looking into the names and will get back to me."

"Yep, that's being a cop. A lot of sitting around and waiting for people to call you back." Kara stood and stretched. "I'm going to head back to the house and take an hour. If you get the emails back from Seattle, let me know and I'll help you go through them. Match up some of these dates that Neil highlighted on the calendar."

Catherine cleared her throat as Kara headed for the door. Catherine said, "Matt sent me your report."

Kara figured he would; she'd given him a quasi-psych profile of McKinnon, but wished she'd managed to disappear before Catherine read it.

And where was Matt, anyway?

"Can we talk about it later? I've been in these clothes all day."

"You should have changed earlier, before interviewing witnesses."

"Yeah, sorry about that. Bombings have a way of messing with your schedule."

Catherine didn't avert her eyes, and neither did Kara. The woman was trying to play the superior game with her, and it wasn't going to work.

Well, it sort of did because Catherine was *in* and Kara was definitely not. But Kara wasn't going to let on that she intimidated her.

Why do you let her? She's doing it on purpose.

Because Catherine was a gatekeeper. Kara had recognized the trait on the first day they'd met. Even before then, when they'd only talked over a team conference call during the Triple Killer case.

She never did well with gatekeepers.

"You wrote that McKinnon had concerns about Officer Anderson following him but that he didn't file a report."

"Yep. He didn't use the word *stalker* but that was the vibe I was getting."

"And this is related to the bombing how?"

"Don't know that it is. It's an outlier. Something we might need to follow up on. It might be a completely separate situation."

"We should tell the sheriff."

"No."

"It's not your call."

"It's not your call, either," she snapped. "McKinnon never filed a report, has no intention of filing a report, and said he doesn't want to make waves. He gets every cop here on his back because he accuses a cop of stalking him? It'll be a mess, especially because this is a small town. He and his girl are back together, he figures no harm, no foul. If Marcy is innocent, you'll screw up her life here. She'd be toast with something like this hanging over her head. And if she's guilty? You give her the heads-up that we're looking at her."

"Guilty? Of the bombing?"

Kara hadn't meant that, but now that Catherine said it out loud, she couldn't get it out of her head. "Low on the list, and not something we can put on the whiteboard—or even talk about here at headquarters. I was specifically thinking of the potential stalking charge, which is why in my report I said I'd get Marcy's side of the story tomorrow morning, when we go running."

"We need to do this officially, formally, keep it in the record."

"If she's innocent you will ruin her life. I'm not going to have that on my conscience."

"Again, not your call, Detective Quinn."

"I thought we were a fucking team, but I guess that's just

bullshit." Kara stomped out of the room and slammed the door closed. In the hall, she almost walked into Matt.

"What happened?" he asked.

"Difference of investigative opinion." She looked him in the eye. "You either trust my judgment or you don't. I'm either a part of this team, or I'm not."

"Let's go back and talk this out."

"You figure it out—you're the boss." She walked away and left the building.

22

After a frustrating afternoon of getting no answers and only having more questions about everything—Marcy and Cal, Neil and his investigation, the plethora of emails the Seattle office sent back to Ryder late—Kara walked to the Fish & Brew at seven thirty to clear her head. It had been a long day and Matt told everyone to take the night off. Clear heads in the morning and all that.

The bombings had Kara and the rest of the team on edge because they made no sense, and everyone handled the frustration in a different way.

But she had some good news. Matt sent her a text that she could follow up with Marcy Anderson as she saw fit; that part of the investigation would be kept in-house only, to be brought to the sheriff's attention when and if it was appropriate.

She didn't feel like gloating. Kara didn't want every investigation to be a battle between her and Catherine. She didn't want to go to Matt like a child, asking a parent to pick sides. She hated being in this position, not knowing where she stood with anyone.

She was angry with Catherine, but also with Matt for reasons she didn't completely understand. Except for one: she didn't feel like part of the team. She wasn't an FBI agent, she wasn't LAPD anymore—regardless of where her paycheck came from. Kara didn't belong anywhere.

She was angrier with herself than anyone else.

She hated this feeling. She'd almost always worked either alone or with one partner. Someone she trusted implicitly to have her back. Someone who literally had her life in their hands, and their life was in hers. Like Colton. The perfect, symbiotic partnership they had was irreplaceable.

And he was dead. Because she'd been on administrative leave and couldn't protect him like she was supposed to.

Everything had changed in her life. She was an outsider.

She wanted everything to go back to the way it was, but that was impossible. She'd had a job she loved. It had excited her, being both dangerous and thrilling. Sure, she'd had no close friends, but Colton had been a rock. He had been her mirror. She missed him—hated that he was dead. Hated that she couldn't say goodbye to him. That he was just *gone*.

She sat on a stool at the bar, still irritated, but the smell of fish and chips made her feel a little better. The pub was nearly full; by the look of it, mostly tourists. The bartender—Damon, the flirty weight lifter Marcy had introduced her to yesterday— was filling an order for one of the servers. Kara waited for him.

Only two minutes later, he came over. "Agent Quinn, right?"

"Good memory. Detective, not Agent. Call me Kara."

"Got it. I have to have a good memory—I'm a teacher. Between 180 and 190 kids in six classes every year."

"Math, right?"

"You have a good memory as well."

"Have to—I'm a cop," she said.

He laughed. "What can I get you?"

"The stout."

"Good choice."

"Pete gave me a taste last night. I came back for more."

"Looking for dinner?"

"Later. I want to savor the pint first."

After Damon put it in front of her, she sipped with great pleasure. "Perfect. Where's Pete?"

"Home. There was a family issue he had to deal with."

"Oh? Everyone okay?"

"Yeah—just…" He glanced around, then lowered his voice. "I shouldn't talk about it, Pete made it clear my opinion wasn't wanted, but basically Pete found out that Ashley was dating a kid he doesn't approve of. Pete's kind of overprotective and superconservative when it comes to his daughters. I told him he needs to give them room, they're great kids."

"I thought so."

"Pete found out that Ashley was sneaking out of the house to see this kid, and then the kid was interviewed by you guys this afternoon."

"Bobby Martin."

"Yeah. So right there that's two strikes against him: sneaking around and trouble with cops."

"I can't talk about the case, but Bobby Martin isn't a suspect."

"But his brother is, right?"

"As I said, I can't talk about the case."

"It's common sense. Craig and his girlfriend vandalized West End last year, and now two bombs?" Damon shook his head. "It's awful. But Bobby is a good kid."

"You knew about their relationship." It was a statement, not a question.

"I figured it out before Pete but decided to keep it to myself. I don't want to cause problems, I love Pete like a brother, you know? He worshipped my sister, and the girls and Pete are my only family left. I'm not going to cause trouble."

"Smart."

Damon nodded toward the server, the bubbly girl Rena who'd served them last night and now wanted him to fill an order, and said to Kara, "When you want food or another pint, wave me down."

"When this is almost empty, pour me another and put in an order for the fish and chips."

He winked and walked away.

She kind of wished Pete Dunlap was there, but then she'd flirt with him and she couldn't exactly follow up on the flirting, so it wasn't fair—to him or her.

She was frustrated because she didn't know what was going on with Matt. After Tucson, they had an unspoken agreement that they were in a relationship. But defining that relationship wasn't something that Kara wanted to do right now. Because part of their unspoken agreement was that when they were working, they were hands off. So last night, in the kitchen, when he clearly wanted to take her to bed, threw her for a loop. Sure, she played along to a point—and if she hadn't been angry with him about siding with Catherine, she might have gone through with it. Because he sure as hell wasn't acting like he was trying to keep their sexual relationship a secret.

To be honest, she didn't care. Kara was no prude; she didn't care who knew who she was sleeping with. But she also didn't talk about it because it was no one else's business. She'd told Matt when they first had sex that she didn't kiss and tell. That was true. But she also didn't lie about it.

Kara didn't like emotional ups and downs. She needed clear rules of engagement with Agent Mathias Costa.

She liked him quite a bit. Honestly, more than she wanted to. Matt was smart. Sexy as anything. Great in bed. And focused. She really liked that he was as dedicated to his career as she was to hers, and that he appreciated her skill set.

Until last night.

It was really bugging her. It had been all night, all day, and she couldn't shake it. If he trusted her, he needed to fully trust her. And if Matt was now listening to Catherine more than her, he clearly didn't trust her judgment. She didn't want every single one of her plans to have to run through a fucking bureaucracy to determine what her course of action was. How could anyone run an investigation like that?

Normally, she didn't care. If a guy was good in bed and not a jerk out of bed, that's all that mattered. But Kara had already let this relationship get beyond physical, and that was probably her biggest mistake. And she didn't know how to put that genie back into the bottle.

Maybe it was impossible.

Double damn.

She sensed someone's approach right before Ryder sat at the bar stool next to her.

She glanced over at him. "I guess I can't convince you to have a beer."

"No."

"Your loss. Did you eat?"

"At the house."

"Everyone still working?"

"No. Matt was serious that he wanted everyone to take a break."

"Clear heads and all that." She nodded toward the thick folder Ryder had brought, now on the bar in front of him. "Breaking the rules, Ryder. I'm surprised at you," she teased.

"I did as you suggested with Neil's calendar, focusing on January first. On New Year's Eve, Brian Stevens was involved in a three-car accident—more specifically, it occurred early in the morning on New Year's Day. The police cleared him of wrongdoing—he wasn't drunk, and the accident was deemed weather related. I've requested all the files from that night."

"Yet Neil had that day circled. Why wouldn't he have the reports?"

"He may have. I'm still going through the emails Seattle sent back this afternoon. He was communicating with a detective from Seattle, Rachel Huang. I put in a call to her, then followed up with an email, so I hope to have more information tomorrow."

"That's great. But you didn't have to come down here and tell me that."

"I had one other thing about Jason Mott. I talked to his sister Jessica again, confirming our meeting tomorrow. I told her specifically what information we needed. Neil was certain that her brother and Brian Stevens were murdered, and he knew who the killer was."

"And the killer is…?"

"She doesn't know. Neil wouldn't tell her, for her safety. She will be here in the morning to go over all the files, because she said Neil was looking into more cases than just her brother's death. For example, four years ago she had sent Neil a report about another suspicious death that was ruled an accident. There's nothing like that in the files from his house, but there are several emails to Tacoma police during that time about the disappearance of a man named Eric Travers. Ms. Mott is going to bring everything she has with her and help re-create Neil's files."

"That's terrific."

"Is it?" Ryder asked. "Because according to Ms. Mott, Neil was concerned about her safety and cut her out of the investigation nearly a year ago, told her not to come up here. They met once since, but in Seattle."

"If Neil was concerned about her safety, that tells me his suspect is on this island."

"Does it?"

"Otherwise, why would he care whether she came up here or not? I'll bet Neil didn't want Jessica's presence alerting his suspect that he was onto him."

"Would you join me for the interview with her?" Ryder asked.

"Why do you sound nervous? Of course I will."

He looked relieved. "Thank you."

"But even if I wasn't there, you've got this. You're a natural."

"I'm good at analyzing information, but I don't know if I'll ask the right questions."

"You know what you're doing, Ryder. Jessica Mott likely knows more than she thinks she does, and now I'm interested in this second so-called accident that Neil was looking into. Neil may have only had a theory, but that theory could have gotten him killed."

Damon brought out her fish and chips and another stout. "Anything else?"

Ryder ordered a club soda with lime. Kara laughed.

"Are you sure you don't want any food?"

"I'm not hungry."

"You can have one of my fish. It's good."

"It's deep-fried."

"You say that like that's a bad thing."

"My dad is a heart surgeon, and I was premed before I joined the Army. I don't eat anything deep-fried."

"Your loss." She took a bite and moaned dramatically. Heaven. So what if it took a couple of years off her life? She was going to enjoy what time she had.

23

Matt sat at the dining table of the FBI rental house reading reports. It was ten o'clock and Kara still wasn't back yet. Ryder had returned thirty minutes ago, said she was at the Fish & Brew, then went upstairs.

Because it seemed the investigation was back at square one, Matt had wanted everyone to get a good night's sleep.

Jim was staying on the mainland tonight since he had been at the ME's office until late. The cause of death for the guard Garrett Washington had been determined to be blunt force trauma. The man was dead approximately three hours before the explosion, which confirmed what they knew—Washington clocked out at 3:03, passed the boathouse on his way back home five minutes later, the bomb went off at exactly 6:30.

Forensics had recovered a cinder block that they believed was the murder weapon, and Jim was working with their crime scene team to confirm. Matt didn't expect they'd get fingerprints off the block, but they might find other trace evidence—something to tie a suspect to the murder. Clothing, DNA, a damn fingernail that broke off. A long shot, but worth pursuing.

Michael Harris wasn't back yet. He was with ATF and their bomb dogs, going over West End and the main harbor for the second time today. Michael was in his element. His report to Matt included technical reports about the bomb and its explosive material. That would be important later when they found a suspect or bomb-making evidence. ATF still hadn't traced the C-4, but they had contacted every contractor in the state of Washington who had C-4 on-site and asked for a full audit. These people knew to comply quickly, or their license to use C-4 could be pulled.

Kara's report was short and to the point. Matt couldn't find fault with it but wished she would be more detailed. Her recount of the second Madelyn Jeffries interview was snide and aimed toward Catherine, but the rest of her report was interesting—though he didn't see how it fit into the case. Did it matter that Officer Marcy Anderson had a previous relationship with Cal McKinnon? Neither had lied about it. And even McKinnon said he wouldn't classify Anderson as *stalking* him—though it wasn't appropriate for a law enforcement officer to use their badge to pull someone over. He sent Kara a note that he approved of her following up on it tomorrow because he didn't see the harm, and Kara knew how to be discreet.

Catherine came into the dining room wearing sweats and a T-shirt and holding a glass of white wine. She sat across from him.

"I should have seen it. You're sleeping with her."

It was a statement, not a question. Matt couldn't deny it if he wanted to—Catherine wouldn't believe him.

But why the hell bring it up now? Because he had agreed with Kara on the approach on one part of the investigation?

"It's a bit more complicated than that."

"*Complicated?* Yes, it's complicated when you're screwing your subordinate."

Matt didn't want this conversation, but now he was stuck. "It didn't start out that way."

"You must know this will not end well."

"We're adults, Catherine."

"Sometimes you don't act like it."

That was rich, coming from her. "We've known each other for fifteen years. I've always had your back. I've always supported you, even when I thought you were wrong. But to state the obvious, you have treated me like shit since Beth was killed." He pushed back from the table, working to keep his voice low. "I didn't deserve it, but I took it because I knew you were in pain. I was in pain, too. *I* found her body, *I* saw what that bastard had done to her. I carried her out of the grave and tried to save her. I loved her—like a sister. Like I love you. And you keep turning that knife because I wasn't *in love* with her. I am not a saint. Beth and I got through it. We were friends. You couldn't accept that. You're a fucking shrink, and you can't see your own issues.

"I'm sorry Beth is dead. God, am I sorry. She didn't deserve it. But *I didn't kill her.* You didn't kill her. And it's time you started living in the present. Because you almost fucked your marriage with Chris. That man is a saint. After what you put him through?"

Matt ran both his hands through his hair. He hadn't meant to say all that to Catherine, but he was at his wit's end. About how she talked to him about Beth, what she thought of him, and yes—she was right about Kara. He was trying to deflect the conversation. He knew he should have kept things professional as soon as they started working together full-time.

He didn't want to give her up. He didn't know how long their relationship—such as it was—was going to last. He didn't want to lose what they had, however unconventional, however brief, however different from every other relationship he'd been in.

And honestly, it was all on Kara. He went where she led. It frustrated him at times, but he knew from the beginning that any relationship he had with Kara was on her terms. And he would take it like that because he was drawn to her, like a fly to honey.

Catherine was right about one thing: Kara was technically his subordinate. He'd justified his relationship because she wasn't an FBI agent, that she was on LAPD's payroll, that she could go back to LA when and if the hit on her was ever lifted. That she would have to go back to testify against the trafficking scumbag she arrested. He convinced himself that she was on his *team*, a task force, a group—not a true boss-and-subordinate situation.

Sigue mintiendo a ti mismo, Mathias.

He was lying to himself. Willingly.

He faced Catherine. Her expression was blank, he couldn't read her, but she was watching him closely.

"I stand by what I said, Matt," Catherine said quietly. "You need to let her go. She's reckless, she's not a team player, and she's psychologically damaged. Anyone would be after enduring some of the cases she's worked."

"You need to give her a chance. She's a great cop."

Catherine stood up, drained her wine, looked him in the eye. "I'll give you until we're back in Washington, Matt. Then I'm talking to Tony."

Before Matt could say a word, she turned and left the room.

It was after eleven when Kara arrived back at the house. She'd had a nice meal, a few beers, and talked for a while with a jolly retired couple who spent every summer on the island. They were in their late seventies and had fascinating stories to tell, and Kara was in the mood to listen.

Sometimes just getting out of her own head was the best way to solve a case.

Kara walked up the porch steps dreaming of sleep. She was exhausted. She put her hand on the doorknob, sensed Matt's presence before he spoke.

"Kara."

"Matt." She should just go inside, go to bed, not have a conversation, but she wouldn't be surprised if her report caused a few problems.

She didn't want this tension; she just wanted to solve this case and any case she was given. She hated inner-office politics at LAPD, and she didn't like them any better here. It's why she preferred working alone, with a single handler. Or a partner who she could trust.

Instead, she dropped her hand from the door.

"This is a tough week," Matt said. "I explained to Catherine why I thought your approach was appropriate for the time being. We'll reevaluate it based on what you learn."

"Fine. Good night."

"Kara—"

She turned to face him.

"You should know, Catherine's sister was murdered last year— it'll be a year on Friday."

"I'm sorry about that," Kara said and meant it. "Maybe she shouldn't be working this case if she's preoccupied."

"Work is the best thing for her now."

"What happened?"

"She took leave from the FBI and was going to resign; I talked her into staying. Her husband and I both did—Chris is one of my closest friends."

Kara had already figured that out, based on partial conversations and observation. But there was a lot that Matt wasn't saying. She could tell when he averted his eyes. And she wanted to know about the murder, because clearly there was a lot more to that story that both Matt and Catherine knew.

"And?"

"I can't— Look, I have a history with Catherine."

Incredulous, she asked, "You dated her?" She could not imagine Catherine as his type.

"What? No." He frowned. "Of course not."

"What are you not telling me, Matt?"

"Catherine and I went through Quantico together. We were in the same class."

"I know that."

He glanced at her. "Did I tell you?"

"No. I dug around. Quietly. Because she hates my guts."

"She doesn't hate you."

"She sure as hell doesn't like or respect me."

"That's not true. While this week is rough, now that she's back with the FBI, she can move past what happened."

"Is that how grieving works? Take time off, wallow in pain and guilt, then move past it?"

Matt frowned.

Kara continued. "I've lost lots of people. Guess what? You don't just forget. You think I'll ever forget what happened to Colton? Or Sunny?" Or any of the other people she'd watched die, by her hand or others. "You deal with it, because if you don't, you go insane. True, work saved me. Maybe it'll save Catherine. But her grief doesn't give her a pass to negate my investigation or informed opinion."

"That's not what she did—"

"Yes, it is. I told her yesterday that Madelyn Jeffries was a low priority; she put her as number one. Then today we have a West End specific target and I question whether it's IP. We don't have enough information—but she dismisses my analysis. You know damn well I'm not saying someone there might not be involved, just that the history of the organization doesn't support this specific type of violent act. But when Ryder gets information, she puts Neil back at the top of the list. Then I suggest that I need to dig around on Marcy—not because I think she's a bomber, but because of something Cal McKinnon said. And she wants to turn a comment into a full-blown investigation. We have *nothing* on Marcy Anderson for *anything* illegal. We blow this, we could blow something big. I know what the fuck I'm doing. I'm following up on everything, doing due diligence, working with the DC office to verify information, but my gut is never wrong."

"Kara, I trust your judgment but—"

"But? Either you trust my judgment or you don't."

"Don't."

"Don't what? Call Catherine to the carpet for the way she's treated me? I'm a cop. Just like you. Just like her. I might not have the rubber stamp of approval by some college or Quantico, but I'm just as smart as either of you."

"What do you want me to do?" Matt asked, clearly frustrated. "When you and someone else on my team disagree, I need to make a call."

"Then make the fucking call! Don't placate me, don't placate her. Don't hem and haw because Catherine is grieving, or you don't want to hurt my feelings. If you think I'm wrong, fucking tell me to my face and give me a damn good reason why you think I'm wrong. I'll listen. I'm not blind, nor am I deaf. I listen better than anyone because that's how I survived twelve years working undercover. If I didn't know how to read the playing field, I'd be dead a dozen times over."

Matt had never seen Kara so angry. So volatile. How could he convince her that he *did* trust her? That he valued her as a member of his team?

He had read her file. It made him sick to his stomach and proud at the same time.

"To be honest," he said carefully, "I've never had a team

of agents who have so much experience. I've always been the leader, I've never had a problem giving orders. But I have multiple leaders on this team. Every one of you is capable of running this investigation."

"But *you're* the boss. Make the call." Kara stared at him with her intense blue eyes as if to tell him he should have known that.

But it wasn't that easy. He respected Catherine and she was an expert in her field, but Kara had a sixth sense when it came to crime. He'd never met anyone whose instincts were so honed. Because they had to be, he reminded himself. She'd be dead if she couldn't rely on her gut. That unnerved him.

"We have a killer on this island," Kara said. "Someone with no remorse for killing *ten people*. But this person is also a coward. They use bombs. Because they get their rocks off watching the explosion? I don't know. Garrett Washington was in the wrong place at the wrong time—he wasn't a target. Maybe the killer intended to take out one of the Colfax family. It was their dry dock; Ted said himself that he does a lot of the boat work. What if he blew it early because the guard surprised him? Are we dealing with a smart bomber or a lucky bomber?"

"Michael is on top of that angle. I trust him."

"Of course you do. This is his wheelhouse. He knows exactly what to do and what to look for."

"Then what's with the tone?"

"Because you need to show me similar respect that I know what I'm talking about. I'm not going to dig into the whys and what-fors that Catherine does. She knows what makes these killers tick. I don't know if I'll ever understand why people do the shit they do. But when it comes to reading people, to observing, I'm the best."

"I'm sorry," he said.

"Don't apologize, Matt. I just want you to do what you do best. I've only known you for a few months, but I've never seen you indecisive. You usually make the right call. But you make the damn call and take responsibility if you fail."

"Fail?" He smiled. He wanted this: the conversation, not the anger. He needed to decompress. Talking with Kara, seeing her, being with her, helped him, especially after a day like this one had been.

"You pretty much admitted you don't think those kids, Craig and Valerie, set the bombs," said Kara.

"Did I?"

"Maybe not what you said, but how you said it."

He concurred. "I don't think they did it. And not just because they had a pretty decent alibi for the first bombing."

"I don't think they were involved, either." She paused. "But I'd tell the sheriff to keep an eye on Valerie."

"I already did."

"You did?"

"I read the initial reports from the vandalism last year. She instigated it. She would have gone further except Craig stopped her. And her punishment was minimal. She's not going to think twice about doing it again if she could get away with it."

"That's what I thought," she said.

"Great minds…"

Matt leaned forward. He wanted to touch Kara so badly, but the house was full of sleeping agents, and he couldn't take the risk…not that he would care if the world knew how he felt. But it wasn't professional, and he was having a difficult time reconciling his two lives right now.

Not to mention Catherine's threat to tell Tony. Matt hoped he could talk her out of it, but Catherine was stubborn.

Last month, when he and Kara had a long weekend at his house in Tucson, everything had been perfect. They walked around naked. They swam in his pool. They had amazing sex in almost every room in his house. She told him how she got every scar on her body. And they even went out for dinner with his best friend and his wife—a real date, where he wasn't self-conscious about how he looked at Kara, how he touched her, how much he wanted her.

It had been a perfect three days. He wanted more time.

Kara tilted her head. "You're not thinking about the case."

"I'm thinking about Tucson. And that last night, when we went to dinner with Tim and Sarah. I wish we were there right now."

She leaned forward, stood on her toes. He leaned forward. Her lips were only inches from his.

She whispered, "Because after dinner we went back to your place and had sex in the pool, and it was pretty damn amazing."

"Kara, it always is," he said, then realized that he sounded a lot more serious than her. If he wasn't careful, they would be making out on the front porch, and then neither of them would be satisfied, just like last night in the kitchen.

She smiled. "Yes, it is."

Then she walked into the house, leaving him physically uncomfortable and with nothing he could do about it.

WEDNESDAY

24

Kara slept like a rock for more than four hours but was still awake before dawn. No one else was up, which was good—she needed time alone to consider how she wanted to approach Marcy. She drank half a cup of coffee with her toast, then left. She stretched her arms as she walked to the harbor. By the time she arrived, she had a strategy.

Marcy knew Kara's style already from the interviews they'd already done together, so straightforward seemed best. She should have talked to her right after the interview with Cal, but maybe this was even better—she was going over her notes, and forgot she'd wanted to talk to her about it yesterday. They'd been busy, blah, blah. Because Marcy was a cop, Kara needed to talk to her like a cop.

Kara arrived first. She stretched while looking around, noticing the other people who were out and about this early. She recognized a few. Kara might have only been here for three days, but she didn't forget faces. Businesses were opening: a doughnut shop on the corner, a coffee shop down the street. Life went on, even after a bombing and murder.

The idyllic town had been hit hard, but they still functioned. Kara admired that. She didn't like many people, but she liked the concept of community; that people had their own businesses, with family and purpose and a sense of belonging.

Even if she had none of these.

She glimpsed Marcy down the street approaching their designated meeting place, but pretended she hadn't noticed her as Kara bent over and touched her toes. Marcy looked different than she had yesterday, but it took Kara a second to realize why.

Yesterday Marcy had worn sweats and a Seattle PD T-shirt. Today she wore black jogging pants like Kara. Yesterday Kara had run in a windbreaker, but left it at the sheriff's station, so this morning she'd only worn her tank top, even though it was cool. Marcy had on a windbreaker this morning—not Kara's, this one had SJSD on the back.

Weird, it seemed, but maybe not. Kara was sometimes *too* observant.

"Aren't you cold?" Marcy asked.

"I won't be in five minutes. Same route?"

"Sure."

Kara started down the road. Traffic was practically nonexistent in the small town in the early morning, even though it was the height of the tourist season. They jogged in the bike lane.

By the time they reached the end of the path at the broken dock, Kara felt invigorated. They stopped, stretched, and drank water. The sun had just broken over the horizon, the sky was clear, it would be a beautiful, warm day.

"I interviewed Cal McKinnon yesterday," she said.

"Right, you said you were going to. How'd it go?"

"I should have talked to you last night, but we were all running around, and then my boss had me writing reports. I swear, the fucking FBI is worse about reports than LAPD."

Marcy laughed as she stretched her hamstrings. "John is cool. I spent almost as much time writing reports in Seattle as I did on patrol. Here, I do it, but it's so much easier. I can usually get it done between calls. In Seattle? We had hot call after hot call. Reports had to wait until we got back to the station."

"FBI is just a bunch of fucking bureaucrats," Kara lamented as she did windmills with her arms. She was cold here on the water, especially now that she was sweating from the run.

"Why'd you leave LAPD?"

Was she intentionally changing the subject or sincerely interested?

Kara said, "It's a really long story."

"That's what you said the other night. A suspect accused you of abuse of force or something?"

"Yep." Kara didn't realize how difficult this was to talk about, even now. She'd given Marcy her snide response the other day. She probably deserved more. "I worked this undercover case, a sweatshop case, Chinese nationals brought in as slave labor. The suspect was a US citizen, owned the sweatshops—and ran a bunch of other illegal enterprises. Anyway, I went deep cover as a buyer for a big-box retailer. Had an informant on the inside, was working it, and had almost enough evidence when my informant was killed. I stayed inside, got what I needed, and when we went in to arrest them, the suspect ran. Fell off a fucking roof and broke his leg. Then his bodyguard threw a knife in my back." She turned, showed Marcy the scar that was only partly concealed by her tank. "I shot him, he died, and I was put on leave, pending investigation."

"Wow. I don't think I've ever had that much excitement on a case, even in Seattle."

"Yeah, it was intense." Not the most intense case Kara had ever worked, but she didn't need to get into more details. If Marcy knew she was an undercover cop by trade, she might not be as forthcoming as Kara needed her to be. She sat on a large rock and leaned forward, touched her toes. She didn't really need to stretch, but she wanted to keep her blood pumping. If sharing her story with Marcy got her talking, it was worth freezing her ass off here on the water.

"Anyway, my boss put me on leave. Mandatory, you know, officer-involved shooting. I was cleared, completely justified—having the knife in my back helped with that. But after all that went down, my partner was killed and my cover was blown. I couldn't go back to my job."

"Why?"

"Like I said, long story, but the suspect has a good fucking lawyer and is walking free right now, awaiting trial." That was only half the truth. The real truth was the LA-FBI was trying to nail her for abuse of power charges and giving Chen a pass if he testified against her. Fortunately, Matt and his boss had intervened, and everything was in limbo. She had no idea what was going to happen, when she would testify, even *if* she would testify. She left that to the lawyers. They'd tell her when they needed her.

She added, "My boss worked out a loan to the FBI, hence me being here and not LA. For my safety, they said. But I always wonder if there's more to it. Some bureaucratic bullshit I don't know anything about."

She stood, stretched her calves.

"You're not from LA, though, right?" Marcy said. "You said you were from a small town."

"Liberty Lake, Washington."

"That's near the Idaho border, right?"

"Twenty miles from. A town not much bigger than Friday Harbor."

Marcy laughed. "Who'd have thought? Ready to head back?"

She motioned for Marcy to lead the way up the narrow path back to the road.

"Oh, I was going to ask," Kara said when they reached the road. "You said you knew Cal from the Coast Guard."

"Right. We used to date."

Marcy had *not* mentioned that the first time, but Kara just nodded, as if she knew. "Yeah. Okay, Cal didn't have much information to help us, but he mentioned that he swapped shifts with Kyle Richards because he and his fiancée had a fight over his ex-girlfriend."

"Shit, I feel awful about that."

"He didn't say much, just mentioned your name, and I meant to follow up last night but…" She shrugged and waved her hand, implying the conversation they'd just had cleared it all up.

"I didn't know Cal hadn't told Jamie that we used to date. I said something, she freaked, and I felt like shit."

"That fits." Sort of. Kara asked, "What did you say that set her off? Or is she just one of those clingy types?"

"I wouldn't say *clingy*. More insecure, you know?"

Kara shook her head. "Honestly, I've never been so into a guy that I worried about his exes. My job has always come first."

"I get that." Marcy nodded. "Cal and I dated, and I should have told you from the beginning that we were engaged. Briefly— kind of a spur-of-the-moment proposal, and then a couple weeks later we realized it was lust, not love. If you understand what I mean."

"Lust? Yeah, I definitely understand that," she said, laughed.

Marcy grinned. "So, we were really good in bed—I mean, so good I thought it was love—but out of bed? Not so much. We ended it. Color me surprised when I saw him here. I was so surprised I pulled him over—stupid on my part."

Kara raised an eyebrow. "You pulled him over?"

"I was on a stupid speed-trap detail—River Road has the

highest fatality rate on the island, so I get it, but I still hated it. I was new, I was stuck with it. And I saw him—he was only going five miles over. I never would have nailed him, except that I was stunned it was Cal, still driving that same old blue truck with a red panel gate in the back. Didn't give him a ticket, it would have been too weird, we talked, and that was it. But Friday Harbor is small, and I saw him with his girlfriend all over the place. I was jogging through the park last week and went over to her when I saw Jamie with their little girl. I was trying to be nice, and I thought for sure he would have told her that we'd dated… I feel like such a bitch for saying anything."

"Honesty is always best. That's on him, not you."

"Yeah. Well, water under the bridge. You ready?"

Kara smiled and started running.

Something didn't sound right. Cal hadn't mentioned they were engaged. She definitely needed to find the truth. If Cal had omitted a key detail when he seemed so forthcoming, that was suspicious.

Whenever something was supposed to be a simple truth and it seemed more complex than it should be? That's where you found the lies.

Matt was dressed and down in the kitchen at six fifteen that morning. Ryder sat at the dining room table, drinking an awful-looking green smoothie and eating nuts and granola. He also had his laptop out and was working.

"You're entitled to eat in peace," Matt said, sitting down at the table with his coffee.

"I'm just looking through a copy of Agent Devereaux's files again in preparation for my meeting with Jessica Mott."

"Do you think that Neil was the target?"

"I don't have a firm opinion, but I can't rule it out. He had extensive information about the Mott/Stevens death investigation, but the FBI and park ranger files don't make it any clearer why he thought they were murdered. I'm hoping Ms. Mott can shed light on his thought process. Then when Ms. Mott mentioned another case Agent Devereaux was looking into, another accidental death, it made me wonder why there's nothing about that in his computer or among his files."

It was slightly suspicious. "The gas company cleared the house, but if you go back bring Kara or Michael with you."

"The sheriff told me the heater was old, but they couldn't rule on whether the leak was intentional or accidental."

"True. They're investigating further, sent all the components to the mainland for a more detailed forensic analysis," Matt said. "Speaking of Kara, I thought I heard her earlier."

"She left to meet Deputy Anderson."

"Right. They went running." Matt wished he could have had backup on her, in case her questioning of Anderson went south.

"Do you think that there's anything to what Kara said?" Ryder asked.

"About Officer Anderson?"

"I was in the conference room when Kara and Catherine were, um, discussing it."

"Arguing." Matt sipped his coffee.

"I asked Kara to join me for the interview with Ms. Mott this morning. I hope that's okay."

"You don't have to ask my permission. I trust you."

Ryder cleared his throat but didn't look at him.

"Do you have something to say?"

"No."

"Is this about the tension between Catherine and Kara? They're resolving it."

"Are they?"

Matt frowned. He wondered if anyone—if Ryder—had overheard Catherine's accusation that he was sleeping with Kara. He didn't want to discuss it with anyone else.

"I know that you and Dr. Jones have been friends and colleagues for a long time. She's well respected and one of the foremost forensic psychiatrists in the country."

"She is."

"And Kara is the exact opposite of Dr. Jones. She's street smart. I heard Jim call her 'a cop's cop.' You have a lot of respect for her, and give her a lot of leeway."

"I give everyone leeway because everyone on this team is the best at what they do."

"But what happens when two of us disagree?"

"We discuss it."

"Not this time. In the Triple Killer investigation, yes—we had discussions and you would consider each theory, and then you made a decision and we all acted accordingly. When we were in Patagonia last month, you gave Kara a lot of leeway because she understands undercover investigations better than most. But this time, two team members have directly opposing opinions—and your decision matters because expending manpower to investigate Madelyn Jeffries or Marcy Anderson or even Neil's cold case takes away manpower from investigating other theories. I've never taken you as a boss who makes decisions on consensus."

"Catherine and Kara resolved it," Matt said. "They went to talk to Mrs. Jeffries again and Catherine cleared her."

"But Kara had already cleared her the day before. I just think… well, my opinion isn't relevant. I shouldn't have said anything."

He looked down.

"I value your input, Ryder. I want to know what you think."

He didn't speak immediately, then said, "When Kara went to the Island Protectors meeting Monday night, to get a sense of their mission and figure out who was who, it was a good idea. She obtained valuable information. And you sided with Catherine."

"I wasn't taking sides."

"You were, and—I shouldn't say this, because it really isn't my place—but Kara was hurt. She acted angry and dismissive about it, but you let Catherine belittle her in front of the team."

Matt opened his mouth to object, then closed it. The last thing he wanted to do was hurt Kara.

"I respect Kara. You know that."

"You didn't show it. Kara *is* a valuable member of this team."

"You don't have to tell me that."

"I don't want her to leave."

"What makes you think she will?"

"Because if I thought that my boss didn't have faith in me, I would be looking for another job. Kara would just quit."

Matt stared at his half-empty coffee. Kara couldn't quit. She was a cop, through and through, and it wasn't safe for her to return to Los Angeles. Would she just…leave?

If she did, it would be his fault.

25

Ryder looked up when the desk sergeant knocked and entered with an attractive young woman. "Jessica Mott is here to see you."

"Thank you," Ryder said. Kara wasn't here yet. Jessica was early, and he really didn't want to do this interview alone. He quickly sent Kara a text message.

The sergeant closed the door, and Ryder stood to shake her hand. "I'm Ryder Kim," he said. "FBI analyst. We spoke on the phone. Thank you so much for coming up here."

"I wish I could have come yesterday, but the ferries were shut down until early afternoon."

Jessica was soft-spoken and dressed simply in slacks and a pale green blouse that matched her eyes.

Ryder motioned for her to sit at the end of the table, then sat in the chair ninety degrees from her so they could comfortably look at paperwork together. "We're still in the middle of our investigation, but we haven't been able to rule out the possibility Neil Devereaux may have been a target for the initial attack. However, what I say here I need you to keep in strict confidence."

She agreed. "Anything I can do to help. I mean that."

He looked at his phone. Kara said five minutes.

"What do you want to know?" she asked.

"I'm waiting for my colleague, Detective Quinn. She's running a little late." That sounded idiotic. "But why don't you start with how you met Agent Devereaux? I've read all his notes, but know I'm missing parts of his files. It's unclear whether you contacted him or he contacted you."

"I reached out to Agent Devereaux four years ago. He told me then that he was retiring at the end of the year and I was heartbroken, because I never believed Jason's death was an accident. I was hoping he could investigate. My parents would never listen to me, didn't want to talk about what happened. Neither did Brian's parents. I was fourteen when they died—who would believe me when I said I thought my brother was killed? It was awful. I missed my brother, and my parents were crushed. I went to college a few years later—University of Washington, just like Jason. That's when I started asking questions. Doing research. Teachers remembered him and Brian—they were inseparable. Best friends from the first day of kindergarten. Funny and happy guys. I mean, he was my brother and he annoyed me—we were seven years apart in age. But he also took me to movies and taught me how to fish—my dad isn't an outdoorsy type—and on my fourteenth birthday, Jason took me in a hot air balloon, though it totally freaked me out. That was the last thing we did alone together before he died...and, well, I now do it on his birthday every year, as a way to, I don't know, remember him. Anyway, my mom sent me to a psychologist in high school who said that I had to accept the truth if I was to get beyond Jason's death. I faked it. Because the more I thought, the more I knew that he was murdered, even though I didn't know who did it or why."

Kara walked in the conference room and sat down. Ryder started to introduce her, but Kara said, "Just ignore me. Keep going."

"Unknown to me," Jessica said, "Neil was suspicious about the deaths and tried to reopen the case, but his superiors said no. And then he was transferred out of state, to DC. I learned all that after we got in touch."

"Exactly when was this?" Ryder asked. "You said before he retired?"

"Yes. The spring before he retired, which was at the end of that year. He'd already planned on moving here, had been looking for houses. Anyway, before I connected with Neil, I became fascinated with cold cases. Mostly missing persons. I read books, watched television, it became somewhat of an obsession—that's what my mom said. Then I was reading the news about a teacher who disappeared while sailing in Puget Sound. His boat was found, some blood, and investigators surmised that he had been drinking—they found empty beer bottles—and when he was adjusting the sails, he messed up and the mast hit him in the back of the head, and he went overboard and drowned. There was some blood found on the mast. It just seemed so much like what happened to Jason, especially when the man's wife said he wasn't drinking, that he had been sober for five years. She was distraught. That's when I reached out to Neil—I gave him all my research into Jason's murder, which wasn't a lot, I'll admit, because there wasn't a lot there. We talked about the teacher in Puget Sound. Neil was interested and said he'd look into it. He asked the investigators if they had checked the bottles on the teacher's sailboat for fingerprints—because he was still with the FBI, I guess they went ahead and did it. There were no prints at all. They didn't find that suspicious because of salt air and water and whatnot, but Neil did. He started looking into that case. When he retired, I came up here to have dinner with him. Neil said he'd found another suspicious death that he was looking into.

"Then last year he got a bit weird. I came up here at the end of last summer to introduce Neil to my boyfriend—we're now engaged." She held up her ring finger, which sported a small but classy diamond. "And he told me not to come again. He said he had a strong suspicion that there was a killer living here, and he needed to further investigate, but didn't want to put me on the killer's radar." She shivered. "You know—I'm getting married in October, and Neil was going to be there. He returned his RSVP right after I mailed them last month. I'm going to miss him."

Kara said, "Everyone who knows him says the same thing. He was well-liked. Did he tell you who he suspected?"

She shook her head. "When I pushed—and I did, hard—he said that Jason was killed because of revenge, both him and Brian, and that three other deaths fit the same pattern."

Ryder pulled out his own notes. "Do you know what three cases?"

"The guy on the boat was Eric Travers, a teacher in Everett—that's north of Seattle. He was in his late thirties, I think. But there should be several articles about him. Four years ago, in September. I sent him links to everything I found. Then there was a woman who went missing when hiking up Round Mountain with friends. They camped for the night, and when they woke up, she was gone. They never found her body. Neil was obsessed with her."

"You remember her name? When this was?"

"It was maybe a year before the teacher drowned. Neither of their bodies have been found. Her name... Missy, I think. I don't remember exactly. But I know he had an article about her disappearance, we talked about it."

"And the third case?" Kara prompted.

"A high school student, his name also escapes me, I'm sorry. It was in Bellingham at the end of last year—right before Neil told me not to come up here. He said he knew who the killer was but couldn't prove it and needed more time."

"When was the last time you talked to him?" Kara asked.

"We talked on the phone a couple times, but he never talked about the case—avoided it on purpose, was my sense. The last time I saw him was in January. He was in Seattle for a football game—he was a huge Seahawks fan—and we met for breakfast the Monday after the game. He was frustrated. He said he didn't believe in a perfect murder, but this was close to it."

Kara leaned forward. "And he never gave you a hint as to who he was talking about?"

She shook her head. "I asked more than once, but he said this guy—he definitely said it was a man—wouldn't think twice about killing someone who thwarted him, and he had to be careful so he didn't tip his hand. Oh!" She sat up straight. "It's someone who is only here in the summers. I can't believe I forgot that!"

"Did Neil tell you that?" Ryder asked.

"Not exactly, but at that breakfast he said he had five months to get his ducks in a row before *he returned*. He was specifically talking about the killer. That made me think it was someone on the island only for the summer. Unfortunately, that's half the people here."

"This is all helpful, Jessica. Thank you for coming to talk to us," Ryder said.

Kara was looking at her phone. "Was that kid in Bellingham eighteen-year-old Billy Clark? A football player who had a full ride to University of Oregon and died in a car crash?"

"That's him. How did you know?"

"Google is my best friend."

★ ★ ★

Ryder stared at all the information in front of him, then glanced up at the whiteboard, on which he had written the names of the five individuals Neil had been researching. He'd easily found the information about Missy Douglas, the woman who went missing on Round Mountain, when he searched for it.

"Someone stole Neil's research," Kara said.

"It appears that way, but there were no prints in the house except for those of Neil and his biweekly housekeeper," Ryder said.

"Gloves. And I'm thinking the heater was intentionally messed with, not an accidental leak. Maybe the killer expected the house to blow up and take everything with it, or he thought there might have been evidence he missed."

"Carbon monoxide is flammable," Ryder said, "but it wouldn't spontaneously ignite. There would need to be a spark, a flame, something to set it off." He paused. "Why not take everything? Why leave the files about Jason and Brian?"

"Because Neil had not been quiet about looking into those specific deaths, and perhaps the killer felt if he took everything, it would be suspicious? It's a theory. It could even be that the *Water Lily* explosion is connected to one of the other three crimes, not Mott and Stevens. We don't know for certain that the five deaths Neil was looking into were all murders, or all the same suspect. In his investigation, he could have stumbled onto another crime, another killer."

Ryder turned back to Neil's computer. "Our data division ran a full undelete on Neil's hard drive and sent me the emails last night and a detailed report this morning. But the emails are spotty—we don't have them all. It appears he only used his computer for email and research. They weren't able to re-create browsing history after fourteen days. But—" Ryder walked over to a second desk he was using where he had a series of emails printed out "—I found an exchange between Neil and the medical examiner who autopsied Billy Clark. Neil and the ME had arranged a time to meet—they would have met the week before he was killed, but there are no follow-ups on that, and I don't know what they discussed. I asked Jim to find out, since he has been working closely with the mainland. Neil also bookmarked every article about Billy Clark and had emailed Billy's father several times, asking for information about his college recruitment and his stats in high school. The kid was a wide receiver, gifted, a once-in-a-generation player, according to people who know about football, which Neil did."

"The question we need to be asking," Kara said, "is what do these five people have in common? What did Neil see that connected them, and how does the killer connect to them? Based on this, it seems Neil believed that these five people may all have been killed by the same person."

"There's one more email I need to follow up on," Ryder said. "Neil had reached out to the campus police at the University of Washington and asked if there was anyone on staff who had been there thirteen years ago. He gave his number and specifically said he was retired FBI, looking into a cold case. There's a response from the police administrator acknowledging receipt and telling him that someone would call him. There was no follow-up by email, but Neil's phone records indicate multiple phone calls to and from a university number at the beginning of this year and again two weeks ago."

"It's worth finding out what he asked and what they told him. And you might want to talk to the shrink about this—because you know what my gut says? If someone went through all the trouble of making evidence disappear from Neil's house, he goes to the top of my target list."

"But what about the second bomb?" asked Ryder. "Why would he set it?"

"*If* Neil was the target, the second bomb was a diversion to distract us and point a direct finger to IP. The guard? Wrong place, wrong time. We weren't seriously looking at IP until the second bomb. We were looking at the victims. We were looking in the right place and the killer knew it." She frowned.

"What are you thinking?"

"Nothing."

"Your face doesn't look like it's nothing."

"Small town," she muttered.

"I don't understand."

"We've been all over Friday Harbor, asking questions, interviewing witnesses, and the killer must have overheard or suspected or observed what our focus was." She looked around the room they were in. All their theories and evidence were posted for anyone to see. "We lock this room at night, but anyone who works for the sheriff—janitors, staff, deputies—would be able to get in pretty easy, right?"

"I suppose."

"Tell Matt to get a lock on this door and only we have the key. I need to look into something."

"What?"

"I don't know," she admitted. It was something in the back of her head. "I have to work through some things."

One thing she'd noticed right away was that the local cops here were friends with everyone. Sheriff John Rasmussen had known everyone by name. People came in with flowers and candy and get-well cards for Tom Redfield, the deputy who'd been hospitalized with carbon monoxide poisoning. Word got around. What if someone let something slip? Innocuous? Without realizing they were putting the investigation at risk?

Or what if it wasn't so innocuous?

"It could also be that whoever lifted the evidence from Neil's house did it *because* of the explosion, but they were not the person who put the bomb on the boat," Ryder said.

"Could be."

"You don't think so."

"Nope. Just call Matt, tell him we need to fully secure this room, or move everything to the house. I have an interview scheduled. I'll be back."

26

Kara looked around the small, tidy house that Jamie Finch shared with her fiancé and daughter. It was cute, a little too frilly for her with lacy curtains and flowery flourishes, but clean and comfortable.

"Thank you for meeting with me."

"Cal said you wanted to talk to me, that we're not in trouble or anything, you're just trying to find out what happened. It's awful."

A little voice came from the adjoining room, joining in with singing from the television. "*PAW Patrol* is the only thing that keeps Hazel entertained for more than five minutes," Jamie said. "But it's cute, so I don't mind."

"She's adorable," Kara said and meant it.

Jamie beamed. "She's a handful, but I wouldn't trade one minute. She's the best thing that has happened to me, Hazel and Cal. Cal told you why I went to my dad's on Friday, right?"

"Yes. But in your words would be helpful."

"I don't understand why. I mean, it has nothing to do with the bombing, right?"

"I need to verify all information surrounding West End Charter and the *Water Lily*. Cal was supposed to work that night, so the fact that he didn't, I need to make sure it makes sense."

"I have a really bad habit of running when confronted with conflict. This isn't anything new for me, and I'm trying to change—really trying. Like, when my mom had an asshole boyfriend—instead of telling her he hit on me—I was fourteen—I went to my dad and begged him to let me move in with him. Everything finally came out, but only because my dad knew I wouldn't just want to move here for no reason. And my old boyfriend—I stayed with him a lot longer than I should have because I didn't want the fight. Anyway, that afternoon I'd taken Hazel to the park when she woke up from her nap. It was a beautiful day, and one of the neighbors has three-year-old twins, so we try to meet up when I'm not working. They had to leave early and so I watched Hazel play in the sand, and then Marcy Anderson ran by."

"She was jogging through the park?"

"Yeah—I'd seen her a few times. Cal pointed her out once, when she said hi, and I asked if he knew her, and he said they were in the Coast Guard together. I asked if we should invite her to dinner, and he said no, he didn't really like her, and that was that. But this time when she passed I smiled at her and she stopped, drank water, and asked if she could sit for a minute. Sure, I said. She commented about how cute Hazel was, how she looked like Cal—which is true, the dark curls and big blue eyes. And then she said something like when she and Cal were together, she didn't think he wanted kids. And I said, together?

Like, together together? I know, stupid, but I don't think well in confrontations, either, and I knew what she'd meant but had to ask. She said yes, didn't Cal tell me? They dated for a while when they were in the Coast Guard, split, but got together a few times after. Including a few years ago in Seattle when they were at a mutual friend's wedding. She said that was probably before he met me, but it wasn't—and I guess I thought then that she *knew* it wasn't, and she was being mean. I remembered that weekend—Cal and I had gone out a couple times, and he asked if I wanted to go with him to the wedding, but I thought it would be too much, too fast, so said I couldn't get off work. But it was after he came back that we really, I don't know, got serious, I guess. But the way Marcy said it then made me think she and Cal had this mutual attraction thing even now, and I left. I mean, not right that second, but I left Cal a note in the morning and took Hazel to my dad's. He wasn't there—he has a condo in Seattle he stays in most of the time, because of his schedule. But I needed to think, you know?"

"Cal mentioned that Marcy had pulled him over for speeding but didn't give him a ticket. Do you know about that?"

"No. I mean, not specifically. This weekend he told me that she'd been popping up in odd places since she moved to town and he should have told me everything from the beginning, but after that wedding he didn't see her or talk to her until she moved here. He loves me—I believe it. And I just let my insecurities get the better of me."

Hazel ran into the room. "Mommy, Mommy, Mommy, I'm hug-ry."

"It's not lunchtime yet."

"Snack?" she asked, her eyes big and wide. She looked over at Kara and put her head in her mom's lap, then looked back over at Kara and climbed into her mom's lap. The little kid didn't stop moving. "Peez?"

"When *PAW Patrol* is over, we'll have a snack."

"Okay!" She climbed down and ran over to Kara. "Name?" She pointed to herself. "Hazel." Then she pointed to Kara.

"Kara," she said with a smile.

Hazel grinned. Her teeth were tiny with a little space between the two front teeth that made her even cuter. "Hi!"

"Hi."

"Sweetie, go back to the *PAW Patrol*, okay? We'll be done in five minutes."

"Five minutes!" Hazel exclaimed and ran back into the other room.

Kara said, "I know you're busy. Couple more things. Cal was supposed to work on Friday but called out and saw you."

"Yes, and he's all torn up inside. And I'm so glad he's okay, but also I'm upset about Neil. And Kyle and everyone, of course, but I loved Neil. He was sweet and kind and funny. He babysat sometimes when I was really stuck. And he came by the Fish & Brew several times a week. Always sat either in my section or the bar."

"Cal said you were friends with him."

"Who wasn't? Neil was a great guy. Just a really good man, deep down, you know?"

"Did he talk to you about a cold case he was investigating?"

"About those college boys who drowned a long time ago? Yes, I knew about it, but he only talked about it in passing. Things like that upset me—I don't like violence and sad things. I felt so bad for them and their families and I didn't even know them. Cal says I internalize other people's pain, that I have too much empathy, but I don't think you can have too much empathy."

"It's an admirable trait," Kara said. Cops had empathy, but they learned early on in their careers to bury it. Otherwise, they wouldn't last long on the job. "When was the last time you spoke to Neil?"

"Um, I don't remember exactly… Tuesday or Wednesday, I

worked both days, he was there one of those days. But we didn't have a conversation, really, just said hello."

"Do you know how he seemed? Was he upset, worried, preoccupied?"

"I can't really say. Well, maybe preoccupied. He didn't sit in the bar, but he didn't sit in my section, either. And—now that I think about it, he didn't eat. He ordered, but then asked for a to-go box, said he wasn't that hungry."

"Thank you for your time."

"That's it? Did it help?"

Kara rose. "I'll call you if I have more questions."

Kara tracked Matt down when he was leaving West End Charter.

"Anything new?" she asked with a nod to the building.

"Michael and I have been reviewing security footage from every camera in a six-block radius. I'm brain-dead."

"Where is Michael?"

"Getting Jim at the airport. They'll meet us at the station. You asked Ryder to get a lock for the conference room. Why?"

"Small town."

"Explain."

They were walking back to the sheriff's station because it was only a few blocks.

"Everything is pointing to Neil Devereaux as being the target. Then we get a second bomb. Slightly different design, not as big an impact, same chemical makeup so we know it's the same guy. West End the clear target."

"Diversion, I get it, but I don't understand about the lock."

"Friday Harbor is a small town on a small island. Everyone knows everyone, just like Liberty Lake and Patagonia. Someone could wander in and deputies wouldn't think twice. A cousin of Bob, a sister of Sue, they're not a killer, right? They could look at our board and see that we weren't even looking at Island Protectors on Monday. They were way down on our list—but Neil was at the top. Targeting West End on Tuesday refocused our investigation. We have Ashley's pictures printed and posted, we have Craig and Valerie listed on the board, they come in, know the diversion was successful. Does that mean he hits a third West End target? Just to make sure we're doing what he wants us to."

"We can pull security cameras from the sheriff's station."

"We should, but we also have to consider basic gossip."

"Deputies talking out of school."

"Exactly."

"Okay. I'm with you. I already told Ryder to do it, but I just needed to hear your reasoning." He stopped while they were still across the street from the sheriff's station. "Learn anything from Marcy Anderson? Do we have reason to pursue her?"

"I don't know," Kara said. "Either she lied or Cal lied. I don't know who."

"About?"

"Being engaged. She said they were engaged for a few weeks, and told Jamie Finch that they'd dated for 'a while.' Cal said they were never engaged, that the relationship wasn't all that serious, they only went out a few times, and he made a mistake sleeping with her after a wedding when he was drunk."

"Does he have reason to lie?"

"His girlfriend. He didn't tell Jamie about his relationship with Marcy, even after she moved here, even when he had an opportunity. He didn't tell her about being pulled over or running into Marcy all over town, until after Marcy outed their relationship to Jamie at the park. Marcy admitted to pulling him over and outing their relationship, said she assumed Jamie knew. She feels bad."

"You don't believe her?"

"I don't have any reason to *not* believe her."

"But."

"But." Kara wanted to know who was lying. If Cal was lying, the reasons could be innocuous—he didn't want to hurt his fiancée. It didn't bode well for their future, but hey, at least it would make sense.

But if Marcy had lied, that was a whole other problem.

"She wasn't suspicious with your questions?"

Kara tilted her chin up. "I'm insulted."

Matt looked at his phone. "Catherine has a profile and Ryder found additional information. Wants us in for a debrief."

He looked at her as if he wanted to say something else, but the streetlight changed, and they crossed the street.

Once everyone—including Michael Harris and Jim Esteban—was gathered and seated in the conference room, Catherine began. She stood in front of the whiteboard, which had been completely erased. Kara was more than a little interested in her profile.

"Kara brought up a point earlier that while the sheriff has been more than helpful, because Friday Harbor is a small town our investigation may be compromised. In light of that, I thought keeping key information off the whiteboard was prudent. But I'm going to use it for the moment to illustrate what we've learned so far. Agent Neil Devereaux thought that five deaths, all considered accidents, were suspicious. In order to come up with a profile, I looked into these cases with the assumption that they were connected as homicides."

She wrote five names on the board:

Jason Mott
Brian Stevens
Eric Travers
Missy Douglas
Billy Clark

Kara leaned forward, interested to hear if Catherine had been able to connect the deaths.

"With Kara's help, Ryder has been instrumental in finding

missing information," Catherine said. "Neil took years to find much of this information because he didn't have a specific direction, but Ryder was able to uncover important facts after recreating Neil's notes and emails in only two days. There are still some holes and some follow-up with local agencies, but we have enough information to put together a profile—accurate if, and only if, Neil's theory is right, and these five people were all murdered by the same person."

Catherine drank some water and continued.

"I managed to reach Travers's wife as well as Douglas's fiancé. Both had spoken to Neil earlier this year but didn't have much new information to share with me. Douglas's fiancé had the impression that Neil was writing a book about missing persons, but he couldn't specifically say that Neil had told him that. Regardless, I was looking to fill some holes in the information we have.

"My profile is questionable for a number of reasons," said Catherine. "It makes several assumptions, including that Neil Devereaux was the target, and the explosion was to hide the fact that he was the target. In my experience, broad acts like the bombing of *Water Lily* rarely have individual targets. At the same time, I trust Neil Devereaux as a reasoned and experienced FBI agent. He had been looking into these deaths, and he either saw something that we don't or his analysis was removed from his possession. If Agent Devereaux had additional information on the Mowich Lake drownings, or the other deaths, where is it? Either he hid the information for some reason, he had it with him when the boat exploded, or it was stolen.

"I'm making more assumptions than I'm comfortable with, but we're also on a clock here, not just because the bomber may seek to further point fingers at Island Protectors, which could result in additional lives lost, but because according to Jessica Mott, Neil believed that the killer was a summer resident. That both helps and hinders our investigation. A resident *all* summer, or someone who comes here for two weeks for vacation?

We don't know. So what I'm focusing my profile on is a person who killed five people over a thirteen-year period. I'm coming at this from the idea that if Neil showed up at my office at Quantico and offered this evidence, what would I say?"

Catherine turned to the board, writing as she spoke. "Neil believed that these five people were murdered and their deaths were made to look like accidents.

"Two college boys who drowned in an icy lake after drinking too much.

"A hiker who disappeared while on a treacherous path, leaving camp early one morning, alone. A teacher sailing alone, got drunk and drowned after being knocked unconscious by the boom on his sailboat. Neither body was ever found.

"A high school senior killed in a single-car crash."

She used magnets to put up pictures of each potential victim next to their name. The college boys and the teacher were white, the hiker was mixed-race Black and Japanese, and the high school student was Black. She didn't believe that these were racially motivated crimes.

"Because each of these accidents appears as it was—an accidental death, and no law enforcement agency seriously considered homicide—*if* they were in fact murders, that tells us the killer is a high-level planner. He is extremely well organized, methodical, patient, with above-average IQ.

"Because the races, genders, and locations were different, I don't think he's a traditional serial killer—someone who is compelled to kill. I initially thought he might be an opportunity killer—on a hike, sees a lone woman, pushes her off a cliff. The boys in the lake—he could have lured them out, pushed them overboard. The water was so cold they had little to no chance of making it to shore alive. Yet the sailboat—a grown man, physically fit, in the middle of the Sound, sailing alone? How is that a crime of opportunity? And the car accident is the biggest outlier. The other four murders were outdoors, recreational areas.

The car accident was a kid driving and hitting a tree. Jim spoke to the investigators and the medical examiner for me because he'd been on shore this morning." She nodded to him. "Please, Jim, add anything that I might have missed. But it appears that the investigation was inconclusive—there were no drugs or alcohol in Billy Clark's system, per the ME. Single-car accident. No sign of any other vehicle, and Billy was only found after he didn't come home on time. The conventional wisdom was that a large animal was in the road—not uncommon in the area, according to the detectives—and he swerved to avoid it, hitting the tree. Or that he fell asleep at the wheel. There were no skid marks indicating braking, but there were swerve skid marks." She put up a photo from the original police report that Jim had emailed her earlier.

"The detective in charge of Clark's death investigation spoke to Neil several times," Jim said. "Neil's questions led him to believe that Neil thought Billy's accident wasn't an accident, that it was intentional. Neil gave him no specific suspect or reason why he thought Billy Clark had been murdered. That annoyed the detective, and he stopped returning Neil's calls."

"If these five deaths are in fact homicides," Catherine said cautiously, "and if they were committed by the same person, then he has a *personal* reason for killing each of these people. That means he knew each person—and if he did, we should be able to find that personal connection."

Matt said, "But even if we do, we won't have any physical evidence tying anyone to these murders—which were all ruled accidental by authorities."

"I think that's where Neil found himself," Catherine said. "He had a suspect but lacked proof. Ryder, please explain the connections you confirmed."

Ryder walked to the board and wrote *University of Washington* to the side. "We already know that Mott, Stevens, and Douglas were all at the University of Washington at the same time. That was easy to confirm. Douglas was a year younger than the two men who drowned. Travers graduated from Washington State in Pullman, and Clark had accepted a football scholarship to University of Oregon, so neither of them had a U of W connection.

"Mott and Stevens were born and raised in Olympia and had been friends before college, roommates in college. Travers was originally from Spokane, and after college he took a teaching job in Seattle, high school. He was promoted to a new position in Bellingham two weeks before he died. Douglas was from the Seattle suburbs, lived at home while she went to college, graduated, went to nursing school, and worked at a children's hospital. She was recently engaged before she went missing. Her body was never found."

"Wait—" Kara said.

Everyone turned to look at her.

"You see something we don't?" Catherine asked. She wished Kara would be clearer and less…*casual*, for lack of a better word. She didn't even dress like an FBI agent.

"Did Mott or Stevens have something good happen to them before they died?"

"I don't understand the question."

"Look—you have it right there. Billy Clark had a scholarship to Oregon, he had his college signing three weeks before his accident. Travers was promoted, about to start a new job—I assume it came with a raise, a better position, whatever. Douglas became engaged. That's generally good news, right? So could the killer target them because of these accomplishments? Maybe because they accomplished something he didn't?"

Catherine was surprised at Kara's psychological insight. Maybe she shouldn't be. Matt had said over and over that Kara was a good cop. Yet she was a risk they couldn't afford, especially in these times. Though Matt irritated Catherine, he was an exemplary agent and had worked hard to create this team. She couldn't let someone like Kara destroy it.

Yet she had a point here.

"That would be a viable motive," Catherine concurred. "Ryder, do you know about the boys?"

"No. Nothing in the file, and Neil didn't make that connection—or if he did, it's with the missing files. I'll reach out to Jessica Mott, see if she knows something."

Kara was staring at the board as if she had more to say but didn't.

Matt said, "This is good, but we still don't have a name or even a direction or one person who knew all those people."

"Well, we have one name," Ryder said. "At least, it's something we should pursue. Damon Avila."

"The bartender at the Fish & Brew?" Kara said.

"He graduated from the University of Washington the year before Mott and Stevens would have—two weeks before they died," said Ryder. "And he dated Missy Douglas for two years."

"Way to bury the lede," Kara said.

"There's no reason to believe that he was involved in any of these deaths," Catherine said. "There is no known motive. He and Missy broke up after he graduated. He didn't share any classes with Mott or Stevens—Mott and Stevens were computer science majors, but Avila was biology and Missy was nursing. And Travers and Clark have no connection to Avila that we can yet find, but Ryder and I only made that possible connection this morning, so we just started the background on him. And even if we did find something, there's no evidence at all—physical or circumstantial—that Avila would have been involved with their deaths, all of which have been ruled accidental."

"Meaning," Matt said, "we have no cause to question him."

"Correct," Catherine said. "And *if* we talked to him about these deaths without having evidence, we'd tip our hand, in my opinion. We need more."

"It would be a balancing act," Matt agreed.

"We have nothing, Matt, and less than nothing for a warrant."

"Neil must have seen something else that we're missing. He spent a lot of time at the Fish & Brew. He knew these people better than we do."

Catherine concurred. "Maybe he found that smoking gun, but it's not here, not anymore."

"If he found it, we can find it," said Matt. "Go back and talk to everyone, find different ways to ask the same question."

Ryder said, "In January, Neil told Jessica Mott that he knew who killed her brother but couldn't prove it."

"Maybe he tipped his hand," Kara said, "and Damon killed him. Framed IP with the second explosion."

"This doesn't leave this room," Matt said. "We have to be extremely careful how we investigate Damon Avila. If we can connect him to the bombings in any way, then that would open a door to a warrant. But if we can't, we cannot overstep or potentially blow the prosecution."

They were all silent. Momentarily, Matt turned to Michael. "Any word about the source for the C-4? Can we see if Avila has any access—friends, family—in construction?"

"ATF is still working on it, but I can look into Avila's friends and family and see if there is any construction connection," Michael said. "Can I read in the ATF about Avila?"

Matt nodded. "Tell them this is on the down-low, need-to-know only."

"Got it." Michael left the room.

"Avila fits what we know from our interview with Mott and reading Neil's notes, but it's still not enough for a warrant or to question him," Catherine said. "And Clark and Travers have no connection to the university."

"But they're both connected to Bellingham High School," Kara said.

"Yes. Though Travers hadn't started working there. He died in May four years ago, would have been moving that summer and starting his new position in the fall."

"What was his promotion?" she asked.

Ryder clicked on his computer. "He was taking over the math and science department and would have been teaching honors classes, plus serving as the assistant dean of students. A pay raise in addition to a title. His wife said that the dean planned to retire in two years and they wanted Travers to replace him."

"Could someone have been overlooked for the position?"

"I can find out," Ryder said. "I'll call the school." He glanced at his watch. "It's after five. I'll leave a message, then call again first thing in the morning."

Catherine said, "Get a staff list. This was four years ago, so find any staff who was there both then and now." She looked at the whiteboard, then said, "Based on Ryder's research, Neil felt strongly that Billy Clark was murdered, but there is no evidence, and he's an outlier in several ways. So we may have to remove him from the pool of victims if a suspect matches perfectly to the other four. Neil may have been mistaken."

"Except," Ryder said, raising his index finger in the air, "that was the case that seemed to jump-start his research into the other four deaths. According to Jessica, he was stumped—until he saw something in *that file*. And he believed that the killer lived here only in the summer. He made that clear to Jessica earlier this year. Avila fits that."

"Avila's a teacher," Kara said.

They all looked at her. She continued. "On Monday, when Marcy and I interviewed the Dunlap girls, she introduced me to Damon Avila. He teaches somewhere on the mainland, works here in the summers. He's their uncle—brother to their mom, who died a few years ago."

"We need a list of all the regular summer people—at least the last two summers, based on Neil's comment to Mott," Matt said. "I'll go over the West End Charter employee files again and see who doesn't live here year-round. Their staff more than doubles around Memorial Day weekend. And an employee of theirs would have easy access to the boats and not be suspicious."

"But are you thinking of this guy as a bomber?" asked Jim. "Because if we think Neil was the target and this guy already killed five other people, he probably just seized on the opportunity."

"But what opportunity? C-4 doesn't fall out of the sky," Matt said.

"Could he be planning another attack?" Jim asked.

"It would be West End," Catherine said. "Because either way—whether the target is Neil, or the target is West End to *distract* us from Neil's investigation—the bomber is going to be consistent there."

"I'm going to shut them down," Matt said. He didn't sound like he was looking forward to it. "This weekend is their biggest moneymaker, but we have no choice. We can't risk it."

Jim said, "How far back are we going here? If we're making a connection to the University of Washington, that's thirteen years."

Catherine replied, "Ryder and I are doing full backgrounds on Missy Douglas and Eric Travers to see if they have any commonalities, and Ryder is waiting for more information from the University of Washington about Douglas and the boys. If we can connect all five of them to Damon Avila, we might have enough to talk to him, but even then it's pie in the sky."

Kara stood, stretched. "If we're done, I'm meeting Marcy at the Fish & Brew."

After she walked out, Catherine glanced at Matt. "Matt, we can't risk exposing our thoughts in this case. I think you need to end this little side investigation of Kara's."

"I'll talk to her," he said and followed Kara.

Ryder took a picture of the whiteboard before wiping it down.

"I'd like to stay here and go over the ME's reports again, talk to him," Jim said. "I have a good relationship with the doc on the mainland. We might come up with a theory."

"Lock up when you leave," Catherine said and handed him a key. "The sheriff also has a key but agreed that he wouldn't let anyone else in here."

After Catherine and Ryder walked out together from the building, she asked him, "What do you think of Detective Quinn?" She really wanted to hear his opinion. Ryder was quiet, smart, and he seemed to observe everything.

"She's a good cop. Dedicated. Hardworking."

She should have known Ryder wouldn't say anything against her. They'd worked several cases together. So Catherine didn't push.

Michael, on the other hand, was more like her. He believed in order, rules, and a chain of command. She would definitely talk to him about Kara later. Because if she couldn't get through to Matt about the need to let Kara go, Michael might be able to.

Someone had to convince Matt that Kara was bad news, because she really didn't want to go over his head to their boss, Tony Greer.

But she would.

"Hold up," Matt said to Kara.

She turned, irritated. Then her posture straightened, and from a slight shift in her expression, he saw her consciously shut down her emotions. He would have missed it if he didn't know her.

"What's your plan?" he asked.

"I told you. I want to get a better read on Marcy. I made a few calls, I'm going to follow up on her background. I know her better than anyone else here."

"You've known her for three days."

"Last night you told me that you trusted my judgment. Do you change your mind depending on the last person who spoke to you?"

His temper flared. "That's bullshit and you know it."

"Do I? You want me off this case, take me off. You want me on this case, you need to let me do my fucking job. Something is going on with Marcy. Is it related to our investigation? I don't know. It might just be personal, a fucking love triangle. Or maybe she has a sense about Damon Avila—she works out with him, she knows him, she might have some intuition there that she's not ready to address because they're friends. Maybe she asked him questions off the record, accidentally tipped him off, I don't know. I need to sit with her, assess her, figure out what's been nagging me about her."

Kara was right. If he looked at the situation objectively, he would have done exactly what she was doing.

"All right."

She stared at him as if she didn't believe him.

"Go. If you get the wrong vibe, if you have any trepidation, alert me, I'll be there. Do you want backup?"

"No, we're going to the Fish & Brew. If I think I need a ride back, I'll call, okay?" She stepped toward him but didn't touch him. "Thank you, Matt," she said, her voice quiet. She'd lost some of her edge, but it was still simmering under her skin, he could feel it rolling off her. "I know this is an unusual situation for you, and I'm cutting you slack because of that. But I'm a cop before I'm your friend; I'm a cop before I'm your lover. Never forget that."

She turned and walked away.

27

"Thanks for reaching out to me," Marcy said after sitting down next to Kara at the bar of the Fish & Brew. "It's been a long week and it's only Wednesday."

Damon came over after serving a couple on the far end of the bar. "Usual, Marcy?" the bartender asked.

"Actually, that looks good," she said, gesturing to Kara's stout.

"Got it." He turned to the taps. "Can I get you fine lady cops anything to eat?"

"In a few," Kara said. "We're going to grab that high-top over there, if that's okay?"

"All yours," he said, putting the pint down in front of Marcy. "Is that a new blazer? Looks good."

"Not new," she said. "Just forgot I had it."

Kara pulled off her own blazer and draped it over the back of the chair at the high-top table, away from the bar where they had a little more privacy. She claimed the best seat, and Marcy sat next to her rather than across from her so she, too, could look out at the restaurant.

"Cheers," Marcy said, holding up the pint.

Kara tipped her glass to Marcy, then drank, put it down. "Long day," she said.

"John had me doing a deep dive on all known IP members."

"West End appears to be the target," Kara said, keeping her voice low. "Shit rolls downhill, sorry. For what it's worth, I had to do a shitload of paperwork this afternoon. I needed this beer."

"Who was the woman you were talking to this morning? The brunette?"

"Oh—friend of Neil Devereaux. Ryder interviewed her, about the cold case Neil was looking into. She's the sister of one of the college students."

"Have to cover all the bases," Marcy said.

"Exactly."

Rena, the cheery waitress from Monday, came over to them. Jamie was also working tonight but she had the other half of the restaurant. If it wouldn't have been awkward, Kara would have worked her way over to Jamie's section, just to see how Marcy and Jamie interacted, but that wouldn't have been natural when the restaurant was nearly full and the bar still had a few tables.

"Hi, ladies, are you ready?" asked Rena.

"I'm going to try the bacon cheeseburger tonight," Kara said.

"Good choice. Regular fries or sweet potato fries?"

"I'm old-fashioned, I'll stick to the regular."

"Same for me," Marcy said.

"Got it! Another round?"

"With the food, if you don't mind," Kara said. She was working, of sorts. She wouldn't drink more than one beer with Marcy just so she could stay on her toes. Catch anything—if there was something to catch.

When Rena left, Kara said, "Did you know about the cold case Neil was looking into?"

"About the college boys? I think everyone knew."

"Did he talk to you about it?"

"Not really. He came into the station a couple of times and talked to John—they'd become friendly. Once I was meeting with John when Neil came into his office, mentioning something about an old case file John had requested from another jurisdiction for Neil. Whatever it was, it hadn't arrived yet. When Neil left, I asked John about it; he said Neil was looking into a closed case of two college boys who drowned, and there was another suspicious drowning investigation from—I don't remember where, someplace in Washington."

"Did the file ever come in?"

"No idea. That was months ago. John would know. So what is it? IP targeting West End or something about Neil?"

"To be honest, we don't know."

"Your boss and another agent—Harris, I think his name was, the tall, dark, and handsome agent? They came in and gave us a briefing this morning about the bomb mechanism and how each one was detonated. ATF has a team of dogs on patrol, and they're bringing in another team for the weekend. But then I heard that West End was going to shut down their weekend charters. It's awful for them—this is one of their biggest weeks of the year—but I understand: for safety reasons, it's wise."

"What's your gut say?" Kara asked Marcy.

"Mine?"

"That's what I asked. You've been a cop for a while, you've lived here a year, you probably have an opinion."

"No one has asked me before."

"I am."

"Well," she said, taking a sip of her beer. A small sip, and Kara didn't think that she really liked it. "After listening to Agent Costa and Agent Harris today, I came away with the impression there didn't seem to be a reason for the second bomb, you know? So I started thinking, well, if someone at IP was involved, why would they kill all those people? Murder sure doesn't help their cause. But I don't understand why people do what they do sometimes. I arrested a perp once, a burglar. Typical, right? Go in, steal shit when the owners were out, leave. But he had this odd MO. Every house he robbed he urinated on the wall. Who does that? Nice thing, though, was that we could trace his DNA to a total of nineteen burglaries."

"Some people are just fucked in the head."

"When I heard that your team was looking into Neil's cold-case obsession, I thought that sounded a lot more interesting, I don't know, motive? But most criminals don't have interesting motives. It's boring, like greed or my wife cheated."

"Can I tell you something? It's part of the investigation, but we're keeping it under wraps for a while."

"I'm all ears."

"We're definitely leaning to Neil being the target." She carefully watched Marcy's reaction. "We think the second bombing was a distraction to refocus our investigation onto IP."

The cop nodded, sipped. "That makes sense. More sense, to be honest, than IP or anyone in that group."

"That's the conclusion we came to, but we still have to cover all our bases. Prove or disprove every theory."

"How can I help?"

"Well, one thing I need to do is find out who lives here only in the summer."

"Why?"

"The shrink has a logical reason, but I don't really want to talk about it here—you never know who's listening. Meet for a run again tomorrow? Then if you can help or give me a direction to get the information, we can go from there."

"Of course. Anything to help. It shouldn't be too difficult—at least, I can pull resident IDs from the county, that would give us a start. And we have a list of rentals, Airbnbs, things like that. *We* don't—I mean, I should say, I know how to get it through the tourism bureau."

"That would be awesome."

Rena came back with their food and another stout for Kara. "You want something else?" she asked Marcy, nodding toward her barely touched beer.

"Naw, I'm just tired, not feeling much like drinking."

"Let me know if you need anything else." Rena walked away.

They ate, chatting about small-town living and the differences patrolling in Friday Harbor versus big cities. Marcy didn't share much about herself, and Kara didn't push. She wanted to know more, but didn't want Marcy to become suspicious.

When she was done eating, Kara leaned over to Marcy and said, "I trust your judgment about people in town; you're new, you don't have loyalties like everyone else. Think about it, okay? About someone you know who isn't year-round, someone your cop instincts might have you doing a double take. You know what I mean, right?"

"I do. I'll think about it tonight."

"Great. Now, I'm getting one more drink, if you don't mind."

"Go ahead, but I'm going to call it a night." She pulled out her wallet.

"Nope, my treat," Kara said. "The FBI gives us an expense account, can you believe that? I can practically eat and drink for free."

"Thanks," Marcy said with a grin. "I'll see you in the morning."

Jamie's shift ended before Rena's, so she asked Rena to take her last table. She had been uncomfortable when she spotted Marcy in the bar. She shouldn't be—she knew that whatever Cal and

Marcy once had meant nothing anymore, over years ago—but she couldn't help but feel like the cop was watching her.

She went to the back to tell Pete she was leaving, but Pete wasn't in his office.

Cal was.

She looked at him, confused, then worried. "Where's Hazel? Is she okay?"

"She's sleeping in her own bed. Like a princess. Just like her mom. Jody came over to watch her."

"Oh." Jody was their next-door neighbor, a sweet older woman who doted on Hazel. "Is something wrong?"

"No. I love you."

"I love you, too. You're kind of scaring me."

"I want to move up the wedding."

"What? Why?"

"I love you, I love Hazel, and I want to marry you. Now. On Sunday. I talked to your dad, he's already changed his schedule, so he has the time off. He'll be here Saturday and said he can't wait. I talked to Ted—he'll marry us out at sea. We'll have our closest friends there, my mom is coming in from Seattle, your dad, and Hazel. If anything, this last week has showed me that time is too short. I'm not perfect, but I will do everything I can to make you and Hazel happy."

Jamie burst into tears. She didn't know why. She loved Cal, and crying wasn't the right response, but she knew why her emotions were all in turmoil.

"What's wrong?"

"I—I'm pregnant. I found out last week and I think—that's why I was so emotional and went to my dad's after—"

"*Shh.* Don't talk about that. Don't talk about anything but *us.* And our family. I'm so happy."

"We didn't plan it! I don't know how it happened—"

"We didn't plan Hazel and she's the best thing that has ever happened to me, other than you."

She nodded as the tears rolled down her face. "I'm a mess."

"A beautiful mess." He held her face in his hands, kissed her, smiled. "When?"

"December. Around Christmas. I think it happened in April when we got a babysitter for the day and had that picnic on Henry Island."

He grinned. "That was amazing. Maybe if we have a boy, we can name him Henry."

"Oh, no. Then we'll have to tell him why!"

"I'm sure one of us has a dead relative named Henry. Only we will know the real truth. And I think it would be cute, to have Hazel and Henry. But if it's a girl, I'll be just as happy."

"You're okay with this? With another baby?"

"I'm more than okay." He put his hand on her stomach, gently squeezed.

A wave of emotion rushed through her and she wrapped her arms around him. "I love you, Caleb McKinnon. But I have a lot to do before Sunday!"

"I talked to Pete. He's giving us a wedding present: ten days paid time off."

"Really? He shouldn't—"

"Don't question it!"

Cal really had covered all the bases. The time off, the money, her dad, Ted marrying them at sea. "I need to go out to my dad's tomorrow and air out my grandmother's wedding dress. I'll see if Jody can make any adjustments real quick, but I want to wear it. I've loved that dress forever."

"It's simple and beautiful and perfect. Just like you." Cal kissed her again. "Let's go home and celebrate."

Rena was preoccupied as she finished her side work—rolling utensils with napkins, filling salt and pepper shakers, topping off the malt vinegar bottles that people here drenched their fish and chips in. She'd never liked vinegar. Give her a good tartar sauce any day—and Pete made the best, from scratch.

She needed to talk to Jamie and Cal. Maybe she should talk to the police, though that seemed a bit of a stretch.

But Jamie was so happy right now, Rena didn't want to throw a damper on it. And Rena was probably mistaken, overreacting because of the bomb and all that. And a baby! Rena was so excited and happy for her. Jamie had rushed out of Pete's office after she and Cal decided to get married *this Sunday!* And asked Rena to be her maid of honor.

Of course!

Rena loved Jamie like a sister, and she thought Cal was the best thing to happen to her. He was a good guy, and he worshipped Jamie. The best dad to Hazel.

Rena would love to have a family and a husband who adored her, but she hadn't found the right guy.

Well, she thought as she glanced at Pete restocking the bar, she *had* found the right guy, but he didn't know she existed. Well, he knew she *existed*, but he wasn't interested. She didn't think he'd actually gone on a date in the seven years since his wife died. Maybe he was waiting until his girls were grown up. Or maybe he just still loved his wife.

It was romantic and sad all at the same time.

After she was done with her side work, she left the restaurant and walked out to the parking lot behind. The bar was open another hour, but the kitchen closed at ten. She unlocked her car, tossed her purse on the front seat, and sent Jamie a text. Want to meet for breakfast in the morning? Talk about the wedding and stuff.

And stuff…or not. Damn, Rena didn't want to make a mountain out of a molehill.

Jamie responded. I'm going to my dad's in the morning. Want to come with?

Rena texted, I'm working the lunch shift, after?

Jamie: I'll be back early afternoon! See you whenever!

She added a half dozen kissing emojis, hearts, and happy faces.

Rena called Cal. His phone went to voice mail. Of course.

"Cal, it's Rena. Can you meet me tomorrow morning for coffee? Maybe after Jamie leaves… I just need to talk to you about something, I don't know if it's important, but it's just weird, and I don't want to stress Jamie out. Text me and let me know what time you can meet. And congrats—I'm happy for both of you."

She ended the call and put her keys in the ignition.

A bright light out the driver's-side window startled her, then her door opened.

Before she could even realize she was in danger, a sharp pain in her neck prevented her from screaming. Warm water rolled down her body.

Not water. Blood. You're bleeding.

Her mouth opened and closed, and Rena tried to reach for her neck, but her hands felt so heavy…

The light disappeared, turned off as suddenly as it had turned on. But in that moment between light and dark, she glimpsed a familiar face. And realized her worst fear was true.

She tried to call out for help but couldn't speak. Couldn't scream. Couldn't beg for help.

I'm dying.

THURSDAY

28

A sharp knock on Kara's door had her out of bed, reaching for her gun. She'd been in the middle of a disturbing dream, remnants still haunting her. She'd pushed her way through an explosion, bodies flying all over the place, only to find her old partner Colton lying in the middle of the street, a bullet in his head.

Then the knock.

"I'm up!" she said before she was fully awake. It was 4:00 a.m. Damn.

Through the door, Ryder said, "There's a body behind the Fish & Brew. Matt wants you and Jim with him."

"Coming. Three minutes."

She went to the bathroom and splashed cold water on her

face. She was tense and felt like she hadn't slept, even though she'd been asleep for nearly four hours.

Her hair was just long enough to put into a ponytail. She brushed water through it and tied it in back. Pulled jeans on over her panties, put on a sports bra, black T-shirt, holstered her gun, and slipped on her comfortable low-heeled boots. Stuck her knife into a slot on the inside of her left boot. It had taken her a few months to get used to walking with the knife there. Now, without it, she felt practically naked. She'd tried an ankle gun, but it was really uncomfortable, and anyone who knew where to look would spot it.

She also had a knife in her pocket, but if she were ever in a situation where she was disarmed and searched, the pocket would be the first place they'd look.

She grabbed her blazer and walked out. Matt handed her a to-go cup of coffee. "It's the waitress at the Fish & Brew."

Something shifted in Kara's mindset. Cal… Jamie… Then Matt said, "Rena Brown."

"She was working last night. She served us, was still there when I left at nine."

"She clocked out at ten thirty. She parks in a small lot behind the Fish & Brew, on the other side of the alley. It's on a slope. No parking in the lot after two a.m., and a patrol found it at three this morning. As soon as they knew they had a body, they called the sheriff, who called me. I asked him not to touch anything, and Jim is getting his forensic kit."

Jim walked in with a large black bag and a backpack over his shoulder. "I could really use the RV about now."

The Mobile Response Team was supposed to have a forensic RV with all the bells and whistles. It was ready to deploy, but this case had been sudden and getting the RV from Virginia to Washington State was problematic and expensive. They would have had to have flown it. Kara didn't think she'd ever see the famed RV in action.

"The sheriff called in the medical examiner from the mainland, but ET is two hours minimum. Because it's a crime scene, I told him not to take the body to the morgue here but wait for the ME to transport it to their facilities."

"Good. I hope nobody touched anything, but I'm not holding my breath."

"The sheriff said he secured the scene," Matt said.

Jim grunted.

Matt drove the short distance to the Fish & Brew. They arrived at the same time as Pete Dunlap. "What happened? Detective Quinn, what's going on?"

Matt stopped Pete from approaching the crime scene. "How did you hear?"

"The bakery down the street—the owner comes in at four thirty in the morning. Said there were police cars and an ambulance here. What happened?"

"We're trying to find out. Stay back."

"There's a body in the— Oh my God, that's Rena's car. Is it Rena? Is she okay? What the fuck happened!"

Matt looked like he wanted to block him, but Kara knew there was no reason not to give Pete some of the information. "Pete," she said calmly, "we just got here. The sheriff called us in. We don't know what's what yet, but Rena was positively identified, and she's deceased. We don't know any more than that, okay? Now, I promise we'll tell you what we can when we can, but for now, let us work."

"She was murdered. Otherwise, you wouldn't be here."

She couldn't argue with the truth. "Why don't you go into your restaurant and brew some coffee? You need it, I need it, the deputies would appreciate it."

"Oh. Of course, yeah, I'll do that."

He turned and strode across the alley into the rear entrance of the Fish & Brew.

Matt caught Kara's eye and nodded. He was about to say

something to her, but Sheriff John Rasmussen approached. "Glad you're here. It's awful."

Jim said, "Everyone away, I need to process the scene. Did anyone touch the body?"

John shook his head. "A rookie found her. Puked in the bushes. Blood everywhere. When he called it in originally, he said a woman was sleeping in her car, might be intoxicated, he was going to approach. Then he shined the light in and saw that she was dead. Swears he didn't touch her or the door."

Jim said, "I need a couple big lights if you can get them. Keep people twenty feet away from the vehicle. And I need one guy who can hold his stomach to help me process the scene."

Jim led the way; Matt and Kara walked behind him. Jim shined his light into the vehicle.

Rena was in the driver's seat. She had been killed where she sat. Her head tipped to the left, and blood covered her neck and chest. At first glance, a novice might think she'd been stabbed to death, but the cut in her neck was so deep it was clear she'd had her throat slit while sitting behind the wheel.

"Get back," Jim said. Matt and Kara each took two steps away and let Jim work. He was methodical and focused. He recorded everything he saw, took pictures, and mumbled to himself.

"Scene outside the car compromised," he said into his recorder. He took close-up pictures of Rena's neck, the car, the ground, took out a tape measure and measured blood spatter on the gravel. Collected samples.

The sheriff approached. "ME just left the mainland. It'll take an hour on the ferry—they have the medical van with them, can transport the body. What the hell happened?"

"Her throat was slit," Matt said.

Jim joined them, removing his plastic gloves. "I need to look at the photos and enlarge a few things, but I can give you the basics. The keys were in the ignition, off. The door was open when she was killed. I thought at first the killer may have been in the back seat, reached around, but the evidence doesn't support that. The killer is likely left-hand dominant. Of course, I need to wait for the autopsy—which I'll assist with—but my guess is that Rena died quickly, of rapid blood loss."

"Are you suggesting she knew her killer?" Matt asked.

"I can't make that determination. The doors were unlocked. The killer likely closed the door after he killed her, to avoid detection or the dome light staying on and alerting someone to the crime scene. There was some indication that the killer walked east, but either got in a car and drove off or put the knife in a pocket or bag. There would have been blood on the killer, especially the hand and sleeve. I printed the door—there was blood on the outside finish, but there were no prints in the blood, so likely the killer wore gloves. I can't give accurate time of death, but full rigor hasn't set in; based on the outside temperature, body temperature, and elasticity of her skin, I can give you a ballpark between ten o'clock and midnight."

"Weapon?"

"None I could see, but we'll need to fully process the scene. It could be inside the vehicle, in the bushes, a dumpster."

Jim handed Matt a phone sealed in a plastic bag. "This was in Rena's purse. She had a text on it that hadn't been read from Cal McKinnon. I didn't unlock her phone."

"May I?" Matt motioned toward the victim.

"I'll do it." Jim was already in his gear. He brought the phone over to Rena and placed her thumb on it, then returned the unlocked phone to Matt.

He read the text.

I'm working at six, but I can take a break around nine—is that too late? Meet at WEC?

He saw that Rena had a one-minute conversation with Cal McKinnon last night at 10:47. Prior to that, she'd exchanged texts with Jamie Finch. He read them. "They were friends?" He scrolled through. She had a few texts between her and Cal, mostly about things like Jamie's birthday, babysitting Hazel. There were hundreds—maybe thousands—of texts between Rena and Jamie. Sharing articles, recipes, pictures, memes, chatting about customers at work. They were close.

He put the phone back in the bag and handed it to Jim. "Kara, find out exactly when Rena clocked out last night. Anything else you can from Pete. Get into her locker if she has one. Roommates, boyfriend, anything you can learn. Then talk to Cal, find out what they talked about last night, if he knows anything. Same questions. No defensive wounds. If the door was open, maybe someone walked her to her car. Or someone she recognized approached. Otherwise, why would she open the door?"

"The car was unlocked. Maybe the killer opened it," Kara said. "Jim, her purse and wallet and everything is there, right?"

"Yes, doesn't appear that anything's missing."

"This has to be a coincidence, right?" John said. "How can this connect to the bombings?"

"Rena could have overheard something at the restaurant. Or witnessed something. We don't know. Or, as you say, it could be completely unrelated. What's the crime rate on the island, Sheriff?"

"You mean homicide? We haven't had any this year, before the bombing. Last year there were two. One domestic, one drug related. We don't get violent crime like this. Property crimes, drugs, robberies? Yeah. But nothing like this. Eleven people dead…that's more than the last four years combined." He glanced behind him at the Fish & Brew.

Kara said to Matt, "I'm going to fill Pete in, okay? Anything you want me to hold back?"

"Just specific forensic details—we'll keep that in-house. But see what you can get out of him. John, I need you to have your deputies canvass the area—potential witnesses, security cameras, whatever you can get, we need. Jim, I assume you're going with the ME?"

"Yes. We'll take everything back to the mainland to process, including having her vehicle towed."

"Send Catherine the photos; she can start working up a profile. Kara, you can have the car when you're done with Dunlap." He tossed her the keys. "John, can I get a ride with you back to the station?"

Kara found Pete standing behind the bar in his restaurant. He turned to her, his eyes red but dry.

"How do you like your coffee?" he asked.

"Black. Thanks."

"I don't know a lot of women who drink black coffee."

She shrugged as he poured, put a mug in front of her. "I got used to it as a rookie."

He stood in front of her with his own coffee, put his forearms on the bar. "I can't get the picture of Rena out of my head."

"I'm sorry for your loss," she said. It sounded stupid to her, as it always did. *Loss* made death sound like a game, or the victim a possession. She wanted to give more, say more, but what the hell could she say?

Nothing would erase the image of Rena Brown soaked in blood, her lifeless eyes, her unnecessary death.

Kara could compartmentalize because she was a cop. She'd seen the dead before. Some deaths were harder than others, but she could deal. What about a civilian? Someone who had never faced such violence?

"You need to talk to me," Pete said after a minute. "Talk. Ask. Anything I can do to help."

"Were you here when Rena left last night?"

He nodded. "I close every night. It's my restaurant, my business. In the winter I'm only open Friday and weekends, so I figure I can put in the time in the summer. But..."

"But?" she pushed when he didn't continue.

"My daughter and I have been arguing. I found out that she was seeing someone behind my back, a kid I don't approve of. And she snuck out of the house to see him, lied to me... I grounded her, but it just— You don't have kids, do you?"

"No."

"I was so angry I didn't listen to her. I wanted to listen but knew she wouldn't say anything to me. It was times like this I need Wendy. I talked to Rena about it at the beginning of her shift, then left to talk things out with Ashley. I don't want to lose my daughter over a boy, but I can't accept lying and sneaking out. I think she understands that now. And I owe that to Rena."

"What time did you return here?"

"After nine. Maybe nine thirty. Jamie had already left, Rena was still here. We close the kitchen at ten in the summer, and usually the bartender can handle the bar himself."

"When did Rena leave?"

"She clocked out at ten thirty. Said goodbye. She was... preoccupied, I think."

"You think?"

"She's usually chatty. She wasn't last night."

"Okay. When did Damon leave?"

"Damon?"

"I was here last night. He was working when I had a beer."

"Right—yeah—last call was at eleven or so, we locked the door at eleven thirty. He called an Uber for a regular who had too much, waited until he left. I left about forty minutes after him. I should have seen her."

"Why?"

"I usually park in the lot. I only live a mile from here, I walk a lot, but we have one car and after dinner with the girls I drive back. But Whitney went with friends to community theater last night, so I said she could have the car. So I just walked down the alley and didn't even know Rena was...was there."

"You couldn't have saved her."

"How do you know?"

"She died quickly."

He didn't say anything, just stared at his coffee.

Kara looked at the timeline that she'd written in her notepad. Rena left at about the same time that she called Jamie Finch.

"You said that Rena was preoccupied. Do you know why?"

"No—but I thought it was about Jamie."

"Why Jamie? They were friends?"

"Good friends. She was preoccupied, but she was also happy. Cal and Jamie decided to move up their wedding to Sunday, and Rena was thrilled. Jamie also announced she's pregnant—I gave her the next ten days off, paid, for the wedding and some time with Cal, after everything that's been going on."

"In the middle of your biggest season?"

"You know, it doesn't matter. Really. I was married for sixteen years. I would give anything to have an extra week with my wife before she died. Anything. So I'm happy to give Jamie and Cal this time. But now... Jamie is going to be devastated." His voice cracked and he looked down at his half-empty mug. "I can't open today."

"Was Rena friends with Cal as well?"

"Sure. Why?"

"The last call she made was to Cal."

"Probably about the wedding. Maybe, I guess, I don't know. They were all friendly, but Jamie and Rena were two peas. And anytime Cal and Jamie wanted some alone time, Rena would watch Hazel. She loved that kid."

"So it wouldn't be odd for Rena and Cal to meet for coffee or lunch, even without Jamie."

"No."

"Did Rena have any problems with anyone who worked here?"

"No."

"What about customers? Anyone who was flirty or thought she gave them bad service?"

"Really?"

"You know what I mean."

"Everyone loved Rena. She was a sweet girl."

"Ex-boyfriend?"

"No. I mean, she probably had one somewhere, but she never talked about it. She relocated here after high school. She used to come here for vacations with her family, she said, and she loved the town, wanted to live here. Odd for a young pretty girl like her, but I understand. I have no intention of leaving the island. When it's in your blood, it's there to stay. If there was anyone, a guy or girl, Jamie would know. But truly, Rena was just a happy person all around."

"Did she park in the same place every night?"

"The lot on the other side of the alley? Yes. It's free, it's safe." He grimaced. "Or it used to be safe. Crime is low here, Kara. Really low. I can't believe what's happened this last week."

"Who was working last night? I was here, but I don't know everyone."

"I'll get you a list. It's a small operation, I just need to double-check who was on in the kitchen."

"I need when they clocked in, when they clocked out. Thank you, Pete. We're going to find out who killed Rena, I promise."

Cal was working at West End, waxing boats and doing light maintenance. Kara found him at the end of the pier.

"Agent Quinn," he said.

"Detective."

He looked at her oddly, but she didn't elaborate. "I need a few minutes of your time. Is there a place we can sit?"

"Jamie—oh, God, is she okay?"

"I'm not here about Jamie."

"Something happened. Just tell me."

So she did. She watched his face carefully. He looked like he didn't believe her, then his face fell. "Oh, God. Rena."

"She called you last night. What did you talk about?"

"She left a message on my cell phone. We were going to meet for coffee at nine."

"Did she tell you that?"

"Yes—no. Actually. She asked to meet, and I texted her, but she didn't confirm. I didn't think twice about it—I should have. I should have called her back. Talked to her."

"Do you still have the message?"

"Yeah, I think so." He pulled out his phone, unlocked it, and handed it to her.

She played the message. Then she played it again and recorded it on her phone.

Rena had something to tell Cal. What was it?

"Did she sound odd to you on the message?"

"I didn't listen—I just read the transcription and texted her back. I thought she might want to talk about the wedding or the baby—Jamie's pregnant. Due late December. We just found out. Oh, God, this is going to hurt so much... Rena and Jamie are close. How do I tell her?"

"Where's Jamie now?"

"At her dad's. She left early to pick up some things, including her grandmother's wedding dress. We're getting married on Sunday... But now, I don't know. I don't know if Jamie... I need to tell her. But not over the phone. Is she going to hear about it on the news? Because I can drive out there right now and tell her."

"The information won't be released by us until Rena's next of kin is notified, but this is a small town. Pete knows, the sheriff's office, ambulance, medical—I can't say she won't hear about it."

"She said she'd be back by noon—I'll call and see if she can come home sooner. I just don't want her to worry—she's pregnant."

So Kara had heard. Several times.

She asked the same questions she asked Pete. Ex-boyfriends, anyone showing undue interest.

"Rena didn't date much. I don't even know if she had someone when she lived in Seattle, but she's always happy. She, um, had a crush on Pete. I don't think he knew, he doesn't date. He told Neil and me once over beers that Wendy was the love of his life. He and Neil used to talk a lot about their wives, they both missed them a lot. And Pete's devoted to his daughters."

That pretty much confirmed what Pete said about Rena. She was a nice girl, happy, no trouble, no violent exes. Who would kill her?

Cal looked around at the West End pier. "Ted is doing everything to keep people safe. More security. He put in new cameras. Even the protesters are backing off this week, finally. But he's shutting down the charters at least for the weekend, and that's going to hurt, a lot."

"I don't expect that to last," Kara said.

"Excuse me?"

She probably shouldn't have said anything. "IP is planning something for Saturday. At least, that's what I heard." She didn't need to go into details about how she went to their meeting on Monday. "Maybe they're going to back off because West End is shutting down operations, but I wouldn't count on it."

"Does Ted know?"

Kara didn't know what Matt had told him. "I don't know. It's not a secret."

"Did they do this? IP? The bombs, killing Rena? Why would they kill Rena?"

Kara didn't think so, but no one knew for certain. "Doubtful, but we're looking at all possibilities. Don't spread rumors, okay? And keep your wits about you, Cal. I don't know what's going on here, but we will find out."

★ ★ ★

Kara looked at her phone and saw that Marcy Anderson had been trying to call her for the last thirty minutes. Kara called her back.

"You got my text about canceling the run?"

"Yes. I heard about Rena. But that's not why I need to talk to you."

"What happened?"

"I'm at the station, but don't want to talk about it here. Coffee? I could use it."

"Okay, that little place across from the sheriff's station, I'll be there in ten minutes."

She called Matt. "Marcy wants to talk to me, I'm having coffee with her."

"In the middle of this investigation?"

"I think she has something important to say. I'll call you right after."

"You're doing this alone?"

"Matt—I'll call you when I find out what's going on. If you don't hear from me in an hour, then you can start worrying."

"I'm in the conference room with Ryder and Catherine. We're digging into Damon Avila's life. We don't have enough for a warrant, but since he and Rena worked together, that's one more connection."

"Going from staging accidents to bombings to cold-blooded slicing a throat?"

"Murder is violent, and killers escalate."

She agreed in principle, but this was violent versus gory. Still…she added, "Because they worked together, maybe she suspected something. Overheard a conversation, or caught him in a lie… It's definitely possible."

"I think a friendly conversation might work. Catherine and I are talking it through now. But I don't want to tip our hand."

"I'll call you when I'm done with Marcy." She ended the call as she parked in the sheriff's lot, then walked across to the coffeehouse. It was a small place but set up with several sitting areas for people to chat. Marcy sat in the corner by the window. Kara sat across from her.

"Coffee?" Marcy motioned to the to-go cup in front of her. "Black, right?"

"Thanks," Kara said, though she wouldn't drink it. The chances that Marcy would poison her were slim to none, but she never drank what she didn't obtain herself. "You look like you haven't slept all night," said Kara.

"Barely. When I got home last night, I watched television to unwind and dozed off. The curse of living alone. I woke up at midnight and had this really uneasy feeling that I knew something important. So I cleaned my whole apartment—I know, that's weird, but when I'm thinking through problems, I clean. Then it came to me.

"I was at the gym working out with Damon. It was a Sunday morning last summer—a week or two before he went back to school, so probably late July, early August. I'd started working for SJSD in May, and Damon was the first person I really got to know outside of work, because of the gym. Damon was angry about something, I could tell by how he was working out and dropping the weights. I asked. He wouldn't talk about it, but then asked me to go to brunch. We had mimosas—Damon started talking about past mistakes biting him in the ass. I asked what he was talking about. He said he couldn't tell me, I'm a cop, and rambled about statute of limitations, but it didn't make sense. Then he said he didn't want anything to complicate our friendship. I said I understood, though the whole conversation seemed weird. Like he wanted to ask my opinion on something, but because I was a cop, he couldn't."

"He could have pulled the standard 'I'm asking for a friend' plausible deniability."

"Yeah, you're right, I didn't think about that. Anyway, the next time I saw him at the Fish & Brew, he was back to his old self. He was gone shortly after that, until Memorial Day weekend. I honestly forgot about the conversation until last night.

"Then this summer, I was at the Fish & Brew one day for lunch before my shift and Neil was there. Damon acted strange. Nothing I could pinpoint, but when he came over to give me the check, I asked him about it. He said Neil was a jerk and should just let sleeping dogs lie. I should have remembered that before now."

"When was this?"

"Beginning of the summer. Four, five weeks ago."

Though Kara suspected she had the answer, she asked, "Where does he teach? You said he taught high school the other day. Math, right?"

"Yes. Bellingham High."

Kara went back to the station, closed the door of the conference room, and told Matt, Catherine, and Ryder what Marcy had told her.

"It fits," Catherine said. "It fits really well. Ryder just talked to the retired campus security chief from U of W."

Ryder said, "Nearly fourteen years ago, in the fall, Damon Avila had been a star football player. He was expecting to go high in the draft but a weather-related accident early on New Year's Day—Brian Stevens was driving—ended his football career. The incident was ruled accidental. The roads were a mess, icy, and Avila was speeding—not above the speed limit, but above what was safe for the conditions. His left leg was shattered. The security chief told Neil this earlier this year—and sent him emails with photos. The reason Avila's name wasn't in the Stevens report was that two different jurisdictions and agencies responded. They referenced each case number, but not the names of the individuals involved. Stevens was not cited, he submitted to a drug and alcohol test, and was clean. He was uninjured. Jason Mott was in the car with him, had a broken wrist."

"Motive," Kara said. "But not enough for a warrant."

"Missy Douglas," Catherine said. "She had dated Avila for nearly two years in college. She broke up with him after that accident. Her fiancé didn't know much about her college years, but her sister did, and I spoke with her this morning. Avila became despondent after the accident, he changed, according to Missy's sister. He accused her of breaking up with him because he was broken. But she had broken up with him because he was verbally abusive and full of self-pity."

"Waiting eight years to kill her? That seems far-fetched," Kara said. "I'm playing devil's advocate here, because Avila looks good for this, but the timing. Why wait eight years?"

"The weekend before Missy went camping, she had publicly announced that she was getting married," Catherine said. "It was all over social media. Her fiancé was a former professional football player. He had played for several years, had health issues, retired early and was coaching college football. Matt tells me his stats were impressive for the time he played. Remember: Damon Avila was a star football player on the verge of being drafted, which is like winning the lottery. Missy's fiancé had done what Avila wanted to do before the accident and he was also marrying the woman Avila had once loved."

Catherine looked down at her phone. "Dammit, but I'm not surprised—Tony says we need more."

"What about the Bellingham connection?" Matt said. "The missing teacher was promoted into a position over Avila at the high school where Avila worked."

"When Travers disappeared, Avila didn't get the job—they hired someone else from the outside to fill it," Catherine said. "And that person is still alive."

"And what about Billy Clark being a student there?" Kara pushed. "Avila must have known Clark."

"Circumstantial," Catherine said. "And Clark's accident is still being called an accident, even though Neil—according to the sheriff's department on the mainland—had been asking them to reopen the investigation, as had the victim's father. One of the problems is that the car accident was in early spring during a rainstorm and any potential evidence was gone before the accident was even discovered."

"I think," Matt said, "we might be able to rattle him. What Officer Anderson gave us is hearsay, but coming from a cop, I put a bit more weight on it. A judge or jury, however, may not. Kara, do you think you can talk to Pete Dunlap? It would be walking a tightrope—we lean too much one side or the other, we either get nothing useful or he slams the door in our face. We need everything to line up."

Catherine said, "We need solid evidence that puts Avila in the same area as one of these deaths. Ryder is already working on that—every public piece of information out there. Remember, if we're right, Neil figured it out as well but felt that there was not enough evidence to turn over. Believing a person is guilty and proving a person is guilty are different. I think Neil found circumstantial evidence related to the three later murders that he was able to connect to Avila, but he couldn't prove Avila killed anyone."

"We need one firm fact," Matt said, "then we have cause to talk to him. We may even be able to get a limited search warrant."

Michael Harris had walked in during the middle of the conversation, and now said, "We may have something. ATF just heard back from the largest construction company in Washington State—they audited their records when they received the ATF order on Saturday, and they are missing three blocks of C-4. It wasn't discovered earlier because the C-4 was ordered for a demolition project that wasn't taking place for another week, and it had been delivered three weeks ago. It was inventoried and stored upon delivery. The good news is that the facility—in Bellingham—is very secure. They are sending all their security footage to the ATF and we should know before the end of today exactly when the facility was breached and who breached it."

"If it's secure, how would someone get in?"

"They're sending over a list of all staff and anyone else with access. This kind of theft is almost always an inside job," Michael added.

"It's all a matter of who you know," Kara mumbled.

"We get one hint that Avila knows anyone on that list," Matt said, "I can get a warrant." He looked at Kara. "Do you think you can work Pete Dunlap?"

"Yes. And he wants to be kept in the loop, so I can go over and tell him…well, I'll tell him we've talked to Rena's family, if he wants to send a message to staff? Then parlay that into a more in-depth conversation. I won't tip our hand, so I might not get anything."

"And you have no reason to think that he would help his brother-in-law."

"No. Pete's protective of his family, but he would never do anything to jeopardize his daughters—and aiding and abetting a killer? I don't see it. Even if it's his sainted wife's brother."

29

Pete tightly hugged his daughters. Telling them that Rena was dead had been one of the hardest things that he had ever done. When Wendy died, that was hard, but they had known she was sick and had time to prepare—though how could you really prepare for the death of your wife or your mother?

Whitney's tears flowed freely. She had always been able to express her emotions—the joy or sorrow—fully. Ashley looked like she was still in shock. But she hugged her dad. "I'm so sorry, Dad."

"The FBI is investigating," he said.

"Why? Is this connected to the bombings?"

Ashley, always thinking two steps ahead.

"We don't know, but they're here, maybe they have jurisdiction." But what Ashley said added to Pete's fear that the bomber was someone close to him. Maybe someone who came into the Fish & Brew. Maybe Rena had overheard someone talking and that's why she'd been killed. He was glad he'd shut down today. He wanted to keep his family far from this violence.

"I was thinking," he said, "that we should take the boat out today, maybe head out to Massacre Bay and swim around Skull Rock like we used to do. Have a picnic. Talk about Rena and anything else you want."

Whitney wrapped her long arms around him. "Daddy, that's a great idea! I'll go pack food."

She jumped up and left him with Ashley.

He was glad of the chance to speak to Ashley alone. "I meant everything I said the other day," he began.

"I know."

"I will never tolerate lies, directly or by omission. But I know why you felt you had to. And I probably judged Bobby harshly because of his brother's actions, and that was wrong of me. I'd like you to invite Bobby to join us today. He deserves to be judged on his own merits, not his brother."

Her eyes widened. "Really? You mean it?"

"Ashley, you are so much like your mother. Your heart is big, your compassion is endless. You are also a good judge of character. If you love this boy, there's a reason. I want to see what you see in him."

"Oh, Daddy." Now the tears came, and she hugged him. "Thank you."

"Can you go pick up your uncle? I invited him, too. I don't want him to be alone today."

"Of course. I'll get him, and then Bobby, if that's okay?"

He nodded, and she ran out.

He didn't know if he was doing the right thing but it felt right, and that was all he had to go on.

He looked over at the wall where a photo of him, Wendy, and the girls had been enlarged and framed. It had been taken a year before her cancer diagnosis. Ashley had been nine, Whitney eight. The girls hated it because they were all limbs and awkwardness, but it was Pete's favorite picture because of the smiles on his girls' faces.

"Thank you, Wendy," he said, believing deep in his heart that his wife had something to do with the words he found today.

30

Kara found Pete Dunlap's house quiet. No one answered the door, and his vehicle wasn't in the carport. She drove over to the high school and learned from the principal that Pete had called in and said he was taking the girls out sailing. The principal had heard about Rena Brown's murder and had questions for her, but Kara managed to quickly end the conversation.

She drove past Damon Avila's house. She couldn't tell if he was home—there was a small garage, but the door was closed. She decided against knocking because he was a potential suspect, and she didn't want to get in a conversation with him right then. She then drove by the Fish & Brew; a sign on the door said they were closed for the day and would reopen tomorrow at 11:00 a.m. Finally, she called the harbormaster's office as she headed back to the station and asked if the Dunlap family had taken out their sailboat, and if so, who was with them. The receptionist was happy to help the FBI and informed Kara that at nine thirty that morning, Pete Dunlap had taken out his family—which included his brother-in-law, Damon—and Bobby Martin.

"Did they file a boat plan?" she asked.

"Excuse me?"

"You know, like a flight plan for airplanes." Kara had no idea.

"Oh, no. Sorry. We don't require anything like that. But I did hear the girls talking about swimming around Skull Rock."

"Which is where?"

"Massacre Bay, near Orcas Island."

Hopefully, the name wasn't a harbinger of what was to come.

Kara reported back to Matt what she'd learned.

"This is good," he said.

"If Avila is a killer, he's out with three teenagers right now," Kara said. "I don't see the good."

"We're close on getting a search warrant. Having Avila out of the picture for a few hours makes it less dicey to execute."

"What happened in the hour I was gone?"

"Michael and ATF have been going through the employee records and video surveillance of the construction company C-4 theft. One of Avila's former students works security for the company—and he was working all three nights of the three-day window the C-4 went missing."

"That seems weak."

"The kid asked for two weeks off on Monday and we don't know where he is. His mother said he and his best friend went camping in Canada, that they got a good deal. She didn't know what that meant, but she was surprised that he just told his employer he was leaving for two weeks without notice. We confirmed that he was issued a camping permit for fourteen days in Yoho National Park. No cell reception, wherever he is."

"Do you think he's going to disappear in Canada?"

"It's possible. His mother seemed surprised by the questions, and his employer says he's been an outstanding employee until he just said he was taking off two weeks, no notice. The AUSA thinks this might be enough for a warrant but is working on how to word it for the judge."

"Are we searching the kid's house?"

"In progress. So far, nothing, but they're being cautious in case there are bomb-making materials or anything potentially dangerous."

"So what you're thinking," Kara clarified, "is that Avila's former student helped steal the C-4."

"It's the most logical answer. Either way, we need to talk to him. Maybe he didn't know what Avila was going to do with it. Then he heard about the explosion and panicked, went to Canada. We'll find him. Canadian authorities have been alerted, and we've flagged his passport. He'll be allowed back in the country, but we'll be waiting for him."

"Okay. And Avila?"

"Just waiting for the warrant. We'll search his house, and if we find anything, we'll get an arrest warrant. This may be the break we've been waiting for."

Kara was worried about the Dunlaps, and said as much to Matt. "We need to keep this under wraps. If Avila suspects anything, he has four hostages right now."

"I briefed Sheriff Rasmussen and he's keeping the intel limited to just our team—plus Deputies Anderson and Redfield, who's back on duty today."

She frowned.

"I know you have concerns about Marcy, but those seem to be personal—her potential abuse of power related to her ex-boyfriend."

Kara still had a nagging feeling that she was missing something, but she didn't know what and couldn't articulate it.

"You're right," she said.

"We'll pass on your concerns to the sheriff when we're done with Avila."

Michael returned to the conference room. "I just sent the information to the AUSA, but we finished going over the ferry records. Avila went to the mainland the Monday before the *Water Lily* explosion, on the last ferry out, with his vehicle. He returned Tuesday on the noon ferry. Early Tuesday morning, there's a glitch on the construction site security tape that I suspect tells us when the C-4 was stolen."

"What kind of glitch?" Matt asked. "Why didn't they notice earlier?"

"The thief wore a hoodie with a reflective material that essentially made the camera blind. We can see that someone was there, but have no visual of that person—face, or even body type."

"Can I see it?"

Michael pulled out his phone and Matt and Kara both leaned in to watch the clip.

It was tagged 3:13 a.m. last Tuesday morning. As they watched, a bright blur came onto the screen and approached the door. The blur stayed there for ten seconds before slipping inside. Less than ninety seconds later, the blur reemerged and left the way he came.

"Two minutes, in and out," Matt said. "Impressive."

"He didn't have a key is my guess," Michael said. "The lock is digital—either a code or a passkey. He was there too long for either, but the company said that the door was accessed with an unassigned code at the same time this recording was made. They aren't alerted when that happens."

"What does unassigned code mean?" Kara asked.

"It's a code the device recognizes but it wasn't attached to an employee. They don't know how that happened and are working with the security company to prevent it in the future."

"Avila is a math teacher," Kara said. "It could be he hacked in or something. That is way over my skill set. I can pick almost any lock, but I can't break into electronics."

"I'm going to push the AUSA. I'll get a warrant. Michael, you and Kara will take the two deputies to search Avila's house. Ryder, you good to join them?"

"Yes, sir."

"Give me ten minutes."

Kara left the conference room to find Marcy. She ran into Deputy Redfield. "Glad you're feeling better."

"I still can't believe they kept me in the hospital. Ridiculous. I'm good. I heard you need me? A warrant search?"

"Yes. Where's Anderson? We could use both of you."

"She left sick," he said. "Maybe thirty minutes ago? She wanted to stay, but after the virus, we have pretty strict protocols, and she had a low-grade fever, so the sergeant sent her packing. She's out for twenty-four hours, minimum. I can tag someone else. Sheriff said anything you need, you get."

"We have enough people. No one is going to be home, so we're not expecting trouble. Ten minutes, meet in the parking lot and we'll give you the briefing."

She walked away, skeptical.

Kara was naturally a suspicious person, and she used to fake fevers when she didn't want to go to school. Easy enough to do. That didn't mean that Marcy did it. And maybe she wasn't sick but didn't want to be around when her friend Damon Avila was brought in for questioning on multiple homicides. Guilt for helping turn him in? Maybe.

She texted Marcy.

Tom told me you're sick. Let me know if I can bring you anything like chicken soup. I can't cook, but I'm happy to get takeout.

A minute later, Marcy responded.

Thanks, but sleep is all I need. Talk to you tomorrow.

Matt came through and the AUSA sent over an electronic warrant. It was limited—they were looking for bomb-making material or C-4, any computers or disks, and any documentation that could be used to make bombs or maps, or evidence of confirmed or potential targets. As soon as they had it, Kara, Michael, Ryder, and Redfield headed over to Damon Avila's house. The deputy stayed outside to make sure no one entered without authorization. Ryder was searching the detached garage and Michael started in the main bedroom of the small two-bedroom house, then would move to the second bedroom. Kara had Avila's small home office, right off the living room. It might have been a formal dining room at one time.

She slipped on gloves and looked through every drawer and cabinet. Though it was a limited warrant, they were allowed to take his computer, which she had already handed off to Ryder to tag and log into evidence. They could access it to check for bomb-making instructions, but she didn't want to do that here in case it was password protected. Ryder could handle that at headquarters.

There was nothing incriminating in his desk. He very well could have taken everything with him, dumping it in a weighted box in the ocean. Kara would have.

Well, no, she would have burned everything and then doused the ash with chemicals, in case something didn't burn completely.

No sign of destruction in the office. No recent fire in the living room fireplace. No smoldering ashes in the barbecue pit. Waterlogged paper was just as good, she figured.

She looked around a second time. Maybe he thought he would get away with it. Maybe he still would. They had nothing to connect him to the five cold-case homicides, but they were specifically looking for something that linked him to the bombings: explosive material or any material that could have been used in the making of the two recovered bombs.

They could also look for journals, writings, or documents that might connect to how to make a bomb. Plans or maps or anything to connect him to the destruction.

If he was hiding evidence here, where would he hide it?

Remember, Ryder thinks that there are missing files from Neil's house. What would he have done with them if he hadn't destroyed them?

If, if, if…

Because she would have destroyed them.

Think like a psychopath.

That was Catherine Jones's job. Kara didn't think like psychopaths. She didn't know why people did the shit they did. She didn't know why her parents liked to con people. She didn't know why criminals trafficked in people. (Greed? Profit? Control? Who the fuck cared *why*?) She didn't know why Damon Avila killed those boys thirteen years ago—because icy roads caused Brian Stevens to swerve out of control? They hadn't caused Avila's accident on purpose! Revenge…yeah, she understood revenge, but this was twisted. It had not been their fault. And what about Avila's girlfriend? Did he kill her because she fell in love with someone else *years* after they broke up? Shit, if every guy Kara walked away from had wanted to kill her, she'd be dead a dozen times over. But it didn't even matter why Missy Douglas had left him. She did, she had every right to, and for years Damon didn't do shit about it…until Missy found a guy she loved, and she was happy. A guy that Damon was jealous of because he had accomplished what had been stolen from Damon, at least in his twisted, petty little mind. He couldn't stand to see his ex-girlfriend happy. That was it. And the fact that Missy was happy twisted him up so much inside that he went out of his way to kill her *eight years* after she broke it off with him.

Perhaps he'd let these slights fester for years. They built up. He must have been watching Missy, following her on occasion. They may have had mutual friends, might have seen each other over the course of the years…and then he pounced when she was at the peak of happiness.

He justified it to himself, she was pretty sure. Most criminals did. Most killers could talk themselves into anything. So did he destroy the evidence? Or hide it?

Kara thought she understood him, at least on the surface, but she still couldn't figure out what he would do with the evidence. At Neil's house, someone had left the box with files related to Mott and Stevens: a cold case, the bodies were found. But Neil was investigating three other murders, and no information about those could be found in his house. Logically, the killer had taken them. Maybe because *that's* where the evidence was. *Those cases* were the connection to Damon Avila.

She looked around. The place wasn't large. They knew from their investigation—short as it was since they'd only ID'd him this morning—that his brother-in-law, Pete Dunlap, owned this house and Damon lived here rent-free every summer. Nice gig if you could get it…but they were family.

It was a clean, tidy place with functional, generic furniture. Everything had been updated, and the only room that Damon really seemed to use was one of the two bedrooms, and this small den off the living room. If he planned on keeping the evidence, he'd want to be able to grab it quickly, but it wouldn't be accidentally found by his family.

She turned around in a slow circle, looking at the walls. A safe maybe? She checked behind the two landscape pictures hanging above the desk. Nope. The walls were panels…and then she saw it.

One panel had a slightly wider gap than the others. She had seen one of these doors before—her grandma Em had them in the basement. Push and they pop open.

She pushed.

It opened.

It was a narrow closet. Hanging were a couple of jackets; on the shelf above was an assortment of junk. On the floor was a lidless box.

Kara was already wearing gloves, so she stepped forward. Looked at what was inside the box, then smiled.

This was it. This was what they needed to nail Damon Avila: Neil's notes, files, and documents.

She called out, "Michael, I found the smoking gun!"

She squatted, picked up the box, stood. It was on the heavy side, so she adjusted it in her arms as she turned around.

That's when she heard a faint click. Not so much a click, but a piece of metal sliding.

She froze.

"Kara, you need help?" Michael walked into the room. "What's wrong?"

She must have looked as terrified as she felt.

"This box I just picked up is rigged."

"Don't move."

She couldn't if she wanted to.

"I'm going to get you out of this, Kara."

"I'm holding you to that," she said. "Or I'm fucking going to haunt you."

Michael walked away, leaving her there. Maybe he knew this was a lost cause. It was only a matter of time before she went boom, and he didn't want to be caught in the fireworks.

If she could move, she'd call her grandma and tell her she loved her. She called her every Sunday, or almost...but had missed this week. How could she do that? How could she forget to call her grandma, the only person on the planet who genuinely, unconditionally, loved her?

She'd been a loner for so long, even when she wasn't alone.

But Em was there for her, she loved her, and Kara didn't do enough to tell her she appreciated it.

I'm sorry, Em. I hope you know you were the best thing that ever happened to me.

Michael called ATF. He talked to his contact, to confirm what he suspected about the bomb on the *Water Lily*. He didn't know how long Kara could stand there completely immobile. Her arms could shake. Her legs might give out. She'd been white as a sheet when he walked in—fear caused people to react in a multitude of ways.

"I'm going to disarm it," he told his contact. "I have experience, I just want to confirm with you."

"We'll be there in ten minutes."

"We might not have that long. It's a motion sensor, and my partner is holding it."

"Got it. We're still on our way."

Michael called Matt while he got his bag from his trunk. As he walked back to the house, Matt answered.

"Kara found the evidence. Notes and documents in Neil's handwriting."

"That's fucking fantastic! Bring it in."

"The box is a booby trap. I'm going to get her out of it. I promise you."

"Explain."

"No time. Just wanted to tell you."

"I'm on my way." Matt hung up.

Great, Michael thought.

He went back to Kara. "Looks like the boss is coming, so let's get you out of this mess before he gets here."

"Just don't make a bigger mess, like with my guts, okay? I kind of like the way my body is all in one piece."

"I kind of like the way your body is, too."

"Flirting, Agent Harris?"

"Just telling it like it is." Michael wasn't looking at Kara, he focused on the box. The angles, the tilt, how much C-4 might be inside, how little motion would set it off. He wouldn't know until he could actually see the bomb. "No matter how the box starts to lean, keep it at exactly this angle. I need to remove the papers so I can see what I'm doing."

"Just do it."

"I need to talk—it helps me with stress, and to work through the problem, okay?"

"Whatever floats your boat."

He started to take out files one by one, carefully putting them on the desk two feet away. He couldn't rush this. If he bumped the box, they were both dead. He had to be methodical. He'd disarmed bombs dozens of times under far more intense situations than this.

"During my first tour we ran an op in Fallujah," he said. "A kid ran up to us. We were nervous—two weeks earlier, a kid ran up to a squad with a bomb strapped to him. Anyway, this time was different. He was six, he and his big brother were playing ball and his brother stepped on a land mine. It didn't go off, but he didn't think he could move. My team went to him—half were watching for snipers, because this was exactly the kind of situation where you get ambushed. But it wasn't a lie.

"That kid, his name was Noor, was a rock. Just like you. And he knew if he moved that mine would explode. Those triggers are touchy. Sometimes you can trick them with a sandbag, sometimes you can't. Some are old as fuck—those are the unpredictable ones. And my commander said we were under no obligation to do this, he would take care of it and we could go. Hell no, so he could have bragging rights? He stayed with me and ordered the rest of our squad to a safe distance. Too many people in the area could set it off, too, you know? So my commander, Sketch—"

"That was his name?"

"His name was Lieutenant Commander Steven MacNamara. We called him Sketch."

"Like they called you GQ."

"I never should have told you about that."

"What? It's cute."

"Cute?" He chuckled. "Shit, girl, it's because I was the most handsome, best-dressed stud in my unit."

"I'll bet you were. What happened to Sketch? Do you still talk to him?"

"Died a fucking hero. But that's another story. Anyway, Sketch filled the sandbag at fifty-five pounds. A ten-year-old kid, fifty-five scrawny little pounds." As he said this, he took out the last of the files on top of the C-4. Looked inside. The level was all the way to the right. Why hadn't it already detonated? Maybe…maybe it had to move back? Did it have to go from one side to trigger, then the other to detonate…? Yeah, that was it. That made sense.

"I told Noor I had him. On three. I looked in his eyes and he didn't want to trust me, but he did. And on three, I grabbed him, Sketch had the bag on the mine, and we bolted."

The good thing about C-4 was that it was relatively easy to disarm. Michael had to get the electric probes out of the clay without disrupting the liquid that would send a spark into the C-4.

He took out his long needle-nose pliers.

"I ran with that kid as fast as these legs would take me. I was in better shape then. I mean, I'm in great shape now, but then? Totally Superman. You would have fallen head over heels for me."

"You're probably right."

Two prongs. There didn't look to be a fail-safe, this was a pretty standard setup. But he wished he could take them out simultaneously, just in case he was missing something.

"What?" Kara asked. "What's wrong?"

"Nothing."

"Don't lie to me." Her voice was steady. Calm. But her eyes... they were terrified. He shouldn't have looked into her eyes. He couldn't screw this up.

"It's the tricky part. But I know what I'm doing."

"Do it. Just do it, Michael."

He took his pliers, said a prayer, and pulled one prong out of the explosive clay. Then he pulled the other out.

They were still standing, in one piece.

"Are you done?" she whispered.

"Almost."

He couldn't risk the prongs sparking, even outside of the C-4. Limited chance of exploding, but it was possible. He put the pliers down on the desk, then reached in and detached the device that was attached to the C-4 and removed it from the box. Put it down on the desk. The level was flat, the prongs sparked, and that was it.

"Okay," he said.

"Okay?"

"Give me the box."

"You're not just saying that?"

He took the box from her arms and put it on the floor. "See? The C-4 is just clay now. It doesn't spontaneously explode."

"I saw those spark." She looked at the desk.

"But they were no longer in the C-4."

"It's okay? Really?"

Kara had been a rock, but Michael just now realized how terrified she'd been. With all her jokes and flirting and banter, she was scared to death.

"I promise. You owe me a beer."

She stumbled, and Michael caught her. She was shaking. She hadn't been shaking when she held the box, but now that the crisis was over, she let it out.

"You have a lifetime of beer on me," she said and spontaneously hugged him.

"You were amazing," he said. "Not everyone could be that still for that long."

"I didn't want to die," she said simply. "And I knew you would fix this."

Michael liked Kara a lot—she was hot, she was smart, she was a great cop—but they'd had some heated arguments. About whether when they caught the Liberty Lake killer if Michael should have let him die—he couldn't, he had to save him. But Kara had shrugged it off as if it didn't matter.

He made his bed…

Then when they were both undercover, he didn't understand how easily she could play a lie, pretending she was something she wasn't. Lying to people she liked, even for the job. The lies he had to tell while undercover kept him up at night. Still did, sometimes.

He'd heard from Catherine of her concerns about Kara and her process and that she might put the Mobile Response Team in jeopardy. Catherine was certain Kara took unnecessary risks, and declared that her record showed a clear death wish. She had asked Michael to talk to Matt about Kara, that Kara wasn't a good fit for the team.

And he'd been considering it. He liked Kara, he worked well with her, but some of what Catherine had said resonated because of his conflicts with Kara.

Yet, when push came to shove, there was no one else—other than Matt Costa himself—Michael would prefer to have his back. She was loyal, she was smart, and while sometimes she crossed lines Michael was uncomfortable even brushing against, she was a good cop. She'd risked her life during their case in Patagonia, but only for others. Not because she was a thrill seeker.

And she doesn't have a death wish.

That was abundantly clear to him now.

Kara stepped back. She was still unsteady. "May I?" Michael asked, offering his arm in support.

She grabbed it. "We need what's in that box."

"I know. I'm going to let the ATF Bomb Squad remove the bomb components first, then it's all ours. Let's get out of here."

When Matt saw Kara walk out of Damon Avila's house, supported by Michael, a flood of emotions ran through him. Fear was still there, but the relief was overwhelming.

If Kara had died, he would have a hole in his heart. Not just because she was on his team. Not just because he was responsible for her. Not just because she was a cop doing her job.

He was in love with her.

Matt had to compartmentalize it. He had to put it aside for now, figure it out later.

Michael brought Kara over and sat her down on a lawn chair. "I'm going to get you some water." He glanced at Matt. "She's fine, just shaky."

"You would be, too, if you were holding a fucking bomb," Kara snapped.

Michael laughed. "And she's almost back to her old self!"

He walked away as the bomb squad drove up.

Matt squatted next to her. He wanted to touch her—and he did. Just her arm. Just to say *hey, you okay?*

"Don't worry about me," she said. "It's one of those delayed-reaction things. Michael had the damn thing defused in less than ten minutes, and I was totally fine throughout. Then it was done and I froze. Well, I was already frozen because I wasn't allowed to move or *boom*."

"That's really not funny, Kara."

"It has to be." She took a deep breath and stared at him, really looked at him. He wanted to kiss her. He didn't.

She sensed it and smiled slightly. "It was Neil's files. Avila put the bomb in Neil's files. That'll give your shrinky friend something to get excited about, and give the lawyers real evidence to nail him."

Michael came back, handed Kara a water bottle, and Matt stood up. "Bomb squad is taking care of it, they just need a little time. They're taking the dogs through the house and grounds."

"Good."

"This is the nail in Avila's coffin," Michael said.

"We definitely have enough to arrest, and I'm going to push him hard. I need to find out if there are any more explosives out there. We know three C-4 bricks are missing—we suspect that only one of them was used in total for the first two bombs. What about the one you just found?" Matt asked, nodding toward the house.

"Half brick," Michael said. "It had a motion trigger, similar but not identical to the first bomb, based on the ATF analysis. But if the chemical analysis comes back identical to the *Water Lily*, it's enough to nail him."

"How fast?"

"Twenty-four hours or less. They have to get it to their lab for an accurate comparison."

"Good, but I'm hoping Catherine and I can get a confession. It'll save time, money, and this town will finally have some peace," Matt said. "But we need to find that remaining C-4. Did you see anything that ties Damon to Rena Brown's murder?"

"Nothing before we found the bomb—nothing visible. But a good crime scene team should go through and look for trace, take his shoes, clothes, the whole nine yards. None of that was on the warrant."

"I'll get another. So after the bomb squad is done, I need a deputy on this house until we can bring in a full team. I'll call in the Evidence Response Team from Seattle." Every major FBI office had a specially trained ERT that focused on crime scenes. The ERT was the framework for Matt's Mobile Response Team.

"Why kill Rena?" Kara asked.

"Maybe she saw or heard him do something that concerned her. They worked together. We've been over at the pub every day since we've been here, that would have put him on edge. Maybe she remembered something."

"Hmm."

"You don't think so?"

"He's not left-handed," said Kara. "At least, he wasn't when working the bar. He works with both hands, like most bartenders, but when he rings up orders, he uses his right."

"I'll check, but ninety percent of the population is right-handed. But if he uses both hands working, he could be ambi-dextrous, or used his left hand to throw us off."

"He's not that smart."

"I beg to differ," said Michael. "Bombers are almost always above average intelligence."

"I didn't say he wasn't intelligent, just that I don't think he would consciously use his left hand to slit a throat just so we couldn't pin it on him because, as you said, ninety percent of the population are right-hand dominant."

"Then Rena's murder is random?" Matt asked, sounding ex-asperated.

"No. But it might not have to do with Avila."

"You can look into it if we find no evidence here that he killed her. But right now, we need to bring him in."

"With his family?"

Matt motioned to the people who had congregated across the road from Avila's house, chatting and watching as a third deputy drove up. "I can't trust that someone isn't going to be able to reach him, or that word isn't going to get out on social media, which could cause him to panic. We need to control this—and I think calling in the Coast Guard is the safest way to bring him in."

"You're probably right."

"About this, I am."

"And do you need me for anything?" asked Kara.

"Not right now. Why don't you take a couple hours back at the house and decompress? What you went through—"

"No, I'm good. Really, Matt," she added. He must have looked concerned. He cleared his expression. "I want to follow up with Jamie Finch about Rena. If Rena said anything to Jamie about Avila, it could give us motive. Cal McKinnon said she'd be back around lunch."

"Do that. Michael can finish supervising the search. Do you want Ryder?"

"Not necessary. I'll let you know if I need anything, but this shouldn't take long."

31

Kara drove just outside the town limits to the house Jamie Finch shared with Cal McKinnon. Jamie's car wasn't in the carport. Kara double-checked her notes; Cal said she'd be back by noon. It was only twelve fifteen. She could wait for her, but it had been a long day already and she hadn't eaten. The extreme fear she'd suppressed while holding the bomb had her adrenaline pumping. But time off at the house wasn't an option. Not only because Damon Avila was still out there, but because sitting around reliving the intensity of her fear would drive Kara crazy. She needed to work. It was calming, purposeful.

She drove to a small sandwich shop downtown, ten minutes from Jamie's house and not too far from the sheriff's station.

She ordered a turkey and avocado—no mayo—and sat outside on the deck, which had a partial view of the water. Under an umbrella, she enjoyed her sandwich. Her heart finally felt like it was beating at normal speed, and she could think. When she was halfway done, her phone rang. It was a Seattle area code... and that's when she remembered she'd reached out to a couple of people about Marcy Anderson.

"Hi, is this Detective Kara Quinn?"

"Yes. This is?"

"Lisa Fletcher, you left a message for me. You said you had questions about my time in the Coast Guard."

"Thank you for calling me back. I won't keep you long. I'm actually calling about Marcy Anderson. You were her roommate for a year, correct?"

"Yes."

"Did you know Caleb McKinnon? He served with you."

"Cal, of course. He and I went through boot camp together."

"Not Marcy?"

"She was in the class before us—maybe two classes before us, I don't remember."

"And you were all assigned to Seattle."

"Yes. I'm an engineer, and Marcy worked in logistics. Cal was maintenance. He could fix anything."

"You're no longer in the Coast Guard?"

"Reserves. I gave ten years and retired last year. I'm back to college for a master's in engineering."

Smart cookie, Kara thought.

"Have you kept up with Cal since he moved to the San Juan Islands?"

"Sort of," said Lisa. "On social media. I mean, that's really the best way to keep up with friends who move away."

"And Marcy and Cal dated?"

"Sort of. Why do you need to know this?"

"I can't say, Ms. Fletcher. It's an active investigation. If you would prefer, I can come down there and interview you in person."

"No, I mean, it's fine. I would just like to know what's going on."

"I understand that," Kara said, but she still didn't tell Fletcher what she was investigating.

"Well, they went out a few times. I never thought they were compatible, but Marcy really fell for him hard. Cal was happy-go-lucky, very sweet, everyone liked him—he's the one guy who would come help you move if he said he would come. But at the time not ready for a serious commitment or anything. I mean, he was like twenty-one, twenty-two? Most twenty-one-year-old guys aren't thinking love and marriage. Marcy's five or six years older than him."

"And how did people like Marcy?"

"I got along with her."

"You didn't answer my question."

"I don't know what you're looking for, Detective Quinn."

Kara thought for a moment, then asked, "Were Cal and Marcy ever engaged?"

"Like, to get married? No. They really didn't date much. It was more like a…well, you know that expression, friends with benefits?"

Boy, do I ever, she thought. "Yep."

"I always thought Marcy kind of pushed Cal that way, and said she was fine with it, but she constantly talked about him, and I knew she was falling for him and it was not mutual. And then Cal put in his papers. He'd given five years and wanted to go to college. He went into the Coast Guard right out of high school. I don't know what happened with college, but he posted on social media that he'd found a dream job in the San Juan Islands and loved that he could work on boats all day long. I congratulated him, we chatted for a while, then nothing—I mean, not nothing, but he doesn't really post much on social media, and when he does, it's mostly pictures of his cute little girl."

"And Marcy?"

"When she left, I didn't keep in touch with her. I mean, she tried—but I was busy traveling for the Guard, and her friendship could be…exhausting. There were some— Well, it's not important."

"It might be."

"Why?"

Kara felt she'd get more information out of Lisa if she gave her a piece in return.

"Marcy moved to Friday Harbor and is now a deputy with the sheriff's department."

She paused. "*Oh!* And that's where Cal lives."

"I'm following through on a complaint—" sort of the truth "—that she abused her position of authority. I need to do a thorough investigation, which means talking to people who knew Marcy when she and Cal were dating."

"First, they dated for a few months, if that, and it was casual. So 'dating' is kind of not what it was."

"Okay. What were you going to say after you said Marcy's friendship was exhausting?"

"Look, this is going to sound weird."

"I can do weird."

"We were roommates for a year. I would have left earlier if I could have, but we had a lease. At first everything was fine, Marcy pretty much kept to herself, worked out at the gym, did her work. But there were a few times I thought she was copying me. Like—okay, this sounds stupid."

"Nothing is stupid."

"At the beginning of the summer, I decided to cut off all my hair. Like, pixie-length short. I had really long hair that I always wore in a bun on duty. I was tired of doing the bun thing. A week after, Marcy got the same haircut—well, not identical, but she cut her shoulder-length hair pretty short. That's when I also noticed she was dressing like me when we weren't working. I've always been a dress girl—I know, sounds weird because I'm in a nerdy job, but I love casual dresses. If I'm not working, I'm wearing a dress. So then Marcy started wearing dresses. I mean, when we moved in together she owned one cocktail dress that she'd bought for an event. Then I saw her in a sundress. And another dress. I commented on it, and she said she just liked my style. But she never looked comfortable wearing them." She paused. "See, it's weird."

Kara considered the blazer last night. Damon commented on it, as if he'd never before seen Marcy wear one. Kara wore a blazer when she was on duty. And also the change in workout clothes.

"Marcy had a boyfriend before she moved to Friday Harbor," said Kara. "When she was in Seattle, working for Seattle PD. Did you know him?"

"I didn't keep up with Marcy. Really. If she had a boyfriend after I moved out, I never met him. But that was five or six years ago."

"What about family?"

"She was from Colorado, that's all I know. She never talked about her family."

Kara wrapped up the call, then made another call to Detective Juan Ortega. Six years ago, he'd been Marcy's FTO in the Seattle PD. Kara had tried to reach him, left a message. He hadn't called back.

This time, he answered. Kara told him who she was and what she wanted to know.

"Is this part of an official investigation?" Juan asked. "Do I need to bring in my boss?" He didn't sound hostile, but maybe a little concerned. She understood that.

"I'm not bringing in my boss," she said. "It's a— Hell, I don't know if it's official or not. Let's just say I'll keep this completely off the record unless I need to put it on the record—then I'll call you back and we'll jump through all the bureaucratic hoops, okay?"

"Give me more."

"I'm investigating the bombings on San Juan Island. And I just had a feeling I needed more information. My boss is pretty certain he's taking the right guy into custody—"

"You have a suspect?"

"We do. It hasn't been announced. We just got the warrant."

"And you still want to know about Marcy Anderson?"

"Yes."

"Okay. What do you want? Off the record."

"You were Marcy's FTO. How did she do?"

"She was a good trainee. Did everything I said. A fast learner."

"But."

"I didn't say but."

"You were thinking it." Kara hoped. She was really going out on a limb here, and cops hated talking shit about other cops. "I'm not IA, Juan. Hell, I've been dragged in front of IA a dozen times over a dozen years. I'm not going to do that to you. But this is important."

"Marcy was a fast learner, like I said, but I also had the sense that she…well, not that she had a crush on me, there wasn't anything sexual about it. But if I ordered a hamburger for lunch, she ordered a hamburger. When we first started riding together, she drank dark, sweetened coffee. I drink mine light, unsweetened. She started drinking it light, unsweetened. I would talk about a movie I saw with my girlfriend, and she would see it that night and want to talk about it the next day. I thought at first she was just trying too hard, I said something, and she toned it down, but it was still there. It was like she didn't quite fit in and knew it, so did everything she could to seem like she was just like me."

"How long did you ride with her?"

"Eighteen weeks. That's our standard FTO period."

"Do you know who her first partner was? Do you have a partner system?"

"Yes, and he's retired. Moved, I don't know where."

"Can you tell me if he had similar problems with her?"

"I wouldn't call this a *problem*, it was just uncomfortable."

"Did she have any close friends in the department?"

"I wouldn't know."

"Not you."

"No, I rarely saw her after FTO. Is that it?"

Juan had confirmed what Kara had been thinking. That Marcy Anderson was whoever she thought people wanted her to be.

But it wasn't enough, and Kara didn't quite know what to do with the information.

"One more question," she said. "Did she ever talk to you about an ex-boyfriend named Caleb McKinnon?"

"Sure. They were living together when she was training."

Whoa. That was not what Cal, Marcy, or Lisa had said. Was this a completely new story?

"Did you meet him?"

"Sure—well, actually, no. I don't think we ever met, though I felt like I knew him. A few months after training ended, Marcy and I ran into each other at a fellow officer's retirement party, and she said that Cal had been transferred to another base and she didn't think their long-distance relationship was going to work out. I had the impression she was hitting on me—it was different than when I trained her—but I had a girlfriend back then—now my wife—besides the fact that I made it a policy to never date fellow cops."

"Thank you, Detective." Kara ended the call before he could ask her any more questions.

She got up and ordered the soup of the day to go. She didn't text Marcy or call her but drove directly to her house.

Marcy lived in an apartment only a few blocks up from the

Fish & Brew. It was a small, clean, generic building with eight units, four up, four down. Redwood trees demarcated the property line. Each unit had both a front and back balcony, and Marcy had the bottom south unit, #4.

Kara knocked.

No answer.

She knocked again, rang the bell.

Though supposedly ill at home, Marcy wasn't there.

Dammit, Kara knew she wouldn't be. She could have saved the eight bucks on the soup.

But it smelled good, and she hadn't finished her sandwich. She sat in her car and stared at Marcy's apartment and ate the soup—some sort of spicy chicken vegetable soup—and considered what this all meant.

Maybe nothing.

Maybe everything.

Fifteen minutes later, she was done with the soup and headed back to Jamie Finch's house.

She wasn't there, either.

32

Matt and Catherine sat in the interview room waiting for Damon Avila to be brought in for questioning.

The Coast Guard had caught up with Pete Dunlap's family while they were sailing in Massacre Bay, across the sound. According to the captain, Avila had come without incident and he had told Dunlap exactly what Matt had suggested: Avila was wanted for questioning by the FBI in an ongoing investigation. They didn't actually arrest Avila, but they would have if he balked about coming in.

But Avila came. Matt asked about the family, and they were concerned and on their way back, so to expect them. But the Coast Guard cruiser was much faster than a sailboat, so Matt had time before he had to face Pete Dunlap and tell him that his brother-in-law was responsible for ten deaths—and likely more. They were only arresting him for the two bombings and the attempted murder of a peace officer—by setting the bomb in his house—but they would be putting a lot more charges on that before they were done.

Matt convinced the sheriff, who wanted to participate, to observe the interview instead of being a part of the questioning. He had been satisfied with the sheriff's team, but they personally knew the suspect and his family, and in this case Matt didn't think that would be a benefit to getting a full confession.

And that's what Matt wanted. He didn't want doubts or questions, he wanted a signed statement and then he would turn Damon Avila over to the Seattle FBI for processing and arraignment.

He had enough information to arrest Damon Avila. While the bomb materials in his house needed to be confirmed to be the same C-4 as was used in the two bombings, the fact was that he *had* C-4, coupled with the fact that documents in Neil's handwriting were discovered in a box that also contained newspaper clippings concerning Avila and his five alleged victims. It was solid circumstantial evidence.

But still circumstantial. They could get him on several auxiliary charges, but Matt wanted to nail him for murder. He might not be able to prove he killed those five people on Neil's list—but Matt *could* prove that Avila had killed the nine people on the *Water Lily* and the security guard at West End Charter.

That would have to be good enough. They could work on the other murders.

"You good, Matt?" Catherine asked.

"Of course. I know what the plan is."

"I meant, this is the first bombing case since the Tucson Bomber."

"I'm okay."

"And Kara was nearly killed today."

"She wasn't."

"What if Michael wasn't there? Do you know if she even should have picked up the box in the first place?"

"I would have," he said.

"You don't know that."

"Catherine, we're not having this conversation now. Avila is on his way in, we need to focus on getting the confession. Barring that, we get him on record with statements we can prove or disprove."

Two minutes later, two deputies escorted Avila into the interview room. Matt asked them to remove Avila's handcuffs. Then he thanked them and they left the room. It was just Matt, Catherine, and their suspect.

Damon Avila was a broad-shouldered, muscular but slender, athletic-looking young man. Brown skin, hazel green eyes, six-one—almost exactly Matt's height. He should have seemed imposing, but he looked terrified, with a deer-caught-in-the-headlights expression.

"Hello, Mr. Avila," Matt said. "We met before. I'm Special Agent in Charge Mathias Costa. This is my colleague, Supervisory Special Agent Dr. Catherine Jones. You've been read your rights. Do you have any questions about those rights?"

He shook his head.

"For your protection, this interview is being both audio and video recorded, so I need you to answer verbally. Do you understand your rights as they have been read to you?"

"Yes," he said. "But I don't understand what's going on."

"The Coast Guard picked you up because you are wanted for questioning in the bombing of the *Water Lily* and the West End boathouse."

Avila was shaking his head. "No. That's just... What? That makes no sense. I don't know anything about those bombings. My God, you don't think I had anything to do with that?"

Avila looked genuinely scared. Good. Denials always came first, and fear was better than belligerence.

Matt slid over a copy of the search warrant. "We executed this search warrant this morning starting at ten twenty-five a.m. You can read it. I'll wait."

Avila picked it up. His mouth dropped open as he read what they were searching for. "C-4? Bomb-making material? You actually think I set those bombs? I didn't. I did *not* do it. I swear to Almighty God I did not have anything to do with those bombs."

"In the closet of your den, we found a box with material that included notes in Neil Devereaux's handwriting. How did that box come to be in your possession?"

"Box? Why would I have anything of Neil's at my place? What kind of notes?"

Matt showed him a photo he'd taken on his phone. "We sent the handwriting to the FBI to confirm, but it appears to match other handwriting that we know to be Neil's. These are journals and notes regarding cold cases that he was investigating."

"About the kids who drowned? Why would Neil give me anything about that? He didn't."

"Actually, these notes were about three other cold cases he was investigating, including the disappearance of your ex-girlfriend, Missy Douglas."

Avila didn't say anything.

"When my colleague picked up the box to log it into evidence, a bomb was triggered. Fortunately, we were able to disarm the bomb, so you're facing an attempted murder charge of an officer of the law instead of murder. The bomb was similar in design to the bomb planted on the *Water Lily*. ATF is currently analyzing the material to determine if it came from the same C-4 shipment that was stolen from a construction company in Bellingham, Washington, which matches the material in both bombs."

Matt stared at Avila, who now looked both worried and confused.

"None of that is in my house," Avila said. "You got the wrong house."

"We didn't get the wrong house." Matt showed him the address on the warrant and additional photos.

"That's not my box. I've never seen it. I swear."

"It was behind a panel in your dining room."

"No, it couldn't have been."

"In the den off the living room."

"See? It's not mine. I don't even use that closet. The house belongs to my brother-in-law. I rent it from him during the summer when I work for him. I mean, he gives it to me cheap—I pay enough to cover utilities and stuff. All the other times of the year he has it up on Airbnb. That's it—whoever was there before me left it. Ask him. He'll tell you."

Avila was grasping at straws, trying to find a way out from under the mounting evidence.

Catherine spoke up for the first time. "Damon—may I call you Damon?"

He nodded.

"Did you know Neil Devereaux?"

"Yeah, of course. You know that."

"I do?"

"I talked to that other agent, the cute blonde. I told her he used to come in a lot."

"Okay. Did you know him well?"

"Like as well as any regular at the pub. He was friends with Pete, my brother-in-law. Talked to him a lot. They, um, both lost their wives to cancer, they just got close, I guess."

"Did Neil ever talk to you about the cold case he was investigating?"

"No. I mean, everyone knew he was looking into it, and he once asked if I'd known Brian and Jason. I said sort of, not really, because I really didn't know them. University of Washington is huge. I mean, I might have known them, but I don't remember, you know."

He was overtalking, which was always a good sign.

Catherine asked, "Do you mean to say that you knew them but not well, or you told Neil you knew them, but you really didn't?"

"The first one—I mean, I might have had a class with one of them or something, it was a long time ago. I knew their names."

Suddenly, Matt saw exactly where Catherine was going with this and he now knew why Neil thought Avila was guilty.

"How did you injure your knee?" she asked.

He stared at her and said nothing.

"Damon, you do remember the accident that shattered your leg, an injury so serious that your football career was over."

"It was a car accident," he said quietly. "I don't like to think about it."

She nodded and removed the accident report from her file. She turned it so he could read it. "Do you see the name on the fifth line? Under 'other vehicles involved'?"

He didn't comment.

"Damon, you see the name."

"Brian Stevens."

"He lost control of his car on an icy road at night and hit your car, which careened off the road. Your left leg was shattered. Now do you remember Brian?"

"I...I didn't know it was the same person."

This guy was not a very good liar, which surprised Matt. Mass murderers could usually lie through their teeth and their own mothers wouldn't know unless faced with hard physical evidence.

"Did you know that your ex-girlfriend Missy Douglas went missing while camping five years ago?"

"Yeah. That was awful."

Catherine pulled out several sheets of paper from her file,

turned them to face Damon. "In April after your accident, Missy broke up with you."

"It was mutual," he said.

"According to this police report, the campus police were called to her sorority three times to remove you from the property when you refused to leave. The first time was when she broke up with you." She turned to the second page. "The second time was a week later, you came to the sorority drunk and wouldn't stop pounding on the door. You broke a window, and campus police cited you. You paid that bill. The third time was in mid-May, shortly before graduation. You entered the property, even though campus police had forbidden you from going on sorority property. This time, Missy threatened to file a restraining order against you. According to the officer who responded, she said quote, 'Damon changed after the accident. I tried to stay with him, but he was mean and yelled at me for no reason and refused to go to counseling or get any help. I don't want to file charges, but I'm scared.' Apparently, she never filed charges with campus police or Seattle PD."

"I felt like crap after that. I loved Missy, I really did, and I treated her badly. I was so... I was fucked. I knew I'd never play ball again."

"That must have been hard for you." Catherine sounded sincere and showed concern. "You were a star player, you broke records in high school and college, and were going to be drafted by the NFL."

"It was the worst time of my life," he said.

"Before Missy disappeared, she had become engaged. To a retired pro football player. Did you know that?"

"Probably, but I didn't think about it. It was all a long time ago." He was looking at his hands, not at Catherine or Matt.

"Why do you think Neil was looking into Missy's disappearance?"

"I don't know."

"Did he ask you about it?"

"No."

"You're a teacher, at Bellingham High School, correct? Math."

"Yeah," he said, glancing at Catherine, clearly suspicious at the change of direction in questioning.

"Did you know Eric Travers?"

"No."

"No?" ·

"I just said no!"

For the first time, Matt saw temper. Not worry, not fear, but anger—anger enough to kill? Could Damon Avila actually plot a murder and wait months...or years...to seek revenge? Plan a bombing that took time and patience as well as a deep, cold spine? To kill innocent people just to kill the man who suspected he was a killer?

"Eric Travers was hired to run the math and science department at Bellingham High School four years ago. You had already been working at Bellingham for five years, and according to the principal—" she looked at her notes "—Monica Jefferson, you had applied for the promotion as well. She wouldn't tell me why you were passed over—employment confidentiality—but I can imagine it was an experience issue. Travers had more than fifteen years teaching and had a master's degree, as well as some impressive credentials working in an underperforming school and turning around math scores. He got recognition in the press—" she put several newspaper articles down "—and recognition by the governor."

"What does any of this have to do with me or with the bombing?"

Catherine stared at him. "Neil believed that you killed all these people."

He shook his head. "No." His voice was a squeak.

"Did he tip his hand? Maybe he asked you a suspicious question—and you thought he might find evidence or just say something to your brother-in-law—like you said, they were friends, good friends. They even went to a football game together last year. Even if Neil couldn't prove it, he could damage your relationship with your family. I suspect you didn't want to kill anyone else—you just wanted to kill Neil. Maybe you set the bomb and expected it to go off when only Neil was on board. You went to his house, took all the files about Travers, Douglas, and Clark—you didn't take the two college boys because everyone knew that Neil was looking at that case. Then you were worried because the FBI was here, we were asking a lot of questions, and looking at Neil's cold-case investigation, and you panicked. You sabotaged the heater. Maybe you hoped that the leak would destroy the house, but you couldn't count on it, so you took the incriminating files. Then, it wasn't unreasonable to think that we would look for suspects among the members of the Island Protectors, so you set a smaller bomb at the West End boathouse. You didn't mean to kill Garrett Washington—he was at the wrong place at the wrong time."

He slammed his fist down on the table. "No! I didn't set any bombs."

Matt said, "Don't do that again."

"I didn't kill all those people! I swear to God!"

It was unclear whether Damon Avila was talking about the five cold cases or the people on the boat.

Matt said, "We have a wealth of evidence tying you directly to the bombings. We found C-4 in your house. We found Neil's files—again, in your house. We have security tape of you at a construction facility in Bellingham where the C-4 was stolen on a night that a student who you taught for two years was working." It wasn't true, but Matt put it out there to see if he would cave. "We have—"

"I want to see that tape *right now.* I didn't steal C-4, I didn't plant a bomb. I want to see the tape. It's not me *and I'll prove it!*"

Matt wasn't quite expecting that level of denial. Or maybe he thought that the tape had been erased or didn't exist. "We know from ferry security footage that you took the ferry to Bellingham the night before the C-4 was stolen. You'll be able to see the tape during the discovery process of your trial, because we're charging you with ten murders with special circumstances."

"No! You can't do that! I didn't do anything with bombs, I swear to God, I didn't!"

Catherine said, "A confession would go a long way to getting the death penalty taken off the table."

Damon began to tremble. He pushed back violently from the table and Matt stood. Though the suspect had been fully searched, he was still in his civilian clothes.

But Damon just put his head in his hands. "I need a lawyer because I didn't put bombs anywhere," he said. "I didn't steal C-4 or anything else. I didn't hurt those people. I need a lawyer."

"All right," Matt said. "One of the deputies will book you, and you'll be placed in a holding cell until we can transport you to the mainland."

"What? No."

"We found C-4 at your house and one of my colleagues nearly died. That is enough to keep you for a long time. You don't want to cooperate? That's fine. Don't. We have plenty of evidence. And you know? I'm going to solve those five cold cases for Neil. I'm going to prove you killed Brian Stevens and Jason Mott because Brian accidentally destroyed your football career. That you killed Eric Travers because he got the job you wanted. That you killed Missy Douglas because she loved another man. And that you killed Billy Clark because..." He was stumped.

Catherine finished for him. "Because you were jealous that Billy Clark was getting everything you wanted."

"So not only will you have ten special circumstance murders on your sheet, you'll have five additional homicides," said Matt. "And you should also know that we have an expanded warrant to search your house and the Fish & Brew for any evidence in the Rena Brown stabbing."

"Oh, God—I did not kill Rena. Please, you have to believe me! I didn't!"

"You've asked for your lawyer, so we cannot ask any more questions. Unless you would like, on the record, to waive that right and continue to talk to us."

He stared at Matt and shook his head.

Now he looked scared more than angry. Even more scared than he had been when he walked in.

"I didn't kill Rena. I liked her! I didn't set those bombs. I never would. I swear."

He didn't say he didn't kill Stevens or Mott. He didn't say he didn't kill his ex-girlfriend, or the teacher, or the student.

Matt glanced at Catherine. She had noticed the same thing. They left the room.

"I thought he was going to confess," Matt said when they were back in the conference room. "You did good."

"He never denied killing the others."

"He had a lot of denials in there, Catherine."

"He denied planting the bombs. He denied killing Rena Brown. He did not deny killing the other five people."

"Maybe because he knows there's no evidence? Hard to prove?"

Catherine frowned, and Matt knew better than to question her judgment on the psychology of criminals.

"We need to talk to that former student who went to Canada," she said.

"We found evidence in Damon's house," Matt said. "You can't possibly believe that he didn't do this."

"I believe he killed the five people Neil was looking at. Neil saw something I haven't yet, if he was as confident as he seemed. I haven't had the time to review all the information we found in

Avila's house. But I'm not sure about the bombings. I'm wondering if someone else is trying to protect him."

"Who?"

"Maybe we should talk to his brother-in-law."

"I'm not about to accuse Pete Dunlap of murder. We have no evidence pointing to that."

"Maybe not, but Neil may have said more to Pete about the cold cases, and Pete was worried about what might happen to his family if Damon was arrested."

"I'll talk to him, but I think you're stretching this. Damon's denying everything because he knows he'll never be free again."

"Maybe you're right."

"There's no other logical explanation."

After a knock on the door, a deputy stepped in. "Pete Dunlap would like to see the agent who arrested his brother-in-law."

"I'll take this, Catherine, unless you'd like to join me."

"No, talk to him. I have a few calls to make."

33

Kara sat outside Jamie Finch's house and called Cal McKinnon.

He didn't answer. She didn't leave a voice mail message. She checked the time on her phone: it was after two in the afternoon.

She stared at the house and considered what to do. Track Cal down at West End? Was he still working? Or find out where Jamie was and drive there, make sure she and her kid were okay? Something was weird.

Matt and Catherine were interviewing Damon Avila and she hadn't heard anything about what had happened there, other than the sheriff's department had brought him in without incident. She felt bad for Ashley and Whitney, who'd had to witness it, but Matt was right—if Avila heard about the search, he could easily head to Canada, only a few nautical miles away. Even if he didn't mean to, he might put his family in danger.

She called Ted Colfax at West End. She'd only met him once, but Matt had been working closely with him since they'd been here.

"Ted, it's Detective Kara Quinn with the FBI Task Force. I'm trying to reach Cal McKinnon. Is he still there?"

"Hold on."

Cal and Jamie lived in a quiet rural neighborhood: small houses and large yards, no sidewalks. Some houses had garages, some had carports. It wasn't far from Damon Avila's house, just on the other side of a two-lane highway that cut diagonally through Friday Harbor until it reached the downtown area.

It took Ted over three minutes to get back to her.

"Cal left five minutes ago. Didn't even clock out, just said he had to go and ran to the parking lot. Is everything okay?"

Almost as soon as Ted started speaking, Cal's old truck ran the stop sign at the corner and turned onto the street, leaving rubber. He passed Kara—may not have even noticed her—and turned into his driveway. He slammed on the brakes, jumped out, and left the truck running.

"I found him." She ended the call and got out of her car. "Cal!" she called out as he ran to the front door.

He abruptly turned, glared at her.

"What are you doing here?" He looked right and left as if he was expecting...what? An attack?

She walked over to his truck, turned off the ignition, and closed the door. She kept his keys.

"Let's talk."

"I don't have time. I gotta go." He opened the door to his house and disappeared inside.

She followed.

"Cal, what happened?"

"You have to go. You're the police." He ran around looking for something—what? "I can't talk to you. Fuck!"

He ran to his bedroom and she heard something slam, then something move. She stood in the doorway and he was standing on a step stool to reach the top shelf of his closet.

Her eye spotted the small gun safe he was unlocking.

"Stop," she told him.

"I don't have time. I gotta go!"

"Cal, do not reach for that gun."

"It's not loaded!"

He wasn't listening to her. She didn't believe that he was going to shoot her, but clearly he was panicked, and she didn't think he'd be able to hit the broad side of a barn right now.

All of a sudden, he stumbled, fell off the stool, then sat on the edge of his bed.

"She has them. She has Jamie and Hazel."

"Marcy Anderson."

He nodded, looked at her, his eyes glassy with fear. "She said if I called the FBI she'd kill Jamie."

From the doorway, Marcy Anderson watched the beautiful little girl sleep in the dim light. Dark curly hair just like her dad, back when he'd let it grow long. Big blue eyes. Chubby little hands. Three years old... Marcy had lost out on the first three years of Hazel's life, but no more. From now on, Hazel was hers.

Hazel should have been Marcy's from the beginning.

She kissed the precious little girl on her forehead and left the room, closing the door behind her. The cough medicine would ensure she slept a while longer.

Marcy walked around the cabin. It was a nice place, clean lines, simple. Hazel's grandfather owned it, but he was rarely here—maybe five, six times a year. There was no clutter. She'd already made sure there were no weapons Cal could use against her—a shotgun, unloaded, was in the corner of the master bedroom closet. The shells were in the nightstand drawer. She moved them to a bathroom drawer on the off chance Cal knew about the shotgun. No knives outside of the kitchen. She hid all those knives high in the cabinets, along with anything that could be used against her. A few heavy objects remained in the living room, but she didn't see Cal grabbing something and throwing it at her, or if he did, being effective before she could respond. And if he did something stupid like grab a gun before he arrived? He would know the bitch he thought he loved would suffer before she died.

It was nearly five. Cal would be here soon. Marcy would be reasonable with him. Sit down and explain how things needed to be. They'd go to Canada and restart their life together—the life they would've had if…

Marcy wasn't stupid. Cal thought he loved Jamie, but clearly Jamie didn't feel the same. He must see that. After all, Jamie kept postponing their wedding. Why couldn't he read the writing on the wall? The woman was keeping him around until she found someone better.

Marcy had loved Cal from the day she met him. They were friends, and they were lovers, and it was good. She was what he wanted. She'd researched him, studied him closely, knew what type of girls he liked (tall brunettes, so she was a natural—Jamie was short with mousy brown hair, so why did he even want her?). She knew what he liked to do (anything with boats, action-adventure movies, and reading science fiction). She had taken a picture of his bookshelf after their first date, picked out one of the science fiction series, bought all of them used and put them in her apartment. She read them so she could talk about the stories. That's what led him to ask her out the first time.

"I've never met a girl who liked Orson Scott Card," he'd said. He'd been impressed that she knew every book, every plotline.

It was great for a while. She wanted to move in, he didn't like the idea. He had roommates…she had a lease…she had a plan to get rid of Lisa, get her transferred, and then ask him to move in and take over her lease. But before she could make that happen, he started pulling away. So she got more inventive in bed, doing things all guys loved, and she stopped taking the pill because if she got pregnant they would get married and every-thing would be great.

But after a month, she still wasn't pregnant and he broke up with her. It didn't even happen dramatically, just one night she went over to his place, and he didn't want to go to bed. He said, "I think we'd be better as friends, Marcy, you know? Just friends."

She'd agreed. If she went all mega-drama on him, she'd never win him back.

So she hung out on the fringes. Did all the right things. Was there if he changed his mind. And waited.

It took years, but then Greg and Diana's wedding came, and they were both there. Cal remembered how much he loved her. He even told Marcy that he'd missed her...and they went up to his hotel room and had sex. It was amazing, his orgasm had been explosive, and she was positive she would get pregnant—it happened at the same time she should be ovulating, proving that fate wanted them together.

So when he left the next day and didn't return her calls, she didn't worry. When she told him she was pregnant, he'd come back.

But she wasn't pregnant.

She slept with six different guys over the next month, all who looked enough like Cal that he would believe the baby was his, and still, she couldn't get pregnant.

Marcy looked down at her hands and saw that her fists were clenched so tightly that her fingernails had left deep impressions in her palms. She shook them out, ignoring the momentary pain.

She had been resolved to forget Cal. He didn't deserve her *or* her child.

And then she found out that he had a baby with another woman.

He had *her* baby—the baby *she* was supposed to carry.

It took her nearly two years to get into the San Juan Islands Sheriff's Department. She had to wait for an opening, and because it was a small department, they didn't have a lot of openings. But she got on the waiting list and *finally* there was an opening for her. She made sure she was exactly what they wanted. She got advanced certifications that would be beneficial in the island community. She hated using the female card, but she did, subtly. San Juan County only had three female deputies. She was qualified, she was a woman, she got the job.

Marcy walked around the cabin. Framed on shelves were pictures of Jamie as a kid, and of Hazel as a baby. One was of Cal, Jamie, and Hazel. Marcy narrowed her eyes and grabbed it. She almost smashed it on the table, but at the last minute she realized that when Hazel woke up, she might cut herself.

She threw the picture in the trash.

Marcy would give Cal one chance to come to his senses. If he didn't, she'd kill him.

After dealing with Jamie, she had considered just leaving. She knew winning Cal over was a long shot. But didn't she need to give the father of her child a chance? One chance to realize *they* were a family?

She looked in her purse, pulled out two Canadian passports. One for her, under the name Anne Elizabeth Porter, and one for Hazel, Elizabeth Hazel Porter. They were perfect and wouldn't garner any scrutiny when crossing the border. She'd picked Edmonton because it was far enough away that it wouldn't be the first place anyone would look. The city was large, over a million people, but there were plenty of smaller suburbs and rural areas. They would live out of town but be able to go into town for supplies. She knew how to blend in, and she'd saved enough money that she wouldn't have to worry about anything for at least a year.

She glanced at her watch. Cal should be here by now. If he'd talked to anyone, she would kill him as soon as he walked in, then disappear. She turned up the police dispatch radio from her patrol car. She'd dismantled the GPS, but she needed the radio. All standard calls. No hint that Cal had called the police or that they were setting up an action on the west side of the island.

She checked on Hazel; she stirred but didn't wake up.

Ten minutes.

Ten minutes and if Cal wasn't here, she and Hazel were leaving.

34

As soon as Kara called Matt, he immediately came over to Cal McKinnon's house with the rest of the team. Time was not on their side, and Cal was in full panic mode. Fortunately, Matt was at his best when he was under pressure, and he listened to Kara's plan while they stood in Cal's small living room.

Cal paced. He was supposed to be at the Finches' cabin by five with a packed suitcase for Hazel, or Jamie would be killed. So Marcy had said. It was quarter to five now.

Kara had been keeping an eye on him as she and Matt worked through her plan, making quick adjustments to the strategy. "Cal, I will not let them die."

She glanced at Matt. He hadn't liked her plan, but he agreed: it was the only way they had a chance against a fellow cop.

"We're too late! She said *five o'clock*. We can't get to Jared's house in fifteen minutes! We have to go, you have to let me go—what if she kills them? What if—"

"They're not dead because she'd have no leverage. And I told you: you're not going. I am."

She turned to the rest of the team. Ryder had downloaded detailed and up-to-date maps of the area. They'd already agreed that Cal couldn't go in—the chances that Marcy would kill him were high. Not to mention that Cal was emotionally involved and there were two other hostages, one of them a young child.

Kara knew there was only one possible way to get everyone out of this alive.

"You know I'm right, Catherine," she said, addressing her comments to the team member who'd had it out for her from the beginning, and the only one who hadn't verbally agreed to the plan she and Matt came up with. "I know Marcy better than any of you. I've talked to other people who knew her well. She will listen to me."

Catherine didn't say anything.

"She started to dress like me. She admires me, looks up to me, wants to emulate me. I can talk to her. You back me up." She pointed to two spaces on Ryder's map. "Two in the back, two in the front. I will find out where Hazel and Jamie are, and you get them while I talk her down. Once they are safe, we take Marcy into custody. If it's not possible to get them, I'm wearing a wire: you'll know. Matt, you can adjust the plan once we have information, but without me being inside, we have no intel and are flying blind."

"I can't let you go in there alone," Matt said. "I wouldn't let any team member risk themselves like that. I like your plan, but we go together."

"And that will set her off. It's my choice," Kara said. "It's why I'm a cop."

Catherine cleared her throat. "Matt, Kara is right. If Marcy can be talked down, it won't be me—she knows I'm a psychia-trist and would assume she's being judged or analyzed. It could escalate the situation. She has high intelligence, and as a law enforcement officer, she would know what my role is. Kara has already developed a rapport with her."

Kara was surprised that Catherine agreed with her so easily.

"However, we all must be very careful," Catherine contin-ued. "Something happened today to escalate this behavior. Why now? Marcy Anderson has been on the island for over a year."

"Friday," Kara said. "It's the only thing that makes sense."

Catherine frowned but said nothing.

"You know what I'm thinking," Kara said. That pleased her. Maybe she and Catherine weren't as different as she thought.

"I don't know that we can make that leap."

Matt said, "What leap?"

"Avila didn't set the bombs," Kara said. "Marcy did."

Matt shook his head. "That's not logical, and we have no evi-dence to indicate such."

"I'll learn the truth when I talk to her," Kara said. "Cal was the target, but she certainly knew about Neil's investigation. I think Marcy knew a lot more about it than she told us. In fact, I think she was helping Neil, just to find out what he knew and how she could use that information to benefit her. I think she knew Neil was looking specifically at Avila, and that's what gave her the idea to bomb the *Water Lily*. But right now we're wast-ing time, we have to go."

A door slammed. Cal had taken off. Michael ran after him.

"Shit," Kara mumbled. "Catherine, I have questions for you, drive with me. I'll leave you around the bend from the cabin. Everyone else will follow."

Cal was screaming outside, and Kara stepped out.

"We have ten minutes to drive forty minutes! She's going to kill my family. I should have gone. I should be there!"

"Text her and tell her you're on your way, you'll turn on your location and share it with her to prove it."

"No!"

"Yes. I'll take your phone with me."

"I'm going with you! Hazel is three years old. She's just a baby." His voice cracked.

Matt said, "Michael, you can take Cal with you, following the tactical van. I have the sheriff read in, and he's doing this off-radio—him and his three most trusted deputies. One in the van with us, and two in a patrol boat. They've already left for the other side of the island. Let's go."

He turned to Kara. "Short leash, Kara. You'll wear a wire. It's small, state-of-the-art, not easy to detect."

She knew better than to argue. The feds did things differently than LAPD Special Operations, where she'd worked undercover, but the wire was a good idea. They needed to know what she knew in order to save Hazel and Jamie.

Kara asked Cal for his phone. He unlocked it, told her the pass code, and she glanced through his messages to see how he texted and adapted his style.

i'm coming! i couldn't help it i'm sorry. don't hurt Jamie, don't touch Hazel i promise i did everything u said. Damon was arrested for the bombs and i couldn't leave wec, but i didn't say a word god i swear plz! i just shared my location with u.

She showed the message to Catherine, who nodded. Kara hit Send.

She still had Cal's keys. "I'm taking your truck."

"She's going to know that it's all a setup when you get out of the truck," Cal cried. "Let me go. Please, this is my family. I'll die to save them, I don't care."

"If she kills you, she'll kill everyone," Catherine said.

Kara concurred. "Trust me," she said, though she was beginning to feel out of her element here.

Catherine followed her out.

Kara had dealt with numerous sociopaths over the years—many career criminals were sociopathic.

But Marcy was a psychopath, Kara was pretty certain. Someone that Kara wasn't altogether certain she could reason with. But she had to try and de-escalate the situation. She and Marcy had a connection, but Kara didn't understand the obsession. Catherine did. She understood people like Marcy Anderson. That's why Kara needed to talk to her.

All Kara could think about was making sure little Hazel was safe. Then Jamie. Children should never be used as pawns in games of grown-ups. It made Kara see red.

Kara drove fast, just as Cal would drive because this was his family. She had navigation working on her phone, and one eye on Cal's phone in case Marcy responded. Catherine stared straight ahead, her hand on the chicken stick above the passenger window.

Cal's phone buzzed, Kara reached for it, but Catherine grabbed it.

"I'll read it." A second later. "She said, 'Don't fuck with me. If you're not here at five thirty on the dot, I'll be gone.'"

Kara glanced at her phone. She'd be there at 5:34. She pressed the accelerator further. She'd make up the time.

"But that's good, right?" Kara said. "Because she didn't say *I'll kill them.*"

"A smart person, even a psychopath, wouldn't put that in writing."

"Thank you for backing me up with Matt."

"It's not ideal, but you made a valid point. You are the closest to Marcy, and while she will be suspicious, you can use your rapport with her to extend the conversation. Matt and Michael will approach the house to search for the hostages as soon as we hear from you where they might be."

"My primary goal is to locate Jamie Finch and her daughter and get them to safety. But I don't know exactly what I'm going into, how I can do that. I need to understand Marcy better."

Catherine said, "From the beginning, you're the one who said there was something off about Deputy Anderson. Maybe you have more insight than you think."

"I find most people a bit *off*. With Marcy, it was because I couldn't read her—and I can read almost anyone."

Catherine gave a little snort. Kara would call it delicate, but it still irritated her.

"You have always been the smartest person in the room," Kara said, doing her own version of a profile. "You expect—mostly deserved—to have everyone defer to you because of your intelligence, education, and experience. When someone pushes back who you feel is beneath you, you dismiss them or shut them out. How dare they doubt you. If someone trumps you on one of those three criteria? You'll listen. I judge people instantly. Bad habit, but when undercover, you develop that skill." Not to mention when you're a con artist. "So do you, Catherine. But I judge them as to their threat level, you judge them based on an intellectual hierarchy."

"I don't know if that is fair, but it's mostly accurate."

"Mostly?" Kara laughed. "Anyway, the reason I sensed Marcy was off was because I was raised by two con artists. I learned how to read people from the first time my parents used me in a con that I understood—I was five. They used me all the time when I was a baby, but I don't remember any of that. My parents stopped trying to lie to me by the time I was nine because I called them on it. My father was going to prison and they tried to tell me he was going to a fucking resort in Bora Bora." She rolled her eyes, but that was the only time Kara had been truly scared. She didn't love her parents anymore, but she had when she was nine, when she feared being alone. "For me, reading people was as much about survival as it was about getting them to do what I wanted. When I worked undercover, those skills finally became useful to someone else. And I was a *damn* good undercover cop."

Kara wanted that back. And she knew she'd never have it. It fucking hurt.

"Marcy put on a face as to what she felt a female cop in a small town would be. I see it now."

"Slow down," Catherine said as they came up fast behind an SUV pulling a boat trailer.

They were on a straightaway. Instead of slowing down, Kara sped up and passed the lumbering vehicle, then moved quickly back into the right lane before she had a head-on with a VW Bug.

If she wasn't so worried about the kid, she would have enjoyed Catherine's white knuckles on the dash.

"She dressed the part," Kara continued. "Lived the part. The way she talked, the way she acted, hell, even the way she ran every morning and worked out. She was the epitome of a female cop. There was nothing...*personal*. I don't know if that's the right way to say it. When we went to interview people, she let me take lead. Not because she was incapable, but I sensed that she wanted to see how I did it.

"I called her former FTO in Seattle PD, and her former roommate. Marcy's been obsessed with Cal for years. Back when they were in the Coast Guard a decade ago. Even after Cal left, moved here, she told her FTO that she lived with her boyfriend Cal, but he never met him. And then at some point, maybe because someone expected to meet him, she told her FTO that Cal was transferred, and she didn't think they'd survive a long-distance relationship. I need to work on the timeline, but that might have been after the one-night stand five years ago. Marcy was a solid rookie, did everything her FTO said, but he never felt a connection with her. He felt she had no personality—at least, that was my sense.

"Her roommate said she thought Marcy and Cal were friends with benefits, but Marcy wanted more. She grew concerned because Marcy started dressing like her, changing her hairstyle, doing other odd things that made Lisa uncomfortable. She said she was still in touch with Cal, but had cut off ties with Marcy. And that had me remembering that Marcy changed her workout attire to match mine. Wore a blazer when she never wore a blazer. And last night when we went to the Fish & Brew for dinner, she ordered dark beer. Damon was the bartender, was going to pour her a blond until she changed it. Made me think she never drank dark, which was confirmed when she only had a couple sips."

"Did you leave before or after her?"

"After, about forty minutes."

Catherine didn't say anything for a long time, and Kara was becoming irritated. She thought this would be a conversation, not a monologue.

She quickly glanced down at her phone. She had almost made up the time, but she had to slow down to go around a sharp curve. It said thirty-five, she did it at fifty. Then she floored it again, passing two cars in a row, earning an obnoxious horn when she had to pull in quickly to avoid an oncoming truck.

Catherine squeaked, then cleared her throat. She said a moment later, "You think Marcy Anderson is responsible for the bombings."

"I do. I don't know if Damon helped her, but I suspect not. If he did, I think she would have killed him to avoid him being able to testify against her."

"And those five murders Neil was investigating were all really accidents?"

"No. I think Damon killed those people. Marcy left them

for us to find, to leave bread crumbs to Damon. If Damon had killed those people, he would have taken the evidence."

"He did. You found it."

"Marcy didn't take all of it from Neil's house because she wanted us to connect the dots to Damon. But she needed some of the files to plant in Damon's house. She didn't want to get involved today, but then this morning she had to, to give us something that might get us a warrant. A statement by a cop holds more weight. She already planned to grab Jamie and Hazel, but needed us occupied with Damon. She had hoped we would come to the same conclusions that Neil did. That's why she put the rest of Neil's evidence in Damon's closet. If it went boom, it was evidence that he rigged his house; arrest him. If it didn't go boom, we have evidence that is less conclusive but still compelling—C-4? Where did he get it? Why did he have Neil's notes?" She passed another car and was relieved it was still light out. She didn't like passing cars in the dark when it was harder to judge distance and curves.

"When Neil told Marcy who he suspected," Kara continued, "—and yes, I think she was very involved in his investigation, though I don't have any hard evidence of that—she came up with this idea. It was just something she said when I asked her if she knew about the investigation—she went out of her way to say no but that she had overheard a conversation between Neil and John, the sheriff. It just felt…out of place. Awkward. Staged. Almost like a cover in case she revealed more information than she intended to, she could point to John as the source. Anyway, if she bombs a boat with both Cal and Neil on it, she'll kill the man who refused to love her and frame Damon at the same time."

Catherine said, "While it's true that obsessive personalities—dangerous stalkers—will kill the object of their obsession, it's usually after a specific betrayal or rejection. Holding on to that without acting on it, even in small ways, is unusual."

"She came here last year with the purpose of being on the island with Cal. I don't know why she didn't try to kill him earlier, maybe because he and Jamie weren't married, she thought she had a chance to split them up."

"Why now?" Catherine asked. "What set her off? She had been planning this for some time—the C-4 was stolen the Monday before, but it would have taken days—weeks maybe—to work out a viable plan to steal it from a construction company that was very loosely connected to Avila through a former student. That takes high-level planning."

"She worked logistics for the Coast Guard—doesn't that practically scream high-level planning?"

"It would," Catherine concurred.

"Like you said, Doc, something changed. What did you mean when you earlier said stressor?"

"I'm not saying your theory is wrong," said Catherine. "The bombing seems to be out of the blue, though we don't know what specifically may have happened between Cal and Marcy in the weeks leading up to this. A stressor is usually a specific event or conflict that propels a sociopath into action."

Now that Kara believed Marcy was responsible for everything, it was all becoming clear to her. "She had to wait until Damon was back on the island," she said, knowing she was right. She glanced at her phone. She needed to make up another minute, so hit ninety on the straightaway, the old truck engine roaring under the strain.

"According to Mott's sister," Kara continued, "Neil told her last year that he knew who the killer was but couldn't prove it. What if he shared that information with Marcy and asked her to help him? She's new, she didn't know Damon and the others, there would be no loyalty or allegiance. And she was a cop, former Coast Guard—his daughter is in the Navy. I think he automatically trusted her."

"That makes some sense."

"But earlier you said that there was a *stressor* that set Marcy off," said Kara. "She's now exposed herself, taken a kid and mom hostage, threatened Cal. That's what I'm missing. Why expose herself when she was on the verge of getting away with the bombings? Because Cal didn't die? I mean, I saw her this morning, and she wasn't all red-eyed wild crazy woman."

"She gave us information about Avila."

"We were onto him, but she gave us the final piece. She wanted us to be distracted today. But why today?"

"Maybe, but that might be a stretch. I'm not sold on your theory, but I think it's worth exploring."

"High praise."

"A stressor is an event or experience that causes stress in an individual, but when the individual has a mental health issue, that stressor can lead to what some people might call a psychotic break. The situation can be perceived as a threat or even a challenge, but for the psychopath, this stress often pushes him to act on his dark impulses. Healthy people who have a stressor in their life—such as someone who loses a loved one suddenly or loses their job—can grieve and find healthy coping mechanisms. Some people fall into a depression. Many people turn their stress inward—they drink to excess, they take drugs, they sleep or eat too much or too little. But generally—some with help and some without help—they can move over the hurdle. A psychopath has always harbored darker impulses, but a stressor causes them to act on those."

"They snap," said Kara.

"That isn't the textbook definition, but you understand the concept."

"Last night, Cal and Jamie moved up their wedding to this weekend."

"That could have been Marcy's stressor."

"And Jamie is pregnant. She told Cal last night, and after him, I guess everyone else. Maybe that final commitment—they were getting married and Cal was never going to go back to Marcy—set her off. But why hurt the kid? Marcy told me that she wanted kids. She was talking about her biological clock ticking and maybe coming to a small island wasn't the best thing for her."

"Interesting."

"And?"

"How did she—? Kara!"

"I see it," she said as she swerved to avoid a too-slow moving car. "Isn't there a law against driving *under* the speed limit? This *is* a fucking highway," she muttered.

Catherine let out a long breath. "How did Marcy know that Jamie was pregnant? That they moved up the wedding? Did they announce it on social media? Have a party?"

It took Kara two seconds but she realized what had happened. "It was last night at the Fish & Brew. Pete Dunlap told me everything, and I didn't see it!"

"Everything what?"

"Cal was at the Fish & Brew last night with Jamie. I thought Marcy had left, but what if she overheard them—or part of the conversation? She left before me. And according to Dunlap, Jamie told him and Rena that she was pregnant. He already knew about the wedding. Marcy blends, she could have been hiding in the shadows, eavesdropping, fuck if I know, but that had to have been what set her off."

Catherine considered what Kara was saying. "I can't speak to what she was thinking at the time, but maybe if Marcy feels she can't have a child, that she's getting too old, or if she hasn't been able to maintain a long-term relationship, maybe Hazel is a shortcut to the life she wants. This is good, actually, because if Marcy thinks of Hazel as hers, she'll protect her."

"I can work with that."

"Be careful. If you're right and she's the bomber, she has the ability to plan multiple steps ahead. She won't be easily fooled."

"I'm not going to try and fool her. I'm going to be as straight-forward and honest as I can."

"I would be cautious in how straightforward you are. Marcy is highly intelligent, and she has shown no remorse for her actions."

Kara considered that, then asked, "Why does she mimic people? Why copy her roommate or me? Why try to be just like her FTO, who was a guy?"

"There could be several reasons. It's not criminal—she'd have never been in the Coast Guard or passed a police background check if she had a criminal past. But most police screenings are exemplary in weeding out sociopaths. Still, very good, very controlled sociopaths, even with psychopathic tendencies, can get in, and Marcy seems to model this—until now. Remember, we still don't know anything about her childhood. Some abuse might not show up in psych profiles, especially if someone is intentionally trying to hide it. Or reveal a small abuse. Such as—why can't you be more like your sister?"

Catherine cleared her throat, and Kara wondered if maybe there was a thread of truth to that statement in the shrink's personal life. But Kara didn't ask. They had four minutes until arrival.

"I need to let you out." She looked for a place to pull over.

"Kara, I told Matt that you should do this, but I am not confident that you're stable enough."

"At least you're honest."

Maybe she wasn't stable. Hell, she didn't know. But what she did know was that she was the best person for this specific job, and damn if she was going to let this shrink demoralize her.

"I think you're reckless and impulsive and are used to doing everything on your own," said Catherine.

Kara swerved over to the shoulder when she saw a spot wide enough for the truck. "Great, go."

Catherine didn't leave. "However, you've shown good instincts, and you know Marcy better than any of us. Because

Marcy fixated on you, you might be the only one who can de-escalate the situation—if it can be de-escalated. She may do something unexpected. Most criminals, if they feel trapped or emotionally exposed, can turn extremely dangerous. But until you can expose her true motivations and why she'd gone to these lengths, she's not going to back down."

Catherine opened the door, then closed it. "Kara, be *very* careful with Marcy."

"*Aww*, you care."

"I'm serious here, Kara. I don't know if Jamie is alive at this point. I think it's fifty-fifty. And while Hazel may not be in im-mediate danger, she could be if Marcy gets it into her head that she wants to hurt Cal by taking away everything that he loves."

Catherine glanced at Kara. "What else did you learn from all these people you talked to?" she asked.

"What are you talking about?"

"After an hour conversation with Madelyn Jeffries, you de-cided that she not only did not kill her husband, but she didn't hire anyone to do so."

"Hour? It only took five minutes."

"You didn't know anything about her background, you based your decision on a conversation and how she answered the ques-tions, how she physically responded. Subtle clues in her psychol-ogy that manifest themselves to a trained eye."

"That's why it pissed me off that you didn't take my word for it. I *am* trained."

"I think I see your point."

Finally, Kara thought, but she kept her mouth shut.

"Watch for subtle clues, both verbal and physical. She has jus-tified everything she's done." Catherine inserted an earpiece. "I'm going to listen to everything, but only you can see her. If her words and tone don't match her actions, let me know some-how. And if there's a point where your life is in immediate dan-ger, you need to let us know."

"I'm going to tell you this because honesty is always the best policy," said Kara. "If Hazel and Jamie are in immediate danger, I'm getting them out and I don't care what the fuck happens to Marcy Anderson."

"She already believes you are her best friend. You come in from a big city and you are who she wants to be. The better rapport you develop, the better for the situation. Get her to relax."

Kara didn't say anything.

"You worked undercover for more than a decade and you lied for a living—you can't lie to her?"

"I can, that's not the issue. I just don't know if it's the best approach."

"Trust me on this, Kara. If she thinks you've turned on her, she'll kill you. It's why I think Jamie may already be dead. Marcy has to believe that you're on her side."

"Okay," Kara said.

Kara didn't think that Jamie was dead. Maybe she didn't *want* to believe it. She asked, "Do you think the fact that Cal didn't die on the *Water Lily* could have been a sign to Marcy that they were meant to be together?"

Catherine tilted her head, considering the possibility. "She might believe that. Cal got a second life, Marcy gets a second chance. And then he and Jamie recommit, set a wedding date, and announce they're having a baby. That could certainly be the trigger for this."

"Okay, I have a plan." She nodded at Catherine. She hoped it worked.

"Good luck." Catherine stepped out of the truck and Kara sped the last mile to the cabin.

35

Kara didn't have time to fully assess her surroundings as she slammed on the brakes in front of the Finch cabin at 5:29 p.m. She'd spun the truck around so she could get out, putting the truck between her and the house in case Marcy decided to just shoot her without conversation.

She jumped out of the truck, but hesitated a brief moment.

The cabin was one story with an A-frame—a loft was upstairs. Five steps up to a narrow porch that wrapped all the way around the property. One window to the right, two windows to the left. Large wood door straight ahead.

From the maps and photos Ryder had obtained, plus Cal's description, Kara knew the rear of the property was all windows with three sliding glass doors. The back deck extended over a short cliff. Not a kill-you-if-you-fall cliff, but you'd break a few bones. The inlet that the cabin had been built on was mostly private—only three other homes were nearby, none of which could be seen from the Finch property, and only one property had a full-time resident. The other two were a vacation home and one currently rented through a house-sharing site.

Her phone beeped. 5:30.

She cautiously approached the house. Marcy opened the door, keeping her body behind it. She had a gun in her left hand, and Kara had no way of knowing if Jamie or Hazel was on the other side of the door, where she couldn't see.

Kara kept her hands visible. She had her weapon in the small of her back, but she made no move to retrieve it.

Marcy was not pleased to see Kara.

Kara held up Cal's phone as she walked slowly up the stairs. "We need to talk."

"Cal called you."

Marcy looked over Kara's shoulder. For Cal? For cops?

"I came alone, Marcy. We're friends and I don't want anything to happen to you."

"Get inside."

After Kara stepped in, Marcy slammed the door behind her, locked and bolted it. She kept her distance from Kara.

Marcy holstered her gun, tucking it under a blazer that looked a lot like one Kara might wear. She didn't take her eyes off Kara, but she clearly didn't think that Kara was going to shoot her since she put her weapon away. A quick scan of her person and Kara determined that Marcy had another gun in an ankle holster. Kara didn't know about sharps, but she had to assume Marcy had at least one knife on her.

"You shouldn't have come," Marcy said. "This has nothing to do with you. Where's Cal? Do not lie to me, Kara."

"I'll tell you where Cal is if you tell me where Hazel is." Kara had immediately determined that neither Hazel nor Jamie was in the great room, where they were standing. The room was spacious, two-story windows looking out onto the deck and the water, trees shooting up to the right and left of the house. A spiral staircase went up to what Kara assumed was the loft—if the girls were there, there was no way Matt and Michael could get to them. There were no external windows in the loft that opened. But Kara could stop Marcy from going up.

A narrow hall was to the left, five doors all appeared closed. From Cal's drawing: bedroom, den, bath, closet, and secondary kitchen door. The kitchen was to the right of the hall, open, but Kara couldn't see everything. On the other side of the great room was a short hall with one door. Master bedroom and bath.

"I'm not negotiating with you, Kara. Where's Cal?"

"She's three years old, Marcy. She's not part of this drama."

"Hazel is sleeping, so keep your voice down."

Kara hoped she was. There were only two bedrooms in the house, though the den was also an option. But, with any luck, Jamie would be sleeping with her. Probably drugged… Drugged was better than dead.

"It's five thirty. Why is Hazel napping so late?"

By now, Kara expected that Michael and Matt would be in position to run the heat-sensing equipment to determine exactly where in the house Jamie and her daughter were. Now Kara just had to delay.

"Where is Cal?" Marcy demanded.

"I wouldn't let him come."

"Really?" she said flatly. She held up her phone. "So this text was from you?"

"He was on his way when I came by his place, and he couldn't lie to me about what was going on. I worried about his safety. So I convinced him that I'd let him go, told him to send the message, and then I handcuffed him and left him there. If he came, he would only get in the way."

"I *need* to talk to him! You don't get it."

"Why Cal? I mean, you could do better." Catherine had said that Marcy admired her, wanted to be like her. Maybe Kara could convince Marcy that she didn't want Cal, that the whole premise of a relationship with Cal was ridiculous. Play to her ego.

Marcy's eyes briefly met hers. "The other day you said something that made sense."

Kara tensed. She'd said a lot of things, and she didn't always think about what words came out of her mouth. She usually spoke the truth, but some things were better left unsaid.

"I usually make sense. What wisdom did I impart?"

"That a lot of women are single moms. And I started thinking, there's no stigma to it anymore. I don't need a guy to support me—I have a good job. Fat savings account. Great insurance. I don't need anyone else."

"Then why do you care where Cal is?"

Marcy didn't answer that question. "I heard on the police scanner that Damon was arrested."

"Yeah. He's in custody, asked for a lawyer. Typical. Nearly got me killed."

"What? He attacked you?"

"He set a fucking bomb in his closet." Kara had to make Marcy believe that *she* believed Damon was the bomber. "I thought I was a goner. Bomb was in a box, I didn't know, picked it up, accidentally triggered the fucking thing. If my partner hadn't been there I'd be in a million pieces."

"I'm so sorry."

"Yeah, well, I'm not in a million pieces, so I'm pretty happy tonight. I'd be happier if you and I were sitting down at the Fish & Brew having a couple beers right now."

"Why'd you come here? You didn't tell anyone on your team?" Marcy sounded skeptical, but didn't outright call Kara a liar.

"I came because I was worried about you. I didn't know what

was going on with you and thought maybe you needed someone to talk to."

"And you didn't tell your boss?"

"I'm not FBI. He's not my boss."

"So everything you told me about LAPD was true? You're
still a detective but you're working for the FBI?"

"Yep. All true. Not perfect, but what the hell is? We all just
do what we need to do to get through each day, right?"

Where the hell were Matt and Michael? She'd heard nothing
in the house. The police scanner was on, but it was low, provid-
ing an almost comforting white noise.

Twice Marcy had glanced down the narrow hall. Was she
thinking of bolting? Grabbing Hazel? Killing Jamie? Kara
needed to keep Marcy talking and buy time.

"What do you want to know?"

"How'd you get the FBI to let you work for them without
having to jump through all their hoops?"

"I helped Costa's team with an investigation, they thought I
did a good job, so when I had that problem in LA with an asshole
who really, really wants me dead, they let me join their team."

"And you caught Damon Avila."

"Yeah. We did. That's where the rest of my team is, either at
headquarters waiting for his lawyer or at his house searching for
additional evidence. And this is partly because of you. You're a
good cop, Marcy. I don't want this bad relationship with Cal to
ruin your career. You're better than that."

"I don't care about Cal. I don't need him."

"See? That's a positive attitude."

"You're playing me, Kara."

"I'm the only one who cares about you," she said. "We all
make bad choices sometimes."

Marcy laughed. "You? You're perfect. You're smart, you have
a great career, you have the respect of everyone who works with
you. You walked into the Fish & Brew and everyone there loved

you, knew you by name and you've been in town less than a week."

"It's because I drink a lot of beer and tip really well."

"No. It's because you have an aura that draws people to you."

She almost laughed but didn't because Marcy believed it. And she knew what Marcy meant—Kara's job this week had been to gather information in order to solve a horrific crime. To do that, she had to make everyone her best friend because they needed to trust her and talk to her. It was a means to an end, and it could be exhausting, but it was not unlike working undercover. You did what you needed to do to get the job done.

"Marcy, what happened last night?"

"How do you do it?" Marcy asked with another glance down the hall. Had she heard something? Sensed something?

"Do what?"

"Have everyone love you."

"It's not true."

"It is. Because you're perfect."

"I'm not perfect, Marcy. The team shrink thinks I'm a borderline sociopath."

Marcy stopped looking down the hall and turned to her in disbelief.

Keep her talking, keep her interested.

"She thinks I'm reckless and volatile," Kara continued. "She has no respect for me because I didn't go to college, shouldn't even be on the team because I haven't jumped through all those FBI hoops."

"How do you work with someone like that?"

"Prove to her that she's wrong. Marcy. Last night. What happened."

She averted her eyes. "I don't know what you mean."

Marcy tilted her head again, listening, then turned to start down the hall. "Don't move, Kara. I need to check on my baby."

Kara had to do something short of pulling her gun.

"Rena Brown."

Marcy whipped around and stared at her, eyes wide.

"Last night before she was murdered, Rena called Jamie, then left a voice mail for Cal. She arranged to meet him this morning. You left the Fish & Brew before me, and a while later I heard about Cal and Jamie moving up the wedding. And surprise, she's pregnant. Did Rena see you eavesdropping? Or maybe she slipped, said something about the pregnancy? I know you killed her, Marcy."

Marcy didn't say a word.

This might not have been the best plan, but it was the only one Kara had to keep Marcy in the room when chitchat wasn't cutting it.

"You're left-handed. Damon isn't left-handed."

Silence. Marcy's face was blank and slack, as if all personality had drained from her body.

"You couldn't risk Rena alerting Cal that she thought you were eavesdropping—that you'd had a bad reaction to the good news. Rena didn't know why it bothered her, but it did. She was doing her side work before she left and spilled a jug of malt vinegar as she was refilling the bottles. She broke a glass. She was distracted...and now I know why."

"Has anyone ever sucker punched you?" said Marcy. "Completely turned your life upside down?"

"We've all been through shit."

"You could never possibly understand. Who do you think you are? Coming here to accuse me of what? Murder? Really!"

A little cry came from down the hall, then "Mommy? Mommy?"

"You made me yell, and now I woke her up."

"Marcy, please stay and talk this through—"

"I need to take care of her."

"Where's Jamie? Where's Hazel's mom?"

"*I'm* Hazel's mom," Marcy said, dead serious.

"What did you do to Jamie?"

Hazel cried louder, then stopped.

Marcy ran down the hall. Kara pulled her gun and pursued. She prayed that her team had Hazel. If the little girl was still in that room, Kara couldn't fire her gun.

Marcy pushed open the bedroom door and flipped on the light. The drapes fluttered around the open window.

She turned around. Kara stood in the hallway, her gun drawn.

"You set this up! You disloyal bitch!"

Kara didn't want to shoot her. She hated this tight hallway, no place to maneuver, no shields. "Hands where I can see them, Marcy."

Marcy didn't hesitate. She rushed Kara.

Kara fired. The bullet hit Marcy in the upper right shoulder, but Marcy didn't slow down. Before Kara could fire again, Marcy had body slammed her up against the wall and punched her in the stomach so hard the wind was knocked out of her. Marcy was strong, she worked out and lifted weights, and Kara felt completely inadequate, like she was Tinker Bell against an Amazon. But she held on to her gun.

Pounding on the front door distracted Marcy for a moment, and Kara, who knew how to fight dirty, used that to her advantage. She hit Marcy on the side of her head with the butt of her gun. Marcy stepped back just enough so Kara could screw her left thumb deep into the gunshot wound. Marcy screamed, stumbled, and reached for her own holstered gun.

"Don't make me kill you," Kara said. She backed away from Marcy, down the hall, her gun aimed center mass. If Marcy pulled, Kara was going to shoot again. Damn, she didn't want to do that! She didn't want to kill her. This whole situation was fucked. "Marcy, I can help you."

"Like everyone else, you lied to me. You lied and stole my baby!"

Kara had backed into the living room to give herself more

room, more places for cover. Marcy stood halfway down the hall, rage and pain on her face, her shoulder bleeding. But she hadn't drawn. That was a plus. Kara could talk her down, she *had* to be able to talk her down.

Out of the corner of her eye, Kara saw Matt, who had broken the front door. He rushed to her side. Michael was right behind him. At the same time, Marcy kicked open the hall door to Kara's right, that led into the kitchen, and Kara lost sight of her. *Shit!* She could easily grab a weapon and Kara would have no choice.

"Marcy!" she called. "We can talk this out. I'm on your side. We can fix this!"

Marcy stepped into the great room from the other side of the kitchen. She had her gun out, but it wasn't pointed at Kara or Matt. It was pressed against her own temple.

She stared at Kara. "I thought we were friends."

"We are friends, Marcy," Kara said firmly. "Put down the gun. *Please* put down the gun. We can get through this, we can work anything out. You don't want to do this, Marcy, please!"

"You betrayed me."

Marcy pressed the trigger and Kara involuntarily screamed.

36

Kara blocked out the vision of Marcy's brains hitting the wall. She turned to Matt. "Tell me you have them, that they're okay, that this is all fucking over."

Michael walked past Kara to verify that Marcy was dead and kick the gun away from her hand.

Matt said, "We have Hazel, she is fine, she's outside with her dad."

"Jamie—God, no. Where is she? Is she—?" Kara hadn't seen her body in the room where Hazel had been. Was that good news? Bad?

"We don't know. There was no other heat signature in the house—you, Marcy, and the kid. That's it."

She was dead. She was here, dead.

Kara searched the house looking for her body. Matt and Michael did the same. They searched the entire property, inside and out, twice, and there was no sign of Jamie Finch, dead or alive.

Kara ended up back in the house and stared at Marcy's dead body.

Damn you! Why'd you take the easy way? Why kill yourself?

"What the fuck did you do with her?" Kara screamed at the corpse.

"We'll find her," Matt said, sounding confident when he damn well knew they had no leads, nothing to go on.

Kara refused to believe that Jamie was dead. It was childish, like believing in Santa Claus, but dammit, she would believe she was breathing until she touched her dead body.

"Where do we start?" Kara said.

Matt motioned for Kara to go outside. There were multiple vehicles pulling up. The tactical van, two police vehicles, the FBI's rental car, more lights could be seen in the distance.

Cal was sitting in the back of the rental car with Hazel in his lap. Catherine was examining her. When she saw Matt and Kara, she stepped away from the child and approached them. In a low voice she said, "She has no external injuries, she says nothing hurts, but she appears sluggish, her pupils aren't dilating properly, I believe from dehydration and whatever she was drugged with."

"Marcy drugged her?" Kara said. She drugged a kid. A little kid. And Kara couldn't yell at her because Marcy was dead.

"I believe so. But she's conscious and talking, able to answer simple questions, which is an excellent sign. She needs to go to the hospital for a full checkup."

Catherine looked at the blood on Kara.

"Not mine," she said.

"You have a cut on your cheek."

Kara couldn't even feel it. Her stomach hurt from where

Marcy punched her, but that was all she felt, and she wasn't complaining.

"I'm fine. We need to find Jamie."

Matt said, "The deputies are searching the perimeter, expanding out. They'll bring in search dogs."

Kara didn't want to hear that, but at least he didn't say cadaver dogs.

Catherine went back to sit with Cal and Hazel, and Michael came out of the house. "There's no indication as to where Jamie is—no notes, no maps. Here's Deputy Anderson's phone. Maybe Ryder can track her movements that way?"

"He's in the tactical van," Matt said.

Michael left to give Ryder the phone. Matt said, "You should take five, Kara."

"I don't want to take five," she snapped. "We have what? Two good hours of light left? I'm going to help search for her." The light was diminishing quickly because of gray clouds that seemed to be thickening as she watched.

"And we will, but we need to be smart about this. Half the C-4 is still unaccounted for. It wasn't in Anderson's apartment, it's not at Avila's house, or McKinnon's house—ATF checked all three while we were here. Now they're on their way here, because this house could be rigged, or Jamie's car—" he motioned to where it was parked in the carport "—or a dozen other places."

Returning from the tactical van, Michael overheard Matt's comment and nodded. "We have to assume that she has one or more bombs already set. They could be motion-triggered or on a timer—ATF found both types of components in her apartment. But there were no maps, nothing to indicate *where* she might have planted them. But they are not at her place."

"We proceed with caution, and on the assumption that Jamie Finch is alive and at risk," Matt said. "Agreed?"

Kara was relieved he didn't think she was dead. Maybe he

did—maybe he was just saying that to make her feel better. But it did make her feel better, and it made her want to do something.

Jim came up with his gear. "Can I process the scene?"

"No," Matt said. "Not until ATF clears the house."

Jim looked at Kara. "I was listening to your wire. You did everything you could."

She didn't want to hear that. Marcy was dead. She hadn't had the words to change the course of Marcy's decision. It hurt. Not because she thought Marcy could be redeemed, not because she thought Marcy was innocent, but because suicide was selfish. To avoid prosecution. To avoid facing her crimes and the victims she killed. To avoid facing the survivors. To avoid telling them what she'd done with Jamie, if she was even alive. If they had a chance of saving her.

Kara should have found a way to stop it.

Kara walked over to the car where Cal and Hazel were sitting. Catherine was still there. Kara didn't want to talk to her, and fortunately, Catherine didn't say anything to try to make her feel better. Kara just wanted to look at Hazel and see the one good thing that had come out of this miserable day.

"Where's Jamie?" Cal said quietly.

"Everyone is looking," Kara said.

Cal kissed the top of Hazel's head, his eyes watering. "Thank you."

"We'll find her."

Catherine cleared her throat. Kara ignored her. She didn't need her negativity. Kara was cynical about everything in her life, but this was the one time she had to believe that Jamie Finch was alive and that they would find her. Until she saw her dead body, she was alive.

The ambulance pulled into the clearing in front of the cabin. When Hazel saw the ambulance her eyes widened and she sat straight up in Cal's lap. "Daddy! It's Marshall!"

Kara had never heard of *PAW Patrol* before Monday; now she didn't think she'd get the theme song out of her head.

Catherine said, "Would you like to take a ride in Marshall's ambulance?"

"Oh, yes, yes! Daddy, can I? Peas? Pity peas?"

Cal was doing everything to not break down. "Of course, honey bunny."

Kara glanced at Catherine. "We have to ask her."

"Ask her what?" Cal said, trying to control his emotions for his kid. "Not about— What if—?"

"Hazel is going to be fine," Catherine said. "She may know something so we can locate…" She didn't continue. Three-year-olds picked up on a lot more than people sometimes thought.

"Be…careful," Cal said. "She's been through so much."

Kara said, "I have an idea. Trust me."

She approached the paramedic. "What's your name?"

"Doug Daniels."

"Do you know anything about the TV show *PAW Patrol*?"

He rolled his eyes. "I have twin five-year-olds."

"That little girl is obsessed with them. We think she knows where her mother might be, but we don't want to scare her."

"Okay. I'll do what I can."

Doug had his bag and walked over to the car. Hazel's eyes got all wide when she saw the paramedic uniform, but she leaned into her father, apprehensive. "Hi, Hazel, my name is Doug. I'm a friend of Marshall's. He wanted to come out here and help you today, but he's on the other side of the island helping another little girl. Can I put this little cuff on your arm and see how strong your heart is?"

She nodded.

Doug talked to her about everything he was doing. He took her temperature, blood pressure, checked her eyes, throat, and ears. Half of which he didn't have to do, but it all made Hazel comfortable, and then she started talking and asking questions about his equipment and if he had ever been on the rescue boat.

"Sure thing, I love boats. Not long ago there was a family that got a leak in their boat."

"Oh no!" Hazel said, but she didn't sound scared. She sounded like she knew the end of the story.

"Yes! And they called search and rescue and I went out and we brought the family back to shore and towed in their boat."

"Do you have a 'overcraft like Zuma, too?"

"It's similar, but not the same. Do you know what that means?"

She nodded.

"Have you been on a boat?"

"Yes. I can swim with my vest."

"You wear a vest? That's so smart. I like boats, too."

"My mommy's on a boat right now! I wanted to go but she said I had to take a nap. I don't like naps. I'm not a baby anymore."

"You're a big girl, Hazel."

Doug looked over Hazel's head at Kara and Catherine. Kara nodded at him to continue. She didn't want too many questions coming from too many people, it might confuse Hazel, but she would take over if she needed, in order to steer the direction of the conversation.

"Do you know what kind of boat your mommy went on? Maybe we can find her, and she can ride in my ambulance, too."

"Really? Um…well… I…" She wrinkled her face.

Kara squatted. "Hey, Hazel, did you see the boat?"

"No." She frowned. "Mommy said I had to stay in the car."

They'd already searched Marcy's vehicle and Jamie's vehicle and there were no clues as to where Jamie might be.

"So you drove someplace and then Marcy and your mommy went to the boat?" asked Kara.

"Mommy said even if I couldn't see them, I had to stay in the car no matter what."

"You're short like me. Cars don't always see us."

"That's what Mommy said. I stayed in the car because Mommy told me to and watched until my mommy and the police girl were teeny tiny specks."

"Did you see any water?"

She nodded. "Grandpa takes me swimming there all the time. Mommy says it's too dan'drous, but Grandpa is with me and he puts on my floaties and a vest." She turned to Doug. "Orange, like Zuma!"

Cal said, "I know where that is. Give me a map."

Kara got the map from Ryder in the tactical van. Cal circled a cove about two miles south of the Finch property near San Juan County Park. "Jared—that's Jamie's dad—takes Hazel there anytime he's in town. There's a shallow area, then this small rocky island about a quarter mile out. There's also a dock, private but everyone uses it. Jamie said she and her friends would swim out to the rocks when they were teens. It's freezing in the winter, but in the summer it's popular. Please find her. Please."

Doug said, "Hazel, let's go take a ride, you, me, and your dad, okay?"

"Is she okay?" Cal asked.

"She's fine," said Doug. "Everything is normal. Her pupils are a little dilated, but that could be from whatever she was given. The doctor will check her out thoroughly."

Kara thought back to everything Hazel had said. "Why did you say your mommy was on a boat?"

"Marcy said Mommy took a boat ride and that we had to wait for Daddy to get us."

"Thank you," Kara said. "You are very helpful."

"Like Marshall?"

"Just like Marshall."

With the information Hazel and Cal gave them, Matt quickly formulated a plan with the help of the sheriff, who knew the area well. The Coast Guard was called in to search the Haro Strait, the major shipping channel west of the island. If Jamie's boat was unanchored, it could drift into an island or rocks or a ship. If there was a bomb on board, and they had every reason to believe there was, then it might be set to explode at a specific time, or be on a motion sensor like the *Water Lily*. Hitting rocks or another boat might trigger it. The fear that Jamie must have, knowing that she was floating on a bomb, had to be paralyzing.

Or Marcy could have killed her and dropped her body in the ocean.

Kara didn't want to think that way, but the thought kept popping in her head.

Matt and Michael were joining the sheriff's search boat that was at a nearby dock. The sheriff drove up then, motioned for Matt that they were ready.

"I'm going," Kara said.

Matt stared at her. She knew what he was thinking.

"I have to see this through." She wasn't going to beg. She wasn't going to pull any card she had in her pocket. The reason was simple, even if it wouldn't make sense if she said it out loud.

Jamie is my responsibility.

What if she had said something different? If she could have talked Marcy out of killing herself? Had Kara done or said something wrong? Kara had to be part of the rescue, if a rescue was to be had.

Matt nodded.

Catherine, Jim, and Ryder were staying at the Finch house until it was cleared by ATF, then Jim would supervise processing the crime scene. Matt, Michael, and Kara piled in the back of the sheriff's Bronco. John had been quiet.

Matt said, "John, you couldn't have known."

"I hired her. She's my cop."

"She deceived a lot of people. We don't know what led her

down this path, but she spiraled out of control these last couple of weeks. That's not on you."

John didn't say anything more, and neither did Matt. What else was there to say?

It was a short drive to the pier. Then the four boarded the search boat and John handed them all life vests.

The captain of the search boat said, "Sheriff, we have word that a fishing trawler is missing from Rogue Cove."

"When?"

"They don't know. Hours up to two days. They had it in for repairs and no one noticed it was gone until the bulletin went out about the missing woman."

"GPS?"

"Not working."

"Shit," John muttered. "Description?"

"Small shrimp trawler, thirty-six feet. We've put the description and numbers out."

"Good. Go."

They headed straight for San Juan Park, the place Cal thought Hazel had referenced. John got a report from a patrol on the shore that they couldn't see a vessel from their vantage point.

The sheriff's department had ordered all civilian vessels on the west side of the island to immediately dock. The navigator of the search boat was focused on radar, and the pilot knew the area well.

The sun was rapidly setting, but the clouds blocked much of the light. In an hour, it would be below the horizon and near dark. Visibility was already difficult with the reflection and angle of the sun on the water. But the biggest problem was the gusts of wind coming from the northwest. They had a search plane out, but if the wind kept up, they would have to turn back.

Twenty minutes into the search, south of the county park and marine preserve, the navigator said, "I might have something." The pilot adjusted his course.

A few minutes later, they came up to a trawler that matched the description of the stolen boat. It had a wide flat deck with railings, and a cabin that appeared closed and dark. The waves seemed to be increasing in size as Kara watched them hit against the boat.

"It's anchored, sir," the pilot said to Matt. "We can't get any closer. There are rocks all over this area. It's well mapped here. The only way that boat could be out there is if it was anchored during high tide."

"Are we at low tide?" Michael asked.

"Yes, sir. The tide's coming back in, but there's also a storm in the north that's bringing these winds. We're not going to see much rain, but we're going to get some of the impact and strong winds. We'd have to wait about three hours before I can safely navigate to the boat."

The trawler they believed Jamie was on was two hundred yards from where the pilot had stopped the search boat. Michael took off his clothes and pulled out a wet suit from his bag.

"Prepared," Kara said with a half smile.

"Always. Can we take the lifeboat?" Michael jerked his finger to the small orange motorized boat attached to the side of the larger search boat.

The pilot looked at the sheriff. "The water is only going to get choppier. I can't advise this."

"It's your call," John told Michael.

"Kara, Matt—I need both of you," Michael said. "Matt, you stay on the lifeboat. Bring Kara and me all the way to the deck. Then you move out, twenty, thirty feet. Circle the area and wait for my signal to come back and get us."

"This is too dangerous, Michael," Matt said.

Michael pulled out one of the coolest toys the FBI had, Kara thought. A military-grade heat sensor, the most sophisticated she had seen. He turned it on, adjusted the settings, and in thirty seconds, he said, "Jamie's there, in the hull, and she's generating heat, so she's alive. I can't face that little girl if I didn't do everything I could to save her mother."

"We don't have time to debate this," Kara said. "Let's go."

John said, "I have the Coast Guard coming in. They have a cutter about twenty-five minutes out."

"That bitch set a motion-triggered bomb that killed nine people," Michael said. "We don't know why this one hasn't gone off, but it could go off in one minute or never. It could be set on a timer. But Marcy didn't just leave Jamie Finch out here for us to find. She left her here to die. Arguing isn't going to save her."

"My life, my choice," Kara said to Matt.

"Shit," Matt muttered. "Neither of you had better die on me."

The three of them climbed into the lifeboat equipped with a motor that Matt used to navigate toward the trawler. He had to slow down almost immediately to avoid a rock just under the surface. The waves pushed them up and down, up and down. Kara thanked whatever angel was watching out for her that she hadn't eaten anything in the last six hours.

Matt clearly had done something like this before, Kara thought, as he adeptly brought the motorboat alongside the anchored boat.

Michael climbed out first, elegantly for a large man, and reached down to help Kara out. He practically pulled her straight up into the bigger boat.

"Do what I say," Michael instructed her. "If I tell you to run, get off the boat. Follow directly behind me."

Matt maneuvered the skiff away from the trawler. Kara could still see him off the bow.

Michael took a bright light from his utility belt. The SEALs really were always prepared, Kara thought. He inspected the deck, then the small cabin, for explosives. "Clear."

A large hatch went down below—where the fish were stored, Kara figured—and that's where the heat sensor had indicated Jamie was being held.

Michael got down on all fours to inspect the seams of the

hatch. Kara held on to the metal railing to prevent herself from falling. How the hell did Michael have such great balance when the boat was continually bobbing in the waves? There were beams all over the place, a hook hanging from the cabin. She had no idea what the equipment did or how it was used, but everything looked dangerous.

"Clear," he said and opened the door. He secured it with a chain that was already there. "Stay until I call you."

"Roger that, GQ."

He glanced at her and gave her a reassuring smile.

She held on because otherwise she would be staggering around like a drunk and probably fall overboard. Michael disappeared into the hull. Kara couldn't hear anything but waves splashing against the side. She was already soaked wet and the cold gusts of wind made her shiver.

"Kara!" Michael's booming voice called.

She let go of the railing and scrambled down the ladder into the hull that smelled like rotten fish. Michael was shining his light in the cavernous space, which wasn't much taller than she was, though long and wide, going the entire length of the boat.

Jamie was tied to the center post, just under the ladder, her hands suspended to a thick pipe that ran along the ceiling. She was unconscious but breathing.

Then Kara noticed what Michael was shining his light toward.

A wire went all around the edge of the hull, and chunks of C-4 were attached in three corners.

"It's on a timer," he said. "We have twenty minutes—I'm going to try to defuse. I need you to get Jamie out. Now."

That was all the motivation Kara needed. She pulled her knife out of her boot and cut the ropes holding Jamie to the pipe.

Michael swore. "What the fuck?"

"I just cut the rope like you said!"

"A wire was embedded in the rope! I didn't fucking see it!

Shit! Get out, Quinn! Go, go, go! Matt!" he said into his comm. "We have two minutes, get your ass here!"

Michael picked Jamie up and threw her over his shoulder like she weighed nothing. Kara was already up the ladder.

Matt was approaching the trawler fast in the orange rescue boat. Kara held on to the railing with both hands as the waves rocked them up and down. Michael swung himself over the railing and held on with one hand like Tarzan, still holding Jamie on his shoulder, while Matt maneuvered the boat underneath them. Matt, who like Michael seemed to be able to balance even on the water, reached up as Michael lowered Jamie to him. Matt grabbed her and set her on the bottom of the boat.

She was safe. She was alive. Kara breathed a bit easier.

Michael reached out for Kara's hand. "Take it," he said.

She did. Michael's large hand grasped her wrist and they were almost out of this.

"Okay, let go. I'll lower you down."

She let go, lost her balance, but Michael held tight.

"You got this, KQ," Michael said with a wink.

A wave fiercely pushed up and tilted their boat away from Matt's skiff. Away from safety.

The hook that had been hanging off the cabin swung precariously toward Kara and Michael. They both ducked to avoid being hit, but the edge of it caught Michael's arm and he grunted in pain, forced to let go of Kara's hand. Gravity and momentum pulled her in the opposite direction, and she slid all the way to the other side of the boat. Michael was holding on to the railing, but the boat was tilting at an unnatural angle. As the boat came down off the wave, the sound of metal crunching on rocks was earsplitting. Was the damn boat going to fall apart before it blew up?

Michael shook the pain from his bicep. The hook had torn his wet suit and he saw blood oozing from the cut. He ignored it. He was holding on as the boat was still trying to right itself.

Michael pulled himself partly up and saw the orange boat. "Go, Matt!" he called out.

"I'm not leaving!"

"One hundred yards—you have to go. I'll get her. I won't let her die. Go *now*!"

Against every instinct, Matt turned the lifeboat away from Michael and Kara.

Michael didn't wait to see if Matt obeyed him. The boat was at seventy-five degrees to the port. Kara was trapped on the other side of the deck, holding on to the railings, her bright orange vest a beacon to him. They had less than a minute before the boat exploded, but only seconds before the waves shifted the boat in the opposite direction.

He had to have Kara secured to him by then, or they were both dead. There was no way in hell he was jumping without her.

He slid down the deck and grabbed Kara around the waist.

"Michael, go. I'll jump and swim."

"You'll never make it in time," he said.

He pulled a hook from his utility belt, pulled hard to release the two feet of attached line, and hooked it on Kara's life preserver.

"I don't want to kill you," she said. "Please! I'm a good swimmer."

"No one dies. Not tonight. We're going under. Do not fight it. I have you."

As soon as the boat tilted to the starboard side, Michael let go of the railing and let momentum take him and Kara to the other side. He took her hand, and they jumped off the trawler into the rough ocean swells. He was more worried about rocks than drowning. But by the grace of God, they missed the rocks.

Michael used every ounce of his strength to fight the current and swim hard to put as much distance as possible between them and the rigged boat. Kara had a grip on his belt, so he knew she was still with him.

He felt a wave of energy hit him, propelling him inhumanly faster through the water. He took a deep breath, knowing he was going under.

Kara was no longer holding on to his belt. He felt her weight dragging down the line that attached her to his belt, but it was jerking, as if she was struggling.

Michael swam hard straight up, breaking out of the water and gasping for air. He reached down and found the line, pulled it up even as it cut into his hands. He felt Kara's hand on his thigh. He reached down, grabbed her wrist, and pulled her to the surface.

She coughed and fought for breath, but that was damn good. She was alive.

Together, they looked back at the boat.

It was gone, just a few flames and a lot of smoke.

He pulled out his flare, cracked it, and light glowed. He tossed it in the air.

"Kara?" he said.

"Let's. Not. Do that again."

"A wave. Take a breath, let it go over us."

He held her as the wave pushed at them. When they resurfaced, Matt was only feet away with the skiff. He helped them into the boat. Then Michael detached his line from Kara.

She sank into the bottom of the boat, next to Jamie. "Is she okay? Matt—please tell me she's not dead."

"She's sluggish, but awake and breathing on her own. She asked about Hazel."

Matt took Kara's hand and squeezed it. "You really okay?"

"I am. And I'm so damn happy to be alive." She looked over at Michael. She had no words. "Thanks doesn't seem like enough, GQ."

"It is, KQ. It's enough."

37

Kara wanted to sleep, dear God, she wanted to sleep, but she couldn't.

They'd arrived back to the FBI house after midnight. She took a very long, very hot shower and still felt cold. Under thick blankets, she willed herself to sleep, but every time she closed her eyes, she saw Marcy kill herself, in slow motion. Watched her brains hit the wall, the blood and bone and gray matter. Kara mentally reviewed every possible scenario to stop what happened, but each time Marcy still ended up dead. She was exhausted, physically exhausted, but could not sleep.

Not to mention that Kara had had two close calls in one day. Must be some kind of a record, she thought.

Finally, after nearly two hours of restlessness, she went out to the porch with a bottle of tequila and the comforter from her bed. She downed a long slug from the bottle. Two in the fucking morning and she couldn't sleep. She drank again, stared into the dark. As long as her eyes were open, she didn't see Marcy's brains outside her skull.

She wasn't drunk yet, but she was getting there.

She heard movement in the house before someone came out to the porch.

Matt.

She wanted to take him to bed because sex would clear her mind. Sex would make her think about herself, and not Marcy, and not the little girl, and not seeing Jamie tied to a pipe or herself holding her breath underwater. But damn, she didn't need to have the critical eye of Catherine watching her tomorrow. This house didn't have thick walls.

Kara knew this wouldn't last. It couldn't.

Nothing good lasted.

Yeah, she was getting drunk. She drank straight from the bottle. It was a good bottle, one she'd picked up downtown to save for after the case was solved.

Damon Avila was in prison, but they didn't know how long they could keep him. Matt was taking another run at him tomorrow. He had a plan, he said, to get him to confess. She wanted to know what it was, but hadn't asked. She didn't know if she could understand anything right now, her mind was numb. Matt wanted him on the five murders, and he was going to do everything in his power to prove it if Damon didn't confess. If not tomorrow, they could still keep him as an accessory to the bombing. Kara didn't know if he was involved—she was pretty certain that Marcy had framed him—but the evidence was at his house, and they could keep him at least until Monday and his arraignment.

She knew how Neil Devereaux had felt. They knew, in their

gut, that Damon Avila was guilty of murder. Proving it was going to be an uphill battle. But they had far more than Neil had, so there was that.

She handed her bottle to Matt.

He took a swig. She admired that.

She reclaimed her tequila.

"I thought you were dead," he said quietly. "When the boat exploded, I hadn't seen you and Michael jump off."

He sat next to her on the love seat. Close. Intimate.

He kissed her.

She needed it.

She put the bottle down and held on to him as she devoured his lips, his neck, behind his ear. He groaned and she murmured, "*Shh*. Don't wake the house."

This would be fun, she realized, taking Matt over the edge and being as quiet as possible. It was a challenge. Because when Kara was with Matt, she liked that they were rough and tumble. She relished the thrill, the satisfaction he always gave her. And she loved how she enticed him to let go. Mathias Costa was far too serious, too uptight most of the time. But not in bed. In bed he was free and sexy and devoted to their mutual pleasure. The intensity of his lovemaking had her hook, line, and sinker.

If someone walked out on the porch, that would be it. Kara knew it, and she didn't want this to be over. She didn't want to give Matt up. If they had to keep it a secret, so what? Couldn't she have one good thing in her life that was all hers?

She wasn't drunk enough to say fuck it.

Reluctantly, she pulled herself away from him.

He pulled her back. "Don't go."

"I have to. Matt—"

"No me dejes amor, te quiero tan mala."

She didn't know exactly what he said.

"I can't have people finding out about this," she told him.

He tensed. And she knew then that someone else knew about her and Matt.

Shit.

Shit shit shit!

"Who?"

"It's not important."

"Dammit, Matt—"

"I'm not going to lose you over a rumor," he said.

"For godsakes, don't let it be easy for them!" She got up and slipped out of his arms. She was cold.

"Don't walk away, Kara. We're good together. You know it, we both know it."

She didn't know what to think anymore. Her life felt like it was in limbo. She didn't know which end was up. She was drunk, but she wasn't stupid. She couldn't blow up her life.

Matt stood, walked over to her, kissed the back of her neck.

She closed her eyes. She didn't want it to end, either. But she didn't think she really had a choice, not anymore.

She turned and looked at him. Something shifted. She couldn't describe it, couldn't put words to these strange feelings, so unnatural for her. Why couldn't she have everything she wanted? Dammit, *why?*

She kissed him, and almost cried. Because she didn't want to pull away. She didn't want to go to bed alone. She didn't want to leave him.

But she did. She walked into the house, leaving Matt alone on the porch.

FRIDAY

38

Catherine had no idea what she was going to do with Matt.

She packed her clothes and toiletries as she finished getting ready to leave. Ryder had moved mountains to get her on a flight all the way to Philadelphia—a short flight to Seattle, then direct across the country. She wasn't going to miss Beth's memorial. She had more important things to focus on other than Matt and his task force. Like her determination to repair her marriage to Chris. Her realization that she needed to be a mother, a full and engaged mother, to her amazing daughter. The last year had been hell on her, but it had also been hell on her family *because* she hadn't been able to face her grief.

Yet Catherine missed her sister Beth something fierce. The

pain and emptiness were always there, a pit in her heart, and she didn't know how to fix that.

Chris had been right about one thing: Catherine still blamed Matt for not loving Beth. Catherine had held it against Matt for a long time. She purposefully hurt him because he had hurt her.

She had planned to skip Beth's memorial because of her mother. Catherine avoided the woman who had birthed her as much as possible. But now Catherine had decided to go for herself. For Chris and Lizzy and Beth. To finally put it behind her.

She had to face her grief if she was truly going to regain her life and have a future.

She picked up her suitcase, took a last look around the room to make sure she hadn't forgotten anything, then left. She said goodbye to Ryder, who was in the kitchen. He was an asset to the team, and someone Matt could rely on. Smart, diligent, and a team player.

Everyone else was likely still sleeping—yesterday had been long and difficult.

She stepped out onto the porch to wait for Matt, who would be driving her to the small Friday Harbor airport.

In sunglasses, Kara sat slumped in a chair, clearly hungover, drinking ice water from a liter bottle. Had she even slept last night? Catherine wouldn't be surprised if she hadn't.

"You're going to your sister's memorial," Kara said, nodding toward the suitcase.

"Yes." Catherine sat down across from Kara. "I wasn't fair to you at the beginning of this case."

"No shit."

Catherine bristled. She didn't like Kara's style, nor did she like her personally. She wasn't someone she felt close to, or someone she could get close to. There were several reasons, some of which she would consider later, when she had time and distance to separate her emotions from her professional opinion.

But Catherine could acknowledge that Kara was a good cop.

"While you took some risks I felt were unwise, you did a good job last night. You handled Marcy surprisingly well."

"Surprising to you," she said.

Maybe, Catherine acknowledged to herself. "Don't blame yourself for her suicide. I listened to the entire conversation. She made the choice to take her life after we rescued Hazel. Once she knew that she didn't have the little girl anymore, when that reality sank in, she was gone, even before she pulled the trigger. That wasn't on you."

Kara drank water, didn't comment. She would probably blame herself in some way, which Catherine understood. She still blamed herself for Beth's murder. Intellectually she knew it wasn't her fault, but in her heart, the pain lingered.

"Your insight into Marcy's psyche helped," Kara said. "I don't think I would have been as effective if I didn't have that perception of her and her motives. I'm not just saying that to make you feel good, Catherine, because I honestly don't care, but we're going to be working together, and you're smart and you understand psychopaths. I respect that."

Catherine nodded. Kara did have an acute understanding of human nature, which made her valuable. But there were some things that couldn't be forgiven, and some things that had to be made clear to her.

"Mathias has worked hard to lead this team," said Catherine. "He and Tony Greer put it together, and Matt likes to give Tony the credit, but he's been talking about a mobile response task force for years. Then everything came together, and he had this opportunity."

"He's good at it."

"But this is a test. Many people above Tony are watching very closely. We succeed, and Matt will be able to replicate this team. Train other teams, other leaders. We fail, Matt will take the heat."

"We haven't failed."

Catherine knew Kara understood the implications of her words—she was not stupid. She wished she could see her eyes, but the younger cop hadn't taken off the sunglasses.

Kara was going to make her say it, so she did. Blunt and to the point, which was how Kara seemed to prefer to communicate.

"If anyone finds out that you're having sex with Matt, your boss," Catherine said, her voice low and clear, "he will lose everything. And so will you. You're not an FBI agent, Kara. You're an LAPD detective who can't go back to that job. Think about that. Whether sex is more important than your future— more important than Matt's future."

Kara's jaw tightened, but she was processing.

Catherine continued. "I've been friends with Matt for a long time. He's my daughter's godfather. He deserves someone who can give him a home base, a place to find peace. Like Chris, my husband, has done for me. You're not peaceful, Kara. You're chaos, and you know it. And the only way this ends is with Matt losing everything he's worked for. He'll land someplace, he always does. You won't. Because I know you have nothing else to fall back on."

"Is that it?" Kara said, her voice low, almost a growl.

Catherine nodded. She got through to her. It might take her a couple of days to accept the truth, but she would.

Catherine rose, picked up her bag, and turned toward the stairs that led to the driveway.

"Catherine?"

She looked over her shoulder.

"You might be the one with the advanced degree, but I see right through you. And don't ever forget it."

A chill went through Catherine, but she held her posture, walked down the stairs, and opened the car door.

"You should come with me to Philadelphia," Catherine said as Matt drove the short distance to the Friday Harbor airport.

"I'm going to get Damon Avila to confess," he said. "And I have to wrap up a lot of things here, you know that. I'll be back in DC on Tuesday, Wednesday at the latest. Once I get a confession, I'll be comfortable with Seattle taking over the investigation."

"Confident, aren't you."

"Do you doubt me?"

She smiled. "No."

Last night they'd discussed how to approach Avila and draw a confession out of him. Catherine had insight there, and Matt had listened, absorbed, and she was confident that he would do well, even without her there. He had a couple of cards to play, and when push came to shove, Matt could take the death penalty off the table. He could even take life in prison off the table. But if Avila didn't play, Matt had a pile of charges related to the bombing he could hold over him.

Neither of them thought Avila had anything to do with the bombings, but the evidence was in his house, and he had motive. It would be hard to get around that.

"I saw you talking to Ryder this morning," Catherine said. "Did he find anything?"

"He's a rock star," Matt said. "He went through the box of Neil's files that we recovered in Avila's house. All Neil's notes, his methodology, and several lines he'd put out to the authorities. There is evidence—not overwhelming, but some, and I'm going to use each piece against him until he confesses."

A moment later, Catherine said, "Come to the house for dinner next Sunday. See Lizzy. Chris."

"I will. Thank you. For what it's worth, Catherine, I'm really glad you're going to Beth's memorial."

"I'm not looking forward to seeing my mother, but I'm glad I'm going, too." She paused, then said quietly, "I miss her."

"So do I."

"I'm sorry for things I said to you. You've been nothing but a friend to me. I could blame my actions on my grief, but that's taking the easy way. I was angry, I was terrified, and…I loved her so much."

"Beth was all the good in the world in one person," Matt said.

"Why didn't you love her? You could have been my brother-in-law. I would have liked that."

"I loved Beth, but I felt she was the sister I never had. We had fun, we could laugh, she brought out the best in me. But it never felt right, not romantically. And I can't explain it any other way." He pulled into the small airport parking lot, turned off the car. He took Catherine's hand. She stared at his hand, because she feared she would cry if she looked in his face. "Cat."

Now she was forced to look. Her eyes were damp.

"Cat, I forgive you. I'm tough, I know you suffered, and I appreciate that you see that now. Not only your own pain, but how you treated me, how you treated Chris. But we move forward from here, and I'm good with that."

She nodded. "Me, too."

He kissed her on the cheek. "I'll walk you in."

He got her suitcase out of the trunk and carried it across the lot to the small airport entrance. She checked in—an easy process for the commuter airport—then turned back to him. "Matt. Be careful."

He stared at her. "Don't."

"I can see that you've developed real feelings for Kara. That's dangerous. Professionally and personally."

"I'm not going to talk about Kara with you."

"Then listen. You have feelings. I see that now. But Kara can't ever be what you need."

"You don't know what I need, Catherine."

"You need your job. *This* job, what you've built, what you've done, is a once-in-a-lifetime opportunity. Don't let a fleeting passion destroy everything you have worked your ass off to achieve."

Catherine turned and walked toward security. She had done what she could to save her best friend. The rest was up to him.

After Catherine left, Kara took four aspirin, finished her water, and went back to bed. She slept four hours on top of the two she'd had earlier that morning. She woke at noon, still a little hungover, but functioning.

Michael was in the kitchen. He'd made breakfast for lunch. "Matt and Ryder are at the sheriff's office dealing with press and paperwork, then Matt is going to interview Avila again. Said if you want to watch, come by. Jim just left for the mainland for Anderson's autopsy, but he'll be back before dinner. Are you hungry?"

"Starving."

"I made plenty, help yourself."

She dished up scrambled eggs, sausage *and* bacon—wow, he even made hash browns!—and a slice of a quiche thing that had green stuff in it, but it smelled good. "You can save lives *and* cook. Lucky me."

She poured coffee and sat down at the table.

"You okay?"

"Peachy."

"Seriously, Kara. I don't usually get to save the life of the same person twice in one day."

"Honestly, that's behind me." Mostly. "You are a rock, Michael, and I'll never forget that. You had my back and I hope you know that I have yours, though you won't see me diving into the ocean or disarming bombs."

"You have your strengths," he said with a grin, then stuffed a piece of bacon in his mouth.

"It's Marcy," she said after a few minutes. Well, it was Marcy *and* Catherine, but for different reasons. "Don't tell me I did everything I could. I know that. It still doesn't stop me from seeing her blow her brains out."

Michael didn't say anything, and they ate in silence. It was a comfortable silence, and she was grateful.

She cleaned up the kitchen while Michael poured them both more coffee. It was the least she could do after the delicious meal.

"How about if we go to the hospital and check on the Finches?" Michael said.

"I'd like that."

The hospital wasn't far, because nothing was far in Friday Harbor. They bought flowers in an attached gift shop, and as they were walking out, Kara couldn't believe what she saw—a stuffed Marshall dog from *PAW Patrol*. She went back to the counter and bought it. Maybe Hazel already had one. If she didn't want it, Kara would keep it for herself. To remind her that she'd done her job: Hazel and her mother were alive.

When they arrived in Jamie's room, Cal was in a chair, looking like he hadn't slept or eaten in days. Hazel was sitting on her mom's bed, looking up at the television, where *PAW Patrol* was playing without sound. That didn't seem to bother Hazel. She probably knew every episode by heart.

Jamie had circles under her eyes. She was hooked up to an IV and had a bandage around her head. Her left wrist was in a cast, and her right wrist was bandaged. She looked at them when they entered and almost smiled.

"You didn't have to."

Her voice sounded off, tired and scratchy.

"Pretty!" Hazel said.

Cal took the flowers and put them on the windowsill. "Thank you," he said. "For everything." He took Jamie's hand. Kissed it, gently.

Kara squatted next to Hazel. "I thought of you when I saw him." She handed her the Marshall toy.

Hazel's eyes widened even more. She took the stuffed rescue dog and hugged him. "I love him!"

Hazel had bounced back. Kara envied her innocence, hoped she held on to it as long as possible.

She turned to Jamie. "We won't stay long. Just wanted to make sure you were doing okay."

Jamie said, "I don't remember much from yesterday, if that's what you want to know."

"Not now," Michael said. "When you're feeling better, you'll need to give a statement, but not today."

With all the emotion in the room, Kara was uncomfortable being there, and she admired Michael for his class. He was a good guy.

"Hazel's a hero," Kara said.

"She really is." Jamie smiled, tears in her eyes. "The nurse told me what you did, Detective Quinn. That both of you risked your lives to get me out of that boat."

"Piece of cake," Michael said. "I'm a Navy SEAL, we can do anything."

"I believe it," Jamie said.

Cal walked them out. He hugged Kara, then shook Michael's hand. "She's okay. Dehydrated, broken wrist, bruises, but she's okay, and so far, the baby is okay. It's a boy. She's fourteen weeks. And I didn't know they could tell the sex that early, but they did a bunch of tests on her and the baby and asked if we wanted to know. Jamie's dad is on his way, he'll be here tonight. We can't go into his house yet, but the sheriff says tomorrow."

"I would get a cleaning crew in first. You don't want to see it," Kara said.

"Yeah, I'll do that. I—I never thanked you for what you did. What you risked for my family, first Hazel, then Jamie. This was my fault. I brought that nutcase woman into Jamie's life."

"No, Cal, this is all on Marcy Anderson," said Kara. "Don't ever forget that."

"Yeah. Well. I, um—I pray Jamie will forgive me."

"Piece of advice? Forgive yourself first. The rest will come."

39

Sheriff John Rasmussen had been having a difficult twenty-four hours from handling the press, multiple agencies, and his own staff who learned about Marcy's crimes, which needed to be addressed. But Matt wanted him in the interrogation room with Damon Avila. Not just because Avila's family was local and the sheriff should be involved, but because it might give him more pieces to the bigger puzzle of how Marcy put together this complex frame job.

Matt debriefed John, and the sheriff was on the same page with him, so when they walked into the interrogation room with Avila and his lawyer—a public defender from the county who looked near retirement age—they had a united front. An assistant US attorney had arrived earlier in the morning and was observing from the observation room. It would help expedite any legal agreements should Avila want to talk. Matt had already received a bit of leeway from the government lawyer, so he didn't have to jump up and down to get permissions.

He went through preliminary questions with Avila and the lawyer. Avila looked like he hadn't slept much, and he was drinking Dr Pepper and water, alternating between the soda and the water bottle.

"Again, Mr. Avila," Matt said, "I appreciate your willingness to answer a few questions now that you have your lawyer present."

"Depends what type of questions," the lawyer said.

"I'm going to lay my cards on the table," Matt said. At least some of them, he thought. "First, we executed a legal search warrant yesterday on Mr. Avila's property that yielded evidence of bomb making. A working bomb was found that nearly killed one of my team members. Files that had been in the possession of retired agent Neil Devereaux were also found in his house. Files and notes that showed that Neil suspected Damon Avila of murder. This is what we call a clear motive."

"I didn't make any bombs," Avila said. "I didn't kill anyone."

His lawyer put a hand on Avila's arm. "I know that the person you suspect of bombing the *Water Lily* committed suicide last night, and that a statement by a victim showed that Ms. Anderson did in fact plant a bomb on a trawler that nearly killed several people. Clearly, the evidence was planted in Mr. Avila's house. He has no expertise in bombs or bomb making."

"A working theory at this point is that Ms. Anderson and Mr. Avila worked together. Ms. Anderson wanted to kill her ex-boyfriend Cal McKinnon, and Mr. Avila wanted to kill Neil Devereaux, who had uncovered evidence that Mr. Avila killed five people over the course of the last thirteen years."

Avila's face paled. He didn't say anything.

"You will not be able to prove any of it," the lawyer said. "My client has nothing to do with the bombings, and the idea that he is some sort of serial killer? You're pulling that out of thin air."

"The evidence will prove it," Matt said. "A bomb in his house. Documents stolen from Neil that include Neil naming Mr. Avila as a suspect in these deaths. I can get a dozen sworn statements that Anderson and your client were friends and spent a lot of time together. Mr. Avila was on the mainland the same time that C-4 went missing, and one of his former students who he continued to tutor in math worked at the construction company where the C-4 went missing from. I can tie this case up with a pretty little bow for the prosecution. And with Ms. Anderson dead, the people will want justice. This is a death penalty case. Murder with special circumstances."

Avila opened his mouth. The lawyer stopped him from talking. "With Ms. Anderson dead, you have no evidence that my client has done anything wrong."

"A bomb was found in Mr. Avila's house in the box of documents stolen from Neil Devereaux. Those documents have already been read and processed—Neil's fingerprints were all over them, the notes were in his handwriting. That is enough evidence to keep your client held without bail. The court system doesn't take kindly to domestic terrorists."

Avila shook his head.

His lawyer said, "You're jumping the gun on this, Agent Costa. I know that a search of Ms. Anderson's apartment yielded more documentation of bombs and bomb making as well as her obsession with her ex-boyfriend. Photos, letters, plans. On her person was found passports for her and the young child she planned to kidnap. It's clear she was the sole bomber."

Someone had talked out of school about the passports. The search of her property? That was very public, but the passports were not. That irritated Matt, but he didn't say anything.

John did, however. "Where did you hear about the passports, Roger?"

"I don't have to tell you that. I know it's true. And you don't have a case."

Matt wondered if Avila had helped Anderson with the passports. Maybe…maybe. But they hadn't found anything that pointed them in that direction at either property.

Matt pulled a file from his briefcase and slid it over to Avila. The lawyer took it first, opened it.

"What am I looking at?" he asked.

"On the top is a copy of the speeding ticket your client received on May 1, four years ago, the day after Eric Travers went missing from his boat. Evidence that your client was in Puget Sound at the time. Then, a hotel receipt where he stayed for two nights, near the dock where Travers kept his boat. Then, a receipt of your client renting a motorboat the same day that Travers went out—from the same dock."

"This doesn't prove that my client had anything to do with his disappearance."

"The fourth page is a photo of your client's vehicle thirteen years ago—a pickup truck he owned at the time—parked at the trailhead leading to Mowich Lake, the weekend that Brian Stevens and Jason Mott disappeared."

"Which means nothing." He frowned, clearly not understanding why there was a photo of his client's truck at all from that time.

"Neil was obsessed," Matt said, "and he spent three years tracking down people who had been at Mowich Lake that weekend. It was Memorial Day, a lot of visitors. He spoke to dozens of people, asked to see any photos they had, looked through social media pages, and one family had taken pictures in the parking lot when they arrived. Mr. Avila's truck was there."

"It's still not going to prove—"

"I'm going to cut to the chase," Matt said. He'd been watching Avila's expression, and he was ready to talk. Matt had to get the lawyer to let him talk. "We have a dozen FBI agents now reopening five cases—five deaths that had been ruled accidental, but Neil Devereaux believed were murder. Mott and Stevens. Eric Travers. Missy Douglas. And Billy Clark."

Avila began to shake.

"Your client killed those five people, and if Neil could get this information—" he gestured toward the folder "—as a retired FBI agent, think what a dozen active and dedicated FBI agents will be able to find."

"I—" Avila began.

The lawyer interjected. "Before my client says another word, I need a plea deal in writing."

Matt pulled out a paper from his pocket. "The best I can do is take the death penalty off the table." He slid over the agreement to the lawyer. It basically said if Avila had nothing to do with the bombings but confessed to any other capital offenses, he would not be eligible for the death penalty.

"I'm going to need more."

"No," Avila said. "No. Just—no. I'm not going to put my family through a trial. Through...everything. I'm just not going to do that. All I want...if my nieces want to see me...after this... after... I...I just want to stay close. As close to them as I can so they can visit."

"That I can do," Matt said, with a glance toward the one-way mirror. There was no knock, no sign to stop the agreement. "I will make it happen, if you're honest with me right now."

"I never planned on killing anyone. It just...happened. I followed Brian at Mowich Lake. It was a fluke, really—I saw them at a gas station in Pullman, I was in town interviewing for a teaching position, and just followed them. They were laughing, and all I could think about was how my life was over. I couldn't play ball. I'd lost my girlfriend. I'd lost everything...and I was going to confront him. But I didn't know what to say, so when they invited me to go midnight fishing, I went. One thing led to another and I pushed Brian into the lake. Jason tried to get him out—the water was cold, freezing. And I pushed Jason in but he hit his head on the boat and he floated. I think he was unconscious. Maybe dead. It was so dark. I took the boat back to the dock. I didn't plan to kill them... I just wanted them to hurt like I hurt."

Neil was right. All along, Neil had been right.

"Missy Douglas."

Tears came. Matt didn't know if they were to try to garner sympathy or if he was truly remorseful. "I loved her. I never wanted to kill her."

"What happened to Missy?"

"When I found out she was engaged, I just wanted to talk to her. Her fiancé wouldn't let her—how could he stop her? He said she didn't want to see me and I...I was so angry. I just wanted five minutes! I followed them to the mountain. She went walking in the morning before anyone was up and...and I pushed her. I didn't want to, it was like I couldn't help myself. I loved her. I'm so sorry."

In the end, Damon Avila confessed to all five murders. Eric Travers because he had been given the promotion that Avila wanted, and Billy Clark out of jealousy. It had been spontaneous, like the first two. He came across Billy on the road. Billy had been driving fast, and it reminded Avila of how he shattered his leg. He didn't intend for him to die, just to be hurt. To know how Avila felt. And it was after that that Avila started to lose sleep, to feel out of sorts. The guilt began to set in, and when Neil Devereaux started looking at him suspiciously, he knew Neil knew.

"Did you work with Marcy Anderson to plant the bomb on the *Water Lily*?"

"No. I swear. I knew nothing about her plan. I don't know anything about the C-4. I didn't take it, she didn't tell me anything. But—she told me that Neil suspected me of murder. She said he'd asked for her help, but that I didn't have anything to worry about because he didn't have any hard evidence, only a theory."

"Did you find it at all suspicious that a local deputy was willing to overlook murder?" John interjected.

"No—not really. We were friends. She said I had been her only friend when she arrived, and she knew how it felt when someone betrayed you."

John leaned forward. "Did you tell her that you killed Brian and Jason? The others?"

"I…I said it was an accident. Which was true about Billy—I didn't mean to kill him. And the others, they were just spontaneous. I didn't really plan it, I just saw red and pushed."

Matt wasn't certain he believed that the murders were spontaneous and unplanned, but Avila confessed to all of them.

And Marcy knew. She knew and that was how she was able to frame him. It was almost a perfect crime.

"Why did you go to Bellingham two weeks ago? You went Monday night and returned Tuesday early afternoon."

"I didn't."

"We have your truck on the ferry. Every license plate is logged when they drive on."

"I loaned my truck to Marcy. Hers was in the shop, she'd woken up to a flat tire, and she had a doctor's appointment. I mean, that's what she told me."

"Can anyone verify your alibi?"

He looked panicked for a minute. Then his eyes widened and he said, "Yes! Yes. Pete called me Tuesday morning—I usually don't work until the afternoon, but he needed me to help stock the bar. He picked me up before eleven. I remember because I had loaned Marcy my truck."

Avila stared at Matt, pleaded with him. "I swear to God, I

swear on my sister's grave, I didn't know anything about the bombs. Nothing."

Matt believed him.

"Write it out." He slid a notebook and pen toward Avila.

The lawyer took the pen and said, "You don't have enough to charge my client with murder."

Matt raised an eyebrow. "I do."

"Not first degree. Not premeditated. Before my client writes a word down, I want a plea agreement. Manslaughter, concurrent sentences."

There was a knock on the window. "That's up to the AUSA. She'll be in here momentarily." Matt got up, John followed suit.

Matt followed John to his office and closed the door. John settled at his desk, looking both defeated and angry, but he was beginning to regain his composure.

"Pete Dunlap has lived here his entire life, except for a few years. He was raised here, raised his family here. I went to his wife's funeral. This is going to tear him up."

"Murder affects more people than the victim. Family, friends, community—all victims."

"I'm so angry, but mostly sad. How this could happen in my town. We're good people here, Matt. Good, honest, hardworking people who care about each other. I brought her in."

Now he was onto Marcy.

"Marcy Anderson had a solid record in Seattle, and she had a background with boats. She was in the Coast Guard. I would have hired her if I were in your shoes."

"She killed ten people. Kidnapped a child. And she was one of mine."

"One of the best things about a small town like this is that people know you. They trust you. They will look to you for guidance. And you'll regain what you had."

"That's not going to be possible, not completely," John said. "No one is going to forget what happened. How could they?"

"But you're not to blame. You need to help return the town to the sanctuary it is for so many people."

John nodded, though he still looked troubled. Matt hoped he took his words to heart.

"I need to talk to Donna. Apologize."

"You have nothing to apologize for," Matt said. "We were following the investigation where it took us. If she can't see that, that's her problem."

"She's still one of my constituents. She's still somewhat of a friend."

"I get that. But I'm telling you—tell her what happened, but don't apologize for doing your job. Because one of these days, one of her people is going to go too far, and you're going to have to arrest them. Just like Craig Martin and Valerie Sokola."

"You're probably right."

"I am right."

It would take time, but Matt was confident the San Juan Islands Sheriff's Department would come back, stronger than ever.

Matt talked to the AUSA and John stayed with her and Avila through the negotiations and written confession. The AUSA was thrilled, said Avila would spend at least twenty-five years in prison. "I wish it could be more, but getting the confession goes a long way. Not going to trial on this—where it would be difficult to prove premeditation—is huge. Honestly, this would have been a hard case to prosecute, Costa. I owe you one."

Matt was pleased with the confession, but didn't feel like justice was truly served. Damon Avila would pay for his crimes, but five people were still dead.

Matt left them to wrap everything up and walked from the sheriff's station to West End Charter, needing the time to collect his thoughts. After a week of intensity, he almost felt a letdown. The bomber was dead. A killer had confessed. But people were still dead, and while justice was being served, Matt would never be okay with the loss of life.

Matt planned to tell Ted Colfax what was going on with the investigation, but Ted was out on the water. Matt walked down to the pier, not knowing if he would wait for him, or if he would come back tomorrow.

Matt saw Adam Colfax sitting alone on a bench at the end of the dock. He approached.

Adam looked up at him, sunglasses hiding his eyes, his mouth in a firm, straight line. His face was damp, and Matt suspected he had been crying.

"Ted's out," Adam said. "Won't be back until sunset."

"May I sit?"

Adam nodded.

They sat in silence for a long minute, staring out at the calm water. The wind and clouds from yesterday had disappeared; the sky was completely blue, the water calm, sparkling in the sun.

"You heard," Matt finally said.

"It's fucked. Just fucked and completely stupid."

"I agree."

Again, silence.

"I keep asking myself *why*," Adam said. "She blew up the boat to kill one person."

"She blew up the boat to kill two people," Matt said. "Cal, because she was a psychopathic stalker, and Neil Devereaux so that she could frame Damon Avila for the bombing. She planned on getting away with it."

"But you figured it out."

"My team did."

"And she killed herself. I can't even tell her how she screwed up my life. All those people, dead, for no reason. My sister told me that Mrs. Jeffries is pregnant. Now the kid won't even know his dad. And Kyle..." His voice cracked. "He was only twenty-two. After he graduated next year, we were going to move in together. I wanted to get married, but Kyle said we had all the time in the world. But we didn't. And now he's gone for no fucking reason."

Matt put a hand on Adam's shoulder, but he didn't say anything. There was nothing to say.

Kara didn't want to talk to anyone else today, but she felt she owed Madelyn Jeffries some closure. She dropped Michael off at the house—he said he would go with her, but she wanted to do this on her own.

She drove out to the Jeffries property. Her hangover was almost gone, but her head was still all twisted from both everything that happened yesterday plus Catherine's conversation with her this morning. Kara had no doubt that Catherine had intentionally tried to get under her skin and manipulate her, but there was a lot of truth in her comments, and Kara couldn't shake the feeling that her life, as she knew it, was over.

Worse, she felt like she was in perpetual limbo, not knowing what to do or who to trust.

She pushed it all aside and walked up the stairs to the Jeffrieses' front door. The day, at least, was beautiful. Eighty degrees, blue skies, birds chirping, and sailboats sailing.

Too beautiful, too chipper, after so much violence and death.

Robin, the fiancée, answered the door. "Agent Quinn."

"Detective," she automatically corrected and felt like an idiot. "Call me Kara, please. I'm sorry to bother you, but I wanted to see if anyone had questions, let you all know what happened and what's going to happen."

"That is kind of you. Come in, please." Robin led Kara to the living room and motioned for her to sit. "May I get you anything? Coffee, water, soda?"

Normally Kara would decline, but she was dehydrated. "Water, please."

She smiled, said she would be back. A minute later she was,

with a tall glass of ice water and Madelyn. "Justin is in town getting some supplies," Robin explained. "We're going to stay a few more days."

Kara drank half the water, put the glass down on a coaster on the glass coffee table.

"This is a small town, I'm sure you heard about what happened yesterday, but I wanted to make sure you have accurate information and answer any questions."

Madelyn sat down on the couch next to the chair Kara was sitting in.

"You are kind," she said. She looked pale and skinny—like she'd lost weight in the week since the explosion.

Robin sat down next to Madelyn and took her hand. Robin said, "The sheriff came by late last night. We know about Deputy Anderson. It's—truly, it's almost unbelievable."

"Senseless," Madelyn whispered. "It's not fair."

She at least sounded a little better than she had when Kara was here with Catherine.

"No, it's not fair," Kara said. Life wasn't fair, never would be. "But she's dead. I wish she was in prison, but this way you won't have to go through a trial and newspaper headlines and media bullsh—" She cleared her throat. "Maybe you'll find some closure knowing what happened."

"Maybe," Madelyn said.

"I don't know if you can tell us," Robin said, "but Justin heard that Damon Avila was arrested for the bombing. Did he help her?"

Kara had a text from Matt that Avila had confessed to five murders. "We initially arrested him because of a bomb found in his house, but we believe that Deputy Anderson was attempting to frame him. Neil Devereaux, one of the other victims on the *Water Lily*, had been investigating Avila for a cold-case murder. Neil was retired, but he was obsessed about the deaths of two college students. Avila confessed to the murders that Neil suspected him of and denied any involvement or knowledge in the bombings. At this point, we believe that Marcy Anderson acted alone."

No one said anything and Kara wondered if she'd said too much. She finished the water, put the glass back down. Looked at the painting above the fireplace, the one of the mountains and Pierce and Madelyn having a picnic. They loved each other. Kara didn't know what that even felt like, if she would ever know what it felt like. If she would even know… Love seemed so foreign to her.

Except when she saw the love in Madelyn for her husband. In Cal for his fiancée. In Justin for his father, in Cal and Jamie for their daughter. The way Pete Dunlap spoke about his daughters, about his dead wife. Maybe it was something she would never have.

Maybe love was something she didn't deserve.

She said, "I need to be going, but if you or Justin have any questions, you can call me and I'll find the answers."

Robin got up to walk her to the door, but Madelyn waved her off and escorted Kara herself. She said, "You were very kind and straightforward with me from the beginning, and I appreciate it. Everyone has been walking on eggshells around me. I finally sent my mother away. Told her to go to my house in Bellingham and start planning for the funeral." Her voice cracked, but her eyes remained dry. "Anyway, thank you for being honest. So I'm going to ask you this: Did you know when you were here with that woman that she was responsible?"

"No," Kara said. "Not then."

"When did you suspect her? Or did you?"

Kara thought back to what it was. Carefully, she said, "It wasn't any one thing," Kara said. "But she said something the morning after we were here the first time, and what she said didn't quite ring true. So I watched her. Listened. Investigated. I didn't suspect her of the bombing then… That took another day. But I was suspicious that she had a secret, that she was up to something. And I followed that doubt until I had proof, one way or the other."

Madelyn stared at her, and Kara couldn't quite tell what she was thinking. "You never thought I was involved."

"No."

"You're the only one. I think…I think Justin even had doubts at the beginning."

"I think," Kara said, "that Justin is grieving like you are, that he wanted answers like you did, and he knows you loved his father. And if he doesn't know that? He's an idiot."

Madelyn's lips twitched up just a fraction. "Thank you for everything. And I am glad she's dead. She doesn't deserve to breathe when she killed Pierce and everyone else on that boat."

Kara couldn't disagree.

40

That night, Matt convinced the team to have an early dinner at the Fish & Brew. Pete Dunlap was behind the bar. He was another one who looked like he hadn't slept much lately.

Kara excused herself and went up to the bar. "Hey. You don't mind if we're here, do you? I know this must be awkward."

Pete shook his head. "Tequila?"

She almost turned green. "Too much tequila last night. Blond, pitcher, for my table." She sat on a stool. "How are Ashley and Whitney?" She motioned to the far side of the restaurant where the girls were sitting with Bobby Martin. She was pleased, at least, that Pete had forgiven Ashley for her deception—and welcomed her boyfriend into their lives.

"Shock. They love their uncle. They can't believe… He really confessed to killing five people?"

Kara knew that Matt had talked to Pete Dunlap earlier, that he'd shared with him everything that he could and confirmed his alibi for the time the C-4 went missing. It was probably little consolation that Damon wasn't involved in the bombings, but at least it was something.

"Yes."

"I keep thinking…should I have known? Damon was always so angry and hurt about what happened to him in college. It was an accident, but he blamed everyone and everything. Yet…I thought he was doing good. He spent every summer here. He loves his nieces. He loved his sister." Pete paused in the middle of drawing the pitcher. "How can someone who can be so good to his family kill others out of jealousy? Anger?"

"Few people are all good or all bad." That sounded lame. Damon was a murderer. There was nothing to sugarcoat that truth.

"I trusted him. I trusted him with my daughters. And he killed a boy—a kid only a year older than Ashley. I never want to see him again."

"You don't have to."

"But do I keep the girls away from him?"

"Maybe you should ask them what they want to do," she suggested. "Maybe they can separate what he did from how he treated them. I don't know," she added quickly. "They're your daughters. But I've found that by a certain age, kids like to be included in these kind of decisions." She paused. "My father was in prison."

"Did he kill someone?"

"No. Not that I know of, but I wouldn't be surprised if he had. He was a thief." Among other things. "But he was still my father, warts and all."

"Do you still have a relationship with him?"

"No." That was too quick an answer. "I don't have a *relationship*. He contacts me when he's in trouble or he wants something. I usually ignore him. But that's my choice."

"You think I should let the girls make the decision."

"I think they're mature enough to at least be part of the decision making."

He nodded, put the pitcher in front of her. "You're a good person, Kara Quinn."

"Just good at my job." She reached out and took his hand. Squeezed it. "You're a good father, Pete, a good man, you raised two great kids. They'll get through this because of you."

She took the pitcher and glasses back to the table, stopped just shy and looked at the group.

Ryder looked relaxed for a change. He seemed to have found his rhythm on the task force. He'd kept his cool the entire time, methodically going over evidence, following where it led, not being sidelined even when he'd been rendered unconscious by the carbon monoxide leak. Even last night, he'd taken the time to review all of Neil's evidence, to give Matt what he needed to draw a confession out of Damon Avila.

Jim, who cared so much about the dead and working the evidence that Kara thought he could *will* answers from a crime scene. He leaned back on his chair, laughing at something Michael had said. Not for the first time, Kara wondered what it would have been like growing up with Jim Esteban as a father. Someone honest, trustworthy, and committed to both his family and justice.

Michael, who'd saved her life twice in the same day. He was everything she wanted in a partner, but Kara feared that Catherine had talked to him. A subtle thing, a shift more in Catherine than in Michael himself. Maybe he didn't trust her. Except, this morning, over breakfast, she felt that they had a bond. That they had an understanding deeper than they could articulate. She could practically hear her grandmother's voice. *Don't borrow trouble, Kara.* She trusted Michael, and trust was hard for her to come by. She would have to trust that if he had a problem, he would tell her. Right now, there were no problems. Why would she try to create one?

And Matt. The team leader. Though the beginning of the week had been rocky when he couldn't decide whether to listen to her or to Catherine, he had shifted, taken back the mantle of the boss, and trusted his team to perform. He'd trusted her— not only when she confronted Marcy, but when she insisted on being part of the rescue. That meant everything to her.

But Catherine was right. It was best for them to cut ties. Best for Matt's career...and Kara's. She didn't want to lose her job. She *couldn't* lose her job, her identity. Cut it all off now, no secrets, no hiding, just end it.

The thought made her sad. She felt hollow inside, as if she had lost her best friend all over again.

Then Matt caught her eye, and she felt a thrill race through her, tantalizing her with promise. How? How could she walk away? Was it just sex she craved, or Matt she craved? How could she tell the difference? How did Madelyn know that Pierce was the *one*? How, against all odds and differences, had she known?

Kara never thought about relationships. She had never wanted one. They complicated things, and she had enough personal and professional complications in her life that she didn't need romantic complications.

She put the beer down on the table. "I need to make a call. Give me five minutes." She stepped outside and pulled out her cell, called her grandmother.

"Hello, Em. I missed our call last Sunday."

"Working, I'm sure! But I'm so happy to hear your voice."

"You sound good."

"I'm better than good. Sally, Flo, and I went to bingo last night at the church and I won! One hundred and fifty dollars!"

She laughed. "What did you spend it on?"

"Well, I gave fifty dollars back to the church, of course, and then the girls and I went out to breakfast this morning and left a ten-dollar tip. My treat. And I *still* have sixty dollars left!"

Kara let her grandmother talk. About bingo, about her friends, about her blossoming garden. At the end of the conversation, Kara said, "I just needed to hear your voice, Em. And—I wanted to let you know I love you."

She ended the call when she spotted Ashley Dunlap step out onto the deck and walk toward her. "Am I interrupting anything?" she asked.

"Nope." Kara pocketed her phone. "Just talking to my grandmother. How are you?"

"Okay. Relieved, I guess, that this is all over."

Kara waited. Ashley had something else on her mind.

A moment later, she said, "Do you go to church?"

"No."

"I do. My dad comes with us sometimes, but it was my mom who took us, and I feel closer to her there, sometimes. And in church we talk about forgiveness a lot. I know I have to forgive my uncle. But I'm having a hard time thinking about what he did. My dad told me he killed five people, but he didn't give me details. Tell me, please."

"Your dad needs to give you the details, or you can find them on your own—it's going to be written up in the newspapers, on the news."

"Why won't you?"

"I will, if that's really what you want. You're seventeen. You're mostly an adult. But I think it should be your dad."

"He's so sad. I thought he would be angry, but he's...just sad."

"He'll tell you. Ask him, he knows you can handle it. And yes, we had evidence, and when confronted with the evidence of his crimes, your uncle confessed."

"I just don't see him killing anyone and it hurts. And I don't want to forgive him because my dad is hurting. But I feel like I have to because otherwise I'm not a very good Christian."

"I'm not the person to talk to about faith, but forgiveness is about you, not him. It's so you can live in peace, not for him to live in peace. You don't want to carry the burden of Damon's crimes or betrayal—because that's what you're feeling, as if he betrayed you and your family—in your heart. It never ends well."

Ashley thought about that, then said, "Are you leaving?"

"In a day or two. Maybe Monday."

"Do you think—maybe—before you go, that we could talk more?"

Kara didn't feel comfortable in this role, but Ashley needed to talk to someone.

"Sure," she said. "But I really think you'll be surprised if you talk to your dad. He wants to help you and Whitney get through this."

"I don't want to burden him."

"He's your dad and he loves you. Talking to him isn't a burden. In fact, I think he wants it, but doesn't know how to start."

"Maybe you're right."

"Maybe I am." Kara wasn't a hugger, but she gave the teenager a spontaneous hug because she clearly needed it.

Maybe Kara needed it, too.

SATURDAY

41

Kara should have left with the others that morning. She technically didn't have to be here on Monday when Matt met with Seattle FBI and the AUSA and went to Avila's arraignment. She'd done her part; she'd even written a full report. With details.

But she didn't feel like she had a home yet—just a mostly empty, generic apartment while she looked for something semipermanent. No friends in DC, no family, not much of anything. She considered visiting her grandmother, but instead she stayed put. Then she and Matt ended up in bed, where they always seemed to be when they were alone and had no crime to deal with.

And damn, it was great. No murder, no bombs, no tears, just

an intense passion that had her wanting more…and fearing her own emotions.

She stared at Matt as he slept heavy, sprawled over her bed, naked. She almost kissed him. Not just because she wanted to have sex again, but because she had feelings—feelings she wasn't quite sure what to do with.

She hadn't felt this way before. Sex with Matt was different.

No, it's not. It's the same. It's just sex. Good sex, orgasmic sex, but only sex. A satisfying, intense, totally hot release, but nothing more.

It can't be anything more.

She hadn't been able to shake what Catherine said to her. Kara might have been tough to her face, but Catherine's every word seemed etched in her mind, and no matter what she did or how much she drank, Kara could not get rid of the sick feeling in her stomach that Catherine was right.

Matt would be damaged if their affair came out, but he would survive it.

Kara wouldn't. She'd be kicked to the curb, homeless, jobless, with nothing.

She had to end this with Matt. She *had* to. For her, for him. She didn't want to.

It was unlike her. She rarely cared what anyone thought of her, her relationships, or anything else. All she cared about was her job and that her supervisors respected her work. Even then, she didn't much care what people thought about how she did her job because she got results.

Why did she care if she was cut from the task force? Just this week she'd been thinking of walking away. She'd recognized earlier that she really wasn't part of the team, that she was different from everyone else. She wasn't an FBI agent. She had no college degree. She would never be one of them…except that she had done good.

And she and the team worked well together. Ryder sought out her advice on how to read Neil Devereaux's cop shorthand. Michael and she trusted each other, they could act without speaking, as if they had been partners for years instead of months. She finally felt that she was important to this team, a valued member. That she had a place. She'd saved lives and taken down the bad guys and that's why she became a cop in the first place.

Well, not exactly. She was a cop because she hadn't known what else to do with her life, and she found out she was good at it. Her mentor in high school told her she had a knack, and she went to the academy on his recommendation because she wanted to please him. She didn't recognize it at the time, but he'd saved her life—not physically, but mentally. She had been in a dark place when she was living with her grandmother. She'd hated her parents, hated who she had become when she was with them. She had the urge to kill her mother's boyfriend—an urge that terrified her. They were con artists, not killers, yet the lives they destroyed... When she was fifteen, she didn't know what options she had. And murder came to mind until her mother sent her to live with her grandmother.

She'd thought a lot about this over the last few days. It was exactly half her life ago—fifteen years—when she had landed on Em's doorstep. Her mother had done it for selfish reasons, but Kara was glad. She had Em and she finally knew what unconditional love felt like.

She took another look at Matt, then slipped silently out of bed, grabbed her tank top and sweatpants, and walked to the kitchen while dressing. She didn't want to wake him up because she didn't want a conversation, not now. Not when she was dealing with this confusion.

Confusion she shouldn't feel because she'd never felt this way before.

It was nearly dark out. She grabbed a beer even though she would rather just drink a bunch of tequila to stop her mind from all this thinking and doubting. She went out to the front porch. They faced the water to the east, and she knew there would soon be fireworks for Independence Day. She'd have a great view from here.

She popped the cap off her beer and drank half the bottle, stared out at the ocean. She could just make out faint lights on the shore of Orcas Island across the strait.

She wanted—needed—this job. Without it, she feared she'd go back to her old ways. To the darkness. She couldn't go back to LAPD. She might not even be able to get a job with any other police department. Her record was solid, but in this climate, her use of force would be questioned. She could justify every situation, she'd been cleared in every mandatory investigation, yet who'd take a risk on her?

And could she be a regular cop? Her entire life had been working undercover. Something she was good at. And working for this task force, she realized she was also good at the investigating. Damn good. But in any other department, she'd have to start at the bottom. She'd have to earn detective, and maybe that's what she should do.

If someone took a chance on her.

Except she liked her team, for the most part. If she didn't particularly like someone—Catherine came to mind—at least she respected them.

Kara didn't want to lose this. This task force might be the only thing left for her. Without her badge, who was she? And if she had to give up Matt to keep this, she would. Because it was just sex.

Don't lie to yourself. It's not just sex.

She pushed the thought from her head, frowned. She loved sex. She'd never become emotionally attached because she had sex with a guy. Maybe with Colton, a little. They'd been friends, partners on several cases, and she'd liked him. But she'd never wanted to be with him all the time, and they'd had an understanding that worked for them. She missed him. His murder was still raw to her. It should never have happened.

But she realized she missed his friendship more than anything else. She missed his *being alive.*

She could easily fall into the same pattern with Matt. She liked him. He was smart. He was hot. He satisfied her on many levels—not only in bed. And maybe at the beginning that's what she was doing, putting Matt into a role that she was comfortable with, a place where Colton had been.

But Catherine's words troubled her. If Kara and Matt continued as they were and anyone found out, the powers that be wouldn't let them work on the same team. Kara would be the one who would have to leave, and likely for good. Matt had worked his ass off to get this position. The Mobile Response Team was his baby. Without him, it wouldn't exist. He was developing the prototype for other mobile groups to roll out over the next few years.

That meant Kara should walk away. She wasn't about to take from Matt what he'd spent his career creating. And if she walked away, she had nothing.

Before he opened the front door, she heard Matt behind her.

He came out wearing sweatpants and nothing else.

Her chest tightened. This might be the last time.

He handed her a beer. He had one for himself and sat next to her on the love seat. It was a tight fit, not really meant for two people. He put his right arm around the back, rested his hand on her shoulder.

"Talk to me."

She had nothing to say.

Bullshit. You have a shitload to say, but you can't say it.

She drank the fresh beer.

Remained silent.

So did Matt.

Kara wasn't one to give in to an uncomfortable silence. And this wasn't uncomfortable—hell, she wanted to take him back to bed. They had the whole house to themselves. They could walk around naked. Have sex in the shower. In the hot tub on the deck. On the kitchen counter. That almost made her smile.

"Tell me what you're thinking."

"Sex."

"What were you thinking about before I walked out here?"

"I wish things were like they were before this week."

"Now I'm confused."

"When it was just about sex. Before I realized we can't do this anymore."

"It was never just about sex, Kara. Maybe that first time, back in March. But our relationship is not solely physical. You know that."

"I'm nothing without my job."

"You are far more than a cop."

"I'm really not. I joined the academy when I was eighteen. And you and I both know now that if our relationship is not secret anymore, I will have to leave the team."

He tensed next to her. "Catherine spoke to you."

"You should have told me, Matt."

"Catherine is not going to Tony."

"This is your team, Matt. Your world. You've been wanting this for a long time."

"What does that have to do with anything?"

"I didn't think I wanted to be part of this. I didn't think I fit in."

"Kara, dammit, you are a crucial part of my team. You're an asset."

"I know. That's not what I meant."

"Then just tell me! You're not one to talk around things. Be straight with me."

"I want to be on this team. I'm good on this team." *I need this team.*

"Oh. Well, good. Then I don't see the problem."

"You're being deliberately blind, Matt. If Catherine figured out we're bed buddies, the rest of the team will, too."

"Bed buddies? Really?" He stood up and walked to the railing. She'd made him angry.

"That's what we agreed to," she said. "Sex is a necessary release, especially with our jobs."

"A release," he said flatly.

"You know what I mean."

He turned and faced her. She couldn't really see him well in the near-dark. She'd turned the porch light off earlier so she wasn't on display for the neighbors. But now she wished she could read his expression.

"I want to be on this team," she said clearly, hoping Matt would understand. "And if our involvement gets out, Tony will cut me loose. I have nowhere else to go." Her voice cracked and she didn't know why. Why was she getting emotional about this? About losing everything…about losing her job, her career…

Losing Matt.

She didn't know what they had, but it was much easier to push it aside than give up her last chance of being a cop.

"Kara, you're not going to be dropped from this team. I won't let it happen."

"You might not have a choice."

"And," he continued as if she hadn't spoken, "I'm not giving you up."

"It's not your decision."

"Oh? I've let you direct this relationship for the last four months. I played by your rules. I pretended I was okay with this whole friends-with-benefits bullshit. I'm not. Because this—whatever we have—is more than sex, and it's more than friendship. You're not so jaded that you can't see that."

"Then it's worse. Because romantic relationships screw everything up, especially on the job."

"How? I didn't want you going to confront Marcy because

I was worried about your physical safety, but I knew you were the best person for the job, the only one who had a chance of ending the hostage situation without innocent people—an innocent child—dying. And you did it. Yes, I worry about you—I worry about everyone on my team. I worry about Michael because even though he's well trained and disciplined, he takes risks because he's braver than anyone I know. But that's what leaders do—anytime we send a team into the field, they could end up injured or dead. But I would never shelter you, put you in a protective box. I respect you far too much. I care about you far too much."

He stopped talking. Matt turned to face the water again.

Kara stared at his back, and the sky lit up behind him as the fireworks show started.

Deep down where the darkness lurked, she knew they couldn't sustain this. Kara wasn't a normal person. And which part of her did Matt care about? Because she didn't even know who she really was. She had never known.

But for the first time, there was a small nugget of hope buried deep inside, a nugget that began to shine a light in the darkness. Maybe it had always been there. Kara wasn't going to examine it too closely. She would shelter it, nurture it. Maybe someday it would grow.

She stood up and walked over to Matt. She was making a huge mistake, but that burn deep down told her to shut up. To just let it ride.

To trust Matt. To trust that she would still have this job… and him.

She stood next to him, watched the fireworks.

"One day at a time, Matt. Okay?"

He took her hand, looked down at her. She saw something in his expression she wanted to dismiss to the shadows and light from the celebration over the water. But what she saw told her that he'd meant everything that he said.

It terrified her, but she didn't run away.

"I can live with that," he said. "For the time being."

Her stomach flipped. Kara was about to argue with him about that, maybe do what she should have done at the beginning and walk away.

But then Matt kissed her.

She moaned and he pulled her flat against him as her arms went around his neck so she could get closer.

He picked her up and carried her inside.

He whispered in her ear. "We are amazing together, Kara. In bed—and out. I will prove it to you every day."

And then he put her down on the bed and touched her so she couldn't think, fireworks exploding outside and deep inside.

Today, this was where she was supposed to be.

Tomorrow, too.

★ ★ ★ ★ ★

ACKNOWLEDGMENTS

Most of my ideas start with a nugget of an idea, a "what if..." I think about a good idea like a piece of sand in an oyster: it starts out small and not that special, but as I let it sit, turning it over and over and looking at the idea from all sides, it grows into a pearl. That's how I feel about *The Wrong Victim*.

The idea sprouted when I pictured an explosion on the water and wondered what happened. Everything else in the story came from that initial vision. Why did the boat explode? Was it an accident or murder? What was the motive? How can my characters solve the crime?

As I started writing, I realized one key flaw: I knew nothing about explosives. I read everything I could find about bombs— I don't even want to know if the FBI has a file on me at this point, because my internet searches would certainly raise some eyebrows. But reading doesn't always mean understanding, so I relied on my friend and fellow author Rick McMahon, retired ATF special agent, for guidance. And my usual disclaimer: if I got anything wrong about bombs and the subsequent investigation, that's on me, not my sources.

Whenever I research a place I haven't been, I first talk to people who live in the area. I know no one who lives in the San Juan Islands. I had wanted to visit, but 2020 canceled those plans. As such, I relied heavily on the internet for this book. I wanted to give a special shout-out to the San Juan Islands Visitors Bureau—the information on their website was invaluable to help me feel like I was there, and I hope because of that, you feel like you're there.

Once again, my friend and retired FBI agent Steve Dupre helped with some of my jurisdictional and "what if" questions. I am always grateful for his input!

And mostly, I need to thank Dana Isaacson, who read an early draft of this book and identified a fatal flaw I had missed. Thank you, thank you, thank you!

A very special thanks to my agent, Dan Conaway, who has stuck with me for more than a decade. When you find an agent who helps keep you sane and focused in this business, keep them. Thanks Dan, and the entire Writers House team, especially Lauren Carsley and Chaim Lipskar.

I've been so happy with the Quinn & Costa series, from my editor's edits to the art director's covers to the marketing team behind the scenes. Thanks to Kathy Sagan for loving this book like I do, and still finding ways to make it stronger. Thanks to the art director, Sean Kapitain—I'm always amazed that each cover is better than the last when they're all so good. And I want to give a special shout-out to Justine Sha, senior publicist, who not only does her job extremely well but answers all my odd questions.

As always, my family is my foundation. Dan and the kids deal with my wild writing schedule and random questions about murder. I don't think anyone else would put up with me. And Mom? You know you get the first copy of everything I write.

And of course, thank you to my readers: without you, I wouldn't be able to do what I love.